Look what people are saying about

Curtiss Ann Matlock

"…this one will warm you."
—*Romantic Times* on *Lost Highways*

"With realistic characters and absorbing dialogue,
Matlock crafts a moving story
about a woman's road to self-discovery."
—*Publishers Weekly* on *Driving Lessons*

"Once again, Matlock delivers a gentle,
glowing tale that is as sweet and sunny as its
small-town setting. Readers will be delighted by this
deft mix of romance and…slice-of-life drama."
—*Publishers Weekly* on
At the Corner of Love and Heartache

"This is a delicious read for a lazy summer day.
It's not overly sweet, and it has enough zing to satisfy
readers thirsting for an uplifting read."
—*Publishers Weekly* on *Cold Tea on a Hot Day*

"Ms. Matlock masterfully takes readers into a world
full of quirky characters and small-town simplicity
where they will wish they can stay."
—*Romantic Times* on *Cold Tea on a Hot Day*

"…this is simply a great read."
—*Romantic Times* on *Driving Lessons*

Recipes for Easy Living

Curtiss Ann Matlock

MIRA®

ISBN 1-55166-753-3

RECIPES FOR EASY LIVING

Visit us at www.mirabooks.com

Printed in U.S.A.

ACKNOWLEDGMENTS

My sincere appreciation to—
Meg Ruley, for her invaluable support
and unfailing encouraging attitude,
and my mother, Anna G. Henderson, who always
gave in when I begged, "One more story, Mama."

The Valentine Voice

Christmas About Town

by Marilee Holloway

Get ready, ladies. The opening bell rings on the traditional start of the Christmas Season with the dawning of this Friday after Thanksgiving.

It is time to clean the china and polish the silver. Time to wash, dust, vacuum, mop, possibly refinish, both the house and yourself. Drag out the decorations, buy decorations, put up decorations, find and haul out all the wrapping paper, ribbons and tags you bought on sale last year, along with those wonderfully priced Christmas cards, decide that none of those will do and buy more, write the annual family newsletter, address Christmas cards, stamp and mail Christmas cards.

Then there are all the delightful goodies in the stacks of catalogs that are proliferating like rabbits in the mailboxes. There's still time to get things ordered in, create crafts with the children, make a wreath from the Martha Stewart pattern, along with the accompanying staircase and mantel garlands, plan and host the family, company, or group parties, bake and bake and bake, get a loan and shop, shop, shop, all the while spreading the good cheer.

To assist in your pursuit and survival of the celebration of the Season, for the next four weeks we are going to focus the *About Town* column on Christmas. We're here to help you shop the sales, find the perfect gift, enjoy the celebrations in your community, cook up scrumptious meals, spread the good cheer and hopefully not collapse while doing it.

Julia Jenkins-Tinsley at the post office starts us off by reminding everyone to mail early, so as to arrive on time. The post office has stocked everything for your mailing needs, from bubble-pack envelopes to heavy duty cardboard boxes and sealing tape, all competitively priced, and the USPS takes credit cards, so you don't have to worry about cash.

The post office will be open half days on Saturdays from now until Christmas, and to be of help in a manner those two other big shipping companies cannot, our postmistress will help you pack right there on the spot, free of charge. What a deal! For the mailing convenience of the children, there will be a special box for Letters to Santa in the post office lobby.

In celebration of the beginning of the shopping season, Blaine's Drugstore will be opening one hour earlier, at 7:00 a.m., and is offering free lattes from opening to closing on Friday. Vella Blaine invites everyone to stop in and have a cup while filling out Christmas cards in peace away from the kids. All cards are sale priced. They have American Greetings and the particular Western favorite, Leaning

Tree, in boxed assortments, as well as elegant singles for that someone special.

The Cut and Curl beauty salon is offering a holiday price on perms, $5 off every perm all month. New owner Charlene MacCoy encourages all those who want to get a perm for Christmas to get it now, so that it has time to relax to perfection by Christmas Day. Also, fellas, gift certificates are available for your special woman.

The annual grand opening of Wilson's Christmas Tree Farm takes place this weekend, with their Saturday night bonfire. They invite everyone to come out and roast marshmallows and sing carols. There will be drawings for fresh pine wreaths and wild turkeys, dead, cleaned and frozen.

Don't forget the annual Valentine Chamber of Commerce toy drive. You can drop off your new, unwrapped toys here at the *Voice*, and you'll receive a light-up angel pin for the effort.

The MacCoy Senior Living Community will be having open house and serving Thanksgiving dinner. The meal will begin at 1:00 p.m., with visiting continuing until 7:00 p.m. All are invited to visit their loved ones, family and friends, and to join in the planned festivities, which will include music by the MSL Barbershop Quartet, a swing-dancing show by Turner and Taylor, a horseshoe toss game, and Mr. Vincent Randall's firsthand account of the bombing of Pearl Harbor.

In our effort to help with the holidays, we will be passing along recipes to make your life easier. We begin with that brunt of Christmas jokes, the fruitcake. While I know that many laugh and turn their noses up at fruitcakes, I happen to love them, and as I don't care to bake one, I like receiving them, especially the one we get from Mrs. Frances Kinsey each year. I found out that it is a no-bake, just mix up and forget for a few weeks cake. It is a favorite over at the Baptist Church, and Mrs. Kinsey reports that once her brother's house in Wichita Falls was burgled, and along with the stereo and television set, the burglars also took the fruitcake out of the refrigerator. She kindly shares the recipe with us.

Frances Kinsey's Fruitcake

Line a tube pan with foil, top and sides, and enough to fold over to cover the top.

Mix together in a 2 quart bowl and let stand:
³/₄ cup canned evaporated milk
3 cups tiny marshmallows
1 small can frozen orange juice

Mix together in a large bowl:
6 cups Graham Cracker crumbs
¹/₂ teaspoon each cinnamon and nutmeg
¹/₄ teaspoon cloves
³/₄ cup chopped dates
³/₄ cup each light and dark raisins
1 cup each broken walnuts and pecans
1 ¹/₄ cup candied fruit

Add the milk mixture and blend with hands until all of the crumb mixture is moistened. Press into the foil-lined tube pan. Cover tightly with foil and store in the refrigerator for at least 3 weeks before serving.

I asked how it might taste if not stored for 3 weeks, and she said she didn't know, but the burglars might, as it had only been in the refrigerator a week before it was stolen.

To be included in future columns this month,

call in your gift ideas, recipes, and sales info to Charlotte at the *Voice*, 555-4743, or e-mail her at charlotteconroy@thevalentinevoice.com.

Again: Ready, ladies? Get set. Go!

I
ꝏ

The spirit that attacks everyone at Christmas time and makes them long for home and family attacked Corrine's mother and kindled in her the gumption to reenter her daughter's life. It happened as she began to take calls for reservations for big families for Thanksgiving dinner in the restaurant where she worked as a hostess, and as she heard the wait staff and chefs speak of their Christmas gift desires and plans, and as she saw the advent items displayed in the store windows she passed on her walk home through the French Quarter.

It was, after all, the season for miracles, and the idea took such a hold on Anita's heart as to make her think a miracle was truly possible and that she could actually be a mother after all.

She looked at the calendar, saw the countdown to Christmas and knew it was now or never. She had relinquished her daughter to her sister's care three years earlier, and three years was a long time in a child's life. Her daughter was to turn thirteen shortly after the new year and enter into the portal of adolescence. If Anita didn't get there quick, her daughter would be lost to her forever.

She got busy breaking the news to her boyfriend of her plans to desert him at the holidays and hocking the good jewelry he had given her in order to get herself home to Valentine, Oklahoma, where her sister, her daughter and her memories lived.

Had Corrine known that her mother was of so serious a mind as to actually take steps in the direction of motherhood, she would have said, when she could find her voice, "It's too late. I'm finally happy now, and I have a whole life ahead of me. Don't spoil it."

At the moment when her mother was drinking strong New Orleans style coffee and attempting to put her life in traveling order, Corrine was awakening from a sound sleep, the way she always awoke, her eyes popping open while she lay perfectly still with hands knotted in the covers, somewhere halfway between the warm comfort of flowered flannel sheets and the edgy anxiety of a mind trying to catch up and realize where she was.

It is first light...it is Willie Lee's cat on her feet...it is Friday, Thanksgiving holiday weekend, and no school, yippee...oh, she got to go see the horses!

In the manner of one who is young enough not to need prying out of bed on a day off, she sat up. Willie Lee's cat, still on her feet, did not move but was dragged along over the covers. She gently lifted him, stroked his soft fur once, then sat him aside, threw back the covers and hopped out of bed.

It was light enough in her room to clearly see the posters and drawings—all of horses—pinned on the walls, and the fuzzy stuffed horses, bears and other beings atop the bookshelf crowded with books. She was glad to have her own room, the first ever in her life.

Before they had moved into the apartment over Papa Tate's newspaper, *The Valentine Voice*—a temporary living arrangement, Papa Tate liked to remind them—she had shared a room with Willie Lee. Even yet, when she awoke, she almost always had to peek into his room to check on him. She did so as she padded barefoot and silent along the cold wood floors of the short hallway, seeing him sleeping soundly, his dog Munro lying on one leg and the other thrown free of the blankets.

She felt relief. She did not want to take him with her this morning. And she could never, ever tell him no, for she loved him more than anyone in the world, except for Aunt Marilee.

Sometimes, in her nature of staying ready for any catastrophe, she would imagine what she would do, should she have to choose between Willie Lee and Aunt Marilee, say if a tornado came, as it had the previous spring, and crashed into wherever they happened to be. Which one of them would she throw herself over? Or if both of them needed all the blood in her veins, which one would she give it to? It was a disturbing proposition that could occupy her for quite a while at times.

In the bathroom, she used the toilet, washed her hands and face and brushed her teeth, then jutted her face close to the mirror, examining to make certain her teeth were pearly-white. She very much admired white teeth and thought hers, all so even, were her best feature. Then she went on to examine her face, looking for any blemishes and studying to see if she might find any signs of looking older.

Her eyes were dark as coffee beans, like Aunt Marilee described them, and her eyebrows just about grew together over her nose. She wound her dark, shoulder-length hair up on top of her head and turned this way and that, thinking that she would just have to convince Aunt Marilee to let her begin using makeup. Lots of the girls her age at school used makeup, at least a little cheek blush and pale lipstick. Using makeup didn't mean she was going to start hanging out on street corners, smoking cigarettes and running with bad boys.

Dropping her hair, she hurried back to her bedroom, where she jerked off her flower-sprigged long-johns and got dressed in her favorite blue turtleneck sweater—after pulling two other sweaters from her drawer but discarding them— Wrangler jeans and Justin boots. A pocketknife went in the right jeans pocket, and three dollar bills and a tube of lip gloss in the left, clear, because Aunt Marilee wouldn't let her use the colored kind.

She brushed her hair and caught it back in a ponytail, the whole time thinking with great anticipation of seeing the horses and Ricky Dale this morning. She and Ricky Dale had set up to strip and rebed the horses' stalls, but she had not heard from him since Wednesday.

She would not call him and ask.

Snatching her jean jacket from its hook, she checked herself in the mirror on the closet door, turning sideways and smoothing her sweater to check how much shape she had. She had something, enough for a double A bra, although a lot of that was hopeful thinking.

Legally, she was still twelve years old. Twelve going on twenty-three was what Papa Tate often said, and she could not figure out if he meant it as a compliment or a complaint.

She felt awfully confused about where she was, which was sort of in a nowhere land, too young to be a woman and too old to be a child. She couldn't ever recall feeling like a child. She was too serious. Just about everyone said so. She didn't seem to fit anywhere in this world.

She had, however, great hope in the fact that in a number of weeks that weren't so long now she would legally be a teenager. At least that had some sort of designation as a point in life.

Grabbing her tennis shoes, she headed for the kitchen, silent in her sock feet.

Papa Tate was just coming out of his and Aunt Marilee's room. In flannel pajama pants and bare feet, he looked like he might have been digging potatoes all night, he looked that tired.

Being a new husband and stepfather at the age of fifty-two was hard on Papa Tate. And Aunt Marilee had decided she wanted a baby before her eggs gave out, so she was keeping him busy. She might should have thought about Papa Tate giving out.

They nodded at each other. Papa Tate disappeared into the bathroom, and Corrine hurried through the apartment, pausing to gaze out the windows that ran along the south wall and looked down onto Main Street. It was going on seven o'clock. To the east, the sky beyond the Quick Shop and the tall, bare-leaved trees of Mr. Hornsby's house behind it was turning golden and sending rays of a promised morning streaming through the window glass with blinds as yet pulled high.

Papa Tate said they lived on the sunny side of the street, which it definitely was in winter. Down below, things were still in the shadows. A car passed, headlights on. Deputy Midgette, who Corrine knew by his thin body and saunter, came out the police station door and headed along the sidewalk to the door to his and Belinda's apartment above the drugstore. He must have had the night duty.

Corrine, who was not a fan of the apartment, because it didn't have a porch or a yard, greatly enjoyed the windows. From them, she saw the town wake up in the morning and go to sleep at night. Most weekday mornings Corrine saw Bonita Embree come in to the Sweetie Cakes Bakery at six— she had missed her this morning—and very often she saw that Mr. Grace did not leave the florist shop until way after nine. She saw the sun rise in the morning to shine on the brick and concrete buildings of Main Street, and saw it cast a sort of benediction glow on them as it went down in the evening, letting the moon take over, as if on guard at night.

From the wonderful vantage point of the windows she had viewed the Fourth of July parade, where the rodeo queen, Melissa Pruitt, had lost control of her horse at one corner of Main Street and had just about run down the high school cheerleading team and then put a dent in the mayor's old Cadillac convertible before being reined in at the next corner by Leanne Overton, a professional barrel racer, and Mason MacCoy, an ex-rodeo cowboy.

And she had seen the Senior Citizen bus crash through the Senior Citizens' Center front window when Mr. Northrupt, who was driving that day, pressed the accelerator instead of the brake and went right up over the curb and across the sidewalk. No one had been hurt, although that strange old woman Mildred Covington had choked on a brownie, and Mr. Winston'd had to do the Heimlich maneuver on her, bringing the piece of brownie popping out. The old woman had eaten it back down, though. Corrine had not seen this from the windows, being too far away, but she had heard all about it when she had accompanied Aunt Marilee to get the details for the newspaper report.

Basically, the windows had proved out as a real asset to them as a newspaper family. After the Senior Citizens' accident, Papa Tate had requested that Corrine take notes as she looked out the window, just in case. Aunt Marilee had fixed a nice window seat for comfortable watching, and a small lined tablet was kept at hand.

After her honoring check of Main Street, Corrine went into the kitchen to get coffee going in the maker, and just as she got out the canister, the phone rang, as if someone had seen the light come on, which was probably exactly what had happened, because the caller turned out to be JoBeth Grace of Grace Florist across the street.

"Tell Marilee to mention in her column that this is an exceptional year for poinsettias, and we are beatin' Wal-Mart's price on the six-inch pot size. Oh, only I don't think she can name Wal-Mart. Tell her not to use that name. Just say Grace Florist and Gifts are beatin' those big-guy's prices."

It was funny how people wanted her aunt to write it up, but they also wanted to tell her how to do it.

Mrs. Grace added that she was sending over a big plant for the newspaper office. "I'll write up what I want Marilee to mention in her next two columns and put it with the plant." Then she added, "But give her this message, just the same."

"Okay, I'll tell her."

They got all sorts of presents from people who wanted mention in the paper. Fred Grace sent over a plant or flower arrangement from the florist just about every holiday. Fayrene Gardner had sent over a plate of each of her new dishes when putting them on the menu at her Main Street Café. Jaydee Mayhall gave them some wonderful blue ink pens and cute little notepads when he was running for

County Commissioner and asked Papa Tate to put in a good word for him in his editorial. Papa Tate said his good words could not be bought with ink pens or any amount of money, but he would mention Jaydee, because that was news. He sure did talk highly of the IGA in his editorial, though, when the grocery sent over a sample packet of steaks from their new specialty line of all naturally grown, hormone-free beef. He said that he had not been bought, but that he had experienced a dang good product and wanted to tell about.

Corrine scribbled the message on a small yellow sticky note paper and stuck it on the end of the counter, along with half a dozen other notes. People just weren't reading the instruction to contact Charlotte at the *Voice* with their info.

Corrine scooped the aromatic ground coffee into the maker and set it to brewing with the efficiency of someone who had been doing it since the age of four, when she had learned that fresh brewed coffee in the morning made big people happy. She'd had to stand on a chair for the job back then, but today getting on her tiptoes sufficed, and coffee still made big people happy.

While the coffee brewed, she cut a chunk from one of the three fruitcakes they had received after Aunt Marilee's column had come out, where she said how much she liked them. Corrine was glad her aunt had said that. She liked fruitcake, too. Enough coffee was in the pot for her to pour herself half a cup, to which she added a liberal amount of milk and sugar, then drank it down somewhat hurriedly, interspersed with bites of the fruitcake.

Aunt Marilee did not approve of her drinking coffee. She said that Corrine needed to be sixteen before she drank coffee because of stunted mental capacities and needless stimulation in a young body. Corrine thought her aunt knew just about everything, but she did not believe her infallible. At twelve she could quite often benefit from stimulation just like anyone else.

Papa Tate was late and would need stimulation, she thought with a glance to the clock.

She got his big stoneware mug from the cabinet and then her aunt's favorite china cup and saucer. Just as she went to pour the coffee, the telephone rang again, and she jumped and sloshed the coffee all over. Then she was in a tizzy to catch the coffee before it ran off the counter, at the same time reaching for the phone.

"Is this the Holloway residence?" an anxious female voice asked, when Corrine forgot and just said hello, because she was anticipating some idiot with news for Aunt Marilee's column.

"Yes." She was immediately curious. The woman's tone indicated intensity. "I would like to speak to the Editor, please. I'm sorry to be phonin' so early to your home, but I've got to get on to work, and I've got somethin' I think he might want to report in the paper." She spoke in a tone and manner that caused Corrine to imagine a tragic figure on the other end of the line gripping the receiver with a bony hand. "Oh, this is Teresa Betts...but he won't know me, so I guess that don't matter."

Such calls were not uncommon, and she was reminded of Papa Tate's instruction to never discourage anyone from reporting information to the newspaper. He said it was the business and livelihood of the newspaper to hear everyone out, and that one could never tell what might be the story of the year and win them a Pulitzer prize. Papa Tate had once, years ago, been nominated for a Pulitzer prize, which, apparently, was a really important deal.

"I'll see if he can come to the phone," Corrine said.

Just then, before she could lay the receiver aside, Papa Tate, wearing jogging clothes and Nikes, entered the kitchen. He was whistling, so Corrine slapped her hand over the receiver, in case she was going to have to make up something about him not being there.

"It's a lady who says she has somethin' to tell you for the paper. Her name is Teresa Betts."

He instantly took the phone and said in his Editor voice, "Tate Holloway here. How can I help you?"

As Corrine finished cleaning up the spilled coffee, she watched his attentive expression and listened to him saying,

"Uh-huh," and "I see," and "Well, by golly, that would certainly surprise me." She would have liked to listen to the entire conversation, but time was ticking past, and she wanted to get gone before Willie Lee awoke.

She got a handful of small carrots from the refrigerator, stuffed them into her jacket pocket and took up Aunt Marilee's cup of coffee, carrying it carefully through the apartment to the bedroom, where her aunt was propped up on two pillows, trying to open her eyes.

"Where are you goin' already?" There was a hint of alarm in Aunt Marilee's tone, and she came up off the pillows, brushing back her short hair, as if needing to get herself ready for some contingency that she had either forgotten or that had just popped up.

"To clean stalls for Miz Overton."

"Oh, yes. I forgot." Aunt Marilee instantly relaxed, falling back into her groggy state. She took the coffee mug in both hands and sniffed over it, smiling softly with pleasure, her eyes going all soft and content.

Aunt Marilee was a pretty woman and perhaps prettiest first thing in the morning, when she seemed soft all over. In that feminine state, it was a little hard to look away from her, and in fact, Corrine had seen Papa Tate sit and observe Aunt Marilee when she was sleeping. Just sit and do nothing but gaze upon her as if he had found treasure.

Right that minute, Corrine was looking at her aunt, at her long dark lashes, flushed cheeks, and then at her left earlobe, with its tiny pinpoint of a hole.

"Can I get my ears pierced?" she asked. "It could be a Christmas present." Sometimes the best time to ask Aunt Marilee for anything was in her groggy moments. She would say yes without really realizing it.

Aunt Marilee cracked an eye at her and said, "Think about it for three days and ask me again." Aunt Marilee had taken to doing this thing with three days ever since the pastor had given a sermon at church about how often in the Bible things happened in three days.

"Who was that on the phone?"

"Which time?" At Aunt Marilee's blank look, Corrine said,

"JoBeth Grace the first time, with information for the column, and just now it was a Teresa Betts for Papa Tate. I don't know what that's about."

"Oh." Then, "Maybe we should get an unlisted number." She often said this.

Papa Tate heard her as he came through the door. "Then we wouldn't get these interestin' phone calls," he said. "That was Missus Teresa Betts, who is a practical nurse out at MacCoy Senior Living. She was given three thousand dollars in cash by some unknown person."

"Well, my goodness!" Aunt Marilee sat up straighter, brightening with interest and expectation of the entire story.

Papa Tate explained that Mrs. Betts had brought her mail in on Wednesday but had not looked at it until this morning, when she found a padded five-by-seven manilla envelope containing three thousand dollars in cash, with a note that said: Merry Christmas from Santa Claus.

"That was it? Just Merry Christmas from Santa?" Aunt Marilee asked.

"Yep. No return address on the envelope, of course. It has a Lawton postmark. She asked me if I thought she would legally be able to keep the money. I told her I didn't see why not, since she hadn't stolen it, but to be sure to keep the envelope and the note. She doesn't have any idea who could have given her the money. Though she was certain that it wasn't her no good husband, who left her six months ago with a broke-down car and three children."

Aunt Marilee made a sound of agreement as she drank from her cup.

Papa Tate added that the children were two preschoolers and a first-grader. The younger children had been sick a whole lot over the past year, one having been hospitalized with some virulent form of infection that had almost killed her. Mrs. Betts had been struggling to pay off medical bills.

"Which she can now pay, thanks to the generosity of this magnificent soul." Papa Tate looked as happy as if he'd given the money himself. "She wants me to put a note of thanks to this Santa Claus in the paper, so whoever it is will know that she appreciates his generosity, and that the money will be used to give her kids a good Christmas."

"*His* generosity? What makes her think it's a man?" said Aunt Marilee, who could always be trusted to think of such details.

"Good point, my sharp wife," Papa Tate said, bending to give her a kiss.

Corrine thought things like this were the neatest thing about being a newspaper family. They got told all the best stories.

In the little vestibule at the bottom of their stairwell, she looked at her bicycle. She would have taken it, but Papa Tate had specifically suggested they go up Church Street together this morning. He was making an awfully strong effort to be a good father, and she didn't want to hamper him.

Out the door, the late November morning hit them, sharp and clear and sweet. Corrine felt the air bite through her jean jacket, but she knew she would quickly warm up with movement. They crossed the street at the light and headed up Church Street. "You can go on ahead," she told him. His purpose was to jog, as he did each morning.

But he said, "No…I need to warm up a little." He made what was clearly a halfhearted attempt at some high stepping.

She cut her eyes to him.

"I'm not sure I can jog today," he admitted with a tired tone.

After a moment she said, "Sure you can. Gotta take care of that heart, 'ol' man.'" And she started to jog.

"You could save that ol' man stuff for when I'm really old, okay?" He gave a grin to cover his irritation and joined her, taking care to match his strides to her smaller ones.

When they reached the intersection of Porter Street, she looked down it, eager to see Ricky Dale coming along on his bicycle. The street was empty.

Papa Tate veered to the far side of the street, opposite the small library building that sat on the corner lot where his house had once sat and where they were to have lived, until last spring, when, right before the wedding, a tornado had taken the big old house. It had not been cost effective to repair, nor to rebuild in the same place. Papa Tate, who had let the insurance lapse on the house, had cut his losses and sold the lot to the city, making a good profit while being something of a philanthropist. Both helped his shame about his mistake with the insurance.

The library building was a temporary and cheap stand-in, until the true structure could be built. It looked ugly on the big sweeping lot. Corrine had noticed that every time Papa Tate saw the library sitting where his house used to be, his eyes sort of winced. She knew what this felt like, a memory of hurts that lived deep down.

Halfway up the hill, Corrine had to quit jogging, because her feet hurt in her boots, and Papa Tate said, "Thank you, sweetheart," because he was plain given-out.

The entire sky was glowing golden now. She turned to look over her shoulder, checking for Ricky Dale. No sign of him. He could already be at the barn. Or maybe he wouldn't come today. Maybe he'd forgotten or simply wanted to do something else and hadn't told her. Thinking of it made her mad already. She didn't want to count on him. If she counted on him, and he didn't show up, she would be disappointed.

They came around the curve and could see the sun rising. A quarter mile further and they saw that Mr. Winston and Mr. Everett Northrupt were preparing to raise their flags. Just then the sounds of patriotic tunes came blaring out. The tunes were "The Star Spangled Banner" from Mr. Northrupt's house and "Dixie" from Mr. Winston's. It was pretty much just a racket by the time it reached where Corrine and Papa Tate stood.

"By golly, we made it for flag-raisin'," Papa Tate said, moving to the sidewalk and putting his hand over his heart.

Corrine followed suit, then heard a car coming and turned to see the green Toyota that belonged to the pastor's wife— Naomi Smith, who had a scarf wrapped around her hair— pull over to the curb. Corrine had heard that since the birth of her sixth child back in August, Mrs. Smith often came to watch the flag-raising, that she said she liked to know the day was going to go on.

Just then, from the opposite direction, came Aunt Vella in her Land Rover. She braked hard enough to squeal the tires. Driving right on through the flag-raising was not a thing to do.

The ceremony had become so important to the town that when Mr. Northrupt had had his heart bypass surgery back in the summer, Papa Tate had been one of the helpers who had come up in the morning to raise his flags for him. Corrine and Willie Lee had come, and once the entire sixth-grade class had come up to do it, as a civic duty.

Likely this was the only town in the entire nation where such a thing went on. Mr. Winston—he was Winston Valentine, but everyone knew him as Mr. Winston—raised the Confederate flag first and then the United States flag, and this upset some people, but Mr. Northrupt countered by raising the United States flag and then a much smaller Confederate flag. He grumbled all the time about the Confederate flag but said he had to do it because of his friendship with Mr. Winston.

Some people said that Mr. Winston was being deliberately rude with his flag, but by and large everyone supported his right to do what he wanted. Mr. Winston was one of the town's oldest citizens and had all those medals from the war—she wasn't certain which war, but some war—and nobody was going to tell him he was not a patriotic citizen, although some who didn't know him or the town tried.

Mr. Winston was tugging on his rope with surprising strength for a man older than dirt, about ninety. Then the flags were up, and Mr. Winston and Mr. Northrupt gave a salute, waved at each other and those looking on, then headed back to their houses.

Papa Tate started off jogging. Mrs. Smith came driving on by, not looking at them or waving or anything. She looked like she was in some sort of daze, actually.

Aunt Vella came rolling past—she had a wreath on the grill of her Land Rover—and stopped, calling out the window, "Well, good mornin', shoogahs. How are y'all this mornin'?" Aunt Vella was Aunt Marilee's aunt. She was a tall, big boned woman with a rather loud voice, which she said she got from trying to talk to her husband, Uncle Perry, who was hard of hearing.

Corrine said fine, and Papa Tate said, "Well, Vella, better than I have a right to be." Papa Tate could hardly ever settle for saying one word, when four more would do.

"Don't forget, today is free latte at the store, so come on over," Aunt Vella said, then hit the accelerator and took off.

"Vella doesn't let any dust settle on her," Papa Tate said. Then he breathed deeply and turned back in the direction from where they had come.

"I'll see you later," Corrine told him, heading off up Mr. Winston's driveway and taking the gravel track that went around the garage and behind the big old house to the far rear of the acreage property, where there was a small horse barn and corral.

Ricky Dale's bike was not in sight, and she felt sharp disappointment.

It would be hard, too, totally stripping and rebedding two large stalls by herself. But she could do it.

Her gaze lit on the two horses in the corral. Sunbeams cut through the leafless trees and shone on them, a paint mare and her yearling, who both heard Corrine coming and turned their heads.

They came prancing to the fence. The yearling gave a welcoming nicker.

Corrine kissed the mare's nose and put her arms around the filly's neck, pressing her cheek to the filly's. The bright sunbeam touched her face, and for those few moments all was right in her world. She was a girl with a horse she adored, a secure and loving family, the exciting prospect of a boyfriend, and the pure magic of the Christmas holidays and blooming womanhood racing toward her.

2

Was there anything better than a horse?

The instant Corrine had seen them, she had been in love.

Ricky Dale was the one who had first introduced her to them. Every time she thought of it, she felt a wellspring of gratitude she would undoubtedly feel for him until her dying day. She remembered the time, last spring, when he had said, "You wanna come see the horses at Mr. Winston's?" She had been so shy of him that she had almost not gone.

At first the horses had been afraid of her, a stranger. The mare had shied away, and the filly, only a couple of months old, had hidden behind its mother.

Now both the filly and the mare followed after her, teasing her ears with their breath, nudging her shoulder, rooting in her jacket pocket where they smelled the carrots. They were big and she was small, but she wasn't afraid. She put her nose on their necks and inhaled the scent of them. The filly had a slightly different scent than the mare. Probably only Corrine could tell.

I will not beg for carrots, the mare said. She knew her worth as a well-formed black and white paint, with a thick, lush tail that was half black, half white.

"Here is one for you, Miss Queen," Corrine said.

Me, too...me, too, the filly said. She, too, was a black and white, with a large black splotch covering one hip and black on her ears, as if someone had painted them. An Indian pony, Corrine always thought.

"Yes, you, too, Sweet Shoo-gah," Corrine said, mimicking Aunt Vella's way of saying sugar.

Corrine had named them, but while the horses resided in her affections, they belonged to Mr. Winston's niece, Leanne Overton, who was a professional barrel racer of considerable standing. Back in the summer, she had gotten so famous as to start doing endorsements for saddles and bits and jeans. *The Valentine Voice* had done a write-up about her. And Corrine had seen her ride in the Fourth of July Parade and rodeo. In pursuit of the runaway rodeo queen, she had jumped her horse right up on the sidewalk and woven between light poles and trees and had not even clipped a pedestrian.

In the secret place of her heart, Corrine dreamed of someday being able to ride like that. She had started getting *Horse and Rider* magazine on occasion from the magazine rack at Blaine's Drugstore and had found a book in the school library about the women trick riders of the old wild west shows. She also had found a magazine left in a booth at the Pizza Hut that had an article about women trick riders who performed today. She dreamed of one day becoming such a rider. She drew pictures of horses and riders, and lay for hours before sleep with movies running in her mind of herself as a daring and flashy rider.

Leanne Overton said not to ride the mare, that she was not fully broke. But Corrine had ridden her once just around the small corral. She kept wanting to do it again.

She threw the horses a flake of alfalfa hay to keep them happy. Just as she went to get the wheelbarrow and rake, she heard a vehicle coming up the drive. She looked up with expectation, thinking perhaps someone had driven Ricky Dale over.

But it was Charlene MacCoy's truck pulling into the yard and stopping close to the back door of the house.

Charlene was Mr. Winston's daughter. She and her daughter, Jojo, a small blond girl who was a year younger than Corrine, carried grocery sacks into the house. They apparently were early risers.

Disappointed that it wasn't Ricky Dale, Corrine went to work on the first stall. They generally stripped the stalls every few weeks. This required emptying every bit of wood shaving soiled by manure and urine, and dusting the hard-packed clay floor of the stall with a bit of lime, then lining the floor again with inches of wood shavings. It was hard work, but the sort that enabled Corrine to think and dream, and she rather liked it.

She was wheeling the first load of soiled shavings out to the manure pile when she looked up to see Mr. Winston's granddaughter climbing up on the board fence.

"Hey," Jojo said.

"Hey," Corrine said. She really hoped the girl wasn't going to hang around. She knew Jojo from school, they shared a class, but in all the months of taking care of the horses, she had seen the girl at the house only a couple of times, until the past weeks, when Mr. Winston's day-help lady had quit. Now Mrs. MacCoy was coming nearly every day to do things for her father. People said Mr. Winston's health was failing, and Charlene MacCoy worried over him.

This was the first time the girl had come out to butt into Corrine's business.

"I can help you," Jojo said.

Corrine's first response was to tell the girl she didn't need help, but this seemed a little risky, since the corral did belong to the girl's grandfather, and also the girl had the look of a little china doll.

She was saved from answering, however, when there came the sound of Charlene MacCoy's angry voice from the house, all the way across the big expanse of yard. She came bursting out the screen door, shouting, "Because I love you,

Daddy, that's why!" The screen door slammed, and she yelled back through it, "Because I need you, damn it! I've always needed you, and you've just ignored that and done whatever suited you. I wish you'd think just a minute about bein' my daddy!"

She was a sight, with her red hair and her hand on her hip, hollering like that. Corrine was quite amazed. Mrs. MacCoy was a grown woman and a Sunday schoolteacher, too. Corrine stood there with her hands on the wheelbarrow, uncertain of what to do. Movement seemed out of place.

Then Mrs. MacCoy yelled, "Come on, Jojo."

The girl ran back across the yard and got into her mother's Suburban, and they drove off.

Corrine, who was wondering if she should go see if Mr. Winston was okay—he could possibly have a heart attack from being yelled at like that—was relieved when he came out the back door and filled the bird feeder hanging from a tree. He waved at her, and she waved back, just as if nothing had happened.

She liked Mr. Winston. She wondered why his daughter had yelled at him. Mr. Winston seemed like a grandfather type, but maybe that did not mean he was a father type. She had thought, though, that by the time people got to be his and his daughter's age, they wouldn't be yelling at each other like that.

Her own mother popped into her mind. Possibly she could yell at her mother, something along the same lines as what Mrs. MacCoy had yelled at Mr. Winston.

She had the first stall halfway emptied of old shavings and was thinking she needed to take off her jean jacket when Ricky Dale came riding up on his bike, with his black lab, Beau, chasing along behind.

Well, goodness. He'd had his hair styled like the high school boys were wearing, short and gelled up, too. He looked like a hunk.

"Hey, Corky. How ya' doin'?" he called as he leaned his bike against the trunk of one of the big elm trees.

He had taken to calling her by the nickname some

months ago. She liked that he would think to give her a nickname, but she also disliked it, because it seemed like something he would call a young sister.

"Hey." She smiled in response to his smile and felt a delicious warm feeling flow over her. It was a feeling that was at once annoying and enticing, and it so jarred her that she had to look away from him.

She stepped back into the stall and returned to forking the soiled shavings into the wheelbarrow. She didn't want him to see her gazing at him like a lovesick puppy who could just not wait for his presence.

Remaining where she could see him, though, she saw that he didn't bother with the gate but came easily over the fence, while Beau scrambled beneath the bottom rail. The horses came forward, and Ricky Dale stopped to pet them. The filly nuzzled him, looking for treats. He produced something out of his pocket for each of them.

"Sorry I'm late." He sauntered into the small barn with his long strides, and Corrine was struck anew by how tall he had gotten over the summer and fall. "I had to get over to Doc Lindsey's first and feed the patients, what with him and Amy gone and not back until tonight."

"It's okay. I got it." She did not want to act like she either needed him or wanted him.

"You didn't have to come, if you were needed at Parker's," she added. She could call Doc Lindsey by his first name because he had been engaged to Aunt Marilee, and Corrine was as much or more acquainted with the veterinarian as Ricky Dale.

"Naw. There was an emergency with a dog hit by a car, but once I got the blood cleaned up, that stand-in vet Miz Andrews said she could handle everything."

She thought he talked about the blood on purpose. Guys liked to talk about blood, plus Ricky Dale was turning into a real vet. He worked all the time. Papa Tate called him a real go-getter. She didn't know any other boy his age, or even older, who worked like Ricky Dale did.

"And hey, this is a big job, and you're pretty little, Corky-girl. Take a break, and I'll empty the wheelbarrow."

She was little? Corky-girl? She clamped her lips shut. To say she was not little sounded like something a little girl would say.

She went to shoveling the manure and wet shavings in an industrious fashion. She could do the job as well as him. Hadn't she been doing this with him for nine months? At first she did it for no pay, either, just to help him out because it had been a big job even for him, a boy. Okay, she had done it in order to be around the horses, and Ricky Dale, too.

But whatever her reasoning, she had done the work. And she had kept Sweet Sugar's cuts medicined up as much as Ricky Dale had, and brushed the Queen until she shone, and she had even ridden the mare, and he had not done that.

Pausing to catch her breath, she leaned on the handle of her manure rake and looked out from the stall to see Ricky Dale in the sunlight filtering through the bare tree branches.

He set down the wheelbarrow and removed his coat, hanging it on a post, then lifted the wheelbarrow again and pushed it to the manure pile to dump the contents. He wasn't so skinny anymore.

Beau, tongue lolling, got in his way, and he ordered the dog to lie down. He had gotten such good command over the dog that it instantly obeyed.

Watching, Corrine slipped back in memory to the previous spring, that first day when Ricky Dale had come riding his bike up to her front porch and brought Beau, the most obnoxious puppy alive, who did not listen to a word anyone said. That was the day Ricky Dale first took her and Willie Lee to meet the horses, and that was the day that Beau had gotten himself kicked in the head by the mare for annoying her. They had thought Beau had been killed by the blow, but then he had revived at Willie Lee's healing touch.

It was sharing the strange experience and the secret of Willie Lee's magical ability to heal animals that had instantly, in one day, cemented their friendship. Back then, well aware of the trouble Willie Lee's mystical gift could bring her cousin, Corrine had sought to protect him and had sworn Ricky Dale to secrecy. Actually, she had threatened to make him out a liar, if he had told anyone. Ricky Dale wasn't the sort who would have been afraid of her threats, though; he had kept the secret because he had promised. He had not told all that he knew, even when Willie Lee had laid hands on the filly after she'd been cut up in the tornado and stopped her bleeding right in full view of Aunt Marilee and Papa Tate and half the town.

All the talk about Willie Lee had died down, and Willie Lee's healing ability seemed to have faded over the summer. But for a while it had been a relief to Corrine to be able to speak honestly with Ricky Dale about it.

Ricky Dale was the first friend Corrine had ever really had. She had never felt like she fit with other kids. She just did not think like they did.

Ricky Dale, too, was a bit different. Not only did he work more than he played, but being the sheriff's son had cut him out from a lot of the crowd. He said that being the sheriff's son was about like being a preacher's kid, that people were always watching to see if he broke a law, or if he acted too good to do so. Then there were a few kids whose parents had gotten traffic tickets from his father or been cited for one thing or another, and even one boy whose father had been arrested by the sheriff, so he did not like Ricky Dale at all.

But over the months since the past spring, both of them had changed. Corrine had started wearing a bra, filled out the bottom of her jeans, and had full monthly periods now, which she would just die if Ricky Dale could tell, so sometimes during her week she avoided him.

Ricky Dale was getting zits, and his voice was changing. Aunt Marilee said this was about like a girl getting a period. He had been on the short side, and then he had sprouted up to become one of the three tallest boys in their class at school, and even taller than a few eighth-graders.

His height seemed to be making up for him being the sheriff's son. Other boys were looking up to him, as if being tall made him know more. Teachers even treated him like he was older, and Coach Pitner was pestering him to join the junior high basketball team. The coach thought that Ricky Dale could be the same great basketball player his father had been. Ricky Dale's older brother had been disappointingly short, plus he was only interested in cars.

The hope was that Ricky Dale could give Valentine High a few winning seasons once he got there, and Coach Pitner wanted to get him started. Ricky Dale never had been much interested in contact sports, didn't even play baseball like other boys, but he said he was considering joining the team. "They need me," he said, "and the coach says I could maybe get a scholarship from it."

Where at first she and Ricky Dale had played tag and wrestled each other like pure children, sometime over the late summer, they both had stopped, as if by mutual agreement.

Corrine was very aware now when her hand touched Ricky Dale. She was very aware of when his hand touched her.

He came back with the wheelbarrow, plopped it down and took up his manure fork. Corrine shoveled a heaping scoop of the shavings she had loosened into the wheelbarrow, just to show she had the muscle and size to do it.

Ricky Dale, however, did not seem to notice. He was frowning as he went to shoveling the shavings. "We got a cat that come in to Doc Lindsey's that got hurt somehow. Its hip sockets are injured. It's less than a year old, and the doc says sometimes young cats can grow their sockets back like normal. It would be interestin' to see if Willie Lee could fix it, though."

Corrine said, "Far as I know he hasn't healed any animal since that last dog you brought over, and he couldn't help it. At least he hasn't said anything about healin' any."

Ricky Dale nodded, and she could tell he remembered how sad Willie Lee got when he couldn't heal an animal. They had agreed that Ricky Dale had best not bring any more animals around.

"What do you think happened with him?" Ricky Dale asked now.

Corrine shook her head. "I'm not sure. It's like whatever

he had faded. Granny Franny says that can happen. That children are close to God when they are young, and as they grow up, they lose that. She says it's the pull of the world."

Corrine had an instant of wondering if all Ricky Dale was interested in was that she was a cousin to Willie Lee. She felt bad for thinking that. She knew it wasn't true. At least, it hadn't been true last summer.

He said, "Last week Doc Lindsey said that when I get ready to go into vet school, he's gonna help me. That's where I'm headed, I told him. He's already givin' me his veterinarian magazines, so I can get a jump-start."

He went on about his plans and recent interesting cases at the clinic, and as Corrine listened, she wondered if he would ever be as interested in her as he was in being a go-getter in the veterinarian world.

Or if he ever might be interested in something she was doing. She never quite knew how to speak about what she did or wanted to do, though. She did not think he would be interested in her drawing or in her desire to be a woman trick rider. Likely he would laugh his fool head off at that.

3

When Corrine entered the newspaper offices, the big room was busy, as it usually was on Friday, the day they put the Sunday edition to bed. Even in the winter, a few of the fans suspended from the tall ceiling revolved, as if joining in to give extra energy. People talked across the wide and deep room of six desks, computers hummed all over the place, and above this was the squeak of desk chairs, the ring of telephones, and the sound of country music playing from a radio on Reggie Pahdocony's desk.

The door to Papa Tate's office was open wide, so that he could pop out and holler something, or anyone could pop in and speak to him. Aunt Marilee said he never wanted to miss anything someone might say or do, and to that he replied, "Yessir, and that's what makes me a newspaper man."

Aunt Marilee had just fallen into the newspaper business, doing, as she said, what she could and had to do to keep body and soul together. Most of the time she had to push herself to write copy. She did seem to enjoy being with Papa Tate at the paper now, though.

Right at the front was Charlotte Conroy's reception desk.

The size of the desk was indication of her importance. She was the receptionist, the office manager, Papa Tate's right hand, and she basically ran the paper.

At the moment, Aunt Marilee, with her reading glasses perched on her nose, was peering over Miss Charlotte's shoulder and dictating as Miss Charlotte typed into her computer. Miss Charlotte could type faster than anyone alive. She really wasn't a Miss anymore, having gotten married back last summer to Sandy Conroy, but everyone still called her Miss Charlotte because Papa Tate did. Sandy was a whole eleven years younger than Miss Charlotte, but the general consensus was that this was the best marriage anyone had ever seen. Aunt Marilee said that biologically women should marry younger men, because women kept stamina longer than men did. She had not followed her own advice. When Corrine had pointed this out to her, her aunt had replied that the heart did not know about biology.

Corrine paused at Miss Charlotte's desk long enough for Aunt Marilee to take note of her safe arrival but did not disturb the women's work. She kept on going through the big room, keeping a cautious eye on Reggie Pahdocony, who liked to hug her any chance she got. Reggie was busy talking on the phone at the moment, though, so Corrine got safely past.

Sandy Conroy, their layout man, waved at her through the glass window of his cubicle, and she waved back, then continued on to the rear cubicle, which had a solid wall with a solid door. It belonged to the newspaper's comptroller, Zona Porter, who did not like to be seen.

Because of traumatic events in her youth, Aunt Marilee said, sometimes Zona went through periods where she didn't want to be seen so badly that she came in to her cubicle before everyone else arrived and left after everyone else had gone, coming out only to slip over to the rest room, which luckily was only a few feet away from her cubicle door. During these times, everyone helped her out by pretending not to see her.

Corrine was fascinated by Zona, but also thought she

could understand her a bit. Sometimes Corrine didn't want to be seen, either.

Today, though, Zona's door was half open, so Corrine knew the woman was having a good day. Corrine stood in the doorway, until the tiny woman at the desk looked up. Zona removed her glasses, and even without them, she had large, dark owl eyes. She smiled.

"The Quick Shop had a new delivery of fig bars, and I got an extra one," Corrine said, and took the small sack to the woman's desk.

"Thank you, Corrine." Zona had sort of a bird voice.

"You're welcome," Corrine said as she left, barely pausing in step.

Then—rats, Reggie Pahdocony was off the phone. She looked up and saw Corrine. "Well, good mornin', sweetie. How are you?" With a lively smile, she wrapped Corrine in a big hug and said how Corrine was just growing so tall.

Corrine had been delegated the job of getting the family mail from their post office box. This was because Aunt Marilee was not a naturally organized person and could become somewhat overwhelmed by incoming mail. She could become so anxious about all the paper and what to do with different pieces that she would actually put off going to the post office box for days. This behavior contributed to even more mail crammed into the box.

One time, during the particularly stressful period of being newly married and just moving into the apartment and trying to sort out all their things, Aunt Marilee opened the door to their P.O. box, looked in, and then slammed it again, waiting three more days, until Miss Julia Jenkins-Tinsley, the postmistress, caught Corrine on the street and handed her a grocery sack filled with all their mail.

"I'm goin' to get the mail," Corrine told her aunt on her way out the *Voice* door.

"Get Willie Lee from the drugstore," her aunt called after her.

Corrine waved that she had heard and headed down the sidewalk, intent on passing by the saddle shop to look in the window. The saddle shop had been closed for just about the whole summer, and then the Silverhorns had reopened it with all new paint across the window and a display of the fine saddles, headstalls and all manner of leather goods that they made. Two weeks ago they had placed a barrel racing saddle in the window.

Of tanned leather, it had fancy tooling and a suede seat. Corrine managed to look at it with adoring eyes while keeping her body moving so as not to appear to be staring. Today she saw in one sweeping glance that a big red bow had been tied on the saddle horn, and in the suede seat sat a white card with fancy lettering: Christmas Sale Price: $1,200.

They had marked it down a whole hundred dollars, she thought, as she hurried to the curb and then across the street to the drugstore.

Someday she would have a saddle like that one. Maybe she would get a saddle and horse instead of a car.

The drugstore had display windows, too. Willie Lee was in one of them, helping Aunt Vella set up a Christmas scene. He had an elf hat on. Corrine waved at him through the window, then entered the door and was immediately surrounded by the familiar scents of the old store—musty wood, barbeque sandwiches, medicine, and now latte from the new machine.

"Corrine! I have been *wait-ing* for you," Willie Lee said, throwing himself at her.

She caught him and set him up straight. His pleasure on seeing her sent a slice of guilt through her.

"I thought you were helpin' me," Aunt Vella said, snatching the elf hat from his head.

"Yes, be-cause Ma-ma would not let me go by my-self to Mis-ter Win-ston's house." He blinked behind his thick glasses and frowned at Corrine.

Ohboy. She had the urge to grab hold of him and hug him tight. Instead she crouched and petted Munro, burying her face for several seconds in the dog's furry neck. He licked her face.

"If you had gone up to Mr. Winston's, you wouldn't have

gotten ice cream. Neither you nor Munro," Aunt Vella pointed out and winked at Corrine.

"Did you and Munro have ice cream without me?" Corrine said, feeling better about the situation.

Munro looked up wide-eyed from where he lay unobtrusively beneath a rack of comic books, while Willie Lee grinned his charming grin at both Corrine and Aunt Vella and said, "Oh, that is right." Then he put his fingers to his lips and told Corrine not to tell. "Aunt Vel-la will get in trouble for not ask-ing Ma-ma."

Just then the bell over the door dinged again, and Mr. Winston and Granny Franny came in. Granny Franny was in front, coming in with a swirl of her deep royal-blue cape and the scent of musky flowers. She had quit dyeing her hair red, and it was pure white, which Corrine had not yet gotten used to. Mr. Winston said to Corrine, "Hello, again." He had on his little roadster cap that Granny Franny had bought him for his birthday and bright white Nikes. Only in between the hat and his shoes was old, Corrine thought.

Granny Franny was Papa Tate's mother and not really their grandmother but said she had assumed the role. She did it quite well, because she always brought them presents. Corrine immediately knew the contents of the paper tote bags she carried would include something for her and Willie Lee.

Sure enough, when Granny Franny laid eyes on Corrine and Willie Lee, she said, "I am glad to see y'all—I've got some things for you." She didn't stop, though, but continued on through the store, plunking her tote bags down at a table in the fountain area and calling over her shoulder, "I have to go to the bathroom, but you wait and don't run off."

"I'll alert the news media," Mr. Winston called after her.

From far in the rear of the store came Granny Franny's voice. "Perry, get out of that bathroom. I gotta go."

Everyone in the store chuckled, and Uncle Perry came out with a red face.

"Well, Perry, did you turn into a plumber now that you're

retired from the pharmacy?" called Mr. Jaydee Mayhall, who was getting an order to go from the fountain counter.

Corrine did not like Mr. Mayhall. Hardly anyone liked Mr. Mayhall. He thought he was a big shot, but right then Corrine did not like his voice that made fun of Uncle Perry. Somehow she felt defensive of the old man, who was big and tall and knew all manner of stuff from all his television news watching and Web-TV Internet surfing but was very shy, just like she herself was. He was sort of like Willie Lee, in that he did not fit in. He was extra smart about facts and details, but totally clueless about everyday life.

"He's a pretty expensive plumber," Aunt Vella said, "but he'll get the job done by and by." She touched his shoulder in a way that made Corrine feel better. Aunt Vella could really pick on Uncle Perry, but she didn't like anyone else to do it.

Uncle Perry sat down with Mr. Winston and still didn't say a word. For a long time when she first met him, Corrine had thought maybe he couldn't talk, but what it was was that he couldn't hear well. He'd finally gotten a hearing aid last month.

She went over and stood beside his best ear and said, "Hey."

"Hey, you," he said and winked at her. That was what he always said to her, "Hey, you." She never heard him say this to anyone else.

"We've come for our free latte, Vella," said Mr. Winston, then asked Uncle Perry what was up.

"Old pipe got a hole," Uncle Perry replied, short and simple.

"I declare, Vella, there's a draft in that rest room with that big hole in the wall. What's goin' on?" Granny Franny said when she returned.

Aunt Vella was just putting two cups of latte on the table. "We had a pipe burst. Those pipes are all only about seventy years old, give or take a bit. We got to have them replaced, and then the building will probably fall down."

"Too bad we people can't replace our pipes like that,"

Granny Franny said, laughing. She motioned to Corrine and Willie Lee. "Some things came in the mail for you today."

She was all the time ordering things through the mail. From one of the cardboard boxes, she produced a compass for Willie Lee.

"Maybe this will help your mother to feel more confident about your not gettin' lost. With that, you can always find your way home. And for you, my dear." She handed Corrine a little case of colored pens and pencils. "I thought maybe the ones I gave you in the spring might be dryin' up."

"Thank you, Granny," Corrine said and kissed the woman's powdery cheek, catching the faint smell of cigarette that she never wanted Papa Tate to find out about. "You'd better chew some gum," Corrine whispered in her ear.

"Oh! Thank you, my dear." Her eyes twinkled with a secret shared as she dug into her purse to find the gum.

Willie Lee was gazing at his compass with a perplexed expression. Aunt Vella asked him if he knew what it was.

"Yes," he said. "It is a com-pass." Then he looked up at them. "But my home is not on here, so how will I find it?"

As they headed out the door of the drugstore, Willie Lee kept dawdling. He was fascinated with his compass.

"Come on, Willie Lee. I want to get the mail and get home for lunch."

"O-kay." He made an effort to walk faster, but it was hard for him. Willie Lee was not made to do anything very fast. He was always looking at things other people overlooked, and, although physically very attractive, with white-blond hair and blue eyes behind his thick glasses, he was small for his age of ten and had difficulty with coordination. It was as if his impaired learning capacity that held him back to a five- or six-year-old's intellect also held back his motor ability.

Corrine felt guilty for rushing him—it seemed she was always rushing him these days—and determined to have more patience.

Next door to the drugstore, they had to walk around Fred

Grace, who was standing on a stool and attaching white lights to the edge of the awning that went clear out over the sidewalk in front of his florist shop. Mrs. Grace was pulling in the potted fall mums and bringing out poinsettia plants.

Just then a city truck, with extension ladders and all manner of power tools, came pulling up to the curb. Men hopped out and went to work removing the fall season flags that fluttered from the light poles. Workmen coming behind them further down the street were hanging glittering figures of angels with trumpets and toy soldiers with gift boxes for Christmas. Another crew worked to string lighted garlands from pole to pole across the street.

"The street is get-ting dressed up," Willie Lee said.

He could say things like that, very insightful observations that made Corrine wonder at the deep workings of his mind, when he had difficulty tying his shoes and learning the alphabet.

Corrine waited while he watched the city workmen for a few minutes, and then she told him to watch his compass while she took his hand and led him on down to the post office. Munro looked up at her as if to say he knew what she was doing.

The postmistress was cleaning the glass door of the post office upon which she had hung a plastic holly wreath. If Corrine had seen the woman in time, she would have turned around and waited for her to disappear.

Another reason Aunt Marilee let Corrine come get the mail was because Miz Jenkins-Tinsley drove her nuts. "I love her, but I cannot stand her," Aunt Marilee said.

Mrs. Jenkins-Tinsley was a busy sort of woman. It was as if she vibrated at an annoying pitch. Corrine could never look at her and not think of how Aunt Vella would go on about how the woman needed to pick one name or the other and stick to it. Corrine tended to agree. She always tried not to have to address Mrs. Jenkins-Tinsley by name, because she felt silly saying it.

The woman had already seen them, though, so there was no getting away.

"Hello, Corrine...Willie Lee." She held the door open for them. "You young'uns out of school for the day, huh?"

Obviously, Corrine thought, but said, "Yes, ma'am."

"Mun-ro is with us," Willie Lee said.

The woman was nice and smiled and said hello to Munro, who went right into the post office lobby with them.

Munro was something of a local celebrity for having secured for Willie Lee a small fortune when a missing computer chip belonging to the Tell-In Technologies Corporation had been found in his dog collar, put there by the dog's previous master. The reward given from Tell-In had given Willie Lee a lifetime of financial security and eased Aunt Marilee's mind considerably. The dog was also considered Willie Lee's guardian, and he went everywhere Willie Lee did, except into the Sweetie Cakes Bakery. The owner of the bakery, Bonita Embree, said she was not too fond of dogs, no matter how special they were. Munro really wasn't supposed to go into the Main Street Café, either, but Fayrene Gardner, who owned it now, said they would all pretend that Willie Lee was blind and needed his dog, should any authorities show up.

Corrine went on to their post office box in the row of bronze boxes along the wall. Still working on her windows, the postmistress commented about having recently seen their Granny Franny.

"She picked up another order from *Fredericks of Hollywood*," the woman said, casting Corrine a look both dubious and curious. Then she said, "What does she order from there, Corrine?"

Corrine simply shrugged. She did know that Granny Franny liked to wear padded girdles, because she said she had no behind to cushion her on hard seats; however, Corrine did not think she needed to discuss Granny Franny's private business with this woman.

The postmistress turned her attention to Willie Lee, asking him, "Have you made out your letter to Santa yet? Look at this special mailbox we have installed here, just for Santa's mail." As she stepped over to a mailbox with snow painted on it, she raised her voice in the manner many people did when speaking to Willie Lee, as if a mental handicap equated to deafness.

"No," he answered in a normal tone. Then, "I am a big boy now, and I know there is not a Santa Claus."

This brought Corrine's head around.

Mrs. Jenkins-Tinsley's eyebrows went up. "You don't believe in Santa Claus?"

Willie Lee shook his head. "No. He is a fair-y ta-ale."

"Who told you that?" Miz Jenkins-Tinsley wanted to know. She shot a gaze over to Corrine, as if to say: *Are you responsible for this?*

"I learn-ed it at school," Willie Lee said, his chin coming up.

Corrine jerked her attention back to the P.O. box, stuck in her key and opened the door, then drew out the big bundle of mail. She had to use both hands.

Behind her, the postmistress was getting quite worked up over Willie Lee's comment. "What in the world are they teachin' up at that school, anyway? They've kicked God out of school. Are they startin' on Christmas now?"

Even if Willie Lee could have given voice to an answer to that, the postmistress did not give him time.

She said, "If there's no Santa Claus, Willie Lee, I don't guess everyone in the world needs to even continue with Christmas. This year Valentine is very special, because we have Santa's very own mailbox. Not every post office has one of these, but I guess I might as well pitch it out, if there isn't any Santa."

"It is a nice mail-box," Willie Lee managed to get in.

He never wanted to hurt someone's feelings, and it did appear that the postmistress was not happy with what he had said. With a protective hand on the special elaborate and large mailbox and the other on her hip, she jutted her face down at him.

Corrine nudged Willie Lee toward the door. She wanted to get away from this discussion. Already she was imagining what was going to be Aunt Marilee's reaction when she learned about Willie Lee's new stance on Santa Claus. Likely the postmistress would call Aunt Marilee right up, too.

"Thank you, Miz Jenkins-Tinsley," Corrine said, further annoyed with the woman because of her cumbersome name.

"Oh...you're welcome, Corrine," said the postmistress, who was adjusting the placement of Santa's mailbox. Then, "Don't miss the postcard from your Grandma Norma. She said she's havin' a good time on her cruise. And there's a card from your mama, too."

At the last comment, Corrine's head came up.

"I wouldn't want you to miss the postcard and envelope in all that wad of mail," the woman said, observing Corrine with high speculation. "Your mother's cards have sure picked up these past months. You've been gettin' them every week, haven't you? How's she doin' down there in New Orleans? Did she get married to her boyfriend down there yet?"

"She's doin' fine...real good," Corrine got out, her cheeks burning. She did not answer the question of marriage but opened the door and ushered Willie Lee and Munro through ahead of her.

Behind them, the postmistress called, "You two might just want to write letters to Santa anyway. Y'all don't want to take a chance about Santa, just in case."

Corrine did not reply. She was heading along the sidewalk at a good clip with her mind racing. All of a sudden, she realized she was halfway down the sidewalk and Willie Lee was not with her.

Turning to look, she saw him and Munro quite a bit behind her. Both boy and dog had their necks craned upward as they watched a workman stringing lights on one of the sidewalk trees.

Corrine slipped onto the nearby bench, took the rubber band off the bundle of mail and flipped through it. There were four catalogs—an L.L. Bean, a J. Jill, a Miles Kimball, a Pecans of Georgia. Christmas brought in stacks of catalogs, and Corrine and Aunt Marilee found them great fun. Aunt Marilee said perusing catalogs was better than taking a tranquilizer. She and Corrine would each take a catalog and look through, and whenever one of them found something tantalizing, they would "ooo-ooo" and show the other.

They didn't order much of anything, though. Money was tight, plus Aunt Marilee said she usually just went on to wanting something else.

There were also a few fliers, a Wal-Mart sale paper, a couple of bills, two fantastic offers for credit cards, and several dire emergency solicitations for charities.

There was the postcard from Grama Norma, who was on a Mediterranean cruise. Grama Norma loved cruises, and this was her biggest yet. She had even gone without her husband, Carl, when he had not wanted to go so far away as Europe. Grama Norma had shocked everyone by not only going on the trip alone, but by saying, "I respect your choice, Carl. You, your beer and your recliner have bonded. I'll bring you back some souvenirs."

Everyone said this was a result of Grama Norma entering therapy and going to a support group. Corrine thought Grama Norma was pretty funny these days. On her postcard, she had written that she was having a *maaarrrvelous* time and was spending lots of Carl's money.

And there was the envelope from her mother, addressed to *Miss Corrine Pendley*. The return address read: Anita Pendley, P.O. box 1515, New Orleans, Louisiana.

If Julia Jenkins-Tinsley had seen the letter, then she already knew that her mother had not married, because she was still Anita Pendley.

Her mother's handwriting was flamboyant, the C with a curl at the beginning and swoop at the end. Corrine could recall how when her mother used to sit down to write something, she would focus with a deliberate expression, and often she would say, "I wasn't all that good at school, but I sure could write beautifully. My papers were always neat as a pin. Keep your papers neat, Corrine, and everyone looks more favorably on what you write, no matter what it is."

For the first two years that Corrine lived with Aunt Marilee, correspondence and telephone calls from her mother had been sporadic at best. Then, last spring, when her mother had gone to the rehab hospital, the cards had started coming once a week. They were of the keeping-in-touch variety in which her mother would write, "It is wet down here in New Orleans...miss you," or "Thinking of my girl, hope you are doing well in school, don't grow too fast, love, Mom."

Aunt Marilee kept a supply of cards for Corrine to send back, and Corrine wrote in them as carefully as she could, although she never felt her handwriting measured up to her mother's, nor did she feel she found satisfactory things to write. She wrote things such as: "It is windy here, very warm for fall," or "I hope you are doing well...miss you, love, Corrine."

She had difficulty writing the word love, although at least she could write it, where she could not say it. She had tried writing, *yours truly, Corrine,* but that just looked too horribly stupid.

She would carefully insert the card into the envelope, lick the flap and put the stamp in place, and take it to the post office, picturing her mother in New Orleans, living in one of the old places in the French Quarter, with a wrought-iron balcony that her mother would lean against in a seductive pose. Not that Corrine had ever seen the French Quarter; she had not seen her mother since her move to New Orleans, but she had seen pictures of the city, and she had seen women very much like her mother on the pages of Victoria's Secret catalogs, beautiful women with off-the-shoulder dresses and sensual expressions.

About twice a month her mother would telephone, and these, too, tended to be rather quick exchanges in which Corrine's mother did most of the talking. Corrine would be excited when she did have something to say, such as the evening her mother called and that very day Corrine had taken first place in the county-wide spelling contest held at their school and won an electronic notepad. Corrine started marking things in the notepad that she might share with her mother and thus not feel tongue-tied and stupid when her mother telephoned.

At that moment, Corrine grabbed hold of passing courage

and tore open the envelope. It contained a card printed with a cute little cottage with snow and animals, and a caption at the bottom that said: There's no place like home for Christmas.

Corrine stared at the picture, then opened the card. Her mother's fancy handwriting flowed in blue ink on the white paper.

Hello, honey. I'm thinking of coming home for Christmas. How about that?
Miss You. Love, Mom.

She read the note twice, then slipped it back into the envelope and stuffed it into her jean jacket pocket.

"Come on. I'm hungry," she called to Willie Lee.

Oh, darn, there she was rushing him again. On the other hand, if she did not, they could still be on the sidewalk this time tomorrow. Willie Lee never tired of watching anything and everything.

When they entered the apartment, they were met with the aroma of grilled ham and cheese. Aunt Marilee had a few staple things she could cook, and grilled ham and cheese was one of these. Aunt Marilee was not given to cooking, and the only reason she did any of it was that she felt so strongly about people, especially Corrine and Willie Lee, eating healthy foods.

She was right then in the kitchen at the stove, making the sandwiches. Papa Tate sat on a low stool at the table, typing away at his laptop computer. He typed mostly with two fingers, throwing in another two every now and then. He was fast at this. Not as fast as Charlotte, but he still was an amazement.

Papa Tate was writing a novel. He preferred to work on it in the apartment in close proximity to Aunt Marilee so that he could holler at her to come read passages he thought were extra clever. Basically, Papa Tate thought just about everything he wrote was clever, and so, it seemed, did most people.

Leaving the mail on the corner of the counter, Corrine went to the refrigerator. "Papa Tate, do you want cold tea?"

He held up a finger, which meant, "I have to finish this thought."

Aunt Marilee, who had picked up the bundle of mail, said, "Oh, good, catalogs!" She grinned at Corrine, as if Corrine had personally drawn them up.

Corrine said, "There's a postcard from Grama Norma. It's small."

The letter from her mother in the pocket of her jacket seemed on fire. She jerked off her jacket and took it clear through the apartment to her bedroom, where she threw it on the bed.

When she returned, Aunt Marilee was at the kitchen window, looking down onto Church Street, saying, "They're putting up the tree over at City Hall. I don't know why they are puttin' it up so early."

She opened a large can of fruit cocktail and poured it into a bowl, then stopped again at the window, bending over and peering harder. "Well, my goodness, they are goin' ahead and decorating that tree, and they haven't anchored it."

The next moment she threw up the window and hollered out instructions. "Kaye, you need to have that tree in more than that little stand, or it's gonna blow away."

That would be Kaye Upchurch, the mayor's wife, who called back up to Aunt Marilee that they were using a heavy-weight iron stand. Corrine went to peer around her aunt and saw the woman below at the edge of the curb across the street, shading her eyes as she peered upward.

"I can't imagine why they are already puttin' up a real tree. It'll be dead by Christmas," Aunt Marilee said over her shoulder to them in the kitchen.

Aunt Marilee removed the window screen, and the two women proceeded to carry on a discussion of the matter, sidewalk to second-story window, while cars passed in the street.

Aunt Marilee was adamant that the tree was going to be blown away, and that it would cause a wreck, probably be blown out in the street at the time some little compact car came along, nail their windshield, and possibly end up killing people and getting the city into all manner of legal troubles.

Papa Tate, who had paused in his typing long enough to lift his coffee cup, said to Corrine and Willie Lee, "Only our Marilee can go from an innocent Christmas tree to people gettin' killed in no time flat."

Corrine, thinking this was a true statement, smiled and ducked her head to hide it.

"Oh, hush, Tate," said Aunt Marilee, who had so rattled the mayor's wife as to persuade her that the anchoring had to be done, and right that instant before catastrophe struck. "People need to think of these things, or the city could get in a good lawsuit. We need to anticipate disaster in order to prevent it." Aunt Marilee had voiced an interest in being the next mayor, and as she spoke, she retrieved her tool kit from the pantry.

Papa Tate reached out as she went stalking past, grabbing her by the wrist and wrapping an arm around her hips, pulling her tight against him. Laughing she resisted, but mildly, just enough so he would hold her bottom tight as he pulled her down and kissed her so hard and thoroughly that when he released her, she missed a step and teetered.

Corrine, whose eyes watched their every move even as she drank from her glass of apple juice, had that peculiar ball of emotion that she often felt when witnessing their passion, which was a swirling mixture of curiosity, suspicion and relief. Her curiosity about the sex life of her aunt and this man she had married aside, Corrine had not been able to banish the conviction that their marriage would inevitably crumble, and that Papa Tate would be off and Aunt Marilee would be crying nights into her pillow and they would all be destitute. She was constantly watching the two for reassurance that the splitting time had not yet come, and that they still loved each other.

Aunt Marilee, her face flushed, went hurrying out, but she returned a second later to caution Corrine and Willie Lee to be careful and not fall out the open window, having known just as surely that they would be peering out to watch what went on, while Papa Tate went back to his novel, his two fingers clicking the keys.

Eating their sandwiches at the window, Corrine and Willie Lee saw Aunt Marilee stride across the street below in the manner that indicated she meant business. Her long legs pushed out her wool skirt with each step. She proceeded to call a city workman off his decorating job on the intersection to bring a ladder that she herself used to climb up and sink fasteners into the brick wall with her cordless drill. Aunt Marilee had been a single woman for many years and could use power tools even better than many men, Papa Tate included.

The workman and Mrs. Upchurch hovered at the foot of the ladder. Mrs. Upchurch liked to give direction as much as Aunt Marilee, so it was a job with great discussion. The workman seemed focused on his ladder and, as far as Corrine could see, never took his hand off of it. At Aunt Marilee's direction, the workman moved the ladder several times, and Aunt Marilee went up and down, and eventually she had a wire tied from the tree to the wall on each side.

Aunt Marilee was fully experienced in doing this, as each Christmas she anchored their tree at home in the same manner, because whatever cat, or cats, Willie Lee had at the time would insist on climbing right up the trunk. And because Aunt Marilee feared somehow, someway, the tree would fall on one of them. She was not about to let that happen.

4

Corrine sat on the window seat at the front of the apartment, looking down onto Main Street, which was lit up with the colorful Christmas decorations. Using what light spilled from the kitchen, she attempted to draw the street but was very frustrated that she could not get her ideas to come out how she wanted them.

As she worked, she reflected that she very often drew in the same manner as Aunt Marilee wrote, which was to say that she thought about a drawing, and thought and thought, and then began with small, uncertain sketches where she had to push herself to make any lines at all, because she was so fearful that none of it would turn out how she imagined in her mind and would cause her horrible disappointment.

After a bit of this painful floundering around, though, all of a sudden, the urge to get the picture finished in any way, shape or form would seize her, and she would begin to draw in earnest, accepting the drawing however it turned out, and simply relieved and joyous to have done it at all.

She looked up to see Aunt Marilee in the kitchen entry, silhouetted against the bright light behind her, wiping her hands on a towel. Instantly Corrine thought about her mother's note and felt self-conscious.

"What are you working on in the dark?" Aunt Marilee came to sit on the window seat.

Corrine passed her the pad. Aunt Marilee was about the only person to whom she would ever show her works in progress. She had to show many things to Miss Dewberry, her art teacher at school, of course, but when drawing for art class, she was always careful to pick simple things that she knew she could draw halfway decent, and things that did not feel private.

"Well, I like this," Aunt Marilee said with warm praise in her tone.

"I do better with horses," Corrine said.

Aunt Marilee smiled. "You've got horses down. It's time to stretch a bit."

"It's all out of proportion."

"Oh, I don't think so.... I like it. You caught the spirit of Christmas." Aunt Marilee could always be counted on to say encouraging things about any accomplishment. "This could be a Christmas card." She gave a questioning look.

Not certain how she felt about that, Corrine shrugged. "Maybe."

Aunt Marilee regarded her in a way that caused Corrine to move her eyes to the left, where her aunt's thick auburn hair was swept behind her ear, where from the lobe swayed an antique style silver and topaz earring.

"I ran into Miss Dewberry this afternoon on the sidewalk. Actually, she almost ran me down while I was crossin' the street."

Corrine felt embarrassed. Likely Aunt Marilee had been out in the street dealing with the City Hall Christmas tree situation. She nudged the embarrassment aside. She wouldn't let herself be embarrassed for Aunt Marilee.

Aunt Marilee was saying, "She said, just as she did at open house, that you have a rare and wonderful artistic talent. Those are her words—rare and wonderful. She said she had recommended you for a special Saturday workshop up at Cameron University next month."

Her gaze asked why Corrine had not mentioned this.

Corrine gave a small shrug. "I'm not sure I want to go...and it isn't free. It costs. Pretty good, too. And I know you and Papa Tate are busy with the paper and all."

"Miss Dewberry said it was just twenty-five dollars. That won't break us. And I can take you. It's a special opportunity. I don't mind taking you. I'd like to."

As she spoke, she tilted her head and crossed her legs in a lazy manner. Aunt Marilee moved sort of like a lazy cat, but like a cat's, her eyes were focused and intense.

"I just don't know if I want to go," Corrine said, feeling that strong grip of stubbornness that she truly disliked but clutched around her for fear of doing otherwise.

"Well, there's plenty of time to decide. Miss Dewberry said that she didn't have to submit your name until a week before the workshop. A number of other students are going. It wouldn't just be you."

That was the problem. Corrine did not want to go off and be crowded all day with a bunch of other people she did not know, nor even with those, like Miss Dewberry, whom she did know and rather liked.

She said, "I'm ready to get my ears pierced. I'd rather not have to wait until I'm eighteen."

Aunt Marilee, rising to her feet, took a deep breath and gave Corrine a look that said she understood exactly the change in the subject. "Okay," she said. "You won't have to wait until you're eighteen. Thirteen will be adequate."

Thirteen again, like one day she was unqualified for pierced ears and the very next day everything changed, and pierced ears were allowable.

"It isn't like drivin' a car," she said.

"No, for that you have to wait until you're sixteen." Aunt Marilee, her earrings swaying, bent to kiss Corrine on the forehead.

The streetlight in a backyard on the other side of the rear alleyway cast a silver glow through her bedroom window and made a pattern on the wallpaper. She lay snuggled down in her bed, listening to Aunt Marilee and Papa Tate getting ready for bed, and then finally to their door being shut, which meant likely they would be involved with each other for at least a little while. Their bedroom, being on the other side of the bathroom and a long closet, was a private sanctuary. "Sanctuary" was how Aunt Marilee referred to it when she had to lie down with a sick headache.

Corrine lay listening to the quiet for some time. She wondered briefly at her aunt and Papa Tate having sex and thus possibly being too involved to hear anything from Corrine's room. Aunt Marilee had the ears of a guard dog. She was capable of being roused by something as slight as one of them turning over in bed. Often her aunt rose in the night to come peek in hers and Willie Lee's rooms in a habit Corrine termed bed-checking.

"Just checking," her aunt had explained to Corrine during those first weeks when Corrine had come to stay with her. Corrine wondered what her aunt was checking for. Did she believe they might disappear in the night? The idea that her aunt believed some such harm could come to them in bed made Corrine, already a nervous child, more nervous.

In those first weeks, Corrine would come bolt upright in bed with some alarm at hearing someone breathing near her bed. After a few times of this, Aunt Marilee would not come into the room but looked from the doorway, not realizing she could on occasion still awaken Corrine, who was equally a light and fitful sleeper and could still hear her aunt's breathing in the dark.

At last, and very quietly, Corrine pulled both her tiny flashlight and her mother's card from beneath her pillow. Pressing on the pinpoint light, she studied the card for a long minute; then she pressed off the light, and tucked it and the card back underneath her pillow.

She lay there thinking of her mother and of all that had happened and what might happen in the future, should her mother actually come to get her, which Corrine did not believe she was going to do.

Earlier in the year, her mother had given Aunt Marilee and Papa Tate legal custody of Corrine, because her mother had gone into a rehabilitation hospital for alcoholics and generally out of control people. That was what Corrine had overheard Aunt Vella call it. Her mother had had a breakdown and gotten picked up in a public fountain in New Orleans. When Aunt Marilee had spoken to Louis, her mother's boyfriend, he had told her that her mother had been awfully beautiful in the fountain. Somehow that had struck Aunt Marilee hard, so Corrine connected there was significance to it but did not understand exactly what it was.

This had all happened back in the spring, at the time of Aunt Marilee's and Papa Tate's wedding. Her mother had been supposed to come for the wedding, but of course something always happened for her not to come, and this time it was her going into the hospital.

Aunt Marilee said, "Your mother is getting the help she needs. She is so brave to do this. It will be hard for her, but I know she's going to do just fine. God has your mother in hand, and we'll pray for her, too."

Corrine *had* prayed for her mother. She did want her mother to be happy and healthy, but she wasn't sure that any prayers from her would help the job. As a little girl, from the time she could remember, she had prayed for her mother to be happy and for God to send a man to be the husband and daddy they both wanted, and for them to be a happy family in a nice house, like her mother was always talking about.

It never had happened.

What had happened was that her mother picked one sorry boyfriend after another. At the outset of each of these relationships, she always said, "Oh, boy, this time, Corrine, honey, our ship has come in," or words to that effect. But Corrine, having that rare understanding of children who grow up too fast, saw that her mother seemed determined to sink her own ship.

Sometimes, after her mother drank a lot of beer, she would begin to cry and to tell Corrine how things would have been different if Corrine's father had not been killed on that drilling rig. "He would have taken good care of us," her mother would say over and over.

Corrine had never known her father. Her mother had no

pictures of him, either. She described him physically as blond-haired and blue-eyed, traits that did not show up on Corrine.

She felt as if she had been a burden to her mother, so much so that finally her mother had called Aunt Marilee to come down to Fort Worth to get her. Corrine, almost ten years old at the time and already mature beyond her years, could see that her mother had been in a desperate situation, without a job and too beaten up by her latest boyfriend to get any employment right away. Deep inside, Corrine even perceived that her mother had done something of a heroic thing in placing her into Aunt Marilee's capable hands, letting go of the one other person in this world who belonged to her.

Sometimes, even though she didn't want to, Corrine could recall her mother's face contorted with despair and her eyes flowing with tears as she had told Corrine that she would have to go live with Aunt Marilee. "Just for a while, my baby...just for a while," she repeated, sobbing and hugging Corrine.

Remembering now, Corrine turned into her mattress, squeezing her eyes closed, wishing to block out the tide of confusing emotions that swept over her.

Her mother would not come, so there was no need to get all worked up over it. And no need to tell Aunt Marilee, either.

The three of them—Corrine, Willie Lee and Aunt Marilee—stood in a line, looking over the display of decorated artificial trees in the Christmas shop at Wal-Mart. Papa Tate had not joined them in the excursion, because he said decorating the house and choosing the tree was women's and children's business.

"Then what is the man's business in Christmas?" Aunt Marilee had asked.

"Lights," Papa Tate said. "Men do the lights, and cut down the tree when required." He said if Aunt Marilee wanted to go to the Christmas tree farm to cut a live one, that as the man of the house, it was his duty to take her. "But women do everything else."

"I have married a tree killer," Aunt Marilee said. "I'm shocked."

Watching her aunt now studying the trees, Corrine tried to judge which way to go on this thing—supportive of her aunt getting an artificial tree, or vetoing it. She herself did not have a strong view either way, but this was not the case with her aunt.

A Christmas tree was really important to Aunt Marilee. This was because, as Corrine gathered from both her mother and her aunt, both women had suffered the lack of an adequate tree and mostly any happy Christmases during their childhoods.

Corrine had heard from each of them as to how they had been poor, and poor in their time was really poor. They had not had a telephone or television at certain times, and Corrine, who had usually had both, except for brief times when her mother was without a boyfriend or a job, could not envision this.

The fact of them being poor may have been one of the few things upon which her aunt and mother agreed. Whenever they got together, there would be a short period when they discussed their deprived childhood. They batted their poor-child statements back and forth like a tennis ball. Aunt Marilee, the older sister, would start off with, "If there was help from the government, we didn't know it," and Corrine's mother would say, "We had church people give us food, and that was mortifying," and then Aunt Marilee might tell the one about Mary Louise Youngblood's hand-me-down dress. "I wore it to school, and Mary Louise told everyone how it had been hers." Both her aunt and her mother told many stories of this nature and had a great time doing it.

The conversation would eventually evolve to how their father, Grama Norma's first husband, had drunk up any money they did have, and how the trees they had at Christmas had been left-over and spindly things with hardly any branches on them.

"Once my father even stole a tree," Aunt Marilee had told her. "He came in a week before Christmas, in the middle of the night, and he had a tree complete with lights and decorations. Even the tinsel. I heard the commotion and snuck down the hall to see him comin' in with this tree. Ornaments flew off like big snowflakes as he staggered around the livin' room with it, still in the stand, too, attempting to get it put in front of the window, while Mama was havin' a hissy fit and tryin' to keep the curtains closed. It was all over town the next day how the Sheriff's tree out front of the station had been stolen.

"Luckily no one ever came to our house, so we didn't have to worry someone might recognize the tree," she added. "Although Mama took the police station ornaments off and hid them in the attic, and got new at discount from Aunt Vella. It was by far the prettiest tree we ever had."

Grama Norma did not appreciate this story. She always said it was not true the way Aunt Marilee made her out as having a hissy fit. She was simply doing what had to be done to live with her first husband.

Corrine thought Grama Norma was a bit odd. She had white carpet throughout her house that she didn't like people to walk on, and she didn't drive too straight, and she didn't see when her husband, Carl, sneaked drinks from a small liquor bottle in his coat. Aunt Marilee had explained that Grama Norma did see, but chose not to.

For her part, Corrine believed Aunt Marilee, because she knew well that Grama Norma, and her own mother, too, could stretch the truth like a rubber band, but Aunt Marilee had never lied to her. That she knew of. This brought up the thought that maybe Aunt Marilee was just a better liar than the other two. Still, she trusted Aunt Marilee more than anyone in the world.

Corrine, who did not think her Christmases with her mother had been real winners, also thought the story of the stolen Christmas tree was rather exciting. Her own Christmases had been more on the dreary side. Usually there had been just herself and her mother, whose attempts at gaiety always made Corrine feel she came up short in that department.

Nevertheless, they always had a particularly lovely tree, because her mother saved for the whole year, regularly putting coins and bills into a coffee tin, in order to buy a tall, thickly branched one. They decorated the tree with glass balls her mother carefully chose and kept in outdated suitcases of the hard-sided variety that weren't made anymore and that her mother got at the Salvation Army store. Her mother kept anything of importance in suitcases, as they could easily be picked up and carried when they did one of their hurried moves in the night.

Each Christmas there would be presents for Corrine beneath the tree, and not just school clothes, but toys, even if they were cheap ones. Aunt Marilee had sent presents every year down to Fort Worth for as long as Corrine could remember, and not just for Corrine, but for her mother, too. Her mother would open them and cry. And directly after, when she phoned Aunt Marilee to thank her, the two would get in a big fight on the phone.

Aunt Marilee went all out on the presents, and Corrine knew from her past two Christmases with her aunt that the closets were filling up. When the tree went up, soon would follow piles of presents beneath it for Corrine and Willie Lee, so many that Corrine would often feel embarrassed. She would think about poor children in China, who weren't even Christians, so they didn't have Christmas, or starving children in Africa, who wouldn't have a Christmas dinner. Thinking of those children made her feel guilty for her bounty.

Often, about this time of year, she would consider growing up and entering missionary work.

After several minutes of standing there staring at the artificial trees, Corrine reached out and touched one.

"Looks real, don' it?" said a man she just then saw nearby. He was an older man, a rancher, with pointy-toed boots and a cowboy hat.

While Corrine was wondering about talking to a stranger, Aunt Marilee said with some wonderment, "Yes, it really does," then reached out and felt it for herself.

Corrine looked at the skinny stick of a trunk on each tree and thought that if the branches could be made to look so lifelike, why didn't some manufacturer think to make the trunk look more real?

The old gentleman said, "They have come a long way in this world. Now people put up a tree on Thanksgiving weekend. Used to, we went out and chopped us down a cedar on Christmas Eve, put it up that night, and took it down Christmas night."

"You on-ly had a tree for one night?" Willie Lee asked.

"Yep. Had Christmas all day long, but that was it. We got back to chores the next day, up before the sun."

Another deprived childhood story. Corrine thought putting up a tree for one night a big chore in itself and not hardly worth it, and if she'd been so poor as to have to work all the time, she sure wouldn't have bothered with the work of that tree.

"We didn't have 'lectricity, so our tree didn't have any lights. Some used candles. My aunt had those. Did you have those?" he asked Aunt Marilee, who said no.

Corrine thought the guy must be really old. He looked pretty good for his age.

"Well, these here trees are practical, I'll give 'em that. Pay once, and keep it. Don't keep payin' year after year, and they're not likely to catch on fire, either. Safer," he said as a last comment before heading off to his wife, who was calling him from over in the shampoo aisle. She looked so old that it was a wonder she could walk.

Corrine swung her attention back to see that her Aunt Marilee had a determined expression. "It can't be too big...where *are* we going to put it?" She slowly walked around the display, measuring with her eyes.

Corrine followed, trying to pick out the one she liked the best. There was one that revolved. She pointed it out, but Aunt Marilee did not seem impressed. She said she didn't know how she would anchor a revolving tree to the wall, so likely the cat could take it down, and then it'd be revolving on the floor and make a real mess. "It wouldn't be safe," she said.

There was a tree that had lights attached right on the branches.

"It's convenient," Corrine offered.

Aunt Marilee studied this one hard, likely looking for any thing in it that might not be safe.

Willie Lee put his nose up to one. "They do not smell."

"No, they don't," Aunt Marilee said with a sigh.

Corrine pointed out spray cans of spruce scent.

Aunt Marilee looked at the cans but did not seem too enthused. After another look at the trees, she said, "These trees will be on sale for five more days. Let's think about it."

While Aunt Marilee went down the health and beauty aisles, Corrine had the good fortune to catch sight of a little girl about to get her ears pierced over in the jewelry department. Pretending to study the cheap jewelry on a large revolving rack, Corrine watched the ear piercing with avid interest.

It turned out to be pretty much of a distasteful sight. The little girl was only about four or five, and cute as she could be, dressed really sweet in a little pink outfit and with her hair carefully braided. Quite shortly Corrine had to restrain herself from going over there and jerking the girl away from her stupid mother, who was as slovenly as cousin Belinda used to be and who kept saying that it wasn't going to hurt, which anyone could see was a big fat lie, because the jewelry clerk had this big gun in her hand. It was like they were going to blow a hole in the girl's ear, which they must have done, because when the jewelry clerk put it to the girl's earlobe, the girl went to screaming.

The gun had put a post earring in the little girl's ear, though, which did seem an economy of motion. But how anyone could say that doing it wasn't going to hurt was beyond Corrine.

She looked around for Aunt Marilee, who she expected to hear the girl's howls and come over and read the women the riot act. This concerned her, too, because then probably Aunt Marilee wouldn't let Corrine get her ears pierced.

But upon watching them shoot the little girl in the other

ear, she thought that she might have to rethink this desire of getting her ears pierced anyway.

When she caught up with her aunt, she studied her aunt's pierced ears. She still liked the way earrings looked on her aunt, and she counted ten women all around, shopping and in the checkout aisle. They had pierced ears and fun earrings and were still alive. One woman had two holes in each earlobe, and there were even a couple of little babies with pierced ears. These were Mexican or Oriental children, who just about always had their ears pierced as babies. This seemed sensible to Corrine, who in her mind saw doctors doing the job. Get it over and done with, because then, when the babies grew into schoolgirls, they would not pester their mothers for pierced ears. These babies had small round gold posts or hoops in their dusky ears and looked so feminine.

Yes, she still wanted her ears pierced, but she did not think she wanted that jewelry clerk coming at her with that gun.

"Aunt Marilee, will you pierce my ears?"

Aunt Marilee's eyebrows went up. "I don't think so," she said very firmly. Then her expression softened. "We'll go over to the earring store at the mall soon. Maybe for your birthday."

Her birthday did not constitute "soon" for Corrine, whose mind was still thinking about the gun in the clerk's hand. "Do they use a gun at the mall?"

"Well, I don't know," her aunt answered absently, because she had begun putting things from the cart up onto the checkout belt.

"Who did your ears?"

"A girl at school. We did each other's ears," said Aunt Marilee in a preoccupied fashion, then realized what she had revealed, and added, "Don't you do that. It isn't sanitary. There are a lot more germs these days. If you still want your ears pierced in two weeks, I'll take you up to the mall."

Corrine, who thought fleetingly that she had no school friend to pierce her ears, anyway, had wanted her ears pierced for way over six months, so she did not think she was going to change her mind now. Except she might if they came at her with one of those guns. She wondered if there was another way to get the job done. Maybe she could find out in the school library.

"Look, Willie Lee, there is a Santa Claus," Aunt Marilee said with excitement.

There were a pair of Salvation Army bell ringers just outside the doors of Wal-Mart, standing with their red bucket. One of them was dressed up as a Santa Claus.

"Here, sugar, go take this dollar and put it in the bucket."

Willie Lee said nothing about the Santa and went willingly over to the bucket. When he dropped it through the wire, which Corrine figured was on top of the bucket so that no one could get their hand in and take *out* of it, the Santa said in this hearty voice, "Thank you, little boy. You'll get what you want for Christmas," and passed Willie Lee a piece of candy.

Uh-oh.

Willie Lee looked at him and said, "How do you know?"

"Know what?"

"That I will get what I want?"

"Well, because I'm Santa Claus."

Willie Lee peered at the man. "Your bea-rd does not look real. If you were San-ta, you would have a bea-rd that grows."

The man smoothed the white fluff that looked more like cotton candy than a beard, and not very good cotton candy, either. The elastic band could be seen going over his ear. It seemed to Corrine that if someone was going to pass himself off as a Santa Claus, he ought to do a better job of it.

The man said, "Well, I'm a Santa Helper."

"Oh." Willie Lee said, staring at him. "Have you seen San-ta Claus?"

"Yes...yes, I have."

"When?"

"Well, at night. I saw him just the other night."

"Where?"

The fake Santa, who was attempting to smile and greet people going past, encouraging them to put money in the kettle, cast Willie Lee an impatient look. "In my backyard."

"San-ta comes to your back-ya-rd?"

Willie Lee clearly didn't believe this, and his slow pattern of speech was an irritation to many people, who don't want to take the extra time. The Santa was not happy about the exchange, plus people were crowding up, and now two little girls holding their mother's hands had brought her to a stop to regard the Santa Claus and listen to him. He said to them, "Ho, ho, ho, here are some sweet little girls who are on Santa's list," and handed them some candy.

The mother dropped money into the kettle, prompting Willie Lee to ask, "Are you help-ing San-ta get mon-ey?"

"Yes."

Aunt Marilee pulled him away then. "We need to get out of the way, honey."

They were driving out of the Wal-Mart parking lot when Willie Lee said, "I guess there are fake San-tas just like there are fake Christ-mas trees."

Aunt Marilee looked at Corrine with a perplexed and dismayed expression. Corrine didn't know what to say and settled for a shrug.

Thankfully, Willie Lee didn't say anything else.

Corrine thought about it as they drove back to Valentine. There were a lot of fake things in the world. Fake Christmas trees, fake pine scent and fake Christmas balls really made from plastic. Fake horse tails—she had seen them for sale in one of the horse magazines. Fake cleavage created by pads to push up the fat. Fake leather that looked just like real but was a lot cheaper, and some cow did not have to die to produce it, either. Some of the fake things worked out, and some of them did not.

That fake beard on the Santa didn't work, was her opinion.

And she decided that maybe she did not want a fake tree, either. Maybe somehow she had inherited from her mother and aunt the desire for a big, beautiful, real tree. Then thinking how the tree was a living thing and would be chopped down made her a little sad.

5

Supper was beef stew. This was one of the staple dishes that Aunt Marilee could manage to get to turn out well most of the time, and something she could throw in the Crock-Pot and leave. It was a sure sign of winter's having arrived, because Aunt Marilee only made beef stew in the winter months.

Aunt Marilee had some particular rules about living in society. She said it was like no one wore white shoes before Easter—and Aunt Marilee was firm on this rule—no one was supposed to make beef stew until the evening temperatures got down to forty on a regular basis.

To accompany the stew they had crisp cornbread and sweet cinnamon apples that Papa Tate decided at the last minute he had to have and was cooking at the stove. Papa Tate was a really good cook, which is why he always said Aunt Marilee married him.

Corrine was helping to set everything on the dining room table when the telephone rang. She heard Aunt Marilee say, "I might as well answer it now as later."

Coming into the kitchen, she saw her aunt jerk up the

receiver and say hello. Then, after a second of listening, "Hello, Julia, how are you?"

Mrs. Julia Jenkins-Tinsley.

"Yes, we are just about to sit down for supper," Aunt Marilee was saying. "Maybe you could…"

She stopped and fell to listening, tucking the receiver against her shoulder as she brought a big stoneware bowl from the cabinet, then plunked it down and took hold of the receiver, straightening as if from an electric jolt.

She said, "Willie Lee is ten years old now, Julia," which was something to reply, without saying right out that she had not known of her son's change regarding Santa.

She listened some more and responded with, "Yes, I'm sorry to hear that, Julia. But it is early." And then, "Yes, I will make sure to mention it in Wednesday's column."

When Aunt Marilee hung up, she stood there for a moment with her back to them, her hand remaining on the receiver and her shoulders slumping.

"What is it?" Papa Tate asked, glancing over from attending to his apples.

"Oh, Tate."

He instantly went to her and put his arm around her, saying, "What is it, honey?"

Aunt Marilee laid her head against his shoulder. "Oh, Tate," she said, about like she'd heard Oklahoma had been bombed, "I knew something wasn't right this afternoon when he saw Santa Claus, but…"

She lifted her baleful eyes. "Willie Lee doesn't believe in Santa Claus anymore."

Papa Tate's eyebrows went up, but immediately he looked enormously relieved, as undoubtedly he had expected something much worse. He patted her shoulder and said, "Well, it was bound to happen."

Aunt Marilee took exception to this. "I don't see why his innocence has to be robbed."

Then she looked at Corrine and demanded to know just what Willie Lee had said that afternoon down at the P.O.

Corrine, in a low voice, gave her aunt a concise version, then gave the opinion that the culprits who had brought this about were Cody Truax and Jimmy Spears, two boys who had a history of bullying Willie Lee. Aunt Marilee listened, her head cocked to hear every word, the whole while she was putting the beef stew into the serving dish and pulling the pan of cornbread from the oven.

After Corrine's tale, she related to Papa Tate what had gone on with the Santa at the Wal-Mart. Papa Tate got a few chuckles out of it, but Aunt Marilee was not happy.

"Tate, I think you should talk to him about this."

Papa Tate looked surprised. "About just what?"

"Well, about believing in Santa. This is not good, his givin' up Santa."

"It happens, Marilee, to all of us."

"Not to Willie Lee it shouldn't. He's gettin' a wrong idea."

Papa Tate rubbed the side of his face and said, "What do you want me to say to him? And maybe you should handle this thing, anyway."

"I want you to convince him there is a Santa, and you need to do it, because you are the best at convincing people of anything in the world."

Aunt Marilee did not realize exactly what she had said. Papa Tate gave her a long look, and then he was wise enough to think on the matter as he poured the apples into a serving dish. Finally he came up with, "Marilee, I don't think lyin' to him will be a help."

"I'm not sayin' lie to him. Just convince him that there is a Santa."

"Oh."

From the outset of supper, Aunt Marilee kept casting Papa Tate glances. She was clearly anxious for him to begin convincing Willie Lee about Santa. When Papa Tate did not open the conversation, she said, "Willie Lee, what is this Mrs. Jenkins-Tinsley tells me that you said you no longer believe in Santa?"

Willie Lee blinked from behind his thick glasses. He bit his bottom lip, and then he said, "I am a big boy now. I know that San-ta Claus is a fair-ry tale. You put my presents un-der the tree."

Aunt Marilee gazed at him, and then she took in a breath and looked at Papa Tate.

"Well, now," said Papa Tate, holding his buttered cornbread to the side as he leaned toward Willie Lee. "You are a big boy...that's true, but we don't want you to dismiss this idea of Santa Claus so quickly."

Willie Lee gazed at Papa Tate, and so did Corrine and Aunt Marilee.

Papa Tate rubbed the side of his face and said, "I'm a big boy, right?"

He waited for Willie Lee to nod, then continued. "Well, I believe in Santa Claus, and I think it is *because* I am a big boy that I can believe in him."

Willie Lee moved his eyes to the table and then back to Papa Tate. "Does San-ta bring your pres-ents?"

Corrine's gaze moved to Papa Tate, and across the table from her, Aunt Marilee did the same.

"Well..." Papa Tate frowned, then he nodded. "I have to say that you are right. Me and your mother put the presents under the tree." He did not like saying it, and his tone faltered as he sent an uncertain glance to Aunt Marilee, who looked about like her dog had up and died.

Papa Tate set down his crumbling piece of cornbread, wiped his hands and started in with his expanding manner that meant he was arriving at an idea. "But that's only so far as that goes. It is the force behind the presence that I'm talkin' about, Willie Lee. I'm talkin' about when you start settin' aside belief in Santa, you are losin' somethin' precious, and we don't want to see that happen to you. Okay, so some boys at school told you there isn't any Santa Claus, but they clearly don't know the entire truth of the situation, and they are missin' out, too." Papa Tate was warming up to the subject.

"I point out that there is at least a Santa or two, because we see them all over the place at Christmas, so there's your answer to the question of is there really a Santa. Yes, in some form, there certainly is. These Santas are out doin' good and making children happy, too, so isn't that the definition of a Santa?

"There are thousands of stories told about Santa Claus, songs sung about him, and people writing him letters. All of that makes a Santa in spirit, and it is the spirit of Christmas. That's why there is a Santa, and that's why I keep believin' in Santa Claus. I don't want to miss out on any of it, and I don't want you growin' up in the wrong way and missin' out on it, either."

Aunt Marilee's expression had turned to one of admiration. Papa Tate, who had become confident in his stance, became even more so. He picked up his cornbread and slathered more butter on it, then pointed the knife at Willie Lee. "Believe in Santa Claus, Willie Lee, because it's good for you."

"Yes, sir," Willie Lee said willingly, and because he was very adept at understanding when adults wanted him to please.

Suddenly Corrine was struck by how innocent her cousin looked, his blond spiky hair catching the overhead light, his eyes blinking behind his thick glasses as he made an effort to understand what Papa Tate was saying, which was all truth. But she had an inkling that she could never have put into words. It was about the reason that Aunt Marilee and Papa Tate and Julia Jenkins-Tinsley—and Corrine herself—wanted Willie Lee to keep believing in Santa. It was because they wanted to keep him all safe and secure.

And on some level Corrine understood that if Willie Lee no longer believed in Santa Claus, then all of them lost belief. If Willie Lee was not safe and secure, neither were any of them.

The Valentine Voice

Christmas About Town
by Marilee Holloway

Thanksgiving's down, Christmas is on full-time. Those of you who are lamenting over how commercialized the holiday has become and that people are rushing Christmas, get over it. This is how things are, and no amount of grumbling will change it. Join us and have all the fun you can.

If you still have pumpkins, Indian corn and scarecrows on your porch, you are late. Get them off and hang up the holly wreaths and Santas. You might want to check out the special insert in today's edition, which features a column from Martha Stewart, as well as one by our own Peggy Sue Langston, Valentine High School home economics teacher, for some quick front door decorating ideas. A cheery front door can make all the difference in a person's mood, both your own and those who come up to your front door. Let's keep that in mind with all the family visiting going on.

If you find that all of your Christmas decorations look like the clothes hanging at the back of your closet, you have the opportunity to correct that by attending the Christmas home demonstration sponsored by the Valentine Women's League, featuring Mrs. Langston and her designs. The demonstration will be held at the Christmas Cottage on Main Street, this Tuesday evening at 7:00 p.m. The cost is $10, and for that you are guaranteed to take home a lovely wreath, plus many ideas to use around your home. Also feel free to bring other craft materials, and Mrs. Langston will try to help you make something from them.

The Christmas Cottage is once again situated across the street from the Valentine Fire Department and is being operated by the ladies of the Fire Department Auxiliary. The Cottage is filled with all manner of beautiful items for the Christmas home and great gift ideas, too. All profits go to help support our Fire Department throughout the year, so be sure to drop in and make a purchase. The home or business you save from fire may be your own.

Many of our merchants and civic clubs have banded together to make a magical wonderland of light displays in the Valentine City Park. If you have not seen the Holiday Lights in the Park, you are missing a real treat. Our thanks to all the men and women who gave up much of last week, including part of their Thanksgiving Day, to help untangle lights from last year.

Let me also set the record straight that it was not Mayor Upchurch who took scissors to two of the more tangled strands; it was our own Editor, who proved capable of getting them put back together with electrical tape, too.

Mark your calendars for the St. Luke Episcopal Church's annual Christmas bazaar. Times are 9-6 Friday and Saturday, and Sunday 1-5. Those of you who have attended before know this is a good place to get that special one-of-a-kind gift, or to see people you have not seen all year. Miss Minnie Oakes will have one of her lovely handmade quilts for auction, even though she is a Baptist. She did say this may be her last year to supply a quilt, so you won't want to miss your chance at getting one. The silent bidding will begin at noon on Friday and continue through to Sunday at 4:00 p.m.

Grace Florist has a fresh supply of the best potted poinsettias to have graced our town in years, and at rock-bottom prices to rival the famous national discount store. They are also stocked with table centerpieces, or they will make one to your specification, and Fred Grace says you can stand right there and direct the making.

The Main Street Café is providing a free cup of hazelnut coffee with a piece of homemade pie, your choice of apple, dried peach or raisin, for every receipt from a Valentine merchant in the amount of $10 or more. Owner Fayrene Gardner says come in and rest your feet for a few minutes, all week long.

Don't forget the annual Valentine Chamber of Commerce toy drive. You can drop off your new, unwrapped toys here at the *Voice*, and you'll receive a talking Santa Claus pin for the effort.

This week's recipe is courtesy of Mrs. Naomi Smith, who gives us a recipe to use the leftover turkey or ham you might have from Thanksgiving. She says, with her crew, she bakes extra meat in order to have leftovers.

Naomi's Turkey (or Ham) and Fruit Salad

1 orange, peeled and sectioned, (or do what I do: 1 small can mandarin oranges, drained.)

15 large grapes, cut in half (If you're stuck using the seeded variety, do remove the seeds.)
Two handfuls of sliced almonds
1 banana, peeled and sliced
1 apple, cored and diced
3 cups cooked white meat turkey, ham or chicken
1 cup mayonnaise (Naomi's a cook and makes hers from scratch, but I advise Kraft Mayo.)

Mix it all up, chill and serve on a bed of lettuce. It looks very pretty.

Please send your news and gift ideas in to Charlotte at the *Voice*, phone her at 555-4743 during business hours, or e-mail charlotteconroy@thevalentinevoice.com. Due to the volume of news for this special Christmas column and the fact that I am not organized, Charlotte is keeping track of everything sent to us. Your cooperation is appreciated.

6

It was Papa Tate's habit to cook breakfast on Sunday mornings and to read aloud from *The Valentine Voice* while they all ate. He was very proud of his paper and liked to make sure they heard some things from it.

This Sunday morning, he read Aunt Marilee's column and about himself cutting the two strings of lights. He said to Aunt Marilee, "You just had to go and tell the world your husband lost it, didn't you?"

Corrine had been there when he'd gotten so aggravated with the tangled strands of lights that he had gone over and plucked scissors right out of the hand of Iris MacCoy, who was using duct tape to attach lights to a snowman form, and cut out the worst knotted places.

It was the first time Corrine had ever seen him really mad, which was strange, when she thought about it, since she had seen him putting up with Aunt Marilee's ex-husband butting into their lives, and with the tornado taking their house, and with people all mad at him about his really hot editorial saying that too much money and time was spent on sports in the schools and not enough on educating.

He sure had been mad at that string of lights, though, and watching him now, Corrine sat very still, wondering if he and Aunt Marilee were about to have a fight.

But then he began laughing, and as Aunt Marilee passed by to go get more coffee, he pulled her down into his lap and kissed her.

Corrine watched them, wondering if knowing how to kiss came natural, and then she got up and took her plate into the kitchen to put in the dishwasher, because she was so embarrassed at the feelings and thoughts that came crawling over her, making her skin fairly itch.

She had heard girls talking about kissing their boyfriends. There'd been a number of girls talking about it at the age of nine, for that matter.

Here she was on the verge of turning thirteen, and she had no experience whatsoever of kissing even one boy. The entire idea of getting close enough to a boy to kiss him was frightening in itself. The only two people she was close enough with to kiss were Willie Lee and Aunt Marilee, and even then, she didn't often do it.

She had almost gotten close enough to kiss Ricky Dale once last summer, but then he had jumped up and started acting stupid. She had been aggravated with him for that, but a little relieved. Maybe he hadn't even known how to kiss back then. She wondered if he knew how now. It would be embarrassing if, when she got to kiss Ricky Dale, he knew how and she didn't.

She had heard a girl say she practiced on her hand. Corrine had tried it, but doing that was just too stupid.

They never attended Sunday school but went to church services. Aunt Marilee, who might have been in favor of Sunday school had it taken place in the afternoon, said the main problem with going to church was that all that was required to get there involved the same routine they practiced all week, getting everyone out of bed, fed and dressed, and finding car keys and purse. All of that proved totally counterproductive to solitary quiet time spent in communion with God.

"It is the constant war between the spiritual life and the earthly life," proclaimed Papa Tate, in his wise Editor voice. He had no answer for the dilemma, except possibly staying home in pajamas and watching television evangelists, which he was not against and thought could pass in times of sickness or depression, but was not satisfactory on a regular basis. He was too much of a visitor with everyone to be happy with television church.

That particular Sunday morning, while in her routine of rushing to get ready for church, Corrine found Willie Lee in a precarious position at the kitchen window, where no one had remembered to replace the screen.

"What are you doing?" she asked, hurrying to him with some alarm, imagining him tumbling out.

He was feeding a pigeon. He had gotten it a dish of water and a handful of dried oatmeal.

"He is ti-red, Cor-rine. He is sick."

Corrine knew to trust her cousin's judgment about animals. The bird did look exhausted. It sat plopped down on its feet, its little eyes blinking in a droopy manner.

"It's a pigeon, Willie Lee. Maybe it's a homing pigeon. Have you picked it up? There may be a band on its leg."

"Oh...I will see." He put his hand out to stroke the bird, and then he gently lifted it inside. The bird cocked its head back and forth, regarding Willie Lee and not frightened at all.

It did have a band on its leg. Corrine explained about the band and how it was put on homing pigeons for the purpose of identification.

"He belongs to someone, so maybe you shouldn't feed him. He needs to go home to whoever owns him," Corrine said.

"I have to feed him. He is tir-ed and hung-ry. And he needs to stay here where it is warm."

"Not inside," Corrine said firmly. "He'll poop all over. Put him back out on the windowsill so that he can fly away when he is ready."

Willie Lee did so with great reluctance. Corrine didn't put the screen in, but she did shut and lock the window, saying that she didn't want Willie Lee to fall out.

"I do not think I will fall out," he said.

"Well, I would hope not."

"Why?"

"Because it would be awful." The image of him all broken and bleeding on the sidewalk filled her mind, but to speak of this seemed too horrible and possibly harmful to Willie Lee's psyche, so she said, "We would all be upset."

"*I* might be up-set," Willie Lee stated, blinking behind his thick glasses.

Corrine shut her mouth and went to check her image in the dining-room mirror, where, if she stood back by the table, she could almost see her full self.

She was wearing a rose-pink sweater and the long black skirt Aunt Marilee had bought her at The Limited at the mall. She thought she looked good in the outfit. It seemed to benefit her shape. At least in the sweater and slinky skirt she had a shape.

Very often, though, she had trouble trusting her perceptions, and this being one of those uncertain times, she looked more closely, trying to observe herself from someone else's eyes and to ascertain if she had missed something and perhaps really looked silly.

She did wish her hair looked more grown-up. Maybe she could put a rinse on it and make it auburn, like Aunt Marilee did.

Whenever anyone said how pretty her aunt's hair was, her aunt always said, "Thank you, and I thank God for it," making a joke. "One never has to tell everything one knows," Aunt Marilee said, in justifying why she did not tell that she applied color to her hair. She only admitted to the touch-up job, as she called it, when someone asked her point-blank, "Do you color your hair?" She would say, "I touch it up a bit with a rinse." Somehow a rinse was supposed to be more natural than flat-out color.

Since Aunt Marilee was so opposed to her using makeup,

Corrine doubted her aunt would allow her to put a rinse on her hair.

There came the sound of a car honk in the street, and Willie Lee called from the front window: "Pa-pa Tate is ready with the car."

Corrine called to Aunt Marilee. A moment later her aunt came flying out of the bathroom. She looked thrown together, but on Aunt Marilee that generally still looked striking. Her color was high, and she slung a burgundy wool wrap around her shoulders.

"Y'all get coats on. Where's my purse?"

"We don't need coats," Corrine said and handed over the purse from where it sat on the sideboard.

Aunt Marilee, who was clearly about to argue the point on the coats, decided not to and went on through the door Corrine held open, seeming to suck the rest of them along by the force of her movement, down the stairwell and across the sidewalk to the curb, where they threw themselves into the waiting white Cherokee.

"Whew, we made it," Aunt Marilee said when the doors were slammed.

Munro sat in the back seat between Corrine and Willie Lee, panting.

"Did you doubt you would?" Papa Tate asked, as he headed from the curb.

"Yes, Tate, very often I do," replied Aunt Marilee, yanking down the visor and putting her lipstick on in the mirror there.

The sun shone down on the First Street Methodist Church, and the bell in the steeple was ringing out when Papa Tate pulled into the parking lot.

Bong...bong...bong. Corrine loved to hear the bell. It had a friendly tone, as if it were saying: *Wel*-come...*wel*-come.

Even though it was a crisp winter morning, there was no wind. Corrine found the good weather disappointing. How could anyone get into the Christmas spirit with weather like this? The men hanging out on the front lawn and smoking cigarettes did so easily in shirtsleeves or unbuttoned sport coats. They called greetings to Papa Tate and Aunt Marilee. In the friendly manner he always displayed, Papa Tate went to join them, shaking hands all around, eager to find out if there was anything he needed to report in Wednesday's edition, and to just generally be the Editor, as he enjoyed doing.

Corrine saw Sheriff Oakes, one of Papa Tate's good friends and Ricky Dale's father, among the men. Ricky Dale's big brother was with the sheriff, but she didn't see Ricky Dale. She headed on up the stairs behind Aunt Marilee, Willie Lee and Munro, and entered the high-ceilinged sanctuary.

The light in the sanctuary had a golden cast, caused by the five windows of opaque ivory glass on either side of the room and the single round stained-glass window above the altar. Corrine, having the artist's appreciative eye for color and light, never failed to be affected. It was like entering a holy place, where angels might be seen at any minute, except right that moment there was all the commotion of people arriving and calling greetings to each other. Three little kids were running up and down the center aisle. Pastor Smith, who had done away with the church nursery so that all children would be with them during services and maintained that he could speak above any crying child, was fond of saying, "Suffer the young children to come unto me." Since he seemed eager to have children in the sanctuary for church service, Corrine wondered at that word "suffer."

Aunt Marilee led the way to their accustomed seats in the second to the last pew on the right side.

Aunt Vella, standing with some other women near the middle of the sanctuary, called a greeting in what she meant as a hushed voice but wasn't much of one. "Hi, Shoo-gahs!"

Immediately Aunt Marilee was surrounded and holding court. This was a regular occurrence, as people wanted to tell her things for her column. Corrine and Willie Lee were used to getting themselves out of the way, and this time they moved extra fast. Corrine shoved Willie Lee to her far side, and Munro slipped further beneath the pew, where he must have been faced with ankles all around and, had he not been such a sweet-natured dog, might have gotten in a good bite or two.

Corrine busied herself with looking up and bookmarking in three hymnals all the songs that they were to sing, which were listed in the bulletin. She used little pieces of paper that stayed in the hymnals from week to week, since these were their regular places and books. While doing this, she kept a lookout for Ricky Dale. She would raise her head and eyes just enough to scan the area but not appear as if she were looking for anyone.

There were his mother, with her bright, naturally carrot-colored hair, and older sister sitting up in their pew, four rows up, on the extreme right. Sheriff Oakes liked to sit on the outside aisle in case he needed to get out quickly for an emergency, like a car wreck, a fire, or some domestic dispute. Ricky Dale was not with them.

Another glance around the sanctuary and she saw Anson Brown, one of Ricky Dale's friends, talking with Paris Miller. Paris had her hair cut short as a boy's and wore black lipstick. She was fourteen and in the eighth grade, having been held back a year. She came to church by herself, which was always some amazement to Corrine.

She did not see Ricky Dale. Maybe he was sick. She had never known Ricky Dale to be sick.

Just then Lila Hicks started playing the piano, the indication for everyone to get to their seats. Mrs. Hicks was somewhere on the other side of fifty-five, to use Aunt Marilee's expression; she had bright yellow hair and a rather round figure. She favored formfitting clothes, not the most wise choice. Corrine had heard Aunt Marilee and Aunt Vella say that Mrs. Hicks loved m and m's—men and music. Everyone did admire her piano playing. Right then she was playing "We Three Kings," with closed eyes and a happy smile.

The knot of women around Aunt Marilee dispersed, and Aunt Marilee sat down and breathed deeply. People came trailing in through the front doors and the side entry from the fellowship hall and Sunday school rooms, gathering their children and settling into the pews. The small choir assembled at the side of the altar.

Corrine, still watching for Ricky Dale but about decided he was not there, suddenly saw him come through the side entry. She almost did not recognize him. His hair was carefully styled, as it had been on Friday, and he wore a sport coat. Brown tweed. It was too big for him, probably belonged to his older brother.

And he was with Melissa Pruitt.

Corrine sat back at this fact, forgetting to pretend casual attention. Her gaze fastened like a magnet on the two, Ricky Dale all brown and Melissa all blonde. Melissa frosted her hair; Corrine had heard her talking about it at school.

She watched them stop and speak to Ricky Dale's mother. Melissa smiled in the fashion of a beauty queen, which indeed she was, having been in beauty pageants since the first grade, and then the Fall Queen for their middle school, as well as Rodeo Queen that past summer, the one who had lost control of her horse. A person became a rodeo queen by how many rodeo tickets they sold, not by how well they could ride. Corrine thought quickly and uncharitably that horses were not as impressed with the girl as were humans.

She watched Melissa and Ricky Dale proceed down to the front and back up the center aisle to the pew where Melissa's parents were sitting.

Just then Ricky Dale looked right at Corrine, and seeing this, she came to her senses and quickly averted her gaze to Mrs. Hicks playing on the piano. Out of the corner of her eye, she saw Mr. Pruitt get up to let his daughter and Ricky Dale slip into the pew.

She had not taken note, but she did not think the two had been holding hands. Even though they were now sitting shoulder to shoulder and could be holding hands, she told herself that most likely Mrs. Pruitt sitting right next to them prevented them from doing so in the pew.

She rather wished Ricky Dale would attempt to hold Melissa's hand and that Mr. Pruitt would smack him upside the head for the attempt.

* * *

"You go on," Aunt Marilee told Papa Tate when services had ended and everyone was rising and leaving.

Most Sundays after church they went down to Aunt Vella's and Uncle Perry's drugstore, where they had bar-beque sandwiches and ice-cream sundaes for lunch. "I'm going to the meeting for the Christmas pageant. Aunt Vella is stayin', too. She'll give us a ride after."

Papa Tate was going out the door before Corrine could jerk her attention away from watching Ricky Dale and Melissa and think up an excuse to go with him.

The subject of the Christmas pageant had come up earlier in the week, as well as again that morning at breakfast, when Aunt Marilee had mentioned the meeting. Both times Corrine had told her aunt then that she did not think she wanted to be in the pageant.

What she meant was that she *knew* she did not want to be in it, as she had not wanted to for the past three Christmases that she had been with her aunt, but she could not bring herself to say other than, "I do not think I want to." Aunt Marilee had said fine, but that Corrine could of course help this year.

This was the first year that Aunt Marilee was involving herself in the pageant, and she was pretty much going to drag Corrine along with her, in some capacity, as she usually did with things.

Seeing Ricky Dale with Melissa Pruitt had sent the matter of the pageant, and all other matters, right out of her mind. She had not heard the sermon, had barely followed along with the songs, and when Mrs. MacCoy had announced the meeting would take place, Corrine had heard but gone on thinking of how she might get Aunt Marilee to let her get her ears pierced and use makeup, just like Melissa, and preferably right this minute.

Melissa was in her same grade at school. She had a real figure and the biggest breasts of anyone in their grade. Despite all that Aunt Marilee and the physiology teacher said about people growing at different rates—which was proven out a lot by Ricky Dale—Corrine suspected that

Melissa could be a year or two older than twelve and managing to keep it secret.

Corrine ended up following after Aunt Marilee and Willie Lee and Munro, who were going down the center aisle to the front of the sanctuary, where Mrs. MacCoy was attempting to gather everyone, which was no easy task. At least in staying, Corrine could see whatever went on with Ricky Dale and Melissa. She wondered if they would stay.

As she passed where the two were still hanging out in the pew, talking with the Pruitts, she kept face forward. She didn't want them to think she had any interest in them whatsoever.

Just as she reached the front of the sanctuary, Mrs. MacCoy called out, "Up here, y'all. Anson…Paris…and you, too, Ricky Dale and Melissa. Y'all get up here."

Paris Miller, who was near the doors, went racing out, but Anson Brown was not so bold, probably because his father was a deacon. He came down the aisle, clowning with elaborately slumped shoulders, while Ricky Dale came striding past him in a cocky manner, his too-big sport coat fluttering out behind him. Melissa came more slowly, looking for all the world like she was walking along a beauty contest ramp. She didn't so much walk as she glided, smiling at those she knew, or at least imagined, were watching her.

All she lacked was the wave, Corrine thought.

Melissa and Ricky Dale fell in with the other young teens and a few of the bigger grade-school kids standing around, joking in whispers and trying to look cool. There were no high school kids, because to begin with there were only six in the congregation who came regularly and they all refused to do the pageant, even the pastor's teenage kids. Being senior high school teens, no one expected them to do the pageant. This was a clear demonstration to Corrine's mind that she would reach an age where she could do what she wanted.

Right then, though, she definitely felt uncertain as to where she fit in. She was not an older teen, but she stood with the adult women. She looked over to Ricky Dale and his crowd, but she couldn't move over there with them; she felt that she didn't fit in there even more.

So she turned to doing what she normally did, which was to attend to Willie Lee and in the process all the younger children, helping them to sit in a group on the carpet. When they were settled, rather than sit with Aunt Marilee and the other mothers in the front row, Corrine eased herself to a spot on the altar step, a vantage point where she could remain unnoticed but watch everything that went on.

To her surprise—and annoyance—Jojo MacCoy sat herself down on the step, too. She cast Corrine a quick half smile.

Corrine simply returned a blank stare. She had the urge to tell the girl to go find her own place, but she was stopped by the thought that, when considering first rights, it was God's step.

Melissa Pruitt was chosen to be the main heralding angel, who pronounced the big greetings to the shepherds and did a lot of narrating and got to stand in a spotlight. She about knocked out a fourth-grader for the part, while trying to appear like she had not volunteered. Corrine thought the girl would prove to be a great actress.

Ricky Dale was drafted as a wise man, as were Anson Brown and Anson's younger brother, Gideon. Corrine knew them slightly, because their mother, Imperia, sold advertising for the *Voice*. Anson was a real cut-up and showoff, so he was given the main wise man speaking part. He was going around saying, "This looks like mixed casting to me—two black dudes and a white wise guy."

Pastor Smith's middle son, Shad, was chosen to play Joseph.

"He even looks old," Jojo said in a low voice to Corrine, who spared her a glance but did not give voice to her thought of agreement.

She didn't know what the girl wanted, and she did not want to encourage whatever it was, although she would have to say that the Smith boy did look like a little old man. His real name was Shadrach, and his mother readily admitted she had been out of her mind after thirty-six hours of labor when she consented to letting her husband name him. He was eleven, skinny and had an unusually long face. A fake beard would be great on him.

The part of Mary settled on Jojo. No one said it aloud, but plainly there were only two other girls who looked innocent enough to portray the Virgin Mother. One of these said she was going to be out of town, and the other said very desperately, "No, I can't," and looked as if she might cry or throw up at the prospect of having to perform in front of an audience. Corrine felt such sympathy for the girl that she couldn't stand it and had to look down at her skirt.

"Jojo," her mother called, causing Corrine a little jolt, since Jojo was sitting right next to her.

Mrs. MacCoy glanced about for her daughter, and then all eyes came to the altar steps, where Jojo was reluctantly standing up. The attention spilled over to Corrine, who saw Ricky Dale looking right at her. His expression was pointed and curious.

She returned a pointed and curious look of her own, and then shifted her gaze to Jojo, who was walking over to take a copy of the play from her mother. Her mother had that expression of firmness, and Jojo took the manuscript without protest, other than her shoulders all slumped.

Three shepherds were chosen next, and Willie Lee was one of these. He was thrilled. He said that Munro could play a real sheep dog. "The shep-herds would have a dog," he told Mrs. MacCoy, who looked at him with pleasant surprise and said, "Well, yes, I imagine they would, Willie Lee."

Small parts as the innkeeper, his wife and daughter, and a boisterous inn visitor, were handed out, and then the three children who were left were given a choice of being nonspeaking crowd people or working on the set design.

Corrine did not say anything and went unnoticed, but when Aunt Marilee jumped in and volunteered to help with the set design, she said, "Corrine will help with the sets."

Mrs. MacCoy then smiled at Corrine. "Well, that's excellent!"

Corrine smiled in return, as was clearly expected.

7

Corrine had not seen Aunt Marilee as delighted with anything in a long time as she was with the prospect of this Christmas pageant. In fact, since they'd had to move into the apartment over the newspaper, Aunt Marilee had very often been subdued. It was as if she had repeatedly been putting on a happy face for everything, while continually being disappointed.

While she did have Papa Tate now, and having him made up for a lot, she did not have her spacious kitchen, with its lovely backyard view. She did not have her porch swing, where she liked to sit with a cup of coffee. She did not have the small office area she had so anticipated sharing with Papa Tate in his big house that had been taken away by the tornado. Added to that, she did not have the new baby that she so desperately wanted with Papa Tate.

Corrine saw all this in an instant, as her aunt came up between Corrine and Willie Lee, put her arms around their shoulders and said in a bubbly manner, "This is going to be such fun. And your Papa Tate is going to be able to have a part in this, too, because he can have the programs printed, and maybe even get us paper we can use in makin' our sets."

She fairly beamed at them.

Aunt Vella gave her opinion that it was a good thing Charlene MacCoy had taken over producing the pageant. "Pastor Smith is beyond fine at preachin', but I don't care if he does have six kids, he does not know how to make them behave. Last year one of them tied his shoelaces together, while some other little devils kept diverting him off to the Pizza Hut and leaving him with the bill. And when it came to this pageant, well, Pastor Smith was a dud. Attendance has been fallin' off so much that practically the only people to come last year were the parents of the kids in the pageant."

She spoke this in her loud voice, and Corrine glanced around to see if anyone might have heard her. Luckily the parking lot was deserted; they were the last to leave.

"I'm so glad you're with us, too," Aunt Marilee said, dropping back to link arms with her aunt. "All of us together—this is a real family endeavor."

Corrine thought Aunt Marilee was awfully sentimental all of a sudden. Christmas did that, though, and she thought fleetingly of her mother.

"What's this I hear that you don't believe in Santa Claus anymore, Willie Lee?" Aunt Vella tossed over her shoulder to the back seat.

"I am a big boy now, and I know San-ta Claus is a fan-ta-sy," Willie Lee replied, after a moment's thought.

"You don't say? Are you sure about this?"

Now that was a question, considering all the Santas in view at every turn.

Willie Lee appeared to be given pause by it, too, as his answer came slowly. "Yes." Then he added more firmly, "My ma-ma and Pa-pa Tate put my gifts un-der the tree. I know this."

"Well, where do they get the gifts? Maybe they get them from Santa."

"They get them from the store," Willie Lee said.

He spoke with such practicality that Aunt Vella shut her mouth and regarded him in the rearview mirror.

Willie Lee did not say anything else but sat in his usual calm manner. There was never any telling what Willie Lee might be thinking.

Papa Tate, Uncle Perry and Mr. Winston were waiting at the drugstore, sitting around one of the small soda fountain tables.

Corrine experienced a small disappointment in that Granny Franny was not there today. When Aunt Vella asked where Franny was, Mr. Winston said, "She's partakin' of the new Sons of Light church that's moved into the old Hardee's building out on the highway. They hold services for just about all day, and Franny wanted to see if they were worth anything."

Granny Franny was an irregular churchgoer, and she did not believe in belonging to just one church but liked to scatter herself about, as she said.

Uncle Perry and Mr. Winston had empty plates in front of them, but Papa Tate had been waiting for them to arrive to eat lunch.

"I'm sure glad you got here," Papa Tate said. "My stomach thinks my throat's been cut."

He got up and went behind the soda fountain to make their barbeque sandwiches, even though Belinda was working the counter.

Belinda, who was Aunt Vella and Uncle Perry's daughter, had the attitude that family could serve themselves and save her the trouble. Since taking over management of the drugstore last spring, she hired help for every day except Sunday, when the store only opened for the afternoon. She was looking for extra help for the Christmas season and apparently had not found anyone yet. Belinda could be a little hard to please. She mostly stood behind the counter and watched the television up on the wall, which she kept tuned to a shopping channel.

Having become an avid television shopper, she had Buddy, the UPS man, stopping at the drugstore several times a week, bringing items. Aunt Vella was a little upset that Belinda had become a TV shopping junkie, but overall her daughter's appearance had improved to such an extent that

Aunt Vella repeatedly commented on how pleased she was that at last Belinda had taken an interest in fixing herself up. Belinda had lost twenty-five pounds and wore fashionable clothes and also shoes, rather than flip-flops all the time.

Corrine took note that today Belinda had on a red Christmas sweater with glittery designs, and gold and red Christmas stocking earrings.

Corrine wished she could do some television shopping.

"It's all about money," Deputy Midgette said, dropping the comment and then going on to dig into his banana split.

"What are you talkin' about, Lyle?" Belinda said in the annoyed manner that she often used, especially to Deputy Midgette, who was her significant other, which was more than a simple boyfriend, since they lived together in the apartment over the drugstore. Corrine gathered that significant other meant they had sex.

"What?" the deputy said, looking surprised.

"What is all about money? Not that I'm probably goin' to find it enlightenin'."

"Oh. Santa Claus." He waved his spoon. "Your mother was talkin' about Santa Claus, and I just put in that Santa Claus has become a real moneymaker."

He wiped his new little mustache with a napkin, and said, "People will buy anything that Santa is sellin'. Look right there on the TV. They got Santa sellin' fancy nightgowns at a hundred dollars a pop." He shook his head in disbelief, but then he stared at the model displaying one of the sultry items, even while he spooned ice cream into his mouth.

The television camera zoomed in to show Santa holding one of the gowns. He went to ho, ho, hoing over how satiny the fabric was, and then the camera panned back to show the gown on the beautiful model.

"I think I'm goin' to get that gown," said Belinda, picking up the cordless phone that she kept within easy reach and punching the button for the number she had on speed dial. "My Santa Claus is my credit card," she said while waiting for an answer on the other end.

"*I'm* her Santa Claus," said Uncle Perry, causing a moment

of surprise, since none of them were used to him saying much. Then they all laughed, and Uncle Perry sort of beamed.

Corrine was proud of him.

Aunt Marilee and Aunt Vella were talking with Mr. Winston and Uncle Perry, and Willie Lee had joined them. Corrine took the opportunity to wander over to the revolving makeup displays and consider how far she might go with buying and applying makeup before Aunt Marilee had a conniption.

While she stood studying the small packages of Maybelline and Cover Girl, two high school boys, of the cool sort, came in. Corrine had seen them at school. One had blond hair cut short and styled messy, and the other one, with dark hair, she knew was Darla Rae's brother, Michael. He was a junior and on the football team. Darla Rae, who was one of the cool girls in middle school, was all the time saying, "I'm gonna tell my brother," to any boys who bothered her. Michael didn't look so tough to Corrine. He looked a little on the skinny side.

The boys went over and ordered barbeque sandwiches and Cokes to go. Papa Tate ended up fixing for them, since Belinda was still busy with her television purchase. When they left with their drinks and greasy sacks, Michael looked at Corrine.

She quickly averted her eyes, but then she could not help herself and glanced through the window as they went out the door. Michael looked back at her, and he winked!

As embarrassed as if she had gone suddenly naked, she instantly turned. *Ohmygosh, ohmygosh!* She looked upward to the mirror in the makeup display rack, wondering what in the world the boy could have seen.

Probably he saw someone who looked like his kid sister. This thought was so depressing that she couldn't look at the makeup anymore, which was just as well, because Aunt Marilee called her to come eat her lunch.

As she slipped back into her chair, Uncle Perry leaned close and said, "You choose whatever you want off that makeup rack and tell 'em I said to let you have it."

She was astonished, but then she shook her head. "Thank you, but Aunt Marilee doesn't let me wear makeup."

"Ah...she knows best."

Everyone got sat down around two of the small soda fountain tables, and someone asked Papa Tate about Mrs. Betts and the three thousand dollars she had gotten from the anonymous Santa. Even though Papa Tate had decided not to write a piece about it, the news was all over town.

Papa Tate said that he didn't know any more about it than anyone else. "I just know what Mrs. Betts told me. She showed me the cash and the note, too."

"Are they gonna let her keep it?" Belinda asked.

"Well, I mentioned it to Neville, and he said just let it ride, that he had no legal reason to question her about it. We just don't want some FBI types or somebody lookin' into it, which was why I decided not to do a write-up about the incident." Instead, he had put in a little box advertisement that said: Teresa Betts thanks her Santa Claus.

"I got to thinkin' that it was possible some authorities might tie up her money while they investigated. I'll write it up a little later, after she's spent it."

There was a lot of debate about where the money might have come from, and Aunt Marilee said, "See there, Willie Lee. There *is* a Santa. He gave money to Mrs. Betts, and he signed his name."

While Willie Lee looked thoughtful, Papa Tate cleared his throat and said, "Well, it was a typed note."

"Still counts," Aunt Marilee maintained.

"What is this I hear that you have given up on old Saint Nick, Willie Lee?" asked Mr. Winston.

Corrine wished everyone would drop the subject. She did not like all the frank talk about Santa around Willie Lee. The way everyone was talking, he sure couldn't ever believe in the guy now.

"I am a big boy now," Willie Lee said, "and I know Santa Claus is a fair-ry tale."

"Uh-huh." Mr. Winston nodded. "So, have you come by this because of your age, or because of someone else's opinion, or because of your own deduction?"

Willie Lee's eyebrows wrinkled.

Mr. Winston said, "What I am asking is did you come by not believin' in Santa Claus by yourself, or did someone tell you the idea and you believed what they said?"

Willie Lee bit his bottom lip for a few seconds, then said that Jimmy Spears had told him, and then he had asked DeeDee Redbird, and she had said it was true.

"Two opinions...sound reasoning, mostly," Mr. Winston said with a nod. "But what if both of those people are wrong?"

Willie Lee gazed at the elderly man.

"There are other people who say there is a Santa. Which people are right?"

Willie Lee said, "Do you say San-ta is a real per-son?"

Corrine wondered what Mr. Winston would say to that and watched the older man sit very still, thinking.

"Well, I cannot say I have ever seen the real Santa Claus," Mr. Winston said. "But I cannot say that I have *not* seen him, either. Maybe I did and did not know it."

Boy, a conversation like this could go on forever.

Mr. Winston said, "Do you understand that you can be any age and believe or not believe in Santa?"

Willie Lee appeared to think hard, then said, "Yeess."

"There are those people who believe in Santa, and those who do not. Maybe a few of the ones who do not believe are older, but that does not mean they are right. Older people make a lot of mistakes. Can we agree on that?"

Willie Lee's eyes behind his thick glasses swept around the adult faces and went lastly to Corrine, who, she was sure, revealed an expression of agreement despite herself.

"O-kay," he said slowly, watching Mr. Winston carefully.

"Each belief—whether for Santa or givin' up on him—has some very good facts behind it. I have read that there was a real Santa Claus many years ago, and there are a few people running around who call themselves Santas today."

"I know," Willie Lee said. "Up at Wal-Mart."

"There you go," said Mr. Winston.

"He had a fake beard," Willie Lee said.

"Ah. Well, Willie Lee, I don't know about there being a

Santa Claus in person, but I do know that there is a lot of belief in Santa Claus. And I do think it quite possible there is magic in the belief. Maybe it is a magic that only those with believing hearts can experience. And maybe Santa Claus is an angel who only comes to people who believe in him."

Mr. Winston leaned forward on his cane and said, "It is never good to take someone else's belief. We have to find things out for ourselves. I think you should do an experiment before you give up on Santa Claus and enter a world of total reality."

Willie Lee's eyes were glued on Mr. Winston, and so were everyone else's. A half a dozen times, Aunt Marilee looked about to say something, but then she would close her mouth.

"I think you need to write Santa Claus a letter and tell him something that you want, and that you haven't told anyone else about wantin'."

He let that sit there a few seconds, then gave a wave and said, "Now, I'm not talkin' about world peace or gettin' more courage, goin' to heaven, or wantin' to do better with your homework or be kind to everyone. All that is God's business, and God isn't some Santa Claus, no-sir. What I'm talkin' about are things, like a basketball, a pair of Nike tennis shoes, a watch…stuff such as that. These are matters for Santa Claus, and for angels, too. You do believe in angels, don't you?"

"Yes. I have seen an angel. I think."

"Well, there you go." Mr. Winston ducked his head to look Willie Lee right in the eye. "Write your letter to Santa Claus and ask for something you really, really want. Somethin' little tiny counts, but it has to be dear to your heart, because Santa Claus is in the business of givin' people special gifts, not just any old things. And make it somethin' you haven't told anyone else that you want. Then see what happens. That's a better way to decide what you want to believe, rather than trusting the opinions of someone else."

"Did you write to San-ta Claus?" Willie Lee asked.

Mr. Winston sat back. "No, sir, I have not. But that's

because I didn't think of this idea until this minute." He used his cane to push himself to his feet. Mr. Winston had been a big, tall man—it was said he had carried three men to safety all by himself in the war—but he was stooped now. "I think I'll go home and write my letter. I advise you all to do the same, just to see what happens."

"I need a new gun," Deputy Midgette said.

"Well, now you've gone and told and it won't apply," Belinda said.

"I didn't tell the sheriff. He's the one that'd get me a new gun. Don't you tell. That's what I'm gonna write about."

Mr. Winston, hand on the door handle, turned and told them, "If you don't write your letters, then you don't really believe, now do you? You are all wantin' this boy to believe, so it seems you'd better follow your own words."

The bell above the door rang as he opened it and left.

"That's a right smart idea," Papa Tate said. He was making a note on one of the little cards he kept in his pocket, and likely Mr. Winston's suggestion would turn up in a future editorial.

"Be home by five-thirty," Aunt Marilee said in a hushed voice, because of Willie Lee sleeping on the living room floor.

"I will." Corrine slipped swiftly out the door and down the stairwell, while Aunt Marilee came to the door and hollered down at her to not go anywhere else, other than the corral, just in case she would need to find her.

"I won't," she called back, and added, "I'll be careful," before Aunt Marilee could say it.

She felt a little guilty for leaving while Willie Lee was asleep, again. If she kept doing that, he was going to get the idea that she didn't want him with her. That was the truth at the moment, she supposed, but it did not mean she didn't like him around her most of the time. If there was anyone she could be around just about all the time, it was Willie Lee. He was easy. She could be herself, no matter how she was, with Willie Lee.

She wheeled her bike onto the sidewalk and across Main Street, then got on and took off pedaling up Church Street.

She wondered if she might run into Ricky Dale at the corral. Maybe he would just decide to come over for no particular reason, or maybe he would come to grain the horses. Leanne kept a big bale of hay in the feeder for them, but she liked to grain them at night, and if Leanne needed to be off somewhere, she sometimes asked Ricky Dale to do it.

Oh, she didn't even care about running into him. She would enjoy the horses just the same. She didn't mind cleaning their stalls, and likely Ricky Dale was over at ol' Princess Melissa's and had forgotten all about his responsibility.

The sun had passed its warmest, and the air was growing sharp in the shadows of the buildings and trees. It was beginning to look more like Christmas, with the garlands on the light poles, and further up Church Street, just about everyone was getting all manner of decorations put out. She passed a man lining his yard with little plastic candy canes, and another yard where people were setting up their nativity scene and singing Christmas carols as they went about it.

There was the faint scent of wood smoke in the air from fireplaces, but as soon as Corrine started pumping hard up the Church Street hill, she began to sweat beneath her pink sweater and jean jacket.

When she came across Mr. Winston's large rear yard, the mare saw her first and nickered and hurried toward the corral fence, while the filly pranced and kicked with sudden excitement. Corrine left her bike against one of the big elms and climbed up on the board fence. She dug the bag of sweet baby carrots out of the pocket of her jean jacket, put several in her palm and fed them to the horses, which kept nudging each other out of the way. She put her nose to their velvety noses, first the mare's and then the filly's.

"I love you," she whispered to each.

She finished feeding them all the carrots and then dropped herself into the corral and strode to the barn, where she got the fork and wheelbarrow and quickly cleaned each stall. It was easy, after all of her hard work on Friday.

As she haltered the mare and began brushing her, her heart sank a little because Ricky Dale had not miraculously appeared.

Any boy who was interested in Melissa Pruitt was too stupid for her.

With a startling suddenness, she broke into tears and leaned her head against the mare's neck and sobbed. The mare did not move but stood perfectly still. The filly came over and nudged Corrine in the neck until Corrine finally turned and wrapped her arms around the filly's neck.

Stopped crying, she stepped back and wiped the tears from her face.

Then, hardly thinking, certainly not thinking about someone seeing her, she untied the mare from the post, led her to the corral fence, climbed up and slipped over onto the mare's back.

The mare was warm beneath her legs and bottom. She stood still, waiting. Corrine clucked to her, and the mare began to walk at a smooth gait around the corral, then to trot ever so lightly, while Corrine kept her legs tight around her sides.

A magical joy flowed over Corrine. She felt the cool air on her face and the warmth of the intimate contact with the horse. Three times around the corral, and Corrine was one of the trick riders, just as they were in an old Wild West Show. With the lead rope like a rein, she directed the horse into the middle of the corral, where she stopped. With eyes closed, she imagined putting her arms out, while the mare did a glorious bow.

And then something, some shift of the horse, caused her eyes to fly open, and there was Ricky Dale at the fence.

"You get off her before you get your neck broke."

His tone and words swept down her spine and then back up like a flash of fire. She stared at him, then, very slowly, holding on to the mare's mane, slipped her body to the ground. In a dramatic manner, she took the halter off the mare and walked to the barn to hang it on its hook.

When she turned around, Ricky Dale was coming through the gate. "What's wrong with you, Corky? You know you're not supposed to ride that mare. She's not full broke. You could get really hurt."

"You aren't my boss," she shot back at him, her tone so sharp she surprised herself, and clearly Ricky Dale was stunned. He stopped short, opened his mouth and then closed it in an angry line.

Corrine said, "For your information, you aren't the only one who knows a little somethin' about horses. I have ridden that mare before. So if you want to run and tattle, go on. And what's wrong with you? You used to be fun. Now you just think you're way too cool."

Stepping around him, she went through the gate, got her bicycle and rode away with her back straight.

Within five minutes, she began to feel like a fool, which caused her to pedal furiously all the way home, her face burning. Ricky Dale probably thought she was a real idiot.

Oh, what did she care?

Winston Valentine came out of his kitchen and stopped, struck by the darkness of the house. The sun had finished setting while he'd finished the dishes. No one had turned on lights or the television, because Mildred Covington had been moved out to MacCoy Senior Living Center two months ago, and there were only himself and his niece Leanne in the house these days.

He had thought he would miss Mildred, and he'd sure fought the social worker in moving her, but when all was said and done, he was now mostly relieved. Mildred had worn him down with her sneaking all the food she wasn't supposed to eat. She was like a dachshund he'd had once; he'd had to be vigilant at every moment or she would have eaten herself clean to death.

He hated feeling relieved about her being gone, though. It made him feel he had given up.

The house was often lonely, but he was managing. His niece Leanne just being in the house at night was sort of nice. She spent most of her time upstairs. Right then a glow from her room filtered down the stairs, along with the sound of country music from her radio.

For a split second Winston was fifty again, and the music was Hank Williams singing "Kaw-Liga" on his wife's radio. It was as if Coweta was up there, and he was about to go up and kiss her neck and see if he could stir up some good man-woman relations.

He blinked and came back to the present, which was that his wife was long dead and he was eighty-nine years old and standing there in the dark, having a little vertigo.

One thing about living in a house as long as he had lived in this one, and that was that he knew the placement of everything. He went over to his desk in the corner of the dining room and switched on the leather-shaded lamp without feeling around.

Sitting at the desk, he found a piece of plain linen stationery. Coweta had left behind so much fine stationery that his daughter would likely be able to use it for her entire lifetime and still be able to pass some on to the grandkids. He picked up a pen, thought for a moment, and then began to write.

Dear Santa,

Maybe I wrote you as a boy, so you will know me. But I don't remember writing to you, so maybe you don't know me. Mostly I remember having to work hard as a boy, chopping wood and cotton and anything else that my daddy wanted chopped. I'm glad not to be a boy anymore, but I am not glad to be an old man. It stinks.

I am glad to have my memory, though. Lots of people I know have lost that. I have the memory of some fine Christmases, and it seems like the ones I remember best are ones where we had a good snow. I call your attention to one not so long ago, in the '80s, when Coweta was still here and the kids gone, and she and I could still get together. That Christmas we got snowed in for a day, and we went to the grocery story on our horses, even at our age then. And we had sex in front of the fireplace, our last time, which wasn't bad at our age.

I want snow this year. I want to see snow once more before I die, and we know that at my age, that could be soon, so I'll take snow any time between now and Christmas and consider it proof of being from you.

Thanks,

Winston Valentine

Winston reread what he'd written and was annoyed that he had dwelled so much on his age. But, he saw clearly, no matter what age a person was, from infant to elderly, age was a determining factor to all that went on in life. Anyone who thought different was just fooling himself.

He thought maybe he should tear the letter up and ask for a family reunion, but he figured that fell more into God's department, because it was dealing with a whole bunch of people. Besides, he'd had a reunion of his children on his last birthday, and one time of that was enough. They all got a sad, worried expression when they looked at him, and it made him nervous.

Maybe snow was really in God's department, too.

Well, considering he was writing to some being that didn't quite exist, he supposed he could ask for snow. It was snow he wanted.

Leanne came down the stairs. "Whatcha' doin', Uncle Winston?"

"Writin' to Santa Claus." He folded the paper.

"What?"

"I said I wrote a letter to Santa." He inserted the paper into an envelope and began to address it.

Leanne came to stand beside him and watch.

"Haven't you ever heard of writin' to Santa?" he asked, then licked the flap and sealed the envelope.

"Well, yeah." Her pretty eyes regarded him like she was thinking of calling his daughter because he'd gone round the bend.

"Ask and you shall receive, darlin'. You can't get what you want if you don't ask. You might want to write a letter to Santa, too."

Leanne gave him a skeptical look. "What did you ask for?"

"My secret."

She smiled at that, then went into the kitchen and came back with a dish of ice cream. "Maybe I'll write Santa and ask for a husband," she said.

To that, Winston said, "You need to be on your knees in church for that one, girl."

8

Pale morning light was flooding through the east windows when Corrine got up and found Willie Lee with his forehead pressed up against the pane.

"My bird is gone," he said.

"Well, it was time for him to go. He had to go home. That's what a homing pigeon does, and probably his mother and father missed him. And you got him better enough to go by givin' him food and water. You made him well, honey."

Willie Lee nodded and looked a little brighter.

Corrine lifted the window and brought in the small dish of water.

"May-be he will come back," Willie Lee said hopefully.

"Maybe," said Corrine.

When she could get away unnoticed, she went downstairs to check the sidewalk to make sure the bird hadn't died and fallen off the windowsill. She didn't want Willie Lee to see it dead on the sidewalk.

The coast was clear. The bird evidently really had flown away.

* * *

Going to her locker first thing, Corrine looked down the hall and saw Ricky Dale at his locker, too. He was gazing at her. What was even more wonderful was that he had a truly perplexed and pained expression upon his face.

She let herself look straight at him, and she waited for him to come forward to say something to her, expecting it to be along the lines of how he was sorry for his rude treatment of her the day before and for being so stuck up lately. Her mind got so carried away that in that split second she had him leaning over to kiss her, too.

This was not what happened.

Anson Brown called to him from down the hall, and Ricky Dale turned. Anson was standing with Melissa Pruitt and her gang of cool friends.

Ricky Dale cast Corrine a glance and then walked away to join them with his cocky stride.

Corrine shut her locker door, hitched her backpack onto her shoulder and, spine straight, headed in the opposite direction down the hall, with her momentary triumph turned to stoic disappointment wilted around her shoulders.

Later, in algebra class, Ricky Dale came in carrying Melissa Pruitt's books. He had to walk right past Corrine's desk, and she had the urge to stick her foot out and trip him. She did not do this because of the nagging voice in her head that wouldn't let her make a spectacle of herself, but for some moments afterward, she felt thorough regret at her lack of action. She thought maybe tripping Ricky Dale might have been worth a few minutes of embarrassment, but now she wouldn't know, because she hadn't been able to bring herself to do it.

After that she didn't allow herself to look in Ricky Dale's direction, even to see if he was looking or not looking at her.

Jojo MacCoy was in her English class, which was an accelerated class for those middle school students who tested gifted in reading ability.

For the first time taking full note of the girl, who was small and fair and cute as a bug, to use one of Aunt Vella's expressions, Corrine was surprised to realize that Jojo was doing the same thing as Corrine herself usually did—reading from a book opened atop her English text.

Much of their English studies was at a ninth and tenth grade level, and even then, Corrine, whose mother'd had her reading the newspaper to her at the age of six, and who was surrounded by the written word so prevalent in a newspaper family, was very often bored. For much of the previous year and all of this one so far, when the class was reading some lesson in their English book, Corrine had a paperback novel stuck in it, tilting the larger school text so that it was the only book visible to the teacher.

So far that year she had reread *Black Beauty* and was currently working her way through *The Saddle Club* series. Undoubtedly the English teacher knew full well what Corrine did, but she pretended ignorance and made no attempt whatsoever to correct her. There was no reason to scold her, as she got straight As. Besides, it was a little annoying for a teacher faced with a student who almost always knew the answer when called upon and whose papers were always correct. After a while the teacher quit calling on Corrine and seemed to forget her existence.

If Corrine could have been left alone in the library to learn all she needed to learn, she would have been happy. She felt so totally different from everyone else as to be from another planet, and she got through by doing her best to be invisible.

After class, Corrine found herself next to Jojo as they went out the door.

"Hey," she said to the younger girl.

"Hey," Jojo said in return and grinned in an eager fashion. The girl smiled a lot.

The next thought to occur to Corrine was that if more students began reading from books in their English text, there was going to be big trouble.

A glance around at the other students and their silly and flirtatious behavior reassured her that a break-out in novel reading throughout middle school was not likely to happen.

* * *

When Corrine and Willie Lee got home from school, walking in the obnoxiously balmy weather, Papa Tate was up on a tall ladder, attaching lights to the bottom of the outside sills of their apartment windows. Aunt Marilee was hanging out one of the windows, directing matters and lending a hand wherever possible. Sandy Conroy was helping by feeding up the string of lights and assisting Papa Tate in the frequent moves of the ladder. Sandy could do this easily because he was about six foot four. There were five windows, and Papa Tate had to go up, attach the string, then come down and move the ladder and go back up again.

Corrine, standing with Willie Lee on the sidewalk and watching the progress, worried that either Papa Tate was going to fall off the ladder or Aunt Marilee was going to fall out the window. Aunt Marilee was particular about the drape of the light string and kept trying to see how it looked, which was not truly possible from inside the apartment.

"I'll go across the street and look," Corrine said, when she noticed Papa Tate starting to get a little annoyed.

"Up a little higher...no, that's too much, down some," she guided, yelling across the street.

Fayrene Gardner, who lived in the apartment above her Main Street Café, came driving up and saw what Papa Tate was doing. She liked it so much that she asked him to do her windows, too.

"I don't have a ladder that tall," she said, a poor excuse if Corrine had ever heard one. MacCoy Feed and Grain had things like ladders, not to mention she could have borrowed one.

But Papa Tate liked to please, so pretty soon there he was doing the windows of Fayrene's apartment above the café, and Corrine had to move down the opposite side of the street in order to help guide him in the draping of the light string.

Standing on the curb and hollering across the street, she suddenly realized that she was acting just like her Aunt Marilee.

"Come on, Marilee...kids," Papa Tate called to them as soon as it got dark enough for the streetlights to begin coming on. "Let's go see how our lights look."

He was about as excited as he had been on his and Aunt Marilee's honeymoon down at Disney World, when he had rented a boat and driven them around the lake, calling himself The Captain of the *Minnow*. The boat was not named the *Minnow*, it was named *Cruiser 1*. When Corrine had pointed this out, Papa Tate had said he had just changed the name. He and Aunt Marilee had thought this so cute, and Aunt Marilee had kept calling him Captain, but Corrine did not get it.

They all, even Munro, followed him outside and across the street to stand in front of the police station and view the lights on their building. It did look great. Papa Tate had used the new big lightbulbs that he said were not new at all but had been the style when he was a kid. He had put them around the front doors of the *Voice*, too, and Aunt Marilee had hung a lighted wreath on the glass door of the offices, and upstairs she had put electric candles in each window. It sure seemed like she was following her own advice in her column to get decorations up.

Fayrene Gardner was putting white light wreaths in her apartment windows. She only had two windows. She came running down to see how it all looked, too, hurrying across the street to join them, then standing there in her thin sweater with her skinny arms wrapped around herself, thanking Papa Tate over and over.

After several minutes of admiring their buildings, they all checked out the rest of the street. Jaydee Mayhall had not done any decorating down at his end, where he had his law office and also the Family Pool Hall, which was closed.

Aunt Marilee said she would speak to him about it.

Other than that, Main Street looked really dressed up, and they all sort of *oohed* and *ahhhed*. Papa Tate and Aunt Marilee gave each other "the look," and he slipped his arm around her.

"We ought to get a group to go caroling this year," he said.

Corrine thought of it, and immediately pictured them in

a horse-drawn sleigh, but after a minute she realized they would need snow for a sleigh, and that was not likely, especially as it remained so warm none of them even wore a coat right that minute.

Behind them, Belinda and Deputy Midgette, and Lori Wright, the desk clerk, came out of the police station and admired the lights, and then Belinda told Lyle, "You have got to get lights up outside our apartment, too."

"I'm afraid of heights," he said. "Think you could string lights under our windows, Editor?"

Corrine lingered down on the street, studying the looks of it, intently taking in the details and how it all made her feel in order to attempt another drawing of it. She gazed at the engraved concrete letters of *The Valentine Voice,* which took on a glow from the colored lights strung above. "The voice of Valentine," Papa Tate always said.

Her eyes moved left, across the narrow alley, and then she saw Fayrene Gardner's shadowy and lonely looking form at her apartment window, and further along the street, the overhang of the old Opry building had been strung with icicle lights, and they looked almost like real icicles, or maybe how the front of the Opry might have looked back when it was a real theater with lots of lights out front. She could almost hear the sound of people and vehicles that had once moved along the streets of this town at Christmas. She saw now a car coming down the street slowly, its red finish gleaming in the lights.

Turning, she looked at the intersection of Church and Main Streets, with sparkling decorations on each corner streetlight. Just like in that song Aunt Marilee sometimes sang, the red, yellow and green stoplight blinked out Christmas. City Hall, on the opposite corner of Church and Main, was decked out with wreaths on the double doors and lights around the top, and the Christmas tree lights twinkled merrily out front.

A warm feeling flooded Corrine's heart. In that moment she loved this town and everyone in it, and she never wanted to leave. In the space of seconds all the dreams she had ever dreamed went racing across her mind. She wanted to grow up here and be with Willie Lee, Aunt Marilee and Papa Tate, Aunt Vella and Uncle Perry and Mr. Winston, and even Ricky Dale, because she knew that someday she and him would make up. She would be a famous and rich artist and buy them a big house on a farm, where they could have horses and dogs and all the animals Willie Lee wanted, and she would have a big room with sunny windows that looked out over her pasture of horses. She would also take Aunt Marilee's place at the paper when Aunt Marilee retired and did nothing but read and drink tea and eat chocolate. She would keep the *Voice* going and be the conscience of the town, like Papa Tate said, and every Christmas she would decorate the *Voice* building and make sure everyone else decorated, too, so there was always a cheery Christmas just like this one.

"Cor-rine!"

Just entering the stairwell from the sidewalk, she looked up to see Willie Lee on the landing at the top, in the yellow glow of light falling through the apartment door.

"Ma-ma says to come on." He gulped air in, trying to get his words out with speed. "Your mo-ther is on the phone!"

Oh! Oh, rats! Her mother would probably tell Aunt Marilee about sending the note about her coming.

When Corrine came through the apartment door, Aunt Marilee had the phone pressed to her ear and was pacing with the anxious expression she usually had when speaking to her younger sister. Upon seeing Corrine, she focused on her with an intense gaze and raised eyebrow.

"I think that's the best idea," Aunt Marilee said into the phone. "Here's Corrine now."

Aunt Marilee, not removing her gaze from Corrine's face, passed her the phone.

Her mother's voice came over the line. "Hello, sweetheart."

"Hello, Mama."

Aunt Marilee kept standing there. Corrine looked at the floor and held the receiver tight to her ear.

"Marilee didn't know about my idea of comin' for Christmas," her mother said. "Didn't you get my card? I mailed it way the beginning of last week."

She looked at Aunt Marilee. She wanted to say she had not gotten the card, but what came out was, "Yes, I got it. I just forgot to tell her."

There was silence on the line for several seconds, and then her mother said in a soft voice, "Well, honey, I'm comin'. I'll be there on Saturday afternoon."

"You will?"

"Yes, and I'm so excited! I can't wait to see you." There was a pause, and then she said, "Aren't you excited?"

"Yes, I am," Corrine said instantly, giving her best effort at excitement. "That'll be neat." She closed her eyes, wondering where she'd come up with that lame phrase.

Her mother didn't seem to find it a lame phrase. She was already launched into the details of how she was just about all packed and all about her plans to drive up from New Orleans.

Aunt Marilee walked away into the kitchen. Corrine watched her back as she disappeared around the corner.

When her mother fell silent, Corrine asked, "Is Louis coming, too?" This seemed somehow a crucial question.

"No," her mother answered slowly. "Louis isn't comin'. Just me."

Corrine thought immediately that Louis had left her mother. Another boyfriend down. That was probably why her mother was coming. She wanted to ask about the situation with Louis, but she could not bring herself to do so.

Her mother went on to say stuff about planning to stay out at the Goodnight Motel, and maybe Corrine would want to stay out there with her some. "We can have sleepover parties."

Corrine, who was still preoccupied with the fact that Louis was not coming, did her best to respond to the idea of sleepover parties. She said, "That would be neat," and thought, Ohmygod.

When she finally got off the phone, she had to go into

her bedroom to rest up from all her emotion and collect herself before she could face Aunt Marilee, who she knew would be coming to find out why she had not told her of her mother's planned visit.

She didn't get to rest long before Aunt Marilee came tapping at her door. Her eyes were on Corrine like magnets, strong ones. Aunt Marilee possessed the ability to read minds, most especially Willie Lee's and Corrine's. Corrine did her best to make her mind blank.

"You didn't tell me you got a card from your mother, sayin' that she was comin' to visit." She spoke gently, her eyes asking more questions than her voice.

Corrine shrugged. "I didn't think of it." She got busy hanging up her jean jacket and a few other pieces in order to have somewhere to look besides at her aunt. Her room was neat to begin with, so this did not take long. In the process, she picked up the card from her mother and passed it to her aunt.

Aunt Marilee looked at the card and then asked in about three different ways wasn't Corrine excited about her mother's coming and didn't she think it was a grand thing.

"She's really comin' this time, Corrine," Aunt Marilee said at last.

Corrine looked at her, curious at her tone but unable to read her expression. "She's said that a lot of times before."

"Well, I think she *will* come this time," Aunt Marilee said. "She wants to see you. She wants to be with family."

A little bit later, as Corrine was working on a new drawing of Valentine at Christmas, the thought popped into her head that maybe her mother was sick. Maybe she had some terminal cancer or heart disease, and that was why she was coming home, and why Aunt Marilee was sure she would come.

This idea scared her, but right in the midst of it, she thought that if her mother died, that would not make any difference in her life. The cards and phone calls and the occasional little gift that was usually way too young for her anyway would quit coming, and that was the extent of it. She could let go of the dream of ever visiting New Orleans, an idea that wasn't too strong to begin with, except she had wanted to see cemeteries that were walled.

A sadness crept over her as she realized that when she had been planning her future down in the street, she had not thought at all about her mother. She had not included her mother in the faintest fashion. Should her mother die, it would make no difference at all in her life, except to mean she really and truly did not have a mother.

This thought brought tears to her eyes, which she did not thoroughly understand.

She decided that she had to talk to Aunt Marilee and apologize for hiding her mother's letter, and maybe she would find a way to ask if her mother was dying. This possibility had lodged in her mind and was about to drive her crazy. She really was afraid to open up such a conversation, though, so she went to take a hot bath first.

Running the water very warm into the tub, she dumped in fragrant beads Aunt Marilee kept on the nearby shelf and which Corrine was allowed to use as much as she wanted. She stepped into the tub and had the water so hot that she had to sit down very slowly.

She loved baths. She had ever since she was a little child. Her mother had said that Corrine had never screamed like most babies when put in a bath, even when getting her hair washed.

Right next to where the bottle of bath beads sat was Aunt Marilee's package of Lady Shavers. Corrine gazed at them for a moment, then slipped one out. She did not want to ask Aunt Marilee about using one and risk being told to wait three days, or even that she was not old enough at all to shave her legs. She had hair on her legs. That meant she was old enough.

She shaved in the bubbly bathtub, stretching out her legs and admiring them in the manner of a picture she had seen of a cowgirl in a bathtub. Her legs felt so smooth after she finished shaving them, although there was the matter of a few nicks.

When she got out of the tub, she had to apply bits of

tissue to the nicks until they quit bleeding. One nick she resorted to putting a Band-Aid over. Then she smoothed on Jergens lotion from the pump bottle on the counter, just like Aunt Marilee did.

In the mirror, she parted her wet hair on the side rather than the middle.

Pausing to observe herself, she decided that she looked a little older with it parted that way.

Once Granny Franny had commented that Corrine looked like Audrey Hepburn, a famous and beautiful old movie star, Granny Franny said. Corrine had kept a lookout on the old movie channel. Finally she had seen the woman, who she thought was quite pretty but was so skinny as to look like a pure child, so Corrine did not find Granny Franny's reference such a compliment.

Her world was filled with a lot of old people, she thought as she slipped into flannel pajamas with kittens all over them.

When she came out of the bathroom, the television was turned off and the living room dark. The apartment was quiet, except for the murmur of Aunt Marilee's and Papa Tate's voices in the kitchen.

Instantly she knew they were talking about her and her mother.

She stood there for a moment, gazing at the light falling from the kitchen entry. Then, peeking into Willie Lee's room, she saw the low light on over his mouse condominium. Willie Lee was already asleep, with Munro lying in bed beside him. She quickly stepped in and turned the light off over the mice to let them sleep in peace, then came back out and headed for the kitchen, walking on tiptoe.

She felt a little guilty at sneaking but did not stop. Slipping up to the edge of the darkness just outside the kitchen, she heard Aunt Marilee saying, "But not to say anything to me, Tate...not a word."

Corrine's chest began to squeeze.

"This is just one thing, Marilee. It isn't a sign that she can't talk to you if she needs to," Papa Tate said in his practical tone. "And likely she didn't take Anita's note seriously."

"Well, Anita would have done better to show me the courtesy of talking to me before tellin' Corrine."

A chair scooted, and there was the sound of movement as Papa Tate said, "You and Anita do have a bit of trouble talkin' to each other, darlin'." It sounded like he was pouring coffee. "And what would you have said to her, anyway? That she couldn't come? You've been after her to come up here."

Aunt Marilee didn't answer that right away. Probably because she was having trouble arguing against the truth of the statement. Probably her mother wouldn't even have come, except for Aunt Marilee pushing her, Corrine thought, squeezing her eyes closed.

Basically Aunt Marilee and her mother did not see anything the same way. Aunt Marilee was the older sister, and, not meaning to fault her, she liked to act like it. Any time her mother and Aunt Marilee got together, either on the telephone or in person, they ended up in a quarrel. The two could not be on the telephone for any length of time before one of them hung up on the other.

Once Aunt Marilee was pacing during one of their telephone arguments and got furious because she thought her sister had hung up on her. It turned out what had happened was that Aunt Marilee had forgotten that she was not using the cordless and had pulled the telephone cord clean out of the jack. She had been compelled to call Corrine's mother back and apologize, and then Corrine's mother had hung up on her.

What the sisters seemed to argue over mostly was Corrine herself.

"I just don't think Anita needs to keep her plans a secret, Tate. That's not helpful. It more makes me wonder what's goin' on with her."

"You've known that Anita has been trying to get strong enough to come back for Corrine. You yourself said somethin' to me about how nice it would be if Anita could come for Christmas."

"I know…I know," said Aunt Marilee in a painful tone that shot clear through Corrine.

Leaning against the wall, she sort of melted downward.

Then she saw the big mirror across the dining room over the sideboard and in it the shadowy reflection of Aunt Marilee and Papa Tate in the kitchen. The light over the sink was bright and cast a yellowy glow on them sitting at the table, talking over coffee cups.

Aunt Marilee was unwrapping a Hershey's chocolate Kiss. She popped it into her mouth, and for a long minute, neither she nor Papa Tate said anything.

Then her aunt said in a tired voice, "I want Anita to come. I want to see her, and I want her and Corrine to—" She broke off and pushed herself up from the table. "Oh, I'm lyin' to say that I want them to get back together. To be mother and daughter. Oh, Tate, I can't…"

Watching, Corrine could not breathe.

Papa Tate rose and went to Aunt Marilee, pulling her into his arms. They talked in voices too low to be heard, but the raw emotions vibrated from the room, hit the mirror and bounced straight into Corrine's chest, which squeezed so tight it hurt.

Suddenly she saw her aunt break away from Papa Tate and wipe her eyes, saying, "I need to check to see if Corrine's out of the bath."

Ohmygosh! Racing across the dark living room on tiptoe, she dived through her bedroom door and into bed. Grabbing up a book, she stuck it in front of her face and tried to get her breathing slowed down. Luckily she discovered that she had the book upside down and got it turned before Aunt Marilee's head poked through the door.

"All ready for bed?"

Corrine nodded. Her heart was hammering; she hoped it didn't show. *She had to close her mind or Aunt Marilee would read it.*

"You look awfully flushed," Aunt Marilee said, and checked her forehead for a fever. Corrine had to convince her that it was the hot bath.

Later, lying in the dark, she decided that Aunt Marilee

did not have the powers of perception that Corrine had formerly attached to her. She also decided that there was probably little chance that her mother was dying, since Aunt Marilee and Papa Tate had not mentioned anything about it in their conversation.

Of course, there was still the chance that her mother was dying but had not told Aunt Marilee. This possibility made her nervous, but there wasn't any sense in discussing it with her aunt, who obviously didn't know and hadn't thought of it. It never paid to give Aunt Marilee cause for worry.

As for apologizing to her aunt about not telling her about her mother's letter, well, that no longer seemed so necessary. The adults were all the time keeping secrets from her.

The Valentine Voice

Christmas About Town

by Marilee Holloway

If you haven't seen the Holiday Lights in the Park or along Main Street, give yourselves and your family a treat and cruise both in the evening this month to see the magical wonderlands and get into the holiday spirit.

To celebrate all the lovely displays in neighborhood yards around town, *The Valentine Voice* will sponsor a contest for an Outstanding Christmas Yard Award. Entry forms for nominating yours or your neighbor's yard can be found at the IGA, the Quick Shop on Main Street and here at the *Voice* offices.

Prizes will be awarded for First, Second and Third places, and ribbons given for three Honorable Mentions. Prizes are still being assembled, but all winners will receive a color photograph of their yards printed in the *Voice*, plus a framed copy for keeping the memory. The judging panel is made up of Ms. Franny Holloway, Peggy Sue Langston, Pastor Stanley Smith, Father Martin Buckley, Doris and

Everett Northrupt, Gabby Smith and Willie Lee James. In the case of a tie, Editor Tate Holloway will make the deciding vote. The deadline for entering is December 13th, so get busy decorating your yards.

Here's a wonderful new service! The Merry Christmas Maid Service. Starting at $49.99, Stella Purvis and her all-male Christmas maid team will clean you up in a jiffy. Give yourself and your family the gift of both a comfortable home and more time. Call Stella at 555-3323.

All Christmas craft demonstrations that were to take place at the Christmas Cottage will now be held across the street at the Fire Department. This change is due to a fire Tuesday morning at the Christmas Cottage, when, during preparations for the upcoming demonstration, a glue gun was accidentally left touching a pinecone wreath and caught it and then the demonstration table on fire. Thanks to the skill and quick response of the Auxiliary ladies, only the one room of the Cottage, the crafting table and a few boxes of stock received damage.

The Christmas Cottage has reopened for business and is now offering a printed handout on Christmas fire safety to everyone who drops in. No purchase necessary.

Keep in mind that there are more fires at the Christmas season than at any other time of the year.

Someone appears to have started the nasty rumor that Santa Claus is a fake. Julia Jenkins-Tinsley, our postmistress, wants everyone to know that there is an official postal box just for Santa Claus down at the post office, and the USPS could not have such a box for an imaginary person, as that would be mail fraud. All letters in the mailbox will be delivered to

Santa. This service is free of charge, no stamp required, and letters are guaranteed to reach Santa, if mailed by December 21st. After that date, they are still free, but not guaranteed to reach Santa.

I would also like to call everyone's attention to a wonderful and generous gift given to one of our citizens by Santa Claus himself. He even left a note that said, "Merry Christmas from Santa Claus." That is evidence to contradict those of you passing along the rumor of his untimely demise.

Friday night begins the live nativity scene taking place out at the Sons of Light Church, located in the old Hardee's building. It will be a drive-thru event and will take place this weekend and next weekend. Since it is taking place inside and viewed through the big windows, weather will not be a consideration.

Beginning this Friday, as well, the Main Street Café will be open until 10:00 p.m. on Fridays and Saturdays throughout the rest of the month.

And once again, don't forget the annual Valentine Chamber of Commerce toy drive. You can drop off your new, unwrapped toys here at the *Voice*. We are out of Santa Claus pins, but can offer you a free cup of coffee in a *Voice* mug to keep, as long as supplies last.

Our recipe today comes by way of our Editor, who got the recipe handed down to him from his great-aunt. It is a favorite at our house, and sometimes he makes a double batch in order to have some left over for Sunday breakfast, if it's allowed to last that long.

Aunt Lizzie Lee's Cornbread

Sift together:
1 1/2 cups cornmeal

1 teaspoon salt
3 tablespoons sugar

Mix in 2 cups boiling water.
Add and mix:
2 beaten eggs
1 tablespoon cooking oil
1 cup milk

Pour mixture into a greased 10 inch iron skillet or ovenproof baking dish of the same size. Bake at 400° for 45 minutes.

Please send your news and gift ideas in to Charlotte at the *Voice*, phone her at 555-4743 during *Voice* office hours, or e-mail her at charlotteconroy@thevalentinevoice.com. You can e-mail me at marilee@valentinevoice.com E-mail is the preferred method of communication and will almost guarantee your information gets included. Your cooperation is appreciated.

9

Corrine's biggest question of her Aunt Marilee would have been: What are you going to do about this situation with Mama? For surely her aunt would do something. Her aunt always did something about a crisis. Sometimes she would throw up her hands and say that she couldn't do anything and was giving it over to God, but the very next minute, she would be right back there doing something. Somehow, in Corrine's experience, Aunt Marilee always managed to make everything all right.

Aunt Marilee often said of others she thought were being lax: "Why doesn't she do somethin', even if it's wrong?" She had often said this of Corrine's mother.

Corrine felt Aunt Marilee's close attention after the news of her mother's planned visit, and a number of times she happened to see the look on her aunt's face that indicated the wheels turning in her mind, so she suspected that her aunt was thinking about how to handle everything. This gave her at least a bit of reassurance.

Also, she decided that there was plenty of time before Saturday for her mother to decide not to come. Her mother had said a number of times in the past that she was going to come visit, or was going to be a private secretary and make lots of money, or marry a rich man, like marrying Louis, and she had never done any of those things, so Corrine didn't see why she should start now.

After the first day of nervousness at her mother's proposed visit, she saw that Aunt Marilee had settled down, too, and probably thought the same thing: that the possibility of her mother carrying through was slim, so there wasn't any need to worry over it.

At school Corrine had a bunch more to think about than her mother. Usually she was thinking about being anywhere else than school, mostly at the corral with the horses. She was also thinking about not making some dumb mistake, in either her schoolwork or with other kids or the teachers, about what the school lunch would be, since Aunt Marilee insisted she eat a hot lunch, about Ricky Dale possibly looking at her, or not looking at her, or generally anything of a worrisome nature.

She still wasn't letting herself look at Ricky Dale, so she didn't know if he was looking at her or not.

Between classes, Anson Brown came up to her and said, "Ricky Dale wants to know why you aren't talkin' to him."

Corrine was so surprised that it took her a few seconds to answer. She finally got out, "I can't talk to him if he doesn't come around to talk to me."

Imagine, putting the whole thing off as her fault.

The short conversation with Anson was entirely silly and unproductive, to her notion, but she smiled as she thought about the true fact that Ricky Dale had sent Anson to ask.

She continued to have the feeling that Ricky Dale would show up at the horse corral at the same time she did, and that way they could be alone. She had this fantasy that he would tell her he was sorry for deserting her for Melissa Pruitt—maybe not those exact words, but something like that—and they would make up and be friends like before.

She had decided she would kiss him, and this idea began to consume her thoughts. She preferred it to any thoughts about her mother's possible visit, which gave her a helpless feeling. Although the prospect of kissing Ricky Dale brought anxiety, too. She was a little uncertain about her nerve and bringing herself to initiate the kissing, but mostly she thought she could do it. She knew she was fantasizing, but she figured something like that could happen, even if it was just that Ricky Dale and she began talking and looking after the horses together again.

However, her hopes in this direction were frustrated a great deal, as heavy rain set in, and then cold temperatures, and Aunt Marilee would not let her go to the corral. The cleaning of the stalls was not crucial for a few days, since the horses were not shut into them. And really, the idea of standing around in the cold wet barn with the horses doing nothing other than standing around wasn't all that inviting.

She was so mad at that Melissa Pruitt! That girl was worse than Corrine had imagined. She sure was smarter than Corrine had imagined.

First the girl had stolen Corrine's boyfriend. That did not seem in any way Christian, no matter how much Melissa went to church.

Okay, the point could be made that Ricky Dale had not exactly been Corrine's boyfriend, but he could have been. He had certainly been her friend, and was on his way to being her boyfriend, and he was more her boyfriend than anyone else's, until Melissa had stepped in with her two goodies—her big boobs that no boy of Ricky Dale's age could resist. And it was well-known that Melissa made out with boys, too. Then she had to go and do this and just ruin everything for Corrine.

What Melissa had done was be nice, and right in front of half the girls in the class, too.

It had been raining cats and dogs right before school, and the rest room was packed with girls trying to fix themselves up in the two mirrors there. When Corrine came around the partition and saw the bunch, she paused, quite fascinated and a little disconcerted at the sight of so many girls stuffed into one small space.

She stood back like she always did, waiting until there was plenty of space at the mirror, and while she waited, she watched those girls fix themselves up, in order to learn about it. Natalie Sproul, who had great hair, was bent over, hanging her hair and spraying the daylights out of it. Paris Miller, who had her arms lifted in an effort to brush her short hair more spiky than it already was, showed her entire bared middle, with a ring in her belly button.

And here Corrine was having to badger Aunt Marilee for pierced ears. She could imagine what would happen if she wanted a pierced belly button. Aunt Marilee would probably jump out a window.

Corrine watched Melissa Pruitt carefully put her frosted hair into place. The next instant, the girl said to her, "Here, Corrine...take my place. I'm all done," just like she'd been saving mirror space for her, which was something only friends did for friends.

Melissa was stuffing her brush back into her book bag and backing up to give Corrine room. There was nothing for Corrine to do but mumble, "Thanks," and slip in and take a brush to her hair and apply lip gloss. She felt everyone's eyes on her, too, and she heard some mumbling and knew it was about her. Melissa never said another thing but left with her crowd of in-girls, chattering and laughing out the door.

She never in her life had imagined that Melissa Pruitt would be so clever as to be nice to her. She was furious with herself for not thinking of it. She had, in fact, been spending a lot of time dreaming up ideas of mean things to do to Melissa, such as pulling out her chair at the last minute when she went to sit down, or putting horse apples in her book bag, or at the least knocking her drink in her lap at lunch. Of course, these things were too stupid to do, and she wasn't likely to be able to get a chance to do any of them, either, since she didn't get around Melissa at all, but what was really aggravating was that even if she were a bold person and decided to find a way to do all three, she was prevented from doing them now, because she would look lower than snake-poop, after Melissa had just been nice.

The awful thought came to her that Melissa's action could

look like she had been giving her, the nerdy, unpopular girl who couldn't keep a boyfriend, a charity kindness.

Aunt Marilee picked Corrine and Willie Lee up at school. On the way to the drugstore for an after-school snack, she dropped Corrine off at the post office to get the mail. Willie Lee, who usually went everywhere with Corrine that he could, declined going to the post office. Likely he didn't want to run into the postmistress and be challenged again about Santa Claus.

Holding her coat up over her head against the cold rain, Corrine jumped the big puddle in front of the curb, then raced down the sidewalk and into the building. She saw that the postmistress was busy behind the counter with a line of customers, everyone holding a parcel or two.

Mrs. Julia Jenkins-Tinsley was happy as could be to have so many people using the P.O. She had on a Santa cap, with a bell on the end of it. She had also suspended this enormous sign over the special Santa Claus mailbox that said: Drop Letters To Santa In Here. The USPS Delivers On Time.

Corrine thought the postmistress was getting a little carried away about Santa Claus.

She got the mail from their box and ran through the rain down to the drugstore, where it was quite crowded. With the cool, wet weather, a number of people were getting lattes. Aunt Vella was really proud of her latte machine, the only one in all of Valentine, and apparently it was a big hit.

Along with shoppers in the pharmacy and health and beauty aids areas, there were several people browsing the small gift area, and teachers and high school teens coming over to the fountain counter for Cokes, barbeque sandwiches and nachos to go.

Leanne Overton was sitting at the counter, and when Corrine saw her, she felt this bit of excitement she often felt when she saw Leanne. She wanted to be a lot like Leanne when she grew up, be able to handle and ride a horse, although when it came to attire, she hoped to be more refined, like Aunt Marilee. Leanne wore shirts and sweaters that showed what she had, which was considerable, and skintight jeans. Perhaps she needed to wear those to ride well. Leanne did have strong legs. She worked out a lot. Corrine had once heard Leo Pahdocony at the newspaper say that Leanne had thighs that could kill a man. Corrine figured that meant really strong ones.

With Leanne were Charlene MacCoy and Jojo. Charlene and Leanne were cousins, and seeing them side by side, they looked some alike, too.

Sheriff Oakes, Ricky Dale's daddy, was also at the counter, his big body hunched over one of his about a dozen cups of coffee he would have at one time, one right after the other.

Sitting at tables were Granny Franny and Mr. Winston, and the pastor's wife, Naomi Smith, with her baby, and her eight-year-old son and six-year-old daughter, who looked enough alike to be twins and were taking turns sticking a spoon on their noses.

Aunt Marilee, Willie Lee and Aunt Vella had the usual family table. Willie Lee was eating a dish of vanilla ice cream, and Munro was underneath the table, licking at his own dish. Aunt Marilee had a Coke float waiting for Corrine.

As she came around and sat down, Mr. Winston was asking Willie Lee if he had written his letter to Santa yet.

"No," Willie Lee said, keeping his gaze on his ice cream and playing his spoon around in it.

"Do you want something special for Christmas?" Granny Franny asked him.

He looked thoughtful and then shrugged. "May-be I would like a Pok-e-mon."

"Uncle Winston wrote his letter to Santa the other night, but he won't tell what he asked for," Leanne said. "I'm thinking of askin' Santa for a husband, and I've got a list of what I want." She really did. She brought a paper out of her pocket and read it.

"I want a man who loves horses and all animals, even small dogs and cats. I want him to be kind and considerate and like to have adult conversation. To believe women are equal, and to dislike television wrestling, boxing and football, and to never yell or hit."

Her voice was very stern on this point, and Corrine's gaze was drawn to the small scar line across the side of her cheek to her ear. It was common knowledge that one of the reasons Leanne lived with Mr. Winston was that her former significant other had beaten the daylights out of her, and she had finally hit him with a frying pan and run for it. He had ended up with most of her money and two of her horses, though.

"And I want him to want to get married," she finished.

"I think that should be number one for any husband," Granny Franny said.

"What do you mean by adult conversation?" Sheriff Oakes asked her.

"Talkin' about feelings and hopes and dreams."

"Yeah, that's what I thought you meant," he said. "You can get all you need of that on *Oprah*."

Corrine noticed that Jojo kept turning around on her stool and looking at her with a strange expression. It was sort of an adoring look. Corrine didn't know how to respond. She felt a little silly and embarrassed.

Belinda came hurrying over from the perfume counter she had installed for the Christmas season, saying that she wanted the trip to the Virgin Islands that QVC was offering. She snatched up the remote and turned up the volume on the television.

On the screen was a contest for a magical seven-day cruise and stay at a beautiful and exotic resort. An all-expense-paid trip of a lifetime for you and that someone special. A Christmas gift to some lucky winner.

"Mama, I'm gonna enter as you," she said to Aunt Vella, and explained as she dialed that only one entry per person was allowed, and she'd already entered herself and Lyle. "All of y'all enter, and if one of you win it, I'll go with you instead of Lyle."

Everyone let that pass. Probably no one would want to go on a cruise with Belinda. She had a complaining personality. Corrine sure wouldn't want to spend a week trapped with her.

Charlene MacCoy said that if she thought it would work,

she might ask Santa Claus to make her children young again, but not even God could do that. "I'll settle for havin' a good old-fashioned Christmas with my family," she said. "That's the perfect Christmas gift." She smiled at Mr. Winston, as if she had never yelled at him, and touched Jojo's hair.

Corrine, watching the tender gesture, suddenly felt a great hole open up inside of her. She averted her eyes to her tall float glass and stirred the spoon in the murky liquid.

"I want a Game Boy," said Gabby, Naomi Smith's youngest girl.

"Aw, all you're gonna get is coal in your stockin'," her brother said.

"I am not."

"I want Stanley to have a vasectomy," Mrs. Smith said all of the sudden, as she rose to jiggle her baby who had started to fuss.

Corrine was astonished at such a comment coming from a preacher's wife. She also did not think the woman should have said such a thing in front of her children.

Then Aunt Marilee went over and took the baby from Mrs. Smith and began swaying him back and forth in her arms, smiling at him and saying soft words. Aunt Marilee wanted a baby so bad. She was just the picture of a mother, too.

This was another example of the way things were mixed up in the world. Aunt Marilee was praying for a baby, and undoubtedly Mrs. Smith was praying not to have any more, and here she had five and Aunt Marilee had just one—well, two, counting Corrine—and would really like another. What could God be thinking? No wonder people lost faith. She really thought God should not make believing any harder than it already was.

Mrs. Smith began tucking her other two children into their raincoats and fastening up their hoods. She even kissed each one on the forehead, and, seeing this, Corrine felt reassured that she could like the woman again, since Mrs. Smith really did care for her children.

Later, after everyone had left and the store was about to close, and Corrine was helping Aunt Marilee and Aunt Vella clean up, she heard Aunt Vella say in an achy voice to Aunt Marilee, "You know what I'd like for Christmas? I'd like Margaret to come home."

Her Aunt Marilee put her arm around Aunt Vella's shoulders and pressed close, in the manner of helping to hoist up a burden. Watching the two women, Corrine had a strange feeling, as if suddenly seeing far down through her own years.

As they drove the short distance around the block to the parking area behind the *Voice* building, Corrine asked about Margaret, who she knew was Aunt Vella's and Uncle Perry's oldest daughter. There was a picture of Margaret on Aunt Vella's dining room wall.

"Where is Margaret? Is she still alive?" Corrine asked, imagining the woman off in the secret service, maybe, or shut up in an insane asylum. She had only heard mention of the woman several times, in the context of the past.

"Oh, yes. She lives out in Atlanta. She's a travel agent."

Aunt Marilee glanced at her, and then took on that expression that said she was thinking about what to say. "Margaret likes to travel the world, exotic places. She never much liked Valentine, and as soon as she was old enough, she moved off. She's a real sophisticated woman of the world. Each Christmas she goes to some place like London or Paris or Rome."

Corrine imagined that, and it seemed awfully wonderful, but then she thought of Aunt Vella and the longing on her face when she mentioned Margaret.

"Has Aunt Vella asked her to come home? Maybe she would come if Aunt Vella asked her to." Corrine wanted Margaret to come, if only for a few days.

"Well...Aunt Vella and Margaret have a hard time communicating. Aunt Vella thinks that Margaret will come when she gets ready."

Corrine thought that did not seem to be working.

And then she thought of her own mother. She halfway wanted her mother to come, just for a visit. She did not want her mother to come and take her away.

10
಄

The skies were finally clearing when Aunt Marilee dropped them off at school. It was cold but was supposed to warm up, and Corrine would get to go to the corral that afternoon. She decided that she was going to try to find a way to speak to Ricky Dale. She could ask him if he was going to the corral. After all the rain, they would need to attend to the stalls for sure.

On her way to her locker, she saw Ricky Dale talking to Coach Pitner. Right after that, Ricky Dale came over to her. She saw him coming out of the corner of her eye but didn't look at him until he spoke, and then she acted like she was surprised at seeing him standing there, which she sort of was.

He looked a little anxious, so right off she said "Hey," in a friendly manner.

Relief instantly passed over his features. "Hey," he said, and leaned on her locker. "Uh, were you plannin' to go over to the corral this afternoon?"

"Yes," she said, hardly believing the exchange, wondering what Melissa Pruitt would say about this and watching his eyes carefully and eagerly. They were green as cat-eye marbles, and she averted her gaze to his nose before she did something silly because she was just so thrilled.

Then he came out with, "Well, good. Could you feed the horses, then? Leanne called me this mornin'. She's goin' down to Fort Worth, and she wasn't sure if she was comin' back tonight or not. She asked if I would feed them when I cleaned the stalls, and I said I would, but now I need to go to the basketball meeting after school, and then I have to get right over to Doc Lindsey's."

She stared at him, at his green as cat-eye marbles eyes that began to look a little worried the longer she stood there staring at him, so then, like an idiot, she told him, "No problem. I can handle it fine." Which she could, but she didn't want him to use her like a friend, when he wasn't being all that friendly with her.

"Well…thanks." He looked like he had something else to say and then came out with, "I got to get to class," and took a couple of backward steps as he continued to look at her in a curious manner. "Catch ya' later." He turned and hurried off.

She slammed her locker closed and wondered what happened to her being too small to clean the stalls all by herself.

Why didn't he ask Princess Melissa to go over there and feed the horses and muck stalls? Now that would be a sight.

She went into her history class, which she didn't much care for, and doubly so in that moment of thorough disgust with life. In the minutes before the second bell rang, she deliberated about going down to the nurse's office and saying that she had started her period and was sick and needed to go home. She had never done this, but she had heard girls talk about doing it. She deliberated too long, though, and the bell rang and class started. She wouldn't be allowed out of class unless she told Mr. Humphrey why she wanted to see the nurse, and she wasn't about to do that.

It turned out that she got to miss history class anyway, because five minutes into it, the art teacher, Miss Dewberry, came and got Corrine and two other of her art class students and took them to join other students in the cafeteria, where she told them that they were excused from all their morning classes in order to paint Christmas scenes on windows all over the school.

"This school is too drab, and we're goin' to do something about it," Miss Dewberry said. Everyone knew her opinion that the school lacked tasteful character.

Miss Laura Dewberry was somewhere over thirty, really beautiful, with big dark blue eyes. Corrine thought she looked a lot like the country singer Martina McBride. She was from a rich family over in Memphis, and why she would want to come from there to teach in a tiny town of south-western Oklahoma was a mystery to Corrine. The general story was that she had come out to marry her boyfriend, who was a pilot in the Air Force up in Lawton, but he'd been killed in a freak airplane accident before they got married. That story didn't answer the question of why she had not gone home to Memphis and her rich family. Their school was lucky to get her was most thinking people's opinion, according to Aunt Marilee, who, along with a few other parents, had been responsible for getting the school board to hire Miss Dewberry full-time. The job did not pay much and called for her to teach all the grades, first through twelfth. She did not appear to need money, and she loved art and she loved children. Since the first of the year, she had been doing her best to improve the building in which they all spent so much time.

She said now, "I want you to Christmas this place up!"

She was getting half of her students in the morning and the other half in the afternoon. She divided them up into groups, mixing ages and grades. Quite suddenly Jojo MacCoy appeared at Corrine's shoulder, slipping up beside her like some little elf, and Miss Dewberry put two boys with them and told them that they would be painting the large hall window into the library. The two boys were a fourth-grader named Mike, who looked like a miniature cattle baron in starched shirt, pointy toed cowboy boots and a Western hat, and Anson Brown's brother, Gideon, a sixth-grader like Jojo.

Miss Dewberry thrust a Christmas card into Corrine's

hands and told her to use it for an idea and to direct her crew. Corrine felt instant alarm at not only being in charge of other kids but being responsible for producing a picture adequate enough for everyone to look at. Jojo and the boys were standing there gazing at her. She considered saying that she had a sick headache, which she was suddenly getting, but she did not think this would come off very well. She was stuck.

Before they started on painting the window, Corrine looked over and saw Gideon drawing a black mustache on Mike. She sure hoped the paint would wash off.

The image on the Christmas card Miss Dewberry had given them to copy was of Santa in his sleigh with his reindeer, riding off to the moon. Corrine sketched in the basic image. When she was stretching to reach the top portion of the window, Jojo appeared with a library chair to stand on.

Next Jojo jumped right in to start painting in the team of reindeer. Corrine gave over the chair to her; then she set Gideon to working on Santa and the sleigh, pretty easy, because the view was of the back of Santa. She showed the smaller Mike how to make snow-covered pine trees peeking out of the bottom of the window, which was the only place he could reach easily.

Corrine painted Rudolph at the head of the reindeer team, stopping every so often to lend a hand to the others and to make corrections in the proportions. Before she realized it, Gideon had painted Santa with a face.

"You made him a black man," Corrine said, thoroughly surprised.

To that, Gideon replied, "Well, yeah...what of it, girl? Who says he ain't?"

Corrine decided she wasn't going to say he wasn't. And Gideon had given him merry eyes and rosy cheeks. She did fairly itch to make corrections to the sleigh, which looked more like a lopsided box, and to some of the trees, which looked like blobs, but she restrained herself. Miss Dewberry said there was no such thing as constructive criticism.

Throughout the work, she was aware of Jojo watching her and studying her drawing of Rudolph. She also noticed that

Jojo had pierced ears. Her earrings were tiny gold balls, like the sort the little girl at Wal-Mart had gotten. Corrine wondered if Jojo'd had them put in with a gun.

Finally she asked her, "Did you get your ears pierced up at Wal-Mart?"

Jojo's eyebrows went up, and then she shook her head. "Un-uh. I guess I got them when I was a baby. I've just always had them."

Corrine thought Jojo was really lucky.

While they were working, the elementary school principal's secretary came by and brought them some cookies, and the librarian and her helper kept coming out and saying how great their painting was.

The picture did turn out better than Corrine had expected. Lots of people complimented it, and she didn't think all of them were saying it just to be nice. The secretary who had brought them cookies came through taking pictures. Some of the kids wanted to have a judging of the pictures, but Miss Dewberry said, "We do not need competition in art. It is a matter of taste and opinion."

Corrine wondered how college scholarship committees and state fairs would feel about that.

She went through the line and got her lunch—meatloaf, yuk.

Glancing around for where to sit, she saw Ricky Dale sitting between Melissa Pruitt and Anson Brown at their usual table on the far side of the cafeteria.

At the start of school, she had always sat with Ricky Dale, and then Anson and a couple of others began joining them. Lately Ricky Dale and Anson had joined Melissa Pruitt and her crowd. The others could get too noisy to suit Corrine, and she had felt such an outsider that after a couple of weeks, she had moved over to sit at the same table as another girl in her class, Becky Rhudy, and Natalie Sproul and Paris Miller, both eighth-graders. They were all quiet and reserved, like herself. Mostly they did not so much sit together as sit at the same table.

Paris Miller maybe wasn't so reserved as antisocial. That

was what the Social Studies teacher, Mrs. Mullins, had called her, and to her face. Aunt Marilee said she doubted Mrs. Mullins would have another year at their school, because she was a rude individual.

Corrine suspected that a girl such as Paris, with black lipstick and hair gelled up like a guy's and an earring in her belly button, wasn't inviting to most adults, although Corrine found her fascinating and admired her, too, for doing just what she wanted to do with herself. Besides, when someone had been given such a name as Paris, what did people expect? If the teachers didn't like the way Paris looked or acted, they should take it up with her parents, who'd named her.

Corrine went over and sat at the table with the girls, who didn't even say hello but simply looked at her in a casual accepting fashion.

Then right behind her came Jojo MacCoy, just as if she were with Corrine.

"Did y'all hear about the picture on the window in the art class door?" she said, sitting down with her tray as if she had been invited.

Asking a question like that was a good way to get into a group. Natalie Sproul asked with high curiosity, "No. What about it?"

Jojo said, "Johnny Thomas and Sondra Smith painted it as a surprise for Miss Dewberry. They made the window look like a Christmas card, with the edge to open. The only trouble was that it was a scene of the baby Jesus with a star with beams that made a cross, and the superintendent said they had to get it washed off'a there before the school got sued."

"Did Miss Dewberry get to see it first, before they had to wash it off?" Becky Rhudy asked. She was a pudgy girl with a porcelain complexion and a generally anxious expression, which might simply have been the result of thick eyebrows that grew together over her nose.

Jojo shrugged. "I guess she did. She was standin' there."

After a minute Natalie Sproul said, "Corrine, yours and Jojo's window looks great."

Corrine looked up in surprise.

Paris Miller said, "Yea, it's pretty cool." She had a husky voice, like maybe she already smoked cigarettes.

"Thanks," Corrine and Jojo said at the same time, then looked down at their plates and over to each other.

When they'd finished lunch, Corrine and Jojo decided to go over to check out the art room window, sort of as an after-look. Becky Rhudy came hurrying to join them.

The hallway and the art room were empty, the window wiped clean.

"Let's paint another picture there," Corrine said quite suddenly, and without waiting for any sort of reply, she flew into the art class, where the small jars of paint and cleaned brushes were sitting ready on the long worktable. Jojo came after her, the both of them grabbing what they needed, while Becky said, "You'd better not make any religious picture."

Corrine told her to go to the corner and watch down the main corridor for anyone coming. She did not have to tell Jojo anything. Jojo said, "I'll hold the paints," and stood by while Corrine quickly painted a donkey and put Mary atop it, holding a baby. Then she painted what she hoped looked like an angel above them. It was all done with economy of motion and without true detail, except for the donkey, which actually dominated the scene because he was the easiest for her to draw. The whole time Corrine could not believe she was painting so fast, and that it actually came out pretty good without her agonizing over every stroke.

She wanted to write God bless us all, but all she got down was God, and then Becky came running up to them.

"Some kids are comin'!" She looked a little hysterical, as if she were about to be caught robbing a bank or something.

The three of them jumped into the art class. Corrine threw the brushes into the sink, then stepped to the counter to arrange the paint jars. Becky started to hide, and Corrine pulled her over to the counter. "Just clean."

The kids went on past in the hallway, their voices fading as they entered another classroom further along.

Jojo was giggling and trying to hold it in, and Becky,

about to cry, said she had to go to the bathroom really bad and took off down the hall.

Corrine didn't think she wanted Becky Rhudy around in any truly extreme situations, if painting a picture on a window was going to do this to her.

Jojo followed Corrine to her locker.

"Miss Dewberry's gonna know you painted the window," Jojo said.

"Becky's probably gonna tell." Worry washed over her. She did not like to stand out.

Jojo shrugged. "Maybe, but Miss Dewberry'll know anyway because of the donkey. No one else could draw a donkey that good."

Corrine didn't even know why she'd done it. She'd wanted to give Miss Dewberry a surprise. And she'd needed to do something a little daring, although now the entire endeavor seemed much less daring than just plain stupid. She wasn't so worried about getting in trouble for painting something she shouldn't have as she was terrified of calling attention to herself. Thinking of it almost caused her to quit breathing.

The rest of the day, she kept waiting for someone to come get her and take her to the principal's office for painting a religious picture where she wasn't supposed to. When no one did, she vacillated from high relief to high disappointment. When she could, right before her last class, she got a peek at the art class door. The glass was washed clean. She didn't know whether to be glad or sad about that. She hoped Miss Dewberry had seen the picture before it got washed off.

Aunt Marilee picked her and Willie Lee up after school. The sun was out strong, warming things up. Not at all like a month for Christmas, and Aunt Marilee complained about that as she drove them over and dropped them off in front of Mr. Winston's house. From there she was going on down to Aunt Vella's. Aunt Vella was getting rid of old Christmas decorations, and Aunt Marilee wanted a chance at first pick, because likely some of them were antique items.

Corrine was struck suddenly with eagerness at being able

to go to the corral after the days of rain. She told Willie Lee to hurry up, took his hand and helped him to run up the gravel track around Mr. Winston's big house. It was a wonderful old house, she thought, looking upward at the fancy round leaded glass that was likely the stairwell, and further upward to the windows of the second story.

When she grew up, she was going to have a house like this one, and with big trees just like were around it, although she would have it out on a ranch.

They came around the corner of the house, and there was Leanne Overton's big red one-ton sitting out by the corral, after all. And beside it was a shiny green Chevy pickup, with the words *Littleton Ranch* printed in fancy silver letters in the rear window. A cowboy-looking guy was with Leanne in the corral. They had Sweet Sugar in a halter.

A horrible dread came over Corrine as she watched the man pet the filly on the neck. The man had come to buy Sweet Sugar. She knew this in the way that she often knew things without being told.

As she and Willie Lee walked across the yard, Leanne let the filly out of the halter, and instantly Sweet Sugar turned and raced away, kicking up her heels. Leanne and the man turned to come through the gate and saw them.

"Well, hi, you two. I got back a lot quicker than I was intendin'," Leanne said. "I'm glad you're here, though. Wade, these are the children I was tellin' you about. This is Willie Lee, who helped save the filly when she went through the tornado, and this is Corrine, who has been helping take care of the filly all these months. Kids, this is Mr. Wade Littleton."

"Hello," Corrine said. The man's eyes were friendly, moving from Willie Lee to Corrine and then back with more curiosity to Willie Lee.

Willie Lee offered up his hand for a handshake, and Mr. Littleton took it. "This is my dog. His name is Mun-ro," Willie Lee said.

Mr. Littleton said hello to Munro. He wore a leather sport coat, and his jeans were creased by the cleaners. He had this big gold ring on his right hand.

The man said, "You seem to have some good hands here, Lee," in the way that adults did when being nice to children.

Leanne told Corrine to go ahead and grain the horses, and then she and Mr. Littleton stood leaning on the corral fence while they talked. Corrine thought Leanne was interested in Mr. Littleton. She stood close to him and smiled a lot.

As she got the buckets of grain and hung them on the hooks outside the stalls, her mind went back and forth from the idea of Leanne being out to sell Sweet Sugar to this guy being someone Leanne wanted to have for a husband.

She gave Willie Lee a brush and told him to brush the mare, while she went to work cleaning the stall. All the while she kept an ear tuned to hear anything she could of the exchange between Leanne and Mr. Littleton. Leanne was sure touching him a lot, but then, she was like that.

As Corrine pushed the wheelbarrow of soiled shavings out of the stall, she heard Leanne say, "Oh, she'll ride, but I doubt she could ever compete on barrels. I don't think her leg would hold up long for much of that."

Corrine thought that she did not care if the filly could not run barrels. She would love her anyway.

"She'll make a good broodmare, though, Wade," and Leanne went to naming the filly's bloodline.

Corrine's thoughts raced ahead to asking Papa Tate for the money to buy Sweet Sugar. If the filly was to be sold, Corrine would buy her. She could get a job at Parker's vet office. She could work to pay for the horse.

Then she heard Leanne say, "I'm askin' fifteen thousand for her, Wade."

Corrine thought she had to have heard wrong.

"Corrine! You and Willie Lee wait up a minute." Leanne came hurrying down the back steps and across the yard, her breasts swaying beneath her close-fitting sweater.

"I have your payment for November. Yours and Ricky Dale's. Do you think you could take his to him? I've given you both a Christmas bonus. I thought you might be able to use it well ahead of time…for buyin' gifts and things."

The woman held two white envelopes toward her. Corrine slowly took them.

"Thank you," she managed to get out.

"Well, you and Ricky Dale, and you, too, Willie Lee, have sure been a lifesaver for me." Leanne fluttered her red fingernails at the horses standing in the glow of a setting sun. "I know you saved her life, Willie Lee, but that filly couldn't have gotten back on her feet and where she is today without a lot of care. Corrine, you and Ricky Dale puttin' in your time and effort to keep the stalls and all around so spic and span was a real contribution to those horses' health. And they're worth a good deal to me."

"Cor-rine likes to take care of them," Willie Lee said, giving a smile.

"I know she does, honey. It's worked out real well for all of us." She regarded Corrine. "You know it's been my intention all along to sell the filly."

Corrine nodded.

"Well, there are several people interested in her, and I'll be makin' a decision in the next week. I know y'all will miss her, but I will see that she goes to a home where she will be well cared for. A place where she can be out in the pasture with other horses and eatin' green grass."

Corrine stared at her.

"I'll be movin' the mare, too, over to a small horse farm I've taken up north about ten miles. I'm gonna start teachin' barrel racing and raisin' up more of my own stock. I'll need your help for the next week or two, though, if you can still come?"

Corrine nodded. "Yes, I can come. I'll tell Ricky Dale."

"Well, good. Thanks a lot. I sure do appreciate it."

They parted, and then Corrine turned back, "Leanne?"

"Yes, honey?"

"How much are you askin' for the filly?" She wanted to be sure.

"Well, I'm really hopin' to get fifteen thousand. Wade Littleton—the man who was just here—he's sayin' he'll go twelve for her." She looked excited. "Because of her, I'm gonna be able to get my place."

Corrine nodded, then said thanks.

As they walked away to the street, Willie Lee slipped his hand into Corrine's.

"Le-anne is sel-ling Ba-by Sug-gar," Willie Lee told Aunt Marilee on their drive home.

"The filly? Really?" Aunt Marilee cast Corrine an anxious, probing look.

Corrine nodded, keeping her gaze out the windshield. "She's always been going to sell her."

"Oh," Aunt Marilee said. Then, "I'm sorry, honey."

Corrine didn't reply. What was there to say? She wanted to scream and beat something, but that would upset Aunt Marilee, and was just too childish.

That night she pulled one of Aunt Marilee's tricks and took a long hot shower in which she cried and cried. No one could hear you crying in the shower. Corrine had once overheard her aunt telling this to Miss Charlotte.

Naomi Smith, baby on her hip, helped her younger children write their letters to Santa. Fisk made a face, but she and Stanley had been very firm with him about not telling Gabby yet about Santa. He was a kind boy at heart and wouldn't do it on purpose, but he might tell her in a fit of forgetfulness. How did one punish forgetfulness? Naomi herself thought she was losing her mind because she forgot so much.

"Go on and get ready for bed. I'll address the envelopes," she told them, hoisting the baby higher on her hip. "Gabby, ask Shad to help you with the water in the tub."

Gabby wanted a Game Boy and had written that three times in her letter, then put in that she also would take a ballerina dress. Then she had written, *Thank you, Santa. I love You,* and drawn three little hearts. Gabby had a heart as big as all outdoors. Naomi felt an ache in her chest. Once she had felt such easy love for everyone and everything. It was hard to hold on to as she got older and lived in the world.

In contrast, Fisk wrote that he wanted a Mercedes-Benz, and next to that he would take his own room with an entire entertainment center. Fisk thought big; they believed he might be a stockbroker when he grew up.

Naomi went over and put the baby in his swing seat and wound it up to get the full length of thirty minutes. She folded her children's letters, Gabby's very carefully, thinking how much time her daughter had put into writing neatly, inserted them each into an envelope, and addressed them to: Santa Claus, North Pole of the World.

Then she sat, tired and worn, gazing at the carpet that needed vacuuming and listening to both the baby and the swing squeak, and the sound of children hollering in the recesses of the house. A sink and counter full of dishes waited for her in the kitchen. Her eldest daughter was working a job at Pizza Hut, and her second daughter was sitting with elderly Minnie Oakes, who wasn't well. Her husband was communing with God and writing his sermon for Sunday.

Didn't anyone ever relax at night anymore? No wonder United States presidents didn't do fireside chats these days. There was no one sitting beside the fireside to listen.

Pulling a piece of the school notebook paper toward her, she took up a pencil and nibbled the eraser. It was silly. And likely pagan. She should pray to God for any of her needs, since she knew there wasn't a Santa Claus. Her father, a fire and brimstone preacher, had not let any of his children begin to believe in Santa Claus. She had determined on a different life for her children.

And for that instant, with the idea of writing to Santa, as she had done in secret when a child, her heart lifted and she felt very much a hopeful child again, as she had not in so very long a time.

Dear Santa,
  I would like...

She stopped, shoulders slumping as shame swept over her for asking for something for herself, and for a moment she heard her father's stern voice in memory. Then—because her father was long gone and she was a woman grown—she jutted her jaw and wrote quickly and deliberately.

...my own chair and ottoman. The salmon colored Henredon set in the window at Morris Brothers. It's on sale. And I want a table right beside it, and a lamp for reading, and an hour a day just for me. Can you do that, Santa?
Thank you. Naomi S.

A smile came to her lips as she put the letter into an envelope and addressed it to Santa at the North Pole of the World.

Later, however, right before going to bed, she got the letter, tore it up and flushed it down the toilet. There was no way they could afford that Henredon chair, and she would just hate for someone to read her letter. It would be like being seen naked. A preacher's wife was expected to have loftier desires than a Henredon chair, desires such as asking for world peace or feeding all the hungry children.

She'd asked for those things all her life, and nothing had ever changed.

That night, when she said her prayers, she asked for a more positive attitude.

II

∽

Papa Tate drove up to the curb in front of the school. "How about if we all go out for pizza tonight, and then drive around and look at Christmas lights? Willie Lee has to get started on his judging."

"Yes!" Willie Lee said.

"Sounds great," Corrine said, putting enthusiasm into her voice. Papa Tate was wanting to make her happy, because of the horses. She sure wished Willie Lee had not been with her yesterday, because then she never would have said anything about the horses. Now Aunt Marilee and Papa Tate kept looking at her with these worried, helpless expressions.

Aunt Marilee had said more than once, "I'm so sorry about the horses, honey," and Papa Tate had said, "When we get our house, we'll see about gettin' you your own horse."

As if they were going to get a house any time in the next hundred years.

Aunt Marilee had marked a jacket with horses on it in one of the catalogs. Corrine was probably going to get all sorts of stuff with horses on it for Christmas, and she didn't like clothes with horses on them.

Through the windshield, Corrine saw Ricky Dale up ahead, getting out of his brother's pickup truck.

She told Papa Tate goodbye and held the door for Willie Lee to scoot out of the back seat. He went off toward the elementary school wing, and she watched to make sure he didn't get sidetracked before getting to the door. When she turned around, Ricky Dale was waiting at the walk to the middle school doors.

"Hey," he said.

"Hey."

"Did you get over to feed the horses yesterday?"

She looked at him. "I said I would."

"Yeah, well, somethin' could have come up, you know."

"Well, it didn't." She felt badly for speaking so sharply. "And anyway, Leanne had gotten back." While she spoke, she dug into her backpack and brought out the envelope. "Here. Leanne gave me this to give to you. It's payment for November, plus a Christmas bonus."

"All-riiight."

He looked so happy. She hated to tell him about the horses, but she felt responsible to tell him. "Leanne says she's only gonna need us one or two more weeks. She's sellin' the filly and movin' the mare."

"What?"

"What I said. She's sellin' the filly real soon. She has a couple of people interested in buyin' her, for fifteen thousand, maybe." She felt his surprise, although she didn't see his face, because she kept looking straight ahead as they went through the double doors of the school.

"Well, that filly's worth pretty good," he said.

"Yeah, I guess. And she's taken a place up north about ten miles. She's gonna be movin' the mare up there with her, where she has pasture for her. She asked if we could continue doin' the stalls and maybe feedin' some for another week or two, and I told her I could. Can you?"

He frowned. "Well, after school, I'm gonna have basketball practice and workin' at Doc Lindsey's. I can help with the stalls on the weekend, though," he said in an eager to please fashion that bolstered her.

"Okay," she said, experiencing a certain sense of power in orchestration. "We should probably strip the stalls on Saturday, 'cause of all this rain."

Ricky Dale agreed to meet her at the corral at noon. They parted, and she went to her locker, which she ended up slamming by mistake, causing several kids to turn and look at her.

They worked with clay in art class and made little Christmas ornaments and figures. While Corrine was working on a couple of rocking horses, Miss Dewberry came up beside her and said in a quiet voice, "Thank you for the picture, Corrine."

Corrine jumped, then looked at the teacher. Jojo had been right; Miss Dewberry had recognized her donkey.

She didn't know what to say. *You're welcome* didn't quite seem right.

"I want you to go to the seminar at Cameron next month," Miss Dewberry said.

This was annoying. Miss Dewberry probably felt like she could push, since she knew something about Corrine now. "I might. I don't know yet. My aunt wasn't sure," she said, lying before she knew it. Then she said, "My mother's comin' for Christmas, and things are sort of up in the air right now."

Miss Dewberry didn't say anything, just gave her a speculative eye and then complimented Corrine's rocking horses.

She had known all along that Leanne would sell Sweet Sugar. Hadn't Leanne mentioned it a time or two? Somehow she had thought it would be later, that Sweet Sugar was too young to sell, but the filly was going on a full year old. She was lucky Leanne had not sold her before now.

Someday she would have her own horse. Someday she would be grown up and have a good job and a house with a place to keep a horse. It would be a big house, like Mr. Winston's, with big trees to shade both the house and the corral. Her bedroom would be big, too, with flowered wallpaper and a window that looked out at the corral. The barn would be real nice, even nicer than at Mr. Winston's, and maybe she would have a whole ranch where she could ride for miles.

What if whoever bought Sweet Sugar didn't take proper care of her?

"Corrine?"

She looked up to find Mrs. Mullins looking at her. "Are you all right?" the teacher asked in an annoyed tone.

Class had ended and the entire room was empty.

"Yes, ma'am." She gathered up her stuff, dropping her pencil and having to pick it up, and got out of there.

Becky Rhudy and Natalie Sproul were at the lunch table when Corrine sat down, and they said, "Hi."

A little surprised, Corrine returned the greeting.

Paris Miller wasn't there, and Corrine wondered about her but was too shy to ask.

Then Jojo came to join them and said, "Did you hear about Mrs. Maldonado?" She was good at having news so she could sit right down.

"What about her?" asked Natalie Sproul, of course.

"Santa Claus sent her a thousand dollars in cash, just to-day, right here to the school."

"Santa Claus?" Natalie looked disbelieving.

"That's what the note said that came with the money. Merry Christmas from Santa Claus."

"Where'd you hear this?" Natalie was still skeptical.

"I had to pay for back lunches, and I heard Mrs. Maldon-ado and the others talkin' about it."

"That's just like that lady out at your mom's senior retire-ment home," Corrine put in.

Jojo nodded vigorously, saying, "I know."

Becky, her thick eyebrows going together, asked, "What is just like the lady out at the retirement home?"

"Mrs. Betts, who's a nurse or somethin' out at MacCoy Acres, got three thousand dollars in the mail, with a note that said, Merry Christmas from Santa Claus," Corrine said.

"Well, my gosh, there is somebody in Valentine is givin' away thousands of dollars?" Natalie said.

"It looks like it."

"Maybe it's somebody from somewhere else," Becky put in.

They all just looked at her.

Corrine hurried to finish eating so that she could go speak with Mrs. Maldonado and get the details for the paper. The one thing she wanted to ask Mrs. Maldonado was if she had written a letter to Santa Claus and asked for money, or if she had asked one of the Santas at the mall for money.

"Oh, *nada*...no," Mrs. Maldonado said, laughing when Corrine asked the Santa question. "I did pray to the Father for help, though. I want to go see my daughter in Mexico, and now I can. My daughter is going to have a baby, and she needs me. My prayers have been answered. It is a miracle."

Corrine scribbled the woman's words down as fast as she could, and right beside her, Jojo was scribbling, too. She had followed along, just as if Corrine had asked her to come. It was sort of fun to have Jojo with her to share the news of the event, and it turned out that today of all days, Corrine did not have change for the pay phone in order to call Papa Tate and make a report of the incident, but Jojo did, and even produced it eagerly.

Basically, Jojo was a handy person. She was sort of like a little adoring puppy, and there was no way not to like her.

It was a really warm day, over sixty, and sunny, so Corrine and Willie Lee walked home from school. They removed their coats and tied them around their waists and walked past houses with Christmas wreaths on the doors and bows on fences and Nativity and Santa figures in yards. It was sort of normal for Valentine, though. Papa Tate kept saying that it was going to turn cold right before Christmas. It always did.

Corrine intended to go to the corral, but she had to go home to check in with Aunt Marilee first. Also, she was experiencing a strange reluctance to go see the horses. It was almost too painful to think of them. It seemed like she might as well break off from them now and be done with it.

She thought about Mrs. Maldonado. She had been hoping that maybe the woman had written a letter to Santa, asking for the money, or had asked a Santa at a mall, but that theory appeared to be out. Still, Mrs. Maldonado had obviously told a number of people her desire to go home to Mexico for the holidays, and whoever was giving out the money had heard her.

Maybe Corrine could start telling people she wanted a horse—wanted Sweet Sugar—and whoever was giving out money would hear and give her some. Although somebody giving her fifteen thousand dollars did not seem likely. Besides, Corrine just couldn't go around saying she wanted a horse. She could hardly say when she wanted an ice-cream sundae.

"Let's go in and get a cake," Corrine told Willie Lee, when they went past the IGA.

"I want a MoonPie," Willie Lee said. "And Mun-ro wants one, too."

Corrine and Willie Lee chose chocolate MoonPies, then allowed Munro to sniff each of the chocolate, vanilla and banana MoonPies, and he chose banana. Papa Tate, a wealth of detail about the past, always said that the only true MoonPie was a chocolate one. That was all they had when he was growing up. Corrine agreed with him. The other flavors were not to her liking.

With a second thought, Corrine got two more MoonPies, one for Zona Porter and another one for herself, in case she might want it later. It faintly occurred to her that she was following in her Aunt Marilee's footsteps of turning to chocolate for consolation during times of disappointment and frustration.

On the way to the checkout, they passed a display for natural lip balms and lipsticks. Corrine stopped. Maybe if it was an all-natural product, Aunt Marilee would let her use it. *Protect your lips in style....*

She deliberated and chose one labeled Peachy. Then she

had to pull Willie Lee away from the packages of plastic farm animals. Usually she bought something for him, but today she had just enough for their snacks and the lipstick, which was almost five dollars alone.

When they got up to the checkout, there was Paris Miller, who hadn't been in school. Corrine was surprised to see her. In that moment, she realized that church was the only public place besides school that she had ever run into the girl.

"Hey," she said, when Paris looked at her.

"Hey," Paris said back. She didn't look friendly, but she didn't look unfriendly, either.

Corrine's gaze moved to the counter and the things the clerk was ringing up: a single big yellow onion, a package of liver—yuk—two boxes of macaroni and cheese, and a bottle of Metamucil.

Then she realized that Paris was counting out money and didn't have enough. She was two dollars short. "I had it," Paris said, checking her small purse and then her pockets. "I counted it just while I was shopping, and I had another five. It must have dropped out of my purse while I was shoppin'. Can't you just trust me for it?"

"You know I can't do that, Paris. You still owe a bill. You'll have to put something back."

Without hardly thinking, while she was taking in Paris's cheap jeans, shirt and thin worn jacket, Corrine dropped one of the fives she had in her hand.

"Oh, Paris...here. Is this the five you dropped?" She bent and picked it up, holding it out to the girl.

Paris cast her an angry frown, but then her expression went blank and she looked at the money and then at Corrine. She took the bill. "Thanks."

Paris gave the five over to the cashier and waited for change.

Corrine said, "Oh, shoot, Willie Lee, I forgot somethin'," turned around and pulled him along with her out of the checkout lane.

She went back to the lipstick display and replaced the peachy lip balm.

"You are not go-ing to get that, Cor-rine?" Willie Lee asked.

"I changed my mind."

When they went back through the checkout, Paris was long gone. Corrine was relieved, because she had begun to be afraid that the girl would be angry with her. Just exactly what Paris might be angry about, she wasn't certain. Perhaps the girl would be angry about the offer of money in the first place, or the silly way Corrine had gone about it. Maybe she should have offered a straight out loan to Paris. She didn't know why she hadn't done that. It was seeing the clerk's impatient face and feeling all these feelings squirming around inside herself.

Thinking about the entire unfortunate incident, Corrine got really mad at Paris's mother, who was responsible for giving the girl the unusual, conspicuous name and also not giving her enough money to buy things at the store.

There were shouting voices when Corrine and Willie Lee entered the *Voice* offices. They were stopped by the most amazing sight of two ladies grappling over near the coffee table. They both had hold of something. It was a *Valentine Voice* mug, and Papa Tate was trying to placate them.

One was a large woman Corrine did not recognize, and the other was Doris Northrupt, who was not much bigger than a minute, Aunt Marilee always said, even though her voice was plenty big at the moment as she shouted at the big woman, "I don't care if you got here this morning at the crack of dawn. Two little teddy bears do not entitle you to a cup. I brought in a whole box, and there's a Game Boy and a remote control Dale Earnhardt Jr. race car in there."

Corrine and Willie Lee stepped over to Charlotte's desk. She was watching the situation and had the phone receiver in her hand.

"Well, now, ladies…I promise you we will get in more cups. They are on back order."

"Wait! I just found this one!" It was Aunt Marilee coming from the back. She thrust forth a gleaming *Voice* mug. "It was back on the stock shelf. The last one. Here, Miz Northrupt. Now there's one for each of you, and we are so grateful for any and all gifts to the Chamber toy drive. Without such generosity, many children would go wantin', you know. You are our little elves helpin' Santa." Aunt Marilee had obviously caught sight of Willie Lee.

"Well...thank you, Marilee." A faintly sheepish expression passed over Mrs. Northrupt's face; then she flashed a scowl at the larger woman and left with swift strides.

The larger woman gave her thanks and went out, too, and Charlotte put down the phone, saying, "I was about to call the sheriff. I thought they were gonna flatten you, Tate."

"Too bad we aren't sellin' those mugs," said Papa Tate, with wonderment on his face. "Maybe I should give up the paper and sell mugs."

To that, Aunt Marilee said, "Well, honey, we wouldn't have any mugs if it weren't for havin' a newspaper. And it was my mug I gave Doris, so I want yours. I just love the shape of the lips on these cups."

"And they call us kids," Corrine said under her breath as she took Zona Porter the MoonPie she had bought her.

Upstairs in their apartment, she opened the refrigerator, and it was as if a trumpet sounded, *ta-da!* After pulling out the carton of milk, she stood there staring at all the food gleaming in the refrigerator light and thought again of Paris at the IGA. This image was followed by faded memories of her own life coming hard and fast, one upon the other. She thought of all the times she'd had to go to the store and return with the same foods: eggs, or macaroni and cheese, or bologna and day-old white bread.

Her mother had quite often sent her to the store with a certain amount of money to get certain things, and very often it wasn't quite enough money, and the clerks, impatient that they could not deal with an adult and feeling sorry for her, a small child, would be angry with her. She always felt so small and afraid when she looked up at the clerks, who would mostly frown at her as she counted out the few dollar bills and quarters, dimes and pennies, which were usually the tips her mother had made at a waitressing job.

She had sure eaten a lot of macaroni and cheese with her mother.

"What is in there?" Willie Lee said, coming to look in the refrigerator, too, then casting her a curious look.

"Oh, nothin'," she said, slamming the refrigerator closed. She got two glasses from the cupboard and then saw across the counter a loaf of bread and boxes of cereal and a package of almonds.

They had all the food they could want, and Aunt Marilee did most of the food shopping, and bought all of Corrine's particular favorites. Aunt Marilee was big on everyone having just what they especially liked to eat, and quite suddenly Corrine realized this was probably because Aunt Marilee herself had grown up poor. Corrine almost always had money in her pocket to buy snacks, like she had today.

While Willie Lee fell asleep on the living room floor with Munro and his cat, Corrine went into her bedroom, which was small but neat and clean and filled with everything she needed, new clothes and the flowered bedspread that she had picked out and matching curtains at the windows.

Deciding that the horses could get along this afternoon without her attentions, she raced down and got the mail and then returned to clean the house and do laundry.

"Well, my gosh, you are a busy beaver today," Aunt Marilee said, when she came upstairs and found the kitchen spotless and Corrine folding towels.

"Yeah...just felt like it," Corrine said.

She wanted to say: Thank you for this home...for how we live here, but all she could get out was, "Some catalogs came in the mail today."

"Oh, good," Aunt Marilee said, and then she kissed Corrine on the top of the head. "Look at them with me?"

So they sat at the kitchen table and *oohed* and *aaahed* together. Corrine gave Aunt Marilee her extra MoonPie and felt strangely both so happy and so sad at once. She did her best to not show her confused emotions.

Tate was busy in his office when his mother came flying through the door in the manner that she always arrived.

She said, "Guess what I found in my cedar chest?"

"I haven't the vaguest idea." His mother was a peculiar woman. For all he knew, she had Houdini's bones in her cedar chest.

"I found two of your letters to Santa Claus. I framed them for you. They're antiques, or soon will be."

That comment struck him like a two-by-four.

"You'll want to show them to Willie Lee."

Before he could say he was busy—he *was* the Editor, and they were on deadline day—she plunked the framed letters down in front of him right on top of an article he was proofing about a local resident's experiences in Hollywood.

Then, as if he could not read, she read aloud, pure delight in her voice: "'Dear Santa, how are you? I am fine. My mama says I have been a good boy this year. I want a Roy Rogers gun and holster set. It has caps. I really want a Schwinn Black Phantom bicycle, so you can bring that if you want. My mama says if you bring that, I still cain't'—look, that's just how you spelled it—'ride it cause I am too small and will break my neck. Please don't bring one to my brother, either. He won't let me ride it. Your friend, Tate Holloway. P.S. I am five years old and wrote this by myself.'"

His mother laughed. "You did, too. I taught you the alphabet when you were only two years old. You were always so smart. And here's the second one.

"'Dear Santa Claus, I want a red wagon with sides on it and a red cowboy hat and a Schwinn Black Phantom. I am six years old now and I swear I will not break my neck and make my mama cry. Don't listen to her. Yours truly, Tate Holloway.'

"Oh, I can't wait for Willie Lee to see these! They will encourage him. I'm sure I was meant to find them for him."

She went on about how it was all mystical and meant to be, because she had come across the letters just after her morning meditation. He nodded and made appropriate replies and noises until the phone rang, and he had to answer it. She waved as she left.

It was the mayor on the phone, with approximate sales figures from the town businesses over last weekend's beginning bang of the season. Tate jotted them down, and when he got off, he went to move the framed Santa letters and found himself staring at them, instead.

He had not gotten the bicycle that Christmas. His father, who had gone off to buy their presents, had instead gone on a three-day bender and landed in jail. Their mother, as incredible as she was peculiar, had managed to get Tate and his brother a red wagon to share, and some other things, and had even filled their stockings. Tate remembered to this day feeling relieved that his father had been gone. And how he and Hollis had hauled that red wagon all over, picking up discarded soft drink bottles and turning them in for the deposit money. They had also gone down every incline and hill that they could find. They had almost killed themselves going down the ramp at the ice house and flying out into the traffic.

He had eventually gotten a bicycle the following summer, he reflected, an old cast-off he'd found in someone's garage. He had never gotten the Schwinn.

As he gazed at the letter, remembering, the longing of a little boy swept over him. He thought of what Winston Valentine had said that day in Blaine's Drugstore, about writing to Santa Claus.

Then quickly, he pulled out a sheet of *Voice* stationery and jotted off:

Dear Santa,
    *This is Tate Holloway all grown up, and I want a Schwinn bicycle, the one I never got. And I want one for my...*he hesitated...*son, too. I will teach him to ride; so we can do it together.   Thank you, Santa. Sincerely, Tate Holloway. PS: We won't break our necks, no matter what the women say.*

He was already imagining what Marilee was going to say about this.

Chuckling, he put the letter in an envelope and addressed it. Tossing the statistics on the Christmas sales to Charlotte as he passed, he hurried down to the post office and dropped the letter in the mailbox. He hadn't really asked for what he wanted, he supposed. What he wanted was for Willie Lee to get back a sense of faith and wonder in himself, as well as in Christmas. Maybe Tate wanted that just as much himself. It had been a hard year. The tornado had taken the house he had planned so thoroughly for him and Marilee and their family, and now he didn't seem able to give Marilee the baby she so wanted.

But right that minute, writing to Santa Claus seemed to raise hope in him that...well, that life was still good and fine and loving.

Glancing over, he saw Julia Jenkins-Tinsley at the counter, regarding him with curiosity.

"Snoopin' into mail that isn't addressed to you is a federal offense, so don't you go peekin'," he told the nosy woman.

"Well, Tate Holloway, if you are implyin' that I open sealed mail..."

He walked out, way too happy to take offense or give any. He began jotting notes of his rapid thoughts. He had a good editorial about the Christmas spirit on his hands.

While he was taking notes, he just about walked right into Winston Valentine, who was coming out of the Senior Citizens Center.

"Guess what I did?" he told the old man with great pride.

Winston blinked. "What do I get if I play the game?"

"I wrote Santa a letter. Man, that feels good. Great idea you had."

"I know it."

12

Papa Tate showed them his letters to Santa from when he was a kid, explaining how Granny Franny had found them and framed them for him. Then he said, "And I've written my letter to Santa for this year, too. I've asked for somethin', just like Winston suggested. Y'all had better get on the ball with your letters."

Willie Lee, who had been thoughtfully regarding the framed letters, tilted his head and said, "Pa-pa Tate, if you wrote the let-ters to San-ta, why did Gran-ny Fran-ny have them?"

Oops.

Even Papa Tate was momentarily stumped at that one. Then he came out with, "Well, these are copies. I had to write the letter twice. I was just a boy, you know, and didn't write so good."

"Oh," Willie Lee said in an understanding tone. "I don't write so good, either."

"I'll help you write your letter, honey," Aunt Marilee said.

But Willie Lee said, "No. Mis-ter Wins-ton said it is se-cur-et."

"That's right, Marilee. Letters to Santa are a secret," said Papa Tate.

"Oh," Aunt Marilee said, deflated.

Later, when Corrine was doing algebra homework, Willie Lee came into her room and asked if she had written a letter to Santa.

"No, not yet," she said, a little preoccupied. But then she hurried to say, "But I'm goin' to."

He used to believe everything she told him, but now he regarded her with a bit of skepticism.

"I think it's a good idea, Willie Lee. It certainly can't hurt anything."

He nodded and left.

Gazing at the empty doorway, she realized that she wanted him to believe in Santa nearly as much as Aunt Marilee did.

Corrine gave much thought to possible requests of Santa.

Dear Santa, please bring me a horse.

Yeah, when monkeys flew.

Dear Santa, please don't let my mother come visit.

Santa was not in charge of such things, and she felt too guilty to make such a request of God. What a bad daughter to wish such a thing.

Her mother had not yet called to cancel and was due to arrive tomorrow. On the other hand, she also hadn't yet called to say she would definitely arrive.

Corrine considered suggesting to Aunt Marilee that they telephone down to her mother. If her mother was not coming, Corrine wanted to go ahead and know it and not be kept waiting to have relief.

In the end, though, she decided she would rather wait and let her mother bear the responsibility of calling them to say she wasn't coming.

Besides, Aunt Marilee was all focused on going driving to see the lights and decorations. She was more excited than Willie Lee, heading out the door first, telling them, "Come on, y'all. I can't wait to see what Odessa Collier has done this year. She has that new boyfriend and his two sons to help. Three men. Imagine the lights they can put up!"

They drove over to pick up Granny Franny to go with them, since she and Willie Lee were judges in the Outstanding Christmas Yard contest. Papa Tate pulled into the yard and went up to get his mother. He never just honked for her. Every time Corrine saw the little house where they used to live, where she had first come to live with Aunt Marilee, she experienced a tug on her heart. Granny Franny had red lights that looked like candles in the windows. They looked cheery.

Papa Tate and Granny Franny came out and got in the Cherokee, and Papa Tate whipped out a piece of paper. It was a list of entries thus far in the yard contest. In his methodical fashion, he had divided the town up into sections to view. Aunt Marilee made him drive out to the east end first, where Odessa Collier's house and big yard were right off the highway.

There were two cars ahead of them when they got there, and Corrine noticed two more coming behind them and slowing down, forming a line of viewers. This was because Mrs. Collier's house was a showplace of light and sound, proof, Papa Tate said, of the power of men with Christmas lights.

The whole house was outlined with lights, and there was a Santa in his sleigh with reindeer on the peak of the roof. In the yard there were a life-size nativity scene and a Santa village with moving elves, and the enormous cedar tree near the road was fully decorated like a Christmas tree in a house, even with wrapped packages underneath.

"Look at that...."

"Ohmygosh, look at that...."

"See that elf...."

"There's music! Roll down your window."

"She's gonna have one heck of a light bill."

"Some dumb a—wiseacre is sure to steal those packages to see if there's anything inside."

"Oh, Tate, don't be so negative."

Corrine didn't think they should have started with Mrs.

Collier's house, because now the others might prove a letdown.

But this wasn't too much the case. Just seeing any lights at all on a house brought them pointing out, "Look...there's one!" There was great anticipation of the magic that seemed to accompany lights strung all over a house and bushes. Corrine thought that it was sort of nuts, but she really liked it.

A couple of times Aunt Marilee almost caused them to be rear-ended by hollering, "Stop, Tate!" or "Turn here, Tate!"

After they had driven up and down any street that could possibly have lights, seen the few contest entries on the east side of town, and were dizzy and bug-eyed from looking, they went to the Main Street Café. It had grown sharply colder with the deepening night, and Papa Tate's suggestion of coffee, hot chocolate and pie was met with enthusiasm all around.

A golden glow spilled through the café's window out onto the sidewalk. It was like a beacon, and parking spaces up and down the street were filled. Papa Tate had to park way down almost to the Little Opry.

Corrine, suddenly struck with enthusiasm, ran ahead with Willie Lee and Munro. But the instant she went through the door and saw Ricky Dale's brother and his date and some other high school boys in a booth, she stopped, jerked her gaze straight ahead, took Willie Lee's hand and walked him, in what she hoped was a graceful manner, to the large round table, responding as she passed to a greeting from old Mr. Stidham and his wife.

Then Papa Tate and Aunt Marilee and Granny Franny were coming in and saying hello to everyone—the Stidhams, who said they were waiting on Ramona's brother to come in on the bus from Dallas, and to Jaydee Mayhall and his young wife, who was hot, according to a number of people including Ricky Dale, and who made a comment about Munro not being allowed in a restaurant.

But Fayrene said, "Dog? What dog? I don't see a dog."

A little boy from a family sitting at the big booth in the corner, with suitcases piled beside it, so they were probably waiting for the bus, too, pointed at Munro and said, "There's the dog," and everyone laughed.

Aunt Marilee had a ten-dollar receipt from where she had bought stuff at Blaine's Drugstore, so she got her hazelnut coffee and pie free. But then Fayrene said that all their orders were free, since Papa Tate had strung her lights. Corrine thought this was not only nice but very fair.

"I would never even have bothered with that hazelnut coffee special, if I'd'a known how much business I was goin' to pick up by stayin' open late on Friday night," Fayrene said, as she scribbled their order on her pad. There were more people coming in, and just Fayrene and her mother working tables, and her mother did not look happy doing it. Possibly she was in pain, because she was rather bent over. She had long fingernails painted a shiny turquoise, though, so Corrine thought she must be pretty lively on the inside.

Fayrene said that Tammy Faye had been supposed to work but had gotten back together with her husband and had to be with him whenever he crooked his finger, and that her mother was driving her crazy by playing Patsy Cline's song over and over on the jukebox. Right then a female voice was singing, "I fall to pieces..." and Fayrene said with gritted teeth, "I'm about to fall to pieces, and my song is the Chipmunks' 'Hurry Christmas.'"

Papa Tate got up and found the Chipmunks song on the jukebox and played it.

Aunt Marilee couldn't stand seeing Fayrene rushing around. She got up to help with their order and came back with the coffeepot. She didn't stop with just Papa Tate's and Granny Franny's coffee, but went around to all the tables. Jaydee Mayhall forgot himself and drew his hand back to pat her behind, and she said, "Do that and die," and held the coffeepot over his lap.

He instantly dropped his hand, but then he had to whistle at her.

"I expect a good tip," she told him.

Papa Tate's eyes moved up and down Aunt Marilee's back and over to Mr. Mayhall, who was being really friendly to Aunt Marilee. Corrine wondered if he might go over there and punch out the man, but he didn't. He didn't quit looking at Aunt Marilee, though. Corrine did not think Papa

Tate had anything to worry about; Jaydee Mayhall wasn't much.

Just as Fayrene's mother was practically throwing their plates of pie down on their table, Aunt Vella and Uncle Perry came in.

"Hey, you," Uncle Perry said to Corrine as he sat beside her, and she said, "Hey," back. She noticed that his hands scooting his chair up were whiter than she had ever realized. He smelled like old shaving lotion.

As Fayrene was flashing past, Aunt Vella held up several receipts. "I want two free hazelnut coffees and pies."

"You have that latte machine. What are you doin' over here, botherin' me?" Fayrene said and kept on going to the kitchen.

"Two apple pies," Aunt Vella called after her.

Aunt Marilee came with coffee for Aunt Vella and Uncle Perry, then finally sat down, and she and Papa Tate and Aunt Vella began to talk about the record-setting sales going on in town, and about Mrs. Maldonado getting money from Santa Claus. They were careful to carry on like it was the real Santa. Aunt Marilee wondered who would be next to get money, and Aunt Vella said, "Maybe no one. Maybe that's the end of it."

Corrine hoped someone else got some. Just two people getting money didn't seem nearly exciting enough.

Uncle Perry didn't say anything until Fayrene brought his and Aunt Vella's pieces of pie, with a scoop of ice cream on Uncle Perry's.

"What's this?" Uncle Perry said.

"That's your pie," Fayrene said. "Apple. Heated, like you like it."

"It's got ice cream on it," he said.

"Well, yes. You've been havin' ice cream on your pie ever since I've known you. What? Did you decide to change your mind and not tell me?"

"As a matter of fact, yes," he said. "No one said anything about ice cream. I wanted pie. That's all."

Fayrene and everyone stared at him.

"Perry, since you have it, just eat it," Aunt Vella said, giving him a curious look.

Uncle Perry pushed the ice cream aside with his fork, then took a bite. He saw Corrine looking at him and grinned. She grinned in return.

While the adults resumed conversation, Corrine idly ate her piece of apple pie and drank her hot chocolate and watched Ricky Dale's big brother with his arm around his date's shoulders. Once he dropped his hand down over her shoulder and right on her breast. The girl looked at him and sort of grinned. She did not move his hand. She had on lipstick that seemed perfect, like she had drawn on her lips, and Corrine wondered how she did it.

Soon enough, though, she tired of watching them, and she looked at Willie Lee, who was leaning against Aunt Marilee, and thought about going ahead and taking him on up to their apartment. Aunt Marilee ordered another cup of hazelnut-flavored coffee. She was going to be complaining about being up all night going to the bathroom.

The Greyhound bus arrived with a whoosh of brakes, stopping in the street the way it usually did when cars were parked in front of the café. The Christmas lights reflected colorfully on its silver surface.

Diesel fumes came wafting through the door when old Norm Stidham and his wife got up and hurried out to greet their relative. The family in the corner booth were hurrying their children and picking up their suitcases. Corrine wondered where they were going as they trooped outside. She sure didn't think she'd want to be in a family going on a bus, but they all looked fairly excited.

Then all of a sudden there was a lady coming through the café door. She was very noticeable because she wore a fluffy fox fur coat. Corrine, always taking note of earrings, noticed the woman had pretty delicate old-fashioned gold earrings hanging from her earlobes.

And then Corrine realized the woman was looking right at her.

"Anita?" Aunt Marilee said in a breathless voice, and the next moment, she threw Willie Lee aside in her astonishment and haste to get to the woman, while Corrine sat there with the realization that she was looking at her mother.

She couldn't move. She watched the women embracing,

and her heart thudded. Then her mother and Aunt Marilee were both gazing at her.

"Baby?" her mother said. There were tears in her eyes.

Corrine forced herself to get up. She felt like running away, and she couldn't do that. She was trapped there, with the two women crying and regarding her expectantly.

"Hi, Mama."

She moved then, one step forward, and then her mother came in a rush of steps and wrapped her arms around Corrine, who felt the rich softness of the fur coat and the scent of fragrant perfume, and thought she heard her mother say, "Ohmygod, thank you," but she couldn't be sure.

"I thought you were drivin' in," Aunt Marilee said. "On Sunday. What happened to—"

"My car died. It was easier and more economical to sell it to a mechanic at the garage and come on the bus."

Her mother's hair was shorter, and her mother was a little heavier, but otherwise she looked just the same. Corrine had forgotten how pretty she was, and how she could command attention. Everyone in the restaurant was staring at her. Of course, her coat was a draw.

"Ma'am?" It was the bus driver poking his head in the door. "I got your bags here on the sidewalk. You want to check to make sure I got them all?"

Her mother, Aunt Marilee and Aunt Vella went hurrying out the door. Corrine followed more slowly and stood back while her mother counted the luggage: a trunk, two big suitcases, a roller.

"There's one more—a tapestry tote bag."

The driver dug an enormous tote bag from the luggage compartment and grunted as he set it with the other bags.

Corrine's gaze fell on the luggage. It sure was a lot of luggage.

There was discussion of what to do with it. Corrine's mother said she would need a ride out to the Goodnight Motel. Aunt Marilee offered to have her stay the night on their couch, and Aunt Vella offered the extra room at her house, but Corrine's mother said she would rather go to the motel. Aunt Marilee and Aunt Vella were put silent at this, but Papa Tate jumped in to say he would load the luggage into the Cherokee.

Everyone bid everyone else goodbye. Granny Franny kissed Corrine and Willie Lee and went along with Papa Tate, who drove her home. Aunt Vella and Uncle Perry headed for their car.

Then Aunt Marilee said, "Come on, kids, let's go home," looped her arm with her sister's, and the two women headed off down the sidewalk.

Corrine, following with Willie Lee and Munro, watched the way the two women's coats swung with their steps and how the Christmas lights reflected on their hair. She had never realized it before, but her mother was just a bit taller than Aunt Marilee.

Directly after getting yet another pot of coffee going, Aunt Marilee went off to put Willie Lee to bed. Having a bit of a panic at being left alone with her mother, Corrine busied herself getting the cups and sugar and cream on the dining room table. Her mother, looking nervous, too, asked in general terms about school, and Corrine replied in general terms, and the entire time they were looking each other over. Corrine decided that her mother did look older. Possibly it was because she was tired after her trip. She was not wearing her usually carefully applied makeup, and her lipstick had worn off. This was a little unusual, as her mother had always been careful about keeping her lipstick applied.

Corrine kept thinking how surprised she was that her mother had actually come. She couldn't figure out how she felt about it, except surprised.

Then Aunt Marilee returned and all three of them were looking each other over while saying things like: "I love your hair short like that," and "Corrine, you are gettin' so tall," and "This coffee is delicious," and "How was the trip?" to which her mother replied, "Long but quite comfortable. So nice to just ride along and watch the scenery."

Corrine imagined her mother in the bus, reclining in the seat, with her head up against the tinted glass window, watching the miles roll along. She heard in her mother's voice what was not said: that her mother had longed to come home.

For a fleeting instant, she understood her mother as having wants and longings like anyone else. She watched her mother and her aunt, both women saying all manner of things without words but with their searching eyes that seemed to ask: Can we be very careful and make this all right?

Corrine very much wanted everything to be all right for her mother and Aunt Marilee. If it wasn't, she would know the horrible sense of being responsible for their unhappiness.

Quite suddenly Aunt Marilee had the thought to call Grama Norma all the way over on her cruise. "We can tell her you have arrived." She consulted the clock. "But I'm not certain what time it is over there," she said with a worried expression. "Maybe we should wait for Tate. He'll know exactly what time it is in the Mediterranean."

"I really am not up to speakin' to Mama tonight," Corrine's mother said.

Aunt Marilee pressed her lips together, then said, "Mama's mellowin', Anita. She's a lot different now."

Corrine's mother looked long at Aunt Marilee but didn't say anything, at least not out loud.

The next moment her mother remembered that she had not called the motel to let them know she would be coming tonight and requested a telephone book to look up the number.

Very glad to do something helpful, Corrine jumped up to get the phone book and cordless phone from the living room. It seemed a minor miracle that the two women hadn't gotten in a fight yet. She wanted to do everything she could to keep them happy.

"Frank Goode says I have a room tonight as long as I get out there before eleven," her mother told them when she finished her call. "That's when he turns off the lights and goes to bed." She smiled at this, then suddenly looked dismayed. "I hope you don't mind terribly takin' me out there, Marilee. I plan to get a car tomorrow. I..."

"Oh, it's all right. Of course I can take you out. Better yet, you just take the Cherokee while you're here. There's no need for you to rent a car."

Corrine wondered at her mother's finances. Renting a car took money. Where was her mother getting the money? Her eyes fell on the fur coat that was slung over a chair back.

"Well, if you won't need it…" Her mother looked uncertain and ran a hand through her hair, then reached for her purse and pulled out a pack of cigarettes.

Aunt Marilee stopped in the middle of saying that they wouldn't need the Cherokee and could get along just fine with Papa Tate's BMW and said, "Anita, I'm sorry, but we don't smoke in our house."

"Oh, I forgot. I'm sorry." Her mother stuffed the cigarettes back in her purse and looked so flustered that Corrine wanted to get the cigarettes back out for her.

Aunt Marilee explained that she didn't want smoke around Willie Lee and Corrine but that she would walk outside with Corrine's mother. "We can go just out the back door onto the landing."

"No, I'm tryin' to quit anyway," Corrine's mother said brightly. "I do not want you startin' to smoke, Corrine."

Corrine said she didn't plan on it. She did not say that she didn't think her mother needed to give her direction in the matter. She was, in fact, so irritated by her mother's attempt to give her direction that she got up and went to the bathroom, stared at herself for a long minute in the mirror, then brushed her hair hard.

When she came back, Papa Tate had returned and was setting himself down at the table.

Just then a ringing sound started up. Everyone sort of jumped, and then her mother went digging around in the pocket of her fur coat that she'd tossed over the chair back.

"It's Louis. I forgot to call him when I arrived," she said, before she even had the phone in hand. She pulled it out and flipped it open, then walked away a few feet into the low-lighted living room as she spoke in a soft tone.

Papa Tate and Aunt Marilee moved into the brighter kitchen, and Corrine was left there at the table in between, wondering exactly what she should do.

She couldn't help but hear just a bit of her mother's conversation, which wasn't really anything but yes, she had arrived safely, was tired, would call him from the motel.

She called him sweetheart. So her mother and Louis had not broken up. This was a perplexing situation. She looked her mother over, evaluating the possibility of some fatal condition.

When her mother hung up from Louis, she said she needed to get going. She wouldn't want to have Mr. Goode decide to go on to bed and leave her out. Even as she spoke, she gathered her things quickly, as if about to run.

Aunt Marilee wanted to go with her to the motel to help with the heavy luggage, but Corrine's mother said, "There's no need for you to do that, Marilee. I got it all to the bus in the first place. I can manage."

Her tone was such that Aunt Marilee not only shut her mouth but backed up a step.

Corrine stood by, thinking that maybe she should offer to go with her mother. She didn't want to, and she hoped her mother wouldn't ask her to go.

"Can I have a hug?" her mother asked, stopping at the door.

Corrine went over to hug her.

Aunt Marilee got her coat and went, too, out the back way, down the iron stairs to the alley. Corrine hurried into her room and looked out her window to see their shadowy forms going down. She heard their voices, but what they said was lost in the creaking of the metal steps.

Down in the alley, the two women stood for some minutes beside the Cherokee, in the glow from the pole light. Corrine's mother lit up a cigarette, and Aunt Marilee took a couple of puffs from it, then stood with her hands in her pockets for about two minutes, and then she was gesturing. Corrine's mother ran her hand through her short hair and blew rapid streams of smoke into the air. If it wasn't an argument, it was close to one. Then Aunt Marilee stuffed her hands again into her coat pockets and stood with that familiar stance of her legs slightly apart.

Corrine's mother blew out a long stream of smoke, threw down the butt of the cigarette and stamped it with her foot. She said something to Aunt Marilee, who then, quickly and undeterred, wrapped her arms around her. After a moment, Corrine's mother returned the embrace, and the two women clung to each other there under the tall lamp light. Watching, Corrine felt a tightness in her throat.

Then her mother got into the Cherokee, and Aunt Marilee bent in the door, probably demonstrating the workings of the vehicle. Aunt Marilee liked to be thorough with instruction. Corrine heard in her mind as surely as hearing her aunt's voice, "Drive careful."

Corrine's mother backed the car out and drove away to the street. Aunt Marilee stood there in the middle of the alleyway, staring after the car.

Quite suddenly she looked upward, right at Corrine's window. Corrine drew back, hoping that her aunt had not seen her watching.

That night Aunt Marilee set a record in her bed-checking compulsion, looking in three times that Corrine knew of. All the coffee she had drunk before bed obviously did not help her to sleep.

Corrine was roused by the flushing of the toilet each time and then heard the board squeak in the hall outside her door and the swish of Aunt Marilee's robe. Once she even opened her eyes a crack and saw the shadowy form of her aunt there in the doorway, her hand clearly visible on the door frame upon which a patch of moonlight shone.

The third time she woke up enough to say, "I'm okay, Aunt Marilee," in a mumbling voice.

That brought her aunt into the room. "I didn't mean to wake you...shush, go on back to sleep...are you warm enough?" She bent and tucked the covers around Corrine, who didn't know how she was supposed to sleep with someone asking her a question.

"Yes," she said, and what she thought was: I'm okay, I will never leave you.

13

While she was loading the washer, Aunt Marilee remembered that Charlene MacCoy had telephoned the previous afternoon about calling a meeting of the prop crew for the Christmas pageant. The meeting was to take place at ten o'clock. It was nine-fifteen right then, and Aunt Marilee was still in her nightclothes.

She came running out of the tiny laundry room, hollering about the meeting and issuing orders for Corrine and Willie Lee to get themselves dressed, and for Papa Tate to go to the grocery store while they were gone. "I want to give Anita a nice welcome home dinner. Please get a good-size salmon filet. It is—or at least it used to be—Anita's favorite. Make sure it is fresh."

Papa Tate's eyebrow was raised. "Fresh salmon? This is Valentine, Oklahoma, Marilee."

"It's not the end of the world. Juice Tinsley gets it flown in fresh every Friday," she said in that tone that said there were many things Papa Tate did not know. "And could you go over and get the Christmas dishes out of your mother's attic? They would be festive for tonight. We are havin' the grand opening of our holiday season with Anita here," she said, encompassing Corrine and Willie Lee in her statement.

Papa Tate, at the moment drinking his coffee and reading the *New York Times,* said he would do all that, just as if he had planned every minute to do those things for her. Aunt Marilee went to describing exactly where in the attic she thought the Christmas dishes were, and then she decided he should also get the boxes of tree decorations and wrapping paper and bows, too.

Corrine, who had been at the window seat working on her drawing of Valentine at Christmas, broke in to tell her aunt that she had to be at the corral to clean the stalls at noon. "I told Ricky Dale I'd be there. We're strippin' the stalls."

She just had to go.

"Oh, we'll be done at church by then," her aunt assured her and reached for the phone. "I've got to call Anita and tell her where we'll be."

Corrine stared at her aunt. She had forgotten about her mother.

Then quite quickly any thought of her mother was eclipsed by the idea that she was likely to see Ricky Dale at the meeting at the church, and she hurried away to get into the bathroom before her aunt took it over. She wanted to get herself looking her best. She thought she still might kiss him, no matter if he was stupid about Melissa Pruitt. And she intended to flirt with him at church, she thought as she put on a second application of lip gloss.

Melissa Pruitt wasn't the only one who could act silly around a boy.

Her determination for flirting deserted her, however, the instant she stepped through the side sanctuary doors. It went away so thoroughly as if never to have been there, making her starkly aware of her lack of ability to join in with all the other kids, who were joking and laughing all over the place. She felt like some alien from another planet.

The only one she could really talk to was Jojo, who came right over to say hey and dance around in her Mary costume. Corrine thought the younger girl looked really cute and told her so.

"Well," said Jojo, "I look like a kid playin' Mary in a play, I guess."

Corrine thought this was awfully funny and laughed, but then she just stood there watching the others.

Ricky Dale was taller than any of the previous wise men, so his robe came up above his ankles. Aunt Vella said he could just wear his black cowboy boots and that would be fine.

Anson and his brother Gideon had drawn mustaches beneath their noses and were busy doing the same with Shad, who was playing Joseph.

The girls and one little boy who were the second, third and fourth angels were pretending to fly around, flapping their arms and walking on tiptoe. Melissa Pruitt, head angel, had a special angel costume that she was modeling for everyone. It was very elaborate and complete with a halo and glistening wings with little feathers sprinkled over them. This was a far cry from the angel of past years, whose wings were made out of thick posterboard covered with tin foil.

Corrine overheard Mrs. Pruitt say that her sister was an actress in Dallas and had gotten it from a costume shop.

The other kids who were supposed to help with sets and props hadn't even shown up. This suited Corrine, who would rather do the job with just Aunt Marilee. With a growing enthusiasm, they began pulling the old sets and props from the storage room next to the kitchen and hauling them down the hallway to the sanctuary.

As Corrine struggled to get through the door with the manger and some large candlesticks, Jojo came over to hold the door, and she hollered at Ricky Dale, "Come help Corrine with this stuff."

Corrine could have died.

"I can get it," she told Ricky Dale, holding firmly to the manger. He took the candlesticks out of it, and after that he and Anson helped get the large cardboard backgrounds hauled over and set up on the altar stage.

The backgrounds had been used for years and looked it. Corrine and Aunt Marilee sighed over them, then sat on the front pew and tossed ideas back and forth of what they might do for improvement, while Charlene MacCoy began a quick run-through of the pageant.

The entire time, Corrine kept one eye on Ricky Dale. She saw him bending down to instruct Willie Lee about something. Willie Lee had a mustache drawn on now and was quite proud of it. Then Willie Lee and Munro, followed by three other shepherds, came on stage and pretended to behold the angels, who spoke to them from where they stood on milk carton crates in the choir box.

Off to the side, Melissa, not yet wearing her wings because her mother wanted to protect them, hollered that she was the angel who was supposed to speak to the shepherds. She began her narration in a loud voice and could be heard easily. It was evident that she knew her way around a performance.

At his turn, Ricky Dale, as the first wise man, confidently sauntered onto the stage and knelt at the manger to present a gift to the pretend baby Jesus. Little Gabby had thrown her baby doll in there. All Ricky Dale had to say was, "I saw the star in the east and came to worship thee, my king." Corrine thought he said it wonderfully, just like a king would.

Jojo wasn't bad at all, either, once she could quit giggling and taking up the baby doll to make it make noise. She looked just like a virgin should look, and that was all she had to do, because she had no speaking part.

And Willie Lee looked on earnestly, just like a true if very short shepherd, holding onto a crooked staff that was as tall as he was, with Munro at his side.

"Isn't he just so cute?" Aunt Marilee said to Corrine, and Corrine agreed, very quietly, because she rather thought Willie Lee would not especially enjoy the sentiment of cute, since he was growing up.

All in all, the first full run-through was pretty good. It helped that many members of the cast had been in the pageant for a couple of years in a row. The problem was when

Charlene made changes in the dialogue or wanted to put in more action. "But we haven't ever done that," was heard more than once.

"Well, you have now," Charlene replied firmly.

All of a sudden, when Corrine was staring at Ricky Dale and watching Melissa touching him while she talked to him, her mother appeared at the end of the pew. "Hello, y'all," she whispered, and came around and slipped onto the spot next to Corrine.

It was a little disconcerting to be looking at a guy and having wishes about being his girlfriend and kissing him, and then to be faced with her mother.

Corrine wanted to get over to the corral directly after the meeting broke up, but Aunt Marilee made her go to the drugstore for lunch. She had a chicken salad sandwich and ate it quick, with an eye on the clock and another on her aunt and her mother, who were discussing with Aunt Vella the whereabouts of this person and that person from their past—many who seemed to be either dead or very old—and speaking to people who came into the drugstore. Her mother knew more people than Corrine had imagined. She also took note that everyone seemed highly impressed with her mother.

There was that about her mother—she was impressive. She was extremely pretty and lit up when greeting people. She was like she was on show. She was also working on her second latte. Corrine figured her mother was using the lattes in place of smoking. Likely Aunt Marilee had scared her to death about smoking around them.

Watching the clock and watching the two women, Corrine felt anxious to leave but uncertain of which woman to ask about going. It had occurred to her that to keep asking Aunt Marilee for permission could be a little rude to her mother. But she could not bring herself to ask anything of her mother. Not only did she simply not want to, but to do so seemed most definitely rude to Aunt Marilee.

She felt torn between them, as if they were vying for her attention. Neither woman did anything solid to give this impression, but Corrine felt the pull and began to get very annoyed. She might have actually taken up the subject at that very minute, saying something like: "Okay, I just need to know which one of you is going to be my mother, now that you're both together."

But she did not think either woman would want such a question, and Corrine herself sure didn't want to deal with it. Her aunt and mother were doing their best to fall all over each other with politeness. And Corrine wasn't about to say anything that might cause her to be responsible for an explosion of a royal hissy fit that would surely prevent her from getting to the corral and seeing Ricky Dale, and possibly kissing him.

It was ten minutes past noon when she slipped into her coat, saying, "Well, I'm goin' on up to the corral. I'll be back in an hour or so." She intended to slip away virtually unnoticed, especially by Willie Lee.

"Oh, we'll drive you up there, honey," Aunt Marilee said. "I imagine your mother would like to see the corral and the horses you've put so much time into."

"Yes, I would like to see these horses, Corrine."

Her mother looked so eager and pleased at doing something with her that Corrine couldn't protest. It would not have done any good, anyway.

They piled into the Cherokee that her mother was now using. Aunt Marilee drove, very slowly, as she had to point out where Papa Tate's house had stood and explain all the plans she and Papa Tate had made about living there. In the back seat Corrine bit her tongue to keep from screaming: "Will you just get a move on?"

Finally Aunt Marilee was pulling up near the corral fence. Corrine's mother said that she recalled the corral and Coweta Valentine having horses. "She was a wonderful barrel racer," her mother said, speaking enthusiastically to Corrine in the back seat. "I used to come here to watch her. I wanted to be a barrel racer, too."

Corrine had not known this. The comment piqued her interest, but only for about a half a second, because she saw Ricky Dale coming out of the first stall wheeling a heavy load of soiled shavings. She got excited about time alone with him and possibly kissing him. That was, if she could get rid of her family, who trailed through the gate behind her. She felt like she was leading a parade.

Before Corrine got to it, Aunt Marilee introduced her mother to Ricky Dale.

"Hey," he said, and shook her mother's hand, giving her one of his friendly grins.

The expression on her mother's face showed that she liked him immediately, in the same way that just about everyone liked him.

The two women made small talk with him for a few minutes, Aunt Marilee asking about his job at the veterinarian clinic and his family, and making it sound like he was about to be a veterinarian in the next year. Then Corrine's mother said she knew his father from high school. This fact and the way she said it was a little embarrassing for some reason.

Corrine stood there hoping the women would leave and take Willie Lee with them, but what they did next was go over to pet the horses that were already crowded up to Willie Lee and Munro. As they petted the horses, they fell into conversation where the sentences kept beginning with, "Remember when…"

Corrine got a shovel and went to work on the stall with Ricky Dale and clung to hope that before they finished they would be left alone.

"It's nice your mom could come for Christmas," Ricky Dale said.

"Yeah," she said and racked her brain for something more. "I think the Christmas pageant is gonna come off pretty good."

He shrugged. "We'll get it done, I guess."

Corrine could not think of another thing to say. Thankfully, moments later, her mother hollered over, saying, "We're goin' in to visit with Winston. We'll wait to take you home. Willie Lee, honey, are you comin' in with us?"

Willie Lee said he would stay and help Corrine and Ricky Dale. Corrine, feeling desperate and attempting to hide it, tried to tell him that it was a two-person job, but he looked so disappointed that she gave him her shovel and said she would be glad to rest for a few minutes.

Ricky Dale said, "I appreciate your help, buddy."

Quite suddenly Corrine saw the three of them as they had been the past summer, just kids and easy together.

Ricky Dale's gaze met hers, and they grinned at each other.

She thought then that she could walk over and kiss him. This possibility so rattled her that she stepped outside the stall quite before she realized it.

Her mother stood in the doorway of her bedroom. The hesitancy in her expression made Corrine somewhat annoyed. She did not want to produce hesitancy in her mother. A mother should not be hesitant but certain.

"You have a lovely room," her mother said.

"Thanks," Corrine said.

Her mother stepped in and looked around, paying particular attention to her drawings pinned on the wall. "Marilee said you were very good, and you are," she said.

Corrine watched her mother's face and decided that her mother truly liked her pictures and wasn't just being polite. Feeling suddenly shy, she sat and removed her boots then put them away, while her mother roamed the small room, picking up a teddy bear and putting it back and going over to the shelves of books.

"You like horse books, too," her mother said, running her fingers over the line of books, then pulled *Misty of Chincoteague* and *Black Beauty* off the shelf. "I can remember reading these when I was about your age. I think we had to read them for school."

"We read them in the fifth grade," Corrine said.

"Ah...well, I never was the great reader that your Aunt Marilee was. She could go through a book in two days. I imagine you are like her in that." She cast Corrine an assessing gaze.

"I read a lot," Corrine said and flopped herself down on her bed.

Her mother replaced the books on the shelf, very careful to put them back exactly as they had been. Corrine noticed that her manicured hands were very graceful. Then her mother was looking at the drawing books and Corrine's sketch pad on her desk.

"I drew a lot when I was young," her mother said.

"You did?" She experienced a fearful reluctance to have something in common with her mother. Maybe her mother was just making it up, anyway. She could not recall ever seeing her mother draw. She could not recall her mother doing any sort of anything.

Her mother nodded. "Uh-huh. I was best with pencil, like you use here, and later I enjoyed pen and ink and water-colors." She touched the wooden pencil box. "This is lovely."

"You gave it to me," Corrine said.

"I did?"

"Uh-huh." Corrine picked up the box and opened it to reveal the pencils and smudging stick and erasers neatly kept inside. "Last spring, before...Aunt Marilee and Papa Tate's wedding." It had come only a couple of weeks before her mother had gone into the hospital. She thought this and looked at the curve of her mother's cheek and the delicate earring hanging from her ear.

"Oh. Well, I have good taste, don't I?"

Her mother's comment and smile triggered a smile in Corrine, who said that she enjoyed the pencil box.

"I have some new pencils," she said on impulse. "And a spare tablet, if you'd like to take it...well, for drawing." She suddenly felt silly. Her mother probably didn't want to draw.

But her mother looked quite pleased with the idea. "You know, I just might enjoy that," she said, accepting the pencils and drawing tablet. "If you have a spare eraser, I would borrow that, too. I'm sure I'll need it." And she laughed gaily.

Corrine, very glad to be giving her mother something, gave over her favorite eraser and then also loaned her a drawing instruction book.

They went into the kitchen, where her mother showed the drawing supplies to Aunt Marilee, who was cooking supper. Aunt Marilee confirmed that Corrine's mother used to draw a lot, saying that as a toddler she had been punished for using crayons on the walls, and in high school she had gone from painting pictures to doing all the girls' makeup.

Her mother took up a position on the stool at the end of the counter and began to read the drawing instruction book aloud and to attempt the beginning lesson, while Aunt Marilee, who swished around the room in her effort to build a true culinary meal, would toss out comments about this and that.

After a few minutes, Corrine decided that she had better step in and start washing up the dishes. Aunt Marilee was making the biggest mess out of the kitchen, using every pot there was. The sink was piled and the counter strewn.

It was also evident that Corrine's mother was not going to lift a hand. She was happily sitting there, letting Aunt Marilee put a cup of tea in front of her, while she worked at drawing her own hand. "I remember having this as a lesson in art class in school," she said.

They had finished supper and were having dessert, and her mother and Papa Tate were talking about restaurants in New Orleans, when Grama Norma called all the way from her cruise in the Mediterranean.

Aunt Marilee asked Corrine to answer the phone. "Just take a message if it's for me. I am not talkin' to anyone who wants to get somethin' into the column."

Corrine raced to the phone on the kitchen wall. When she heard Grama Norma's voice, she sure was surprised. Grama Norma kept saying, "It's me, Corrine. Can you hear me? Can you hear me okay?"

Corrine said that she could, and by then Aunt Marilee figured out it was Grama Norma and came in and took the phone. When Grama Norma found out Corrine's mother was there, she wanted to talk to her, too, so Aunt Marilee had Corrine get the cordless phone for her mother.

Papa Tate and Willie Lee went outside to walk Munro, and

Corrine's mother sat at the table and talked to Grama Norma, although mostly Grama Norma talked. She had a carrying sort of voice, and Corrine could hear her each time she passed as she cleared the dishes from the table and took them to Aunt Marilee to load into the dishwasher.

They had the kitchen just about clean when her mother appeared at the kitchen door.

"Mama seems to be havin' a great time on her cruise."

"Oh. You already hung up?" Aunt Marilee's face sort of froze.

"Yes. Mama said to tell you goodbye."

"Well, I was goin' to talk to her," Aunt Marilee said, then turned and wiped the counter with vigor, saying, "I'm glad she's havin' a good time."

Corrine's mother had always been Grama Norma's favorite. This was no secret.

Corrine's mother said, "She's havin' a great time. I'd say she is dancin' every man under the table and that her life is just one big party."

Aunt Marilee turned to stare at her.

Her mother ran a hand through her hair. "Oh, I'm so tired. It was a wonderful meal. Thank you, Marilee, but I really need to get back to the motel now."

She took time to gather up the pencils and drawing tablet, then cast a quick goodbye to Corrine and left in the manner of not being able to get away fast enough.

Corrine, who stood at the door and watched her mother descend the stairwell and go out onto the sidewalk, was relieved not to have been asked if she wanted to go with her. She decided that she was going to have to figure out exactly what to say if and when her mother ever asked her to go stay out at the motel.

Anita went to the motel office to get a lightbulb for the bedside lamp. When she opened the door a buzzer sounded, and a minute later, Frank Goode appeared through curtains behind the counter. She was expecting to see the aging rough biker-type that she had known, but instead she was presented with Santa Claus.

"Ho-ho-ho, Merrrry Christmas." He was dressed in a Santa Claus suit. He was perfect for the part, complete with his own long full white beard and long white hair to his shoulders.

Anita laughed with delight. "Your eyes are merry."

"And my belly shakes like a bowl full of jelly," he said, his hand on his round torso.

He said he was on his way to his family's annual Christmas gathering, that they were a whopping big family, and he played Santa to all the grandkids.

Just went to show that one could not judge a book by the cover, she thought, regarding him with wonder. She had been a little girl when Frank Goode had been one of the wild hoodlums of their town and had gone off to California to ride with a motorcycle gang.

Age changed people, if they wanted to change.

"And what can Santa get for you?" he asked.

"Oh, I need a new lightbulb, please, for the bedside lamp." She gave him the burned out one, and he disappeared through the curtains and returned a few minutes later with a new one.

"Are you sure that's all Santa can get for you?" he asked. "Would you like to set on Santa's knee, little girl, and give Santa your list of desires?" He cast her a playful leer as he put several packages that were on the counter into a large red plastic bag.

The word desires echoed in her ears. "Ah…do you have some golden balm for regrets in your sack? Maybe in with some bottles of frankincense and myrrh, you might also have a jar or two of hope?" She was instantly embarrassed at having spoken too intimately.

The older man shook his head and straightened with a heavy sigh. "Now, that's a tall order, little girl." His gaze fell gently on her as he put both hands on the counter. For an instant his eyes looked very old and wise as he told her, "No, I'm afraid Santa can't deal with such a request. He tries his best, but he's limited to things like nightgowns or maybe diamond earrings. He's just not powerful enough for anything else.

"But Santa knows someone who is." He pointed upward. "The Man Upstairs. The Head Honcho. He has the good stuff. The pure gold hope...and you don't even have to wait for Christmas mornin', either."

He smiled and winked an eye.

Anita smiled in return. "You're right, Santa. Thank you." She leaned over the counter and kissed his cheek.

He blushed, even underneath his beard.

She left and went along the narrow sidewalk to her room in the first cabin from the office. Shutting the door behind her, she tossed the lightbulb on the bed, and got down on her knees on the circa seventies green shag carpet that had been shampooed many times and felt like it, not even bothering to turn off the television. She didn't hear it.

"God, I hurt my sister and my daughter. I wish I could turn back the clock, but I can't."

You can't do it, but I can. Let me.

She breathed deeply, and tears squeezed out from beneath her eyelids and ran down her cheeks. "You are the only one who can enable me to be any kind of a mother or a sister, God. My hope is in You."

When at last she pushed herself to her feet, she had the sudden, very clear thought that Santa Claus had given her exactly what she had asked for.

The Valentine Voice

Christmas About Town
by Marilee Holloway

The pace is picking up, ladies. There are less than three weeks until Christmas. If your husband hasn't gotten your outside lights hung up by this evening, I'd say don't bother him about it.

However, there is still plenty of time to get your Christmas cards in the mail, and to make Peggy Sue Langston's Last Minute Christmas Wreath in this week's Valentine Living section.

Here's a great idea: Set yourself free of the kitchen for the holiday, ladies, and order in. Yes, take a break totally from cooking, and the IGA and Ryan's Catering are here to help you do it. The IGA is taking orders for apple, pecan and sweet potato pies, all prepared by Virdis Ryan. Also offered are entire Christmas dinners. These are roasted turkey or hickory smoked ham, complete with your choice of vegetables and pie for dessert. The basic is a meal for four, and the supreme a meal for eight. See their ad in the Valentine Living section, and call the IGA today.

Julia Jenkins-Tinsley is happy to report that the number of letters to Santa took a big jump this week, and that you can still mail gift boxes to loved ones overseas and have the package get there by Christmas. She recommends priority postage to be on the safe side.

Stella Purvis of The Merry Christmas Maid Service says that her team of all male maids have proven so popular that she has a limited number of time slots left before Christmas, so book now, if you don't want to miss them. The beauty of men as maids is that they can move heavy furniture for the really deep cleaning. There will be a $5 extra charge if you wish to stay in your home and watch the men clean, just for the novelty of it. Stella does not allow them to take off their shirts while working, so do not ask.

Belinda Blaine will be hosting a QVC Christmas Shopping Experience on Monday at Blaine's Drugstore and Soda Fountain. This is truly one-stop shopping. Gather your friends and get down to Blaine's for a fun day of shopping and visiting with neighbors in the comfort of the soda fountain. There will be a big-screen television and three phones for your convenience. Don't go rushing all over, looking for that perfect gift. Select it easily by television and phone, and take advantage of being guided by Belinda's expert knowledge of television shopping.

In a quick and random survey about town, the gifts most mentioned by women were: quality perfume, genuine silver or gold jewelry, a cashmere sweater, coat or wrap, a silk negligee, plush robe, a vacation cruise and gift certificates.

Gifts most mentioned by men were: power tools, toolboxes, cologne or aftershave, Corvette, videotape of Monday Night Football, subscription to *Sports Illustrated* that includes the swimsuit issue, and more power tools.

I do not contribute to the surveys; I just report them. Men, take note that nowhere in the women's list was electric cookware or flannel pajamas.

If anyone knows who stole the fake presents from underneath the tree in Odessa Collier's yard, please tell them to return them and no questions will be asked. The tree looks naked without them. Let's keep in the Christmas spirit here, folks.

Also, don't forget the annual Valentine Chamber of Commerce toy drive. This is for county-wide distribution. You can drop off your new, unwrapped toys here at the *Voice*. We are sorry to say that we are out of *Voice* mugs, but we will take your name, and you will receive a mug as soon as a new supply arrives.

Our recipe for today is from Julia Jenkins-Tinsley.

Recipe for Happy Christmas

1 pair of capable hands to bake apple or pecan pies, and all those school treats, and to hang decorations and wrap packages.
1 pair of sturdy feet to run all over doing all the above and shopping for the hearts' desires of family, too.
1 sharp mind to know not to wait until the last minute to mail Christmas cards and packages.
1 wide-open eye, ready to see wonder and beauty.
1 closed eye, so as to ignore Scrooges who do not celebrate.
1 willing heart, preferably worn soft.

Put it all together and let bake ten minutes in front of a warm, flickering fire. Then watch the happiness begin to rise.

If you have news, gift ideas, or recipes, you can call the *Voice* at 555-4743 and leave a message. Charlotte and I are too busy to speak personally. This is the Christmas rush for us, too. We trust in your cooperation.

14
∾

Aunt Marilee awakened in a panic that morning at the knowledge they did not yet have a tree. This caused her to decide to give up the idea of an artificial tree and to insist that as soon as they had a quick bite to eat after church, they had to drive out to Wilson's Christmas Tree Farm. There had been all those lovely clear and warm days in which they could have gone out to get a tree, but today, when Aunt Marilee decided, it was cold and damp.

"The only time to cut a tree down is in bad weather," Papa Tate said. "It's a rule of the season."

They stopped at the Goodnight Motel to pick up Corrine's mother and trade Papa Tate's BMW for the Cherokee. Corrine sat up on the edge of the seat and looked over Aunt Marilee's shoulder as they pulled into the gravel lot and over to her mother's room. She suddenly had a great curiosity to see inside the room. She wanted to see her mother's things about the room, and to see how her mother looked in it.

"I'll go in and get her," Corrine said, hopping out as soon as Papa Tate stopped the car in front of the turquoise door.

She knocked, and her mother called for her to come in.

"I'm just comin', Marilee," her mother said from the bathroom.

"It's me, Corrine." She scanned the room, which was almost a replica of the one they had stayed in when the tornado had taken Papa Tate's house. Papa Tate called it an experience in retro living, because hardly anything had changed in the motel since the sixties.

Her mother's head poked out of the bathroom. "Oh, hey, honey." She looked surprised. "Let me just get my lipstick on." She disappeared again.

Corrine looked at the one large bed, all made up, and at the room, which was on the neat side. There was a robe across the end of the bed, and some clothes on the chair. The sketch tablet and pencils that Corrine had given her mother were on the round table in front of the window. Corrine was tempted to look in the tablet to see what her mother had done, but she didn't want to be caught snooping.

The television was on. The memory that her mother always ran the television came sharply to mind. The room smelled of cigarette smoke and sweet perfume. Her mother had always loved perfume. There were several bottles on the top of the dresser.

Her mother came out of the bathroom. "Okay..." She picked up one of the bottles and spritzed her neck. "I'm ready to get this tree." She grinned as she slipped into her fur coat.

The others were all set in the Cherokee, Papa Tate behind the wheel. Willie Lee called and waved through his open window.

When they got into the car, Papa Tate tossed over his shoulder, "My, but someone smells awfully pretty."

Her mother looked pleased. "It's Shalimar," she said.

Corrine saw Aunt Marilee glance over at Papa Tate. After a moment, she said, "It is lovely."

When they pulled into the field of trees at Wilson's, Papa Tate said that he would cut down the tree, but he wasn't getting out until they had chosen the one they wanted. "They" being Aunt Marilee, Corrine's mother and Corrine.

Corrine really didn't want to get out in the cold, but she wasn't going to miss helping to choose a tree, plus, she felt her presence with her aunt and mother was required. They were both looking at her with high expectation.

Willie Lee said he and Munro were not choosing; they were just getting out to run around. "We are guys. We do lights, not trees," he said, and Aunt Marilee gave Papa Tate a look of "see what you did?"

Papa Tate looked at his watch and reminded them that dark came early now and even earlier with the clouds.

Corrine's mother, her head wrapped in a wool scarf, quickly found a tree to her liking. "Look at this one, y'all."

"Well, I don't know. It's a little scraggly," Aunt Marilee said.

"Room for ornaments," Corrine's mother offered.

Aunt Marilee didn't reply but walked off through the trees, until she called, "How about this one?"

"It has a bald spot on this side," Corrine's mother pointed out.

"Oh, yes, it does."

Corrine found a tree she thought would do. "This one looks nice and even."

"Hmm...it's a little short," Aunt Marilee said. "But keep it in mind."

Aunt Marilee went off in one direction, Corrine's mother in another. Corrine thought she would keep near the Cherokee. She wished she had worn a thermal shirt under her sweater, as Aunt Marilee had advised.

A shout would go up. "Come see!"

"Where?"

"Over here."

They would converge around the tree, hugging themselves against the cold damp, examine all the sides, and always find something wrong with it.

"Too tall...it doesn't look so tall out here, but it will in the house."

"You can cut off the bottom."

"Then there'll be a big bald spot there."

"What do you think of this one?"

"Well, it is flat on this side."

"Put it against the wall...and it doesn't look so flat to me."

"Well, it is."

"You don't have to be such a perfectionist, Marilee. You can hang somethin' there." Her mother's voice was sharp.

"I don't want to hang somethin' there, o-kay?" Aunt Marilee's voice was sharp.

"Let's just look at a couple more," Corrine offered.

Corrine passed by Papa Tate in the Cherokee. He was listening to the Prairie Home Companion on the radio. Willie Lee and Munro had returned and snuggled down under the stadium blanket Aunt Marilee kept there for them.

"Make room for me," Corrine told her cousin and the dog as she climbed inside the car and pulled over a corner of the blanket. She could not make herself believe the two women needed her assistance anymore, and she had become so cold that she didn't care if they got a totally bald tree.

"Comin' to your senses, darlin'?" Papa Tate cast over his shoulder at her.

"I don't have any senses left," Corrine said, gathering Munro close in order to warm her hands on his fur.

Through the beads of moisture on the window glass, she saw Aunt Marilee and her mother debating over a tree. Her mother was hunched down in her wool scarf and fur coat, and Aunt Marilee was hugging herself and moving her feet.

Feeling guilty for abandoning them to each other, Corrine put her hand on the door handle, but she didn't open it. She kept telling herself that she would get out in just a minute, as soon as she thawed out.

Papa Tate, who was watching them, too, turned up the radio and did this humming thing.

The women moved out of sight into the trees, and then, five minutes later, they came running and hollering to the Cherokee. Papa Tate instantly lowered the window.

"We can't find Corrine! Have you seen...oh, my goodness, here you are."

Corrine didn't ask what the women thought had happened to her in the small private Christmas tree lot.

Aunt Marilee pushed back her hair, which was by now quite wet, and said, "Okay, Tate, come get this tree over here. Is that one all right with you?" she asked Corrine's mother.

"Oh, just get it!"

Aunt Marilee's mouth went pencil thin, and she might have jerked Corrine's mother around, but then her mother slipped into the back seat and squeezed close to Corrine, leaving Aunt Marilee and Papa Tate to do the work of getting the tree.

Corrine heard their voices through the window Papa Tate had left down, as Aunt Marilee proceeded to instruct Papa Tate as to just how to cut the tree down so it would come out perfect.

"I hope they get enough of a trunk," Corrine's mother said, giving directions even though she wasn't out there, and only Corrine and Willie Lee, and Munro could hear her. "He'll need to cut it right at the ground."

The streetlight was on in the alleyway when they pulled in. It was all but raining.

Papa Tate got the tree put in the stand. This required cutting off some of the trunk, then a couple of the branches, and then whittling on the trunk again. By the time he got it into the stand, it was a foot shorter than planned. "It'll be easier to get through the door," he said to Aunt Marilee and Corrine's mother, who were looking on with expressions that hinted at the possibility of going back to get another.

It was decided that the easiest way to get the tree inside was to take it up the back iron stairs and through the rear entry. If that was easier, Corrine would have hated to see the hard way. She helped Papa Tate bring it up, and her hands got chewed up by the needles. Aunt Marilee came behind her and pushed on her back every once in a while in her anxiety that Corrine might fall backward.

Corrine looked around once and thought that if she did fall, she was going to take Aunt Marilee, her mother, Willie Lee and Munro with her.

They got it inside, positioned in the corner of the living

room, and straightened up in the stand. The pine fragrance filled the apartment.

"Oh, I'm so glad we got a real tree!" Aunt Marilee said, clasping her hands in rapture. The delight on her face made Corrine smile and be glad for bearing the horribly cold trip of getting the tree. Everyone else was smiling, too.

Papa Tate said, "We went, we conquered, we brought the beauty home."

Papa Tate and Willie Lee started hauling out the lights, and Aunt Marilee went away into the kitchen to make hot chocolate. Very shortly she came out bearing a tray of steaming Santa mugs and encouraging everyone to join in singing "Hark, the Herald Angels Sing." The only words of the song that all of them knew were the chorus, but they sang the phrase repeatedly with gusto.

Aunt Marilee anchored the tree with twine to the wall, of course, and then she presided in the hanging of the ornaments. As she took each one out of its box, she would say, "Look! Look!" as if they were being viewed for the first time. "Aunt Vella made this one," she said of the ball with Willie Lee's picture put on it. "I bought these the first Christmas of my own tree, from an antique store," she said of the red glass balls that Papa Tate said looked used, and Aunt Marilee said the look was termed vintage patina.

Then she came to the ornaments Corrine and Willie Lee had made in school projects and at home under her direction. A number of these were plain ugly, but Aunt Marilee fondled them as if they were gold. She told the story of each one, before giving it to Willie Lee or to Corrine to hang on the tree.

"And where are your Christmas decorations, Tate?" Corrine's mother asked. "Don't you have some history to hang on the tree?"

At her tone, Corrine looked around to see her sitting on the arm of the couch, with her arms folded.

Aunt Marilee dropped her hands into her lap.

"Oh, I never did collect any," Papa Tate said in his slow drawl. "I'm gatherin' mine now."

He said this directly to Aunt Marilee, giving her one of his special smiles, but she simply blinked and looked down into the box of precious ornaments. Corrine looked from Aunt Marilee to her mother and to Papa Tate, who was now looking at Aunt Marilee as if to catch her if she fell off the sofa.

Corrine felt a panicky feeling of not knowing how to make either woman feel okay. She knew her mother felt left out and her aunt felt responsible. This was Aunt Marilee's house, and her family, and her tree, while Corrine's mother didn't have any of it, and especially any little handmade ornaments from her daughter. Corrine, who knew she must have made things for her mother—everyone did from kindergarten through the early grades—couldn't recall any. And if her mother had saved them, likely they were gone, lost during one of their many moves. Corrine had the wild urge to run and gather scissors, paper and glue, and make a star with her mother's name on it.

All of a sudden Aunt Marilee shoved the box of ornaments at Corrine's mother, saying, "Here, Anita. Would you get the rest of these things out of the box? I'm goin' to unpack the stockings and figure out where to hang them."

"Oh, Marilee, I don't want to...." But Aunt Marilee was obviously not going to take the box back.

Corrine's mother looked down into it, and after a minute, she began very hesitantly pulling out the small pieces, asking Corrine and Willie Lee the stories behind them.

Mostly Corrine and Willie Lee couldn't even remember making them.

They turned out all the lights and viewed the Christmas tree that glowed like something out of a Victorian picture. Gazing at it, Corrine's heart filled up.

"It's the prettiest tree we've ever had," Aunt Marilee said in a tone of breathless delight and wonder. She said the same thing every year.

"It is lovely," Corrine's mother said and put her arms around her sister. "Thank you, Marilee."

"Well, you helped, too," Aunt Marilee said.

"You picked a wonderful tree, and you are sharin' it with me," Corrine's mother said.

From there they got into a bit of an argument about who had done what good thing.

Corrine's mother asked her to take a walk on Main Street. Obviously she wanted to speak privately.

Corrine felt Aunt Marilee's sharp attention, although her aunt tried very hard to hide this by making a big deal about both of them bundling up—hats, coats, gloves.

In the minute of putting on her coat, Corrine's mind ran with worries: Maybe her mother was going to ask Corrine to go out to the motel with her. Maybe she was going to ask Corrine to stay with her out there at the motel for the entire time she was in town. Maybe she was going to say she was taking Corrine back with her back to New Orleans. Maybe she was going to say she had a terminal illness.

She didn't look or act at all sick, not like Aunt Marilee's ex-husband, Stuart, had appeared. But there surely were all sorts of ways to have a terminal illness.

As she went out the door, she glanced over her shoulder and saw Aunt Marilee standing in the dimly lit dining room, gazing after her.

The sidewalk was wet, but the drizzle had stopped.

"Look," her mother said, and made a puff of foggy air.

Corrine did likewise. Her mother said that she used to love to do that when she had been a kid, and Corrine said she had done it, too. This was the extent of their conversational ability for some minutes, while they walked along with their hands stuffed into their coat pockets. Passing through the low glow falling through the big window of the café, they saw the clean-up man mopping up. As they watched, he turned out the light, and all that was left was the lighted menu back behind the counter.

Next they passed the saddle shop, where the barrel racing saddle and other leather articles glowed in the warm lights of a small Christmas tree.

"Oh, look at that purse," Corrine's mother said, stopping to gaze in the window. Corrine's eye was drawn to the saddle, but she quickly looked away.

Further along the sidewalk, they passed the Little Opry,

and Corrine's mother stopped. "This used to be a movie theater. I can remember coming here right before it closed. I
must have been about eight." She looked the place over and
sighed.

Then she paused and looked up and down the street. "Valentine's a good place for you to grow up. I'm awfully glad
you can have that opportunity."

Corrine didn't know what to say. If she said she was glad
for the opportunity, too, did that reveal that she was glad
she was here with Aunt Marilee? That seemed too cruel to
reveal. But her mother's comment also seemed reassuring,
alleviating to some extent the raw fear that she was going
to jerk Corrine up and take her back to New Orleans.

A pickup truck came cruising down the street. The colorful
Christmas lights reflected on its gleaming black finish. It was
Ricky Dale's brother's truck. Rock music played out the open
windows as it passed, and there was Ricky Dale with his arm
out the passenger window. "Hey, Corrine!" he hollered and
waved.

Corrine, totally surprised and actually thrilled to be yelled
at by a boy in a truck, gathered her wits and waved and
hollered back.

The truck went to the corner of First Street and turned out
toward the highway, probably going to cruise out by the
Pizza Hut and the flat strip toward Lawton.

"You like him, don't you?" her mother said.

Corrine looked into her mother's smiling eyes and then
away, and shrugged. "He's okay."

"I think he's awfully cute," her mother said.

Corrine grinned at that and experienced a tenderness toward her mother that brought with it a strange bit of anxiety.

They went the length of the block, crossed over and came
back along the opposite side, past the colorful bank window,
the post office, where inside there were now lights glowing
from the Santa mailbox. Past the Sweetie Cakes Bakery and
the Senior Center with its decorative lights, Corrine's
mother looked up the block at the *Voice* building and re-
marked on how festive the lights looked on it.

Corrine peered hard to see if Aunt Marilee was at the windows. She did not catch sight of her, but that did not mean her aunt wasn't hiding in the shadows and looking down at them.

At the corner, in front of the police station, her mother stopped walking, looked at her and came out with, "I really need to tell you that I'm sorry, honey."

Corrine stared at her.

"I'm sorry for how hard the early years of your life were. I really wish I would have been a better mother and given you a stable home. I'm sorry for all my lapses of attention. You had a right to have a stable mother. I'm sorry that I couldn't give you that. I hope you can forgive me."

Her mother seemed breathless after that, and some moments ticked by as Corrine frantically tried to figure out what she was supposed to say.

Finally she came out with, "It's all right," which did not seem at all an adequate response.

She hoped that was the end of it, and yet she felt thoroughly short-changed in making the end of it so quickly. A hard heat stirred in her chest, but then the question of her mother possibly having a terminal illness cut across her mind. Before she could decide whether or not to ask about it, her mother went on to say that she was considering staying in Valentine.

"How would you feel about me livin' here?" her mother asked. By now they had crossed the street and reached the corner of *The Valentine Voice* building. Her mother looked down at her.

Corrine shrugged. The question, right out of the blue, annoyed her. How was she supposed to know in one minute about any of this? Her mother seemed to be changing every bit of what she had said she planned, which was to come for a visit.

"I'd like the opportunity for us to get a real relationship, honey. I'd like the chance to do what I can as your mother. Oh, I don't mean for you to leave your home with Marilee...but I'd like to have a part in your life."

Her expression was desperately hopeful, and Corrine

could hardly stand it. She then realized that her mother had said, *I don't mean for you to leave your home with Marilee,* and felt relief, although she was wondering if her mother might change her ideas about that, too, as she had about her visit.

"I'd like that, too," she said, because it was expected. And because there was a bit of her heart that had always longed for her mother and still did.

"Well…good." And her mother hugged her.

Corrine did her best to hug her back. She hoped someday she wouldn't feel so weird hugging her mother.

They went up to the apartment, and once there, her mother bade good-night to everyone. Corrine was a little surprised. And she could sense a disappointment in her mother. Immediately she thought she was the cause, that her mother was disappointed in her own lack of enthusiasm over what her mother had said to her. Wanting to make up for this lapse on her part, Corrine started to go down with her mother to the Cherokee parked in the alley, but her mother said, "No, honey. You don't need to go out in the cold again."

She spoke this very firmly, in a manner of putting up a hand to push Corrine away. She kissed Corrine's cheek and left.

Corrine searched her mind for what she had omitted, but couldn't quite be certain of what she had done wrong. She thought maybe she should have offered to go do a sleepover at the motel. But there was the fact of school in the morning, so her mother probably had never considered it, so Corrine didn't have to feel guilty about not going.

As she was getting into bed, Aunt Marilee came in.

"Did Mama tell you that she is thinkin' of staying in Valentine?" Corrine asked and watched her aunt's face, wondering how she would take this bit of news if she didn't already know.

Aunt Marilee said that she did know. Corrine did not like this fact. She felt her back crawling.

"Who would I live with, then, if she stays?" Corrine asked, sitting in the bed and pulling the covers tight around her waist. She had begun to distrust what her mother had said about not meaning for her to leave Aunt Marilee. It did not seem quite right for her mother to live in the same town and Corrine not to live with her.

"I don't think we would know that for a while," Aunt Marilee said, lowering herself beside Corrine. "We'd have to see how it went and how everyone feels."

This told Corrine that her aunt and mother had talked about her going to live with her mother. There was, of course, the fact that her mother had so often not followed through with what she intended.

Corrine started to say that she didn't want to live with her mother, but she wasn't certain this would matter. Then she studied her aunt's face and said, "I thought you and Papa Tate adopted me."

"It was temporary custody, honey, for the situation at the time," she said. "Your mother can change that now."

Corrine could not look at her.

Then her aunt stroked Corrine's bangs from her forehead, saying that it would all work itself out in time and not to worry about anything.

"It's Christmas," she said. "We don't want to let Christmas pass us by. Enjoying Christmas is what we're doin' now."

Corrine awoke. It was still night. She thought with irritation that she had been disturbed by Aunt Marilee doing bed-checking, but then she heard the faint sound of music.

Slipping from beneath the warm blankets, she padded quietly out into the hallway. It was music, like orchestra music. The glow of the Christmas tree lights, as well as faint music, spilled into the hallway.

She went to the corner and looked into the living room. The lights of the Christmas tree touched the walls, the furniture, and the two people in the room with an ethereal glow of rainbow color. Papa Tate was kneeling in front of Aunt Marilee, who sat on the couch with her face in her hands.

Instantly Corrine knew that her aunt had been crying, and that it was because of worry over her and her mother.

But Papa Tate, sure as the sun, was going to make everything all right. "Come on, darlin'...dance with me," he said in a voice so soft that Corrine more guessed than heard what he said.

He drew her aunt up into his arms and began dancing with her to "Silent Night" sung by the Mormon Tabernacle Choir. Both of them were half naked, Papa Tate wearing only his plaid pajama pants and Aunt Marilee in the latest gown she had ordered from Victoria's Secret. The colorful Christmas lights warmed their bared skin. As Corrine watched, Papa Tate bent his head to kiss Aunt Marilee's shoulder, and her aunt reacted by dropping her head to the side.

Corrine wondered if such intimate actions to the tune of holy music might be sacrilegious. She could not stop looking. She wanted to see her aunt loved and cherished, and to see Papa Tate happy at making her aunt happy. She wanted to press the image of them as they were right that minute into her mind to comfort her when she got afraid that they might break up. And maybe to throw at them when they even considered breaking up.

Then, feeling suddenly very protective of their privacy, as well as overwhelmed by her own feelings, she slipped away back down the hall and into her warm bed. She snuggled under the covers and clutched them tight around her, trying to stop her quivering, which was more from emotion and longing than from cold, although she didn't fully understand what was happening in her body.

Aunt Marilee had told her all about what went on between a man and a woman shortly after Corrine had come to live with her. "I don't want you finding out off the street," she had said. Corrine had never admitted that as a child in the wild neighborhoods where she had lived with her mother, she had already found out off the street. Aunt Marilee's lessons about sex, however, included details about feelings and choices.

"You love yourself first, and then you can really love a

boy," Aunt Marilee said quite a number of times. "And don't even think about it until you are eighteen, or preferably twenty-one," she would add.

Corrine had been relieved to think of the whole thing being so many years in the future as to not be worth a thought. But now she wondered what it would be like when, someday, a boy touched her the way Papa Tate touched Aunt Marilee. Kissed her bare shoulders and her hair and her lips like she was the most wonderful thing in the world. She wondered if someday she would have a man love her the way Papa Tate loved her Aunt Marilee.

And then she thought of her mother. Scenes of her mother and her boyfriends flowed across her mind, memories of her mother's high, expectant hopes as she would make up for her boyfriends and declare, as Marilee did about the Christmas tree, that each one was the best ever, only to have each one eventually leave, and very often after a violent fight.

A deep well of sadness opened up inside of her.

The Valentine Voice

Christmas About Town
by Marilee Holloway

Here's a news flash that I'm putting right at the head of this week's column: Belinda Blaine is offering her professional shopping services. If you hate to shop, feel inadequate doing it and can't think of a thing to get that someone special, here's your answer.

Ladies, you might want to show this column to the man in your life.

Men, if you are at a loss as to what to get your wife, but you want to be a hero for once and for all, call Belinda at Blaine's Drugstore and Soda Fountain for a free initial consultation. She guarantees delivery of your items by December 22nd, if you call her by this Saturday.

On the subject of gifts, here are suggested fragrances for women from a poll Charlotte did on the street: White Diamonds, Rapture, Joy, White Shoulders, Chloé, Chanel #22, Shalimar and Green Tea.

Hopefully your decorations are all up. If they aren't, I would forget it, except for the Christmas tree. I know some people feel that a Christmas tree is a lot of work, but I encourage you to think about how wonderful you will feel when you have that staunch icon of Christmas spirit to view.

The tree does not have to be big or elaborate. Check out home economist Peggy Sue Langston's ideas on page 5 for how to make a unique tree and ornaments from common items you have right in your home.

Wilson's Christmas Tree Farm has only half a dozen of the imported Douglas Firs left, but still plenty of Scotch pines for cutting. Alphie Wilson says that her son's Boy Scout Troop #12 is offering the service of cutting and delivering the small 3 ft. size free of charge to senior citizens or anyone with a handicap, and she says she's playing wide and loose with that term.

Grace Florist has live miniature trees in pots, complete with lights and tiny decorations. Perfect for table displays. Buy one and plop it on the table for instant Christmas spirit.

The Christmas Cottage has just gotten in a supply of boxed artificial trees. They unfold out of the box complete with lights. The only assembly is attaching the ornaments that are included. No searching your attic or having to run to the store.

And for a trip back in time to simpler ways, try the wonderful wild cedar tree. I'm sure many of you can remember when the lowly cedar was made glorious at Christmastime. For a listing of phone numbers of local farmers who will gladly let you cut a cedar free from their land, see the classified section.

And let me also say that there are lots of cedar trees growing along the highway that no one would ever miss. I got a tree in this manner a number of Christmases ago and remember it fondly.

I want to also encourage you all to send Christmas cards, even if it is just a few to your intimate family. E-mail cards are not the same, but I will not discourage you, if that is all you do. This is the time of year to communicate your feelings to family and friends, and pure sappy sentimentality is thoroughly acceptable to the world.

And don't wait until you get the perfect annual Christmas letter written. About half the people will be glad you didn't send it. In my experience, most people do not write a cheery Christmas letter but either fall into the bragging category or down a depressing well with stuff that is not helpful to know. Now, I'm not speaking to the two people from whom I adore getting Christmas letters. You know who you are. That's two people, out of a dozen. Give it up, the rest of you.

Odessa Collier says a big thank-you to the ones who returned the fake presents under the tree in her yard. Her great-grandchildren were thrilled.

The Valentine Chamber of Commerce toy drive is officially over today. We are pleased to say that this year was a record year in giving. Santa and his elves congratulate all of you. To those of you who have called about your *Voice* mugs, we will get them to you as soon as they arrive, sometime after the first of the year.

I've been asked several times to print Aunt Vella Blaine's recipe for holiday sweet potatoes. Here it is, by her own account.

Holiday Candied Sweet Potatoes

4 or 5 medium-sized yams
cinnamon to taste

¹/₂ cup honey
¹/₂ cup brown sugar
Juice of 1 orange
3-4 tablespoons butter

Cook the yams in the microwave for 12 minutes, or in the oven, or parboil them, any way you want to get them beginning to soften and the skins to come off easy. Then cut them lengthwise and arrange in a casserole.

Sprinkle with cinnamon to suit your taste.

Mix the honey, sugar and orange juice, and drizzle over the yams.

Dot with the butter.

Pour ¹/₂ cup boiling water over yams.

Cover and bake at 350° for 15 minutes. Then uncover, turn the yams and bake for another 15 minutes. You might want to add a bit more water. Suit yourself. I always do.

If you have news for this column, you can call the *Voice* offices and leave a message. If necessary, we'll get back with you, so please don't forget to leave your name and phone number. We do not have caller ID and cannot return calls when you don't leave your name and number. We don't recognize everyone's voice. Thank you.

15

Corrine knew on Tuesday, well before the news came out in the *About Town* column, that Belinda had set herself up as a shopping consultant. Everyone agreed this was perfect for her. Aunt Vella said on the phone to Aunt Marilee, and loud enough that Corrine could hear her, "Glory hallelujah, my daughter has found herself at last!"

Aunt Marilee said to them when she got off the phone, "Belinda is living proof that people can and do change, so none of us should give up."

"I think Belinda must have bought some gumption on one of those channels," Papa Tate said, giving a wink.

In hopes of beating the swarm of people, Corrine got herself over there to Belinda and asked for help. She had to gather all her courage to do this, because she had never in her life asked anyone except Aunt Marilee for anything, and also because she did not have much money. In the past, Aunt Marilee had helped her buy things, taking her up to Lawton, as shopping was limited in Valentine. This year, Corrine wanted to do it all on her own, since she was almost thirteen.

Before she had quite gotten the question out of her

mouth, Belinda agreed to help her, surprising her totally by saying, "Oh, yes, I can help you, honey!" She seemed quite thrilled, perhaps because Corrine was one of her first customers. "And...since we're cousins, how 'bout for payment, you draw me up a picture I can use to make Christmas cards? I want to hand them out with my card inside. I saw the idea on Melody's Small Business Show."

Corrine was struck by Belinda's suggestion. Belinda seemed very eager to have a drawing from her, and she was amazed that she had not before realized that Belinda was indeed her cousin. She had not thought of herself as being anyone's cousin, except Willie Lee's. She always sort of saw herself as alone in the world.

"Okay," she said to Belinda's plan, and immediately Belinda whipped out a jewelry catalog and pointed at a pair of silver and turquoise earrings that Corrine had to agree would be perfect for Aunt Marilee.

"But I was sort of thinking to get a set of perfume," Corrine said. "Aunt Marilee wears something called See-est-la-vee." She said the word how it looked to her, and was annoyed at herself for not writing it out.

Since Sunday, when Corrine's mother had displayed her expensive perfume, Aunt Marilee had been wearing her own perfume. Corrine had seen her dabbing it on her throat and wrists from a small bottle on her dresser. There was only the one small bottle, though, and not much left in it.

"Oh, that's C'est La Vie!" Belinda said, rattling off the name in a way that brought Corrine's eyes wide. "Wonderful choice for Marilee. I don't have it at the counter, but it's been on one of the shopping channels. I'll get it directly. It's a little costly, honey."

She whipped out a paper with fragrances and prices. Corrine was disappointed to see that she could only afford the smallest bottle, but Belinda assured her that it went a long way.

Belinda's suggestions were a folding pair of binoculars for Willie Lee and a book of quotes by famous Texans for Papa Tate. Corrine was awed by how perfect the ideas were.

As for Corrine's mother, Belinda insisted on a silk scarf

and that she would find a nice one Corrine could afford on one of the shopping channels. Corrine felt Belinda knew more about such things than she did. She felt bewildered in trying to choose something for her mother. What did a child with fifteen dollars get a woman who wore a fur coat?

In payment for her consulting services, Corrine gave Belinda the drawing that she had done of Main Street. She had not intended to do this, but when she went home, she saw the drawing on her desk and realized it would work perfectly, and she was anxious to get rid of her debt. She very quickly, during government class, added a couple of touches to the drawing, and in the upper corner, she wrote: Peace on Earth.

She liked it very well, and so did Belinda, who amazed Corrine with her response of near excitement.

It occurred to Corrine that when she was pressed by panic, she could draw her best.

Also, Belinda's shopping consultant business was great. Fifteen minutes, and Corrine's shopping was done.

Corrine was hurrying Willie Lee in their walk home, because she wanted to get there and see how her Aunt Marilee and her mother were getting along. If they seemed to be doing well, she was getting herself up to the corral.

The previous days after school, Corrine had come home to find the two women wearing themselves out contradicting each other as to memory of their childhoods. Aunt Marilee's theme seemed to be that Corrine's mother had not known the hard life that Aunt Marilee had known as the big sister, and Corrine's mother's theme seemed to be that Aunt Marilee was a bossy prude. The only story they seemed to totally agree on was the one about their father stealing the Christmas tree. This may have been because Corrine's mother had been too young to have a full memory of it, and had in the first place been told about it by Aunt Marilee.

Corrine was simply, for lack of a better word, fascinated by her aunt and her mother together. The two women were much like shimmering powers of energy, and both in the same room were almost overwhelming, but Corrine wanted to be with them, was afraid she might miss out on something if she was not.

She found herself envious of them being sisters, and quite annoyed with God that she did not have a sister. The women had not gotten into a terrible argument yet, at least not one that Corrine had witnessed, and she couldn't make up her mind if they were not going to argue, or if it just had not happened yet. She didn't know if she were relieved about them not having a big argument, or disappointed. She kept watching, prepared to help, should an argument break out.

The women each needed her, she felt, and she did her best to split her attentions between them. Her mother wanted a relationship with her. She was not certain what this required from her, but she was fairly certain it meant being around and talking. At the same time, she didn't want to slight Aunt Marilee, who meant the world to her.

All this responsibility with the two women had prevented her from slipping away to the corral, and Corrine was mulling over the possibility of being able to leave the women alone long enough to go to the corral, when someone hollered, "Hey, Corrine, wait up!"

It was Paris Miller. She hurried along the side of the black-topped road in her stacked boots. Corrine was fascinated at how fast and firm Paris could walk in such thick-soled boots.

"Here." The girl stuck out a folded bill.

"Thanks," Corrine said after a few seconds of surprise in which she had to dig around in her memory for why Paris would give her money.

Taking the bill, she stuffed it into her jacket pocket without looking at it. She was highly relieved that the girl did not seem to have taken offense. For one thing, Paris was about a head taller than Corrine and could easily knock her winding.

"What are you lookin' at, kid?" Paris said to Willie Lee, who was peering hard up at her.

"Are your lips real-ly black?" he asked.

"Yeah. Are your eyes really that big?" Then she took off

across the road in rapid strides, hiking her book bag up on her shoulder.

Willie Lee looked at Corrine and asked, "Are my eyes big?"

"No," Corrine said. "She was just jokin'. Your glasses make your eyes look bigger because they're thick."

She glanced at Paris, who was walking fast along the opposite side of the road. "It really wasn't nice for her to speak to you like that, but she didn't mean anything by it. She didn't understand that you were simply askin' a question."

Willie Lee nodded. He understood, because it happened to him a lot.

"And her lips aren't black. It's lipstick...you know, like Aunt Marilee puts on red."

For the next two blocks, Paris walked the left side of the street, up ahead just a little bit, while Corrine and Willie Lee continued along the right. Then Paris turned down a side street of small, clapboard houses, the sort of street that had worn brown yards, cars up on blocks, and at least one house with a recliner on the front porch.

She crossed the yard of the second house from the corner, where a man with really long hair waited in a wheelchair on the front porch.

When they arrived home, Aunt Marilee greeted her with the news that her mother was off shopping and would not be there until suppertime, and that Leanne Overton had called to say she was going away to Texas and would appreciate Corrine seeing to the horses each evening through Saturday.

"I told her it was fine with me, and that I thought you would be happy to do it," Aunt Marilee said.

Corrine was thrilled with these two wonderful strokes of luck. Now she had a surefire reason for going to the corral, and, tonight at least, she did not have to feel guilty in leaving Aunt Marilee and her mother to do it.

But there was Willie Lee, who immediately scampered to get his shoes back on so that he could accompany her.

Corrine opened her mouth, then closed it and resigned

herself to his presence, because she could not tell him not to come.

Just then, Papa Tate appeared at the kitchen entry. "Does anyone know this bird? There's a pigeon knocking at the window."

"My pigeon!" Willie Lee, followed by Munro, went racing for the kitchen.

Aunt Marilee cast Corrine a questioning eye, got up from her desk and headed to the kitchen, too.

It was Willie Lee's pigeon, sure enough pecking on the window glass. Or at least it was a pigeon, and what other pigeon would be there except the one that had already visited?

While Papa Tate assisted Willie Lee in opening the window, Corrine explained about the pigeon that had appeared on the windowsill a week ago.

"I told him we couldn't keep it here in the apartment," she said, looking at Aunt Marilee, who had that mixed expression of dismay and indulgence that she got whenever Willie Lee hauled home another animal. The indulgence usually won out in the short term, and then dismay in the long term.

Willie Lee got the pigeon into his hand and showed that this one, too, had a band on its leg.

"He is my pige-on. He stopp-ed to say hel-lo," Willie Lee said, stroking the bird gently and letting Munro sniff it. "He knows I will feed him...right, Ma-ma?"

He gave her his best innocent expression that Papa Tate and Corrine knew he could use at will, but that Aunt Marilee, as sharp as she normally was, didn't seem to have figured out yet.

"Of course you'll feed him, darlin'," she said immediately. However, this brought up the great question of what was best to feed a pigeon. Aunt Marilee went looking through the cabinets and finally decided on Cheerios.

Corrine saw her opportunity. "I have to go feed the horses, Willie Lee, and you have to feed your pigeon."

He looked at her. "Yes, I do."

It was great not to have to be sneaking off. She could

hardly believe her good fortune. She happened to glance in Papa Tate's direction and saw he understood perfectly. He winked.

As she grabbed her jacket from the hook by the door, Aunt Marilee's voice followed after her. "Be home before dark!"

"Yes, ma'am!" she hollered back, then was out the door and taking the stairs two at a time.

She wheeled her bike onto the sidewalk and hopped on to cross the street. The wind was cold and fresh-smelling on her face as she rode her bike hard up Church Street, up the hill and around the curve, then the half mile to Mr. Winston's, veering smoothly at his driveway and following the gravel track around to the back, stopping beneath the tall, bare-branched elm trees.

On sight of her, the horses came trotting toward the fence. She propped her bike against a tree trunk and hurried to the little shed and the grain bin, where she scooped up handfuls of feed to give the horses as treats. Then, not bothering with halters, as they remained with her without any restraint, she brushed them and petted them, and blew into their noses and whispered into their ears.

She became aware of the air, crisp without a stir, and the quietness all around her, so quiet that she could hear the faint buzz of a stray fly that passed. The horses were on either side of her, towering over her, warm, horsey smelling. She laid her head against the filly's shoulder and felt the life of her. The filly went very still, as if listening to Corrine's thinking.

Corrine looked around at Mr. Winston's house. There was no sign of anyone.

Going to the fence, she climbed up on the rails. The filly, who had followed at her shoulder, nudged her body. Corrine coaxed her closer and managed to slip over the filly's back, lying crosswise, with her head dangling on one side of the filly and her feet on the other. The filly brought her nose around and tickled Corrine's head with puffs of breath.

Not yet large and firm-boned enough to be ridden by an adult, Sweet Sugar could nevertheless easily bear Corrine's slight weight of seventy-two pounds. She stood poised, as if awaiting some further development, and Corrine continued to lie like a dead body, with her hair swaying and the blood running to her head.

Then, slowly, the mare moved off and the filly followed, the both of them sniffing out stray weeds. Eyes closed, Corrine felt the rhythm of the horse's movement and inhaled the sweet scent of horse and earth. Her belly was warm against the horse's back, and her hair and fingertips swung above the ground.

Sweet Sugar stopped walking and shifted her body stance. Opening her eyes, Corrine saw a rear hoof coming toward her face.

Instantly, with some panic, she arched her back in an attempt to get off the filly, and in reaction to her sudden movement, the filly jumped. Corrine found herself propelled headfirst into the ground, with the sound of hoofbeats echoing in her ears.

She lay there some seconds, blinking. Sitting up, she pushed her hair out of her eyes and spat out grit.

The filly stood halfway across the corral, gazing at her with large dark and curious eyes. Corrine stared back. Then, in a lazy manner, the filly scratched her belly with her rear hoof.

Corrine laughed. The filly slowly came forward, stretched her neck and sniffed Corrine's face. Corrine wrapped her arms around the filly's neck and let the animal raise her to her feet.

"I was first," she said softly into the filly's neck. "I was first to be on you."

She brought the horses their buckets of grain. They pressed close as she hung the buckets on the hooks outside the stalls. They could have knocked her down and trampled her, but she wasn't in the least concerned.

"Stand back," she said to them. "I'm small and you're big." And they did as she said, as surely as if they spoke the human language. They didn't even shove their noses into the buckets, until she said, "There y'all go," and then they went after the grain in the starved manner of all horses.

She filled their water tank and sat on the corral fence for a long while, unconcerned about time. She was totally in the bliss of that minute, content to watch the horses twitch their ears and swish their tails, watch darkness inch down from the treetops, feel the creeping cold of a winter evening, and catch the scent of thin wood smoke wafting past.

When she finally told the horses good-night, she said, "I'll be back tomorrow."

She rode her bike home easily through the soft winter evening, taking in the houses trimmed in Christmas lights, the decorated trees at a number of windows, the hum of her bicycle tires on the blacktopped pavement.

Papa Tate came to meet her, stopped his BMW and said through the window, "We were worried. It's gotten dark."

"I'm sorry to be late," she said, without feeling very sorry at all.

Papa Tate smiled at her, and she smiled at him and headed on down the hill, while he turned around and came after her.

When she entered the apartment, she tossed her coat on the hook and hurried through to the kitchen and over to her Aunt Marilee at the sink.

"I'm home." She hugged her aunt before she quite knew she had done it.

"And I'm so glad," her aunt said, laughing, then casting her a probing gaze that was looking for something going on.

Corrine, pushing her hair behind her ears, thought quickly of a diversion. "What happened to Willie Lee's pigeon?"

Immediately her aunt's expression changed. "Oh, flown the coop, thank God! Papa Tate looked homing pigeons up on the Internet for Willie Lee and told him all about the band on its leg being clear ownership. We never should have fed it. When they put it out on the windowsill, it flew away."

With her aunt's mind successfully focused on something else, Corrine got the supper plates from the cabinets and carried them in to set the dining table.

She very much wanted to share her experience with the filly with her aunt. She even stopped once and turned toward the kitchen, the words flowing across her mind: *I got on the filly. Me, Corrine. I tried something that I wanted to do, and it felt good, and it was like magic for me. I don't know why it was, but it was.*

That sounded silly, and she doubted anyone, even Aunt Marilee, would understand. And likely Aunt Marilee would forbid her to go to the horses.

Maybe she could tell Papa Tate.

No, because even if he didn't scold her, he would feel obligated to tell Aunt Marilee.

She looked at the telephone, considered calling Ricky Dale, and then scolded herself for being stupid beyond the max. After his attitude before when he had found her on the mare, she felt she could not trust him to understand now. And he didn't deserve to know anything about her.

Just then her mother swept in the front door, bringing her fur coat, Shalimar scent and two hands full of shopping bags. "I come bearin' gifts, y'all!"

Like a female Santa, she had something for each of them, beautifully wrapped boxes that she handed out in an elaborate manner, and then clasped her hands together, urging them to hurry up and open them.

Inside Corrine's square box was an ornate Christmas ball, with Corrine's name on it.

"It opens...see," her mother said, taking the ball to demonstrate. Inside the ball was written, *Love, Mom.* "Perhaps you could store a little treasure in it. You don't have to make a Christmas ball just for Christmas."

"Thank you, Mom...it's really pretty."

"Do you really like it?" Her eyes were anxious.

"Oh, yes. It's beautiful."

Her mother's face lit up like Christmas itself.

Willie Lee's gift was also a Christmas ball with his name on it, and there was a very unique Christmas tree pin for Aunt Marilee, and a Santa tie that played music for Papa Tate. Her mother was as happy giving the gifts as a child who received them.

They all sat down to Aunt Marilee's spaghetti supper, and the night-black windows reflected their images around the table, while Corrine's mother, who displayed the ability to turn each shopping decision and encounter with a salesclerk into both drama and comedy, regaled them all with her experiences of the day.

Corrine was fascinated with watching her mother, who seemed to shine like a star. Everyone watched her, even Willie Lee.

Papa Tate smiled at her, his eyes twinkling in that charming manner as he put in comments with a wave of his fork. Aunt Marilee smiled, too, but Corrine noticed that she said little.

It was the most pleasant time they had all enjoyed together since the arrival of her mother, although Corrine wished her mother would not smile and joke with Papa Tate quite so much.

She made up her mind, and as soon as she heard Papa Tate take the trash out the back and down to the Dumpster in the alley, she moved quick to follow him. When she got down the iron stairs, he was standing there with his hands in his back pockets. He looked surprisingly young in the thin beam from the pole light some yards behind him.

"Stars are bright tonight, with that light out," he said, indicating the streetlight on the pole at the end of the alley. "Maybe they'll leave it out. Maybe I can pay to have 'em leave it out," he said, giving a wink. "Same as I could pay to have one put in right here behind the doors."

Corrine had to smile at his delight in the thought. She stood and looked at the stars with him a minute, and then she said, "Papa Tate?"

"Hmm?"

"Could you pick Willie Lee up at school tomorrow, so I can go right to the corral to take care of the horses by myself? I don't mean he's any trouble. But sometimes I'd just like to go by myself, you know?"

She felt suddenly an awful toad for wanting to leave all of her family behind.

But Papa Tate said easily, "Sure, sweet pea. I got tired of havin' my little brother trailin' after me, too. I'll take care of it. Willie Lee and I need to go do some Christmas shoppin', anyway."

"Well, don't get Aunt Marilee any of that Say-la-vee perfume," she said, doing her best to recall how Belinda had pronounced it.

Looking surprised, he said, "Thanks for the tip. We do need to coordinate these things."

Then it was up to bed, and as they went up the iron stairs, relief followed quickly by joy washed over her. She had known Papa Tate would understand and handle it, just like he handled so many things. She was so filled with gratitude at his understanding that she hauled off and hugged him when they got inside. Then, embarrassed beyond measure at being so silly, she hurried away to her room without looking to see how he had taken her action.

When she got up to her room, she thought how Papa Tate had said that he had gotten tired of his brother trailing after him, just as if he was thinking of Willie Lee as her brother.

It felt like Willie Lee was her brother. She didn't see how she could ever go off and live with her mother and leave him behind. When she thought of it, maybe she and Aunt Marilee could somehow manage, if she returned to her mother, but she sure didn't see how she could ever, ever leave Willie Lee. No one, not even Aunt Marilee, could take as good a care of him as Corrine did.

Except tomorrow, when she went to the horses. And, as she fell asleep, her mind was filled with the horses and the fantasies of the horsewoman she wanted to be.

16

At breakfast, Papa Tate fixed the deal for the afternoon with Willie Lee. He said they were goin' to play Santa Claus and for no one to ask any questions. It was a "guys evening out," and they were not even returning for supper, but were going to get pizza or chili dogs or any other stomach-busting thing they wanted, and then drive around and look at the lights in the yards for Willie Lee's judging job.

Willie Lee asked if Munro could go, too, and Papa Tate said he sure could, and that they would get a leash for him, and Papa Tate would pretend that he was blind in order to go into stores.

They all knew Papa Tate would really attempt to do this, too. Aunt Marilee wanted to go with them, just to see it, but Willie Lee said, "No. It is on-ly us guys."

That afternoon, when Corrine came out of school, she found Papa Tate's BMW parked at the cub, with her bike tucked in the trunk. He got it out for her, then he and Willie Lee left her to pedal off to the corral. In this manner, she did not waste time going home, nor risk being sucked in by her fascination with and sense of obligation to her mother and Aunt Marilee.

The horses came to the fence to greet her, and she forgot anything and everything beyond them. She leaned over the top rail and petted each one, as they competed for her attention. Then she slipped through the rails and hugged them thoroughly. With the horses, she found a part of herself that she had not known existed. It was a strong and confident self, a girl who knew who she was and what she wanted.

She grained them, and while they ate, she did a quick cleaning of the stalls and added fresh pine shavings to them. She cleaned the water tank and refilled it, the water so cold that she had to put her hands up beneath her armpits for minutes at a time. Jumping around seemed to help, too, and when she did that Sweet Sugar jumped and ran. Corrine ran after her, and the two played a sort of tag, while the mare looked on, blinking her big black eyes in a placid manner.

She rode them again, losing herself in the fantasies of the horses being her very own and she a superior horsewoman of mighty daring feats. Sitting on the mare's wide back and using the lead rope as a rein, she rode around the corral fence. Twice around, and she dared to tap the mare's side and go to a trot. She had to hold on tight with the trot to keep from bouncing off. She was jarred so much that she was jarred completely out of her fantasy of being the Best of the Best Wild West Show Girl.

Stopping the mare in the middle of the corral, she attempted to stand on the mare's back. She got her boots off without spooking the horse and managed to get both sock feet onto the mare's warm back, but she could not get further than a squatting position, for fear of falling off the mare, who kept turning uncertainly to look at her. She put her hands out, though, and it was enough to thrill her.

Leaving the mare, she threw herself over Sweet Sugar's back and let the filly walk around while Corrine watched her hair sway above the ground and felt the blood rush to her head. Quite deliberately, she let herself slide off the horse's back to the ground, where she lay while Sweet Sugar tickled her face with her nose.

When she got to her feet and dusted herself off, she looked up to see Mr. Winston, leaning heavily on his cane, approaching the corral out of the shadows of the yard.

Rats. She'd been caught.

She walked to the fence, her mind running with possible excuses that could convince him that she had not really been on the horse. As all of her excuses seemed too outrageous to speak aloud, she prepared to beg him not to tell and to promise she would not do it again.

He said straight away, "Marilee called and wanted to know if you were still here. I told her you were, and she asked that you get on home directly."

They gazed at each other.

"Get on, darlin', afore they come after you."

"Yes, sir. Thanks, Mr. Winston."

He wasn't going to tell on her.

She got on her bike and, as she pedaled off across the yard, she hollered back again, "Thanks, Mr. Winston!"

She rode home as fast as she could, tires singing over the blacktopped pavement. Glancing upward to the apartment windows, she saw the silhouettes of both Aunt Marilee and her mother there, looking out.

Now they were both doing it!

She raced up the stairs and through the apartment door. "I'm sorry I'm late. I didn't notice the time. Did it get cloudy or somethin'?" She went straight to the sink to wash her hands in order to set the table. She tried to keep her mind blank so Aunt Marilee wouldn't pick up anything.

"Was Ricky Dale at the corral tonight?" her aunt asked.

She saw her aunt's and her mother's eyes regarding her with high speculation.

"Yes," she said, seizing the opportunity to please. "Just for a few minutes, then he had to get on...for basketball practice, I think."

Boy, telling a lie made her hot all over. Corrine focused on the plates as she set them around the table.

A little later, when Papa Tate returned with Willie Lee and

Munro, he came into the kitchen, kissed Aunt Marilee's cheek, proudly displayed the raisin pie he had brought up from the Main Street Café, and said to Corrine, "Saw Ricky Dale at Pizza Hut. He said to say hey."

Aunt Marilee cast a quick glance to Corrine, who said quickly, "Oh, yeah? I saw him earlier. Aunt Marilee, do you want me to save the rest of this salad or throw it out?"

One tiny little white lie, and God was out to catch her.

"Some more peo-ple got money from San-ta, and it is old mon-ey," Willie Lee told them as fast as he could, his face excited. "Tell them, Pa-pa Tate."

"Well, you just tell 'em yourself, Willie Lee."

Willie Lee cast down his eyes and shook his head. Papa Tate coaxed him by saying that practice made perfect. "And they are about to jump out of their skins to hear."

He gestured with his coffee cup to Corrine, her mother and Aunt Marilee, who said in an encouraging fashion, "We're listening, honey. Who got how much, and what do you mean, 'old money'?" She cast a curious gaze to Papa Tate, who returned a patient smile.

The three of them were sort of leaning toward Willie Lee. Corrine sat back, not wanting to give him more pressure, although she had to bite her tongue to keep from screaming at him to spit it out already.

"A girl," he said, frowning in the manner of thinking deeply. "She got mon-ey...umm..."

"Two thousand dollars," Papa Tate filled in.

"Yes...and a man who works at the Ford...car sale place...got mon-ey."

All their eyes shifted to Papa Tate, who said, "Four thousand dollars."

Aunt Marilee gasped, and Corrine's mother said, "Good Lord."

"Yes," Willie Lee said, grinning at their reactions. "It was cash...each one. It came in the ma-ail and with the note...Mer-ry Chris-mas, from San-ta Claus. Just like the oth-ers."

They all started to talk, but Willie Lee shouted, "Wait!" and held up his hand.

All mouths closed, and all eyes looked at him.

"I am not fin-ished," he instructed. "The man...Mis-ter Mann..." he giggled "...his lit-tle boy wrote a let-ter to San-ta and ask-ed for mon-ey to help his dad-dy. His lit-tle boy is Kev-in. He goes to my scho-ol. He is in first grade."

The last part came out quite fast, and while the rest of them stared at him, quite amazed by the news. They started to ask more questions, and Willie Lee again held up his hand, so they shut up.

Willie Lee took a breath. "It is ol-d mon-ey. They saw it at the bank. It is from be-fore." He looked really pleased with himself and folded his arms.

No one dared speak, waiting to see if he was done, but they did dare to look to Papa Tate, who was patting Willie Lee on the shoulder and telling him that he did fine.

Aunt Marilee put her hands together and spoke in a crow-ing manner, "Oh, what a great story...thank you for tellin' it, Willie Lee!" With a giant sigh, she said very happily to them all, "See, there is a Santa Claus."

"Well, I never said there wasn't," Corrine's mother said in a defensive tone.

Ignoring her sister's comment, Aunt Marilee asked, "Now, what about the money being old?"

Papa Tate told her that he would explain after she served the pie.

"I'm gettin' it...now tell."

Corrine hopped up to help, while her mother prodded, "Go on, Tate."

Papa Tate always had to work up to things. He first filled in the details that the name of the girl who got the two thousand was either Janet or Janice Murphy, depending on who told the story. She had graduated from Valentine High the previous spring and worked as a waitress out at Rodeo Rio's on weekends, and at the McDonald's up in Lawton during the week. She was saving to go to college and either wanted to be a nurse or an astronaut, again depending on who told the story.

George Mann, who was a recent widower with four children and worked as a mechanic at the Ford dealership out on the highway, had really gotten his money before the Murphy girl, as he'd gotten it in Monday's mail, but he'd gone into something of a shock for a day, and when he had come out of that and accepted that he had not entered a dream but actually had received real money, he had been afraid to tell anyone. He worried some authorities would find out about it and might demand to know where he got the money, and maybe throw him in jail for stealing it.

"What made him nervous," Papa Tate said, his eyes dancing, "is that the money has dates of issue from 1928 to 1933. And quite a number of the bills are silver certificates."

"Silver certificates?" Corrine's mother said with high interest.

Papa Tate, forking a piece of pie into his mouth, nodded. "Oh, yeah. Probably worth more if he sells it to a collector. They went over it at the bank today."

"Was the money the other people received old like that?" Corrine's mother asked in a quick manner. Corrine could see the wheels turning in her mind.

"Maybe. We're not sure yet. All of this was just comin' out tonight. George Mann is the only one of them to do his banking here at the Community Bank, and I guess he's the only one to notice the money was a little different than what we have today. I never thought to look at the money when Teresa Betts called, or even Mrs. Maldonado." He shook his head at his lapse.

"Perhaps it's stolen money," said Corrine's mother, who looked very thoughtful. "Or maybe even some very old counterfeit money, do you think?"

Corrine quite suddenly saw her mother in a different light. Her mother really was more worldly than Aunt Marilee, even if Aunt Marilee had traveled half the world with her first husband and Corrine's mother had never gone much beyond Fort Worth and New Orleans. Corrine saw in a moment the caliber of people her mother had encountered in her life, especially in her years in New Orleans with Louis, who was a bona fide lawyer on a powerful scale.

Aunt Marilee said, "Oh, for heaven's sake. I don't think Santa Claus would give out counterfeit money in Valentine, especially old counterfeit money," she said, as if the idea was not only outlandish, it was sacrilegious, too. "Santa Claus generously and kindly gives gifts to people. Willie Lee, it's time for you to get bathed and into bed. You have school tomorrow."

He protested, but she escorted him away from the table, and as she went, she cast back a look that reprimanded them as if someone had been talking dirty.

Papa Tate looked thoughtful, and when the bathroom door shut behind Willie Lee, he said, "I thought about counterfeit at the beginning, but Marilee's right—this is Valentine, and I can't see anyone here having the wherewithal to print up counterfeit money of any year. Besides, bein' old money would just draw more attention to it, and that isn't how counterfeiting works.

"This seems to be money that has been put away for a long time. Saved, or maybe stolen and hidden away for all these years."

"Who would have stolen money here?" Corrine's mother said.

Papa Tate shrugged. "That's the ripe question—just who is our Santa Claus?"

Aunt Marilee had returned and was clearing the dishes away. She said, "Would y'all watch this sort of speculation in front of Willie Lee? I do not see the need to put bad connotations on these generous donations of a Santa Claus. This is a great gift to all of us. The gift of childlike fantasy and magic. Why try to tear that down?"

"I wasn't tryin' to tear it down, Marilee. Don't try to make me into the bad guy. And good Lord, Willie Lee's a little slow, but he's not so fragile as to need to be kept in a bubble and convinced that there is a Santa Claus."

Aunt Marilee took that in no better than could be expected and came out with, "Oh, and who is this great oracle of motherhood who is speakin'?"

Aunt Marilee looked barely able to contain herself from

slapping Corrine's mother, and Corrine's mother looked like she *had* been slapped.

Watching, Corrine couldn't breathe.

"All right, now, ladies," Papa Tate said, getting to his feet. "I don't want to have to send each of you to the corner."

Aunt Marilee's face crumpled with remorse. "Oh, I'm sorry, Anita." She shook her head. "I'm just so thrilled for this thing to be happenin' with the money and the notes from Santa that I was gettin' carried away."

"It's okay. Doesn't matter," her mother said, as if spitting out the words.

Aunt Marilee clearly waited for an apology from her sister, but one was not forthcoming. Shortly thereafter, looking very righteous, Corrine's mother left.

Corrine walked down to the Cherokee with her, carrying a piece of raisin pie that Aunt Marilee had wrapped and sent, hoping to buy forgiveness, Corrine thought.

"It's real important to Aunt Marilee for Willie Lee to keep believin' in Santa," she told her mother, wanting her mother to understand.

"I've gathered that," her mother said, opening the driver's door. She stopped and looked at Corrine. "I wasn't tryin' to hurt Willie Lee, honey. I didn't say there wasn't a Santa."

"I know," Corrine said, feeling she had said something all wrong and wishing she had kept her mouth shut, because now her mother was getting all wrought up. The entire argument was too weird in the first place.

"Willie Lee is goin' to grow up, and pretending that Santa is real won't stop that. That's all I meant."

Corrine gazed at her, thinking silence the best to keep from saying something else that might not be right.

"Well..." Her mother kissed her forehead and started to get into the car.

"Here's your pie," Corrine said, handing her the plate. "It's really good. We get it a lot in the winter."

"Ah, yes, it's a winter food, isn't it?" She rolled her eyes, then gazed at the pie and smiled softly. "You know, your Aunt Marilee knows I love raisin pie." She spoke with a mixture of annoyance and grudging pleasure.

Then, just as if they had heard her call to them, of one accord Corrine and her mother looked upward at the apartment windows, and there was Aunt Marilee looking down on them. She waved, and Corrine's mother waved back.

As her mother slipped into the seat of the car, she sighed and said under her breath, "Winter food...and she thinks I'm a fruitcake."

Corrine brushed her teeth in the slow manner that was her habit, watching herself in the mirror over the bathroom sink, but her mind was back at what her mother had said about Willie Lee growing up and no amount of pretending about Santa Claus would stop it.

This was true, in some ways. No one really knew how much Willie Lee would grow up. Probably no one really knew this about anyone. Look at Miss Zona Porter, who spent most of her life inside and poring over accounting books until her eyes were ruined. She was old. Maybe fifty-five, which wasn't much older than Papa Tate.

She mused about this phenomenon, thinking that Zona Porter seemed much older than Papa Tate. She seemed sort of like a little old ageless wizard woman, yet like a child in almost everything. The traumatic events of her youth had no doubt arrested her mental and physical development. Corrine's mind took the leap that if traumatic events could do that, lots of people had arrested development. Just look at many of those people who came on some of those television talk shows. Aunt Marilee called these people those of the fornicating, adultery and big boob job crowd.

Until this year at school, Willie Lee had always seen things the rest of them did not see. He would watch flies and ants, and he said he saw angels. Corrine had not realized how much she enjoyed him doing that, and doing it with him, until he didn't do it so much anymore. She felt the loss that he had not said anything about seeing an angel in a long time.

She thought of how Willie Lee had never liked school, but how the world insisted that people go to school, and that there were things there he needed to learn. But he didn't need to learn not to believe in magical possibilities. He didn't need to learn not to be Willie Lee.

Corrine did not think Aunt Marilee was trying to keep Willie Lee from growing up so much as she was trying to keep him being Willie Lee *as* he grew up.

Finished brushing her teeth, she lifted up her hair and turned this way and that, looking at her image.

The startling thought came to her: Maybe she could ask her mother if she could get her ears pierced. Maybe her mother would override Aunt Marilee's command.

Ohboy. That was a dangerous thought.

But now that she'd had it, she couldn't seem to dislodge it.

17

When Corrine paid hers and Willie Lee's school lunch bills, two secretaries were talking of what they would do if they received a gift of Santa Claus money, as it was now being called. One said she would pay off her credit card and buy her boyfriend a pair of snakeskin boots for Christmas. The other one said she would first give ten percent to her church, then buy a bunch of new clothes and go off on a world cruise and see places like Sri Lanka and Istanbul.

The other secretary, who obviously had some common sense, said exactly what Corrine was thinking, which was, "How far do you think a few thousand dollars goes? You'd better scale down your world trip to maybe goin' to see Nashville."

While she was waiting for the airhead girl to give her change, Ricky Dale came to pay his lunch bill, too. He came right up beside her at the counter and said, "Hey."

"Hey," she said. Corrine had not been so close to him since the day she had introduced him to her mother.

The secretary gave her change, and Corrine, not wanting to appear to purposefully wait for Ricky Dale, moved away from the counter, but stopped in the hallway and took a great deal of time to put her change into her small purse. This encounter with Ricky Dale seemed quite good fortune. She had dressed again for going to the corral after school, in jeans and her blue sweater and her good Justins. She thought and felt very competent, and just minutes before she had combed her hair and applied lip gloss. She touched her lips with her tongue, to make sure.

At the exact moment that he turned from the counter, she finished with her purse and looked up.

"What's up?" he said.

She never quite knew what to say to such a phrase. "Oh, just goin' to class."

They quite naturally walked along the hall together, and she frantically thought of something more to say.

He said, "I guess you've heard about two more people gettin' Santa Claus money."

She nodded, relieved that he'd brought up a topic. "Papa Tate told us last night—a girl named Janice Murphy and a man named George Mann."

"Yeah, that's what I heard, too. Did he tell you about it bein' bills about seventy years old?"

Corrine nodded. "What does your dad make of it? Is it illegal money?"

"Not as far as Dad knows. I heard him talkin' to Mom, and he said Gerald Overton says it is genuine money and just as spendable today. Probably somebody's savings, but no one can figure out who, or why they'd give it away. My mom said maybe whoever it is is dyin', so they want to do a good deed. My mom wants my dad to go investigate the money, but he said there has not been any crime committed, and so he has no reason to go pryin' into people's affairs. Usually he hears about stuff, but he hasn't heard anything about this," he added.

"Neither has Papa Tate," Corrine said.

Corrine thought about the sheriff and Papa Tate, who were good friends. If both of them together couldn't figure out who was giving out the money, then likely no one could, and she said as much.

"Yeah," Ricky Dale said. "There isn't much my dad or Tate

don't know around here, and if they don't know, don't nobody know."

They were almost to their classes. Seized by an urgency to grasp opportunity, Corrine said, "I'm feedin' the horses their grain in the evenin', while Leanne is down in Texas. I'll be there after school, and tomorrow afternoon. Maybe you'd want to come by. I've taught Sweet Sugar to get into my pocket for a carrot." She had not really taught the horse. The horse did it naturally.

"That's cool, Corky...but I gotta game tonight. It's down in Waurika, so we'll leave here early."

"Oh, well, good luck for tonight."

"Well, yeah, thanks." He gave her a wave as he headed into his classroom.

She felt silly the entire rest of the day. She should have known he would have a basketball game. Most of the kids went to the games, but Corrine never had. She didn't have anyone to go with, and she didn't even know what girls did at the games. She wished she had never suggested he come to the corral. Boy, was that stupid.

She wished so much that she could be girlish, like other girls. She wished for blond hair and blue eyes. The girls who had that coloring seemed to know a whole lot. Over the rest of the day, she made an observation that seemed quite stunning: every girl whom she judged to be girlish had pierced ears. This fact seemed to hold true even down to little Gabby Smith, the preacher's daughter, who was so cute and all the boys loved her.

Everyone was talking about the Santa Claus money. A couple of the teachers, when scolding students for not doing homework, used the line: "You aren't going to be receiving any Santa Claus money for Christmas with habits like that."

Somehow the amount of money that many imagined receiving had escalated to the million dollar mark, and many kids, who never in their lives would have thought about it, were scribbling letters to Santa.

Natalie Sproul was one of these. At lunch, she read her

letter, in which she said that her father was out of work and that her mother had an incurable disease.

When asked about both facts, she said, "Well, Daddy was off work for a week, when his company was bought out, and he's still tryin' to recover from that, and my mother has chronic acid indigestion, and that is a disease."

Corrine pointed out that of the four people to receive money, only Mr. Mann's son had written to Santa. "It's probably coincidence that his father got the money after the boy wrote the letter. I don't think writin' to Santa Claus is going to make you any more likely to get money."

Natalie was not deterred. She wanted pointers to make the letter sound very pitiful, so that whoever read it would give her money, as he had been doing these other people who were pitiful, as she said it.

"I don't think Mrs. Maldonado is pitiful," Jojo said. "She's one of the happiest people I've ever seen. She's all the time laughin' back there in the kitchen."

"Well, she didn't have enough money to visit her daughter in Mexico," Natalie said. "Not havin' money is pitiful. That's why I want some."

"Maybe there are other people who have gotten Santa money but haven't told anyone," Becky Rhudy said in her manner of putting things in out of the blue.

They all looked at her, even Paris Miller, who had not said anything throughout the conversation but had kept rolling her eyes. Corrine was surprised that Becky could make such sense.

"Have you?" Jojo asked Becky with avid curiosity that perked all of their ears.

"No," Becky said, which brought some disappointment. "But my dad said he wouldn't tell anybody because of taxes. Don't tell anybody and don't put it in the bank, either. He said there is no such thing as free money, and he wouldn't take it, if it came."

"So who would he give it back to?" Corrine asked.

There was no answer for that one.

"Well, I don't care what y'all say, I'm writing Santa and increasin' my chances," said Natalie.

Corrine thought that Mrs. Julia Jenkins-Tinsley was going to be ecstatic with the volume of mail going into Santa's mailbox.

Jojo left the lunch room with her, coming up beside her like a friendly little puppy. "I talked my mom into givin' a party after we do the church pageant. It's her thank-you for a good job."

Corrine, who hadn't thought much at all about the pageant, said, "What if it turns out to be a bad job?"

"Oh, she'll tell us it was good anyway. And what's to compare it to? It's gotta be okay," Jojo said in a way that made Corrine laugh.

Jojo went on to say that her dad would barbeque hamburgers and hot dogs, and that her mom said she would roll up the rug in the family room to make a dance floor.

Corrine attempted to imagine it. She had never been to a party, at least not a real one at someone's house. Aunt Marilee always had a little family party for Corrine's and Willie Lee's birthdays, but those were not the same as a real party for lots of people. That Corrine had never been to such a party seemed a little odd, even pitiful, she thought, remembering Natalie Sproul's comments and suddenly recalling how poor she and her mother had been.

The thought of Jojo's party made her stomach flutter, and she doubted she would go, although she couldn't say any of this to the younger girl.

They had reached Corrine's locker, when they heard someone say quite loudly, "Ewww."

It came from a group of girls nearby—Melissa and her friends. Melissa was holding her nose, and the other three girls were backing away from her.

Blood was coming out of Melissa's nose and dripping on the floor.

Immediately Corrine snatched tissues out of the small packet in her locker and hurried over to the girl.

"Here." She put the tissues in the girl's hands and helped her to press them to her nose. "Put your fingers here...press hard." She attempted to get the girl's fingers pressed under her nose, but somehow she ended up with her own two fingers pressed at the vital spot, while Melissa, quite wide-eyed with panic, as most anyone might get when seeing so much blood as can come from a nose, regarded Corrine in a desperate manner.

The next moment Melissa looked like she was about to faint. As she was sort of melting anyway, it was easy to get her sat down on the hallway floor and her head tilted back against the lockers. One of her friends came closer and said, "She got knocked by Darla's locker door."

"Oh, God...m...godda be dick," Melissa said, pressing her arm over her stomach.

"No, you won't. The bleeding is about to stop," said Corrine in an encouraging tone. Throwing up, and in full view of the school, certainly wouldn't help the nose to stop bleeding.

A teacher and the school nurse came running up. Corrine saw that Jojo had gone to get them. With the nurse's help, Corrine got her fingers removed from beneath Melissa's nose, which truly had all but stopped bleeding, and the girl went off with the two women.

Corrine, whose hand was bloody, realized she was quite the focus of attention and felt terribly self-conscious. With Jojo bobbing along beside her, she ducked into the girls' room to wash her hands.

"How did you know what to do?" Jojo asked.

Corrine shrugged. "I used to get nosebleeds sometimes."

"Really? Why?"

"Just did." She had gotten nosebleeds in the night sometimes when she had been small, and when she came to live with Aunt Marilee, her aunt had showed her how to stop them. After a few months with Aunt Marilee, she no longer got them.

For a while after the incident, Corrine felt everyone staring at her and heard whispering. And in art class Miss Dewberry made it all worse by commending her for her quick first-aid action. Corrine could have gone through the floor. She felt more different than ever before from the other kids. She was not afraid of blood, and she was not afraid of crisis, but she sure did not like to be singled out. She felt nauseous with everyone looking at her.

After art class, Paris Miller came up beside her. "Heard how you did first aid. That's cool, girl." And there was true admiration on her face.

Corrine was totally surprised, and then Paris was going down the hall, and Corrine hadn't said a word.

Papa Tate was at the curb after school, with Corrine's bike sticking out of his little trunk. He took Willie Lee off on another excursion, leaving Corrine to pedal happily over to the corral. It was one of those wonderful warm winter days, with blue, blue sky, blinding bright sun, and air so still birds wouldn't even fly.

When Corrine got to the corral, Sweet Sugar was lying in the sun-warmed hay. Beside her, Miss Queen had her head stuck into the hole she had eaten in the big bale. She looked out only long enough to see that the person approaching was Corrine, and then she went to eating again.

Corrine lay down with her head against the filly's belly, listening to its occasional gurgle and the mare's gentle munching. She was glad that Ricky Dale was not coming, after all, because for that space in time she was not interested in being a girlish, teenage girl. Had she been such a girl, she likely would not have lain down in the dirty hay, with her head in such a precarious but delightful position. She was glad to be exactly who she was: a twelve-year-old child in total contentment at throwing herself headlong into the fantasy of doing all manner of trick-riding gymnastics atop Miss Queen and Sweet Sugar.

She was fairly certain that girls like Melissa and her friends missed out on a lot.

Luckily she had dared only one quick ride around the corral on the mare and was graining the horses when the Cherokee came rolling beneath the tall elms and up to the corral fence. Her mother, alone, waved at her through the windshield.

She had come to suggest that they go to supper and maybe do a little shopping. "Just the two of us," she said.

She spoke in a hopeful manner that made Corrine's heart ache and caused her to reply quickly, "That sounds neat. I just have to fill the water tank."

Her mother smiled a sunshine smile and came into the corral with her. Corrine cautioned her about getting her shoes dirty, possibly stepping in manure, and her mother laughed gaily and said, "Honey, I've stepped in a lot of manure in my life. I know how to be careful...and besides, shoes wash."

There was a tone in her voice, a hint of lessons hard learned, which likely had nothing to do with the manure of horses. There she came, dressed in a cashmere sweater, pleated trousers and heeled pant boots, easily sidestepping horse piles without the blink of an eye.

There was a toughness about her mother, and in that instant Corrine saw her Aunt Marilee in her mother. And herself, too.

She looked away, feeling a confusing sense of admiration and distrust.

She got her ears pierced.

She could plead insanity. She did not know what had possessed her to even ask to have her ears pierced. They were walking past the earring store at the mall. It had been like a magnet for her.

"Aunt Marilee said I could when we got up here," she had said in answer to her mother's question about getting her ears pierced being okay with Marilee.

She had lied. What had she been thinking? She was turning into a flat-out liar. Santa Claus was not going to bring her a single thing, she thought in her panic.

The closer they got to home, the quieter Corrine got. When her mother pulled the Cherokee to the curb in front of the *Valentine Voice* building, Corrine could hardly move her hand to open the door, and her legs seemed frozen.

Totally unaware of the catastrophe that was about to happen when Aunt Marilee saw Corrine's pierced ears, her mother was opening the back seat door, pulling out bags of clothing and gifts they had purchased, and chattering on about what a great time they'd had.

"Did you have a good time?" she asked, pausing to gaze at Corrine, probably noticing Corrine's lack of enthusiasm.

"Oh, yes," Corrine assured her with feeling. She looked at the bags as she pulled them from the seat. New jeans, new shirts, and a skirt, too. Her mother had bought her just about anything she wanted. In fact, Corrine had been more careful about how much money she spent than had her mother. She had felt guilty for taking advantage of her mother's obvious eagerness to please.

Thinking of this made her irritated at her mother for not taking control of the situation.

Her mother said, "I can't wait for Marilee to see this Christmas tablecloth. She's gonna love it." She was thrilled to have bought Aunt Marilee something that she was sure she would enjoy.

"Uh-huh," Corrine managed to get out.

Waiting for her mother to go first up the stairwell, Corrine told herself to gather courage. Very often her Aunt Marilee surprised her. Aunt Marilee had said she could get her ears pierced when she turned thirteen. That was only a few weeks away.

Aunt Marilee's attention was drawn to the many shopping bags that Corrine and her mother brought in. "Y'all must have bought out the stores." She smiled happily, and even wider when Corrine's mother laughed so very gaily.

"Oh, we had a good time!" her mother said.

As her mother drew out the tablecloth she had bought Aunt Marilee, Corrine had a sudden hope that maybe Aunt Marilee would not notice her ears until her mother had gone. Possibly Corrine could kiss them both good-night and get to bed and not be discovered until morning.

But then her mother was urging her to show her aunt what she had bought, and saying, "She got the neatest tops at the Gap, and look…she got her ears pierced."

Her mother reached over to sweep the hair behind her ear.

Aunt Marilee looked.

Corrine, the small gold studs in her ears feeling like tongues of fire, looked at her Aunt Marilee looking.

"You did it without askin' me," Aunt Marilee said. The next instant she turned on Corrine's mother. "How could you do that? You take her to get her ears pierced without askin' me?"

"Well, Corrine said that you were gonna get her ears pierced," her mother responded, clearly confused.

"Don't put this off on her. She's a child. You're the adult, and you are the one who is supposed to use sense. You are the one to be responsible."

Her mother had recovered quickly and came back with, "I was bein' responsible. She wanted her ears pierced, and I saw to it."

"Oh, good Lord, Anita, would you have seen to gettin' her a tattoo because she wanted one? You had a cell phone. You could have called me."

"I do not equate a tattoo with pierced ears, and I do not believe I'm in the minority with that one. And I didn't know I had to ask you in regards to anything I want to give my own daughter."

The arrow went true. Aunt Marilee all but put her hand to her heart. "Your daughter?" she said in fury. "And just tell me where have you been for the past few years? It takes more than sendin' notes and presents, and droppin' in and buyin' gifts, to make a mother. It takes time and judgment, and—"

While this was going on, Papa Tate came from the kitchen and tried to interject, but her aunt and mother were now to the point of talking over each other and jabbing the air with their fingers.

"Oh, come off it, Marilee. It is pierced ears we're talkin' about."

Aunt Marilee drew herself up to full height. "Do not give me your scorn, Anita. Do not discount my feelings. You just do not know what to take seriously. You never learned for yourself, and you can't teach her about—"

"It's about you holdin' on, Marilee. Holdin' on to what doesn't belong to you. She's my child."

"Stop it! Stop it!" Corrine screamed at them. She was horrified yet unable to hold back. The two women and Papa Tate stopped and stared at her.

"*I* did it. *I* wanted my pierced ears, and *I* got them. Me. She didn't do it," she said, jabbing her chest and then pointing at her mother. "And you two..." She felt the tears clog her throat and burn her eyes, and words tumbled out of her mouth. "You two are drivin' me crazy! *Crazy!* I don't know who to please...you or my mother. I want things, you know. I just want some peace. Why can't you both... Ohhhh!"

With a stomp of her foot, she turned and ran into the bathroom and slammed the door. She was in there a full minute before she realized she was in the bathroom rather than her own bedroom, where she had meant to go.

Dang it, dang it! She stomped her foot again. Tears came, and then full sobs. She sat on the toilet and sobbed her heart out.

Then she heard knocking at the door.

"Corrine...Corrine, honey." It was Papa Tate.

"Go away." She shouldn't be mean to Papa Tate. But she was too afraid to come out. She could not face them. She was so ashamed at causing the fight.

Aunt Marilee would hate her for lying. And she had caused her mother to look bad. She was an awful person. She wished she had never been born.

But she had to tell them. She had been holding back how she felt ever since her mother came. Ever since she had come to live with Aunt Marilee, really. Probably ever since she had been born, when Aunt Marilee had been right there with her mother and had helped to diaper her.

Knocking came on the door again. "Corrine, honey, please open the door."

It was Aunt Marilee this time. She was so used to obeying her aunt that she was reaching for the knob before she realized. She stepped back and crossed her arms.

"No. Go away."

How long could she stay in the bathroom?

She wanted to look at her earrings in the mirror, but she

could not bear to do so now. Here she had her pierced ears, and she could not enjoy them.

The young woman who had put them in her earlobes had used a gun, and she had said it would likely hurt a little, that it hurt some people more than others. Corrine had found it didn't hurt all that much.

Aunt Marilee's voice came again, more firmly. "Corrine, you are gonna have to come out of there. There are people out here who have to go to the bathroom."

Oh, they had her now.

She opened the door.

There stood Aunt Marilee and her mother.

Aunt Marilee said very quickly, "See, I can lie, too," and pushed open the door before Corrine could slam it closed. Her mother came right beside her aunt.

"We're sorry," they said, both at once. They had been crying and looked like they were about to break out again any minute.

"I'm really sorry," Aunt Marilee said. "I haven't listened to you. I'm sorry."

"Me, too," her mother quickly followed, as if not wanting to be left behind in groveling.

Corrine thought: They are nuts. The both of them.

She was sure of it when Aunt Marilee said, "Let me just look at your ears and put some alcohol on them. Did they put alcohol on them when they did it?"

"They used antiseptic," her mother said. "I made sure of that."

The both of them went at her ears, getting alcohol dabbed on the back of the lobes, while Corrine said, "Ouch...that burns," and her aunt said, "Oh, that just means it's working," which did not make a lot of sense to Corrine.

Then she was looking at herself in the mirror over the sink, at her pierced ears, at last. She had them now. It wouldn't do any good not to like them.

"Oh, sugar...they do look lovely," said Aunt Marilee.

"Aren't you sweet lookin'?" said her mother.

Her mother's face came next to hers on the left, and Aunt

Marilee's face came on the right. There they were reflected in the mirror, the three of them together.

Her mother and Aunt Marilee smiled at her, each with such love that she thought it might shatter the mirror.

Snuggled into her bedcovers, she stared at the dim pattern of moonlight on the wall and thought about the events of the day. The thought of all of it made her so tired that she was instantly asleep.

Marilee slipped out of bed and looked back to see that Tate didn't move. She had never in her life slept a night through, and she felt guilty for her wakefulness disturbing Tate. He worked hard and needed his rest.

Tying her robe around her, she peeked into the children's rooms, then went to her desk in the living room and turned on the small lamp. As she started to sit, her eyes fell on the Christmas tree, and she went over and plugged in the lights.

Oh, it was beautiful.

She sat and gazed at it for some minutes. She loved a Christmas tree, just like a child. Anita did, too. It was something they had in common.

At that moment her eye dropped to one of the sticky notes on her desk. It read: Do unto others.

Yes.

She had been doing her best, Lord. She needed more understanding in her heart for her sister. She needed more total accepting love. Could You send that? she asked silently.

She had not yet written her letter to Santa Claus, as she had said she would do, although she didn't know what that had to do with anything at the moment.

It had to do with living as she wanted to live. How could she expect her son or anyone else to believe in the magic of Santa, if she did not?

The reason she had not written her letter was that she couldn't figure out what she wanted from Santa. Her desires fell into God's department. She wanted a baby, and she wanted loving forgiveness for her sister in her heart, and wisdom and courage to be and do all that she needed to be and do for her loved ones.

Then, very quietly, came a whisper into her thoughts: There *was* one thing she wanted.

Oh, but she didn't even want to think about it. It was beyond them at this time. She couldn't have it, and she didn't want to acknowledge the want, because then she would just want it more, and perhaps Tate would find out, and he would feel so badly, and she could not bear for him to feel badly.

She wanted a house.

The thought came full blown, and instantly she tried to stuff it back to the inner pocket where it had been, silent and hidden. But it would not go back. It sat there in her mind, taunting her.

She did want a house, one where she could nurture all of her family and have room for guests to come and go. And she couldn't say this to Tate, because he felt so badly about his house that the tornado had taken, and that he couldn't afford to get them one at this time.

However, since she had finally looked at the desire, she supposed she could write Santa about it. Maybe then she would not be tempted to speak of it.

Slowly, hesitantly, she pulled out a piece of stationery and wrote:

Dear Santa,
  Please bring me a house for Christmas. A big house, with enough room for my sister to live with us and we not get under each other's feet, and where we can have guests to visit, and parties, too. Please have it have a fireplace and a wonderful porch for sitting. And at least two bathrooms.

She looked at that last sentence, then crossed out the two and wrote, *three bathrooms.*

Thank you, Santa.
Love, Marilee

She put the paper into a matching envelope, carefully licked and sealed the flap, and addressed it: To Santa Claus. She left it on the dining room table, so she could show Willie Lee that she had written it.

She sure hoped Tate couldn't read her mind.

Please, God, help me not to mess up and say anything about wanting a house.

18

The day dawned gray and cold. As Corrine gazed out the windows onto Main Street, she saw the colorful lights strung from light pole to light pole sway in the wind. Bonita Embree's car pulled up in front of the Sweetie Cakes bakery. Bonita got out, and her hair blew wildly as she went into her store.

The thought of the wonderful sweets of the bakery made Corrine hungry. She hurried into the kitchen, and before making the coffee, she dished herself up some of the rice pudding someone had given Aunt Marilee.

As she was spooning a great lot into her mouth, her ears caught a sound. Something at the window. Even as she turned to look, she thought of Willie Lee's pigeon.

But, oddly, she didn't see anything. Must have imagined it.

She set aside the rice pudding and finished making the coffee and got out her aunt's and Papa Tate's mugs.

The sound came again from the direction of the window. This time she went to peer out, and there, huddled close to the corner of the window and the bricks, was the little pigeon.

Oh, dear, he did not look good.

Turning from the window, she thought of what Papa Tate and Willie Lee had learned, that one should not feed a homing pigeon; let him go, and he would find his way home. This one had determined their apartment was a motel stop-over on his route, and he was going to have to change his mind on that.

She picked up her bowl of pudding and began eating.

Two spoonfuls, and the wind rattled the windowpane. Oh, darn.

When she opened the window, a cold draft cut sharply into the room. "Come on, little guy," she whispered, drawing the bird into the room and shutting the window.

Holding the pigeon with both hands, she looked him over. His eyes blinked slowly, as if they wanted to stay closed. She set him on the floor. He took a fluttery step and then collapsed.

Oh, Lordy, he'd gone and died in the kitchen. What was she going to do now? She had better get rid of him before Willie Lee came.

But he wasn't dead. When she touched him, he fluttered and struggled to get up on his feet.

Poor, poor thing, but why had she ever brought him inside, where Willie Lee could find him? She would have to get him back outside, and better away from that window. What if he died and Willie Lee saw him?

She had the somewhat wild idea that if she could find a box, she could put the bird in it, with some spoonfuls of the rice pudding, and take him out back and let him fend for himself. Get better or die, as Aunt Vella liked to say. A number of distinct hazards to this plan swiftly crossed her mind; however, she opened the shallow pantry in rash hopes of locating a box.

Then she heard behind her, "My pig-eon!"

Rats.

Willie Lee, with Munro beside him, went to his knees and picked up the bird. "He is sick."

"I know. I was just lookin' for a box to put him in." That sounded bad, like to bury him.

But Willie Lee didn't notice. He was gently stroking the bird and showing it to Munro, who sniffed it, on the rear, of course.

Corrine knelt down on the floor with Willie Lee, trying to think of what to do and say. The bird seemed awfully weak.

"Can you tell what's wrong with him?" she asked in a hushed voice, as if already in the presence of death—and with Aunt Marilee and Papa Tate in the back of her mind. "I suppose we could take him to Doc Lindsey. I don't know if he does birds, but maybe him or Amy would know somethin'."

Willie Lee bit on his bottom lip and looked at the bird for long seconds, then said, "He was in the wind. Some-thing in the air hit him." Willie Lee sometimes talked to animals.

"Can you make him better?" Corrine whispered.

Her cousin's eyes blinked with a bit of alarm behind his thick glasses. "I...I do not know," he said, his voice small and his thin shoulders contracting.

It would hurt Willie Lee badly if he tried to heal the bird and it didn't work. Yet she said, somewhat breathlessly, "Maybe you can, Willie Lee. Maybe if you just try, just to see. That's what Doc Lindsey does. He just tries, and sometimes he can't make animals any better, either. That's just how it is. But you won't know unless you try. And if it doesn't work out, we'll get Papa Tate to take the bird to see if Doc Lindsey can help him, okay?"

He looked at her, then at Munro, who gazed back with what Corrine thought was an eager expression.

"O-kay," Willie Lee said.

Corrine watched Willie Lee as he held the pigeon with one hand underneath and gently placed the other hand on top of it. His eyes closed. Munro put his nose on Willie Lee's hands. Willie Lee seemed very pale, and his blond hair very shiny in the single light. The bird looked like it might have been dead.

After long seconds, Willie Lee's eyes popped open, and slowly he smiled. "I think he will be o-kay."

Corrine watched him set the bird on the floor with a careful motion.

"There you are bir-dy."

"Did you see your angel?" Corrine asked with high curiosity.

"Oh, sort of," he replied in a disinterested fashion. He had an avid gaze on the bird, who sat on his feet and twisted his neck to look up at them. Then his wings fluttered. The bird made its little cooing noise and walked around, bobbing its head. It was just a silly pigeon walking around, with Munro sniffing after it.

Good gosh. She felt as if all the air had gone out of her. She regarded Willie Lee for several seconds, debating about finding out what had gone on with him, but then she decided making a big deal out of it was not helpful to him.

She said, "You know, Willie Lee, probably it will be that sometimes you can help an animal and sometimes you can't, just like it is with Doc Lindsey. And it will be a lot better all the way around if you don't tell anyone about helpin' the pigeon. Our secret," she stressed. "Okay?"

He regarded her in the way he did when thinking hard. Possibly he was recalling, as she did, what had happened the last time, when others found out about him being able to heal animals. Aunt Marilee had strived to keep it secret, but one after another had found out. It just wasn't good for people to know about such a thing. They had put lots of pressure on Willie Lee.

"O-kay," he said with earnestness.

She had a sudden urge to hug him and say she loved him. Feeling awfully silly and weird, she restrained herself.

Willie Lee told her that they needed to feed the pigeon popcorn and to give it a deep dish of water. Corrine was struck with his capability concerning the pigeon's care. He said Papa Tate had read to him the instructions from the Internet. He was slow but steady in getting the pigeon what it needed.

He even said, "We will have to read the band on his leg to find the ow-ner."

"Oh," Corrine said, wondering if he meant that he would give up the pigeon but decided not to delve into that question. She could not stand to bring out sadness in her cousin.

She emptied cans of soft drinks out of a cardboard box to use for the bird, but since it could fly now, it flew up to the top of the refrigerator, where it pooped down the side. She hurried to clean that up and thought that the pigeon presented some big problems, especially as it was now pecking on the grapes in a bowl on the counter. She was really glad when Papa Tate showed up to handle the situation.

At first worried that Willie Lee would tell Papa Tate about healing the bird, she decided she had no way to control what Willie Lee eventually said. Leaving her cousin and Papa Tate to discuss their options concerning pigeon management, she went to get dressed and inspect her newly pierced ears, which she had forgotten until she observed herself in the mirror.

Her heart did a little leap of joy as she observed her earrings and imagined wearing dangling ones.

But then she recalled the awful arguing that had taken place.

She would be glad when she could look at her pierced earlobes and not think about the row getting them had caused.

It was decided that letting the bird go out the window would not do this time, and the only place of good release was the rooftop. Papa Tate and Willie Lee seemed to feel a big ceremony was in order. They had decided to mark the bird, to indicate to the bird's owner that he had been handled. Papa Tate took a permanent marker and drew a tiny heart on the smooth feathers at the back of the pigeon's neck. Then they took the bird up on the roof of the building. This was something of a trick, as to get up there, they had to go up the iron ladder from the landing outside the back door.

Aunt Marilee, fresh out of bed when she heard the plans, stood out on the landing, still in her bathrobe, to make sure neither of them fell off the ladder. Corrine, thinking someone should be of real help and able to call paramedics in the case of catastrophe, stood in the laundry room, cordless phone in hand, while watching Aunt Marilee, her robe and hair blowing in the wind, through the opened back door. If Aunt Marilee screamed, Corrine could punch the emergency number on the speed dial.

Papa Tate and Willie Lee, who climbed up the ladder just fine, took the bird up to the roof in a large shoe box. Once let out, Papa Tate said, it walked around and took off.

"Headed northeast," Papa Tate said.

"Maybe he will come back a-gain," Willie Lee said.

To which Papa Tate replied, "Buddy, that appears entirely likely."

The background for the church pageant, which Corrine had all but forgotten about from the moment she had received the call to look after the horses, was to be simple and stark panels of deep navy velvet fabric that portrayed the dark night sky. Understated elegance, Aunt Marilee said. While Corrine's mother had helped with the idea and choosing the fabric, Aunt Marilee had done all the real work, measuring and hemming the fabric and finding and borrowing unused office partitions at the school that would serve as a framework upon which to hang the fabric.

Feeling a little guilty that she had not shown the slightest interest in helping with the project that was important to her aunt, and to furthermore have disappointed her aunt with getting pierced ears, Corrine now threw herself into the job with enthusiasm. She got the folded panels of velvet put into the box that she had been going to use for the pigeon, lining it with tissue paper, and reminded Aunt Marilee of everything she could possibly need—her tool kit, scissors, pins.

She was so helpful that Aunt Marilee finally said to her, "Why thank you, Corrine, honey. You are sure a help."

They went early to the church to get the background set up across the altar before all the others arrived for rehearsal. Her mother also pitched in, arriving right behind them in the church parking lot. Possibly her mother, like Corrine, wanted to make everything up to Aunt Marilee.

The partitions had already been delivered to the church and were stacked against the wall of the hall. The three of them hauled the partitions into the sanctuary and into place across the wide altar, then draped the velvet fabric over them. Unfortunately the effect was not at all the elegance that Aunt Marilee was shooting for. With quite a bit of disappointment, they surveyed the situation, and Corrine's mother came up with the idea to lay the fabric in pleats, which turned out very well to give the illusion of actual curtains. Aunt Marilee was thrilled with the look, and Corrine's mother was thrilled to have provided the answer, and Corrine was thrilled, even amazed, that her aunt and her mother were working very well together.

Aunt Marilee always did best when she had a mission, and apparently Corrine's mother also enjoyed one. The two women sparked energy and ideas from each other, and quite soon were so close in mindset as to finish each other's sentences.

Aunt Marilee said, "Well, this is going to be fine, but...well, it needs..."

"A star," said her mother looking upward. "Could we hang it from that..."

"Light? No, I think it needs to go further back. We can hang it from that vent there, with some..."

"Fishing line. That'll be invisible."

It was as if the argument of the night before had not happened, as if they had not gone at each other like cats and dogs, and as if Corrine had not felt she was going to die. Indeed, at one point she reached up to touch her earrings, to make certain they were indeed there.

From the edge of the altar steps, she looked out to where her mother and her aunt stood halfway back down the middle aisle, observing their handiwork on the stage. Seeing them together like that, she had the sudden thought that perhaps her mother had not come back to make up with her so much as to make up with Aunt Marilee.

"Corrine, honey," Aunt Marilee called to her. "Please go over there and work the light switches, so we can get an idea of how to focus the lights."

Her mother and aunt spent the next fifteen minutes experimenting with the possibilities afforded by the direct lighting. Her aunt went so far as to get a ladder and climb up to reposition a couple of lights, while Corrine's mother held the ladder steady and gave direction as to the best angles.

Corrine stood there turning on and off the switches as she was bade and watching children begin to arrive and play around on the stage. She wondered at her aunt's and her mother's determination to get the effects of understated elegance in a pageant put on by children, who were sporting tablecloth headdresses, Mexican ponchos and, in some cases, drawn-on mustaches.

The only one who really and truly might be considered elegant in any way was Melissa, in her professional angel costume. Her mother let her don the entire thing this time, magical wings included. Melissa went around posing and acting beautiful, especially for the boys of all ages, and most especially for Ricky Dale.

Corrine was a little surprised that Melissa had come to the rehearsal. She had thought maybe the girl would not feel well enough, that maybe her nose would be all swollen or she would have black eyes. It turned out that she didn't have but faint blue circles beneath them, easily concealed with makeup. In fact, the girl appeared to thrive on the attention. Her mother went on to the other women about how her daughter had sustained an injury and almost had her face marred by someone who had opened a locker door in a reckless manner, and kids kept asking Melissa how she felt, to which she replied, "Okay," in a weak fashion.

Charlene MacCoy told Melissa that if she didn't feel like saying her lines, she could just stand in place at the appropriate times. Melissa said that she could say her lines, and she did, too, giving as strong a delivery as ever and several times, too, as she said, "I need to practice the opening one more time, Miz MacCoy."

No one mentioned that Corrine had been the one to apply first aid to the girl, successfully getting her nose to stop bleeding. For all the staring of the day before, today she was her usual invisible self.

The only one who seemed to take note of her was Jojo,

who danced over to Corrine and said in a low voice, "If I have to hear that angel say, 'Hark!' one more time, I'm gonna barf." Just about anything Jojo said came out funny, and doubly so with her dressed like the Virgin Mother Mary.

When the rehearsal was winding up, Corrine went to the fellowship hall to help the eldest Smith girl serve up snacks and punch. She served first to the younger ones, which included Willie Lee, who was really cute to see hanging out with the pastor's young daughter, Gabby Smith. He clearly had a crush on the cute curly-haired girl.

Corrine got her cousin and Gabby sat down with their drinks and cookies, and returned to the table just at the moment to serve Ricky Dale and Anson Brown plastic cups of punch. She thought the two might hang around the table and talk with her, but just then Charlene MacCoy called them to help Aunt Marilee and Corrine's mother clear the velvet covered partitions and a few other props off the altar and into the back hallway.

"Hey, Corrine!" It was Ricky Dale, running over from his mother's car.

Corrine, who was leaving with her aunt and mother, stopped there in the parking lot, while the two women continued on to their cars.

Ricky Dale, shivering and tucking his hands into his coat pockets, said, "I can help you to clean the stalls this afternoon. Are you strippin' 'em?"

She shook her head. "No. They aren't too bad. I'll just clean them a bit, and it won't take me long to feed and water. Leanne should be back tonight."

"Oh, well, I just thought you might need some help."

"No, that's okay." She wondered if she should have said that she would strip the stalls, so then she would need help.

"Okay. See ya'." He turned and loped back to his mother's car.

As Corrine went and slipped into the seat of the BMW, she wished she would have thought faster and changed her mind about the stalls. But she didn't care to have him thinking that she needed him to help her.

"What did Ricky Dale want?" her aunt asked.

"To know if I needed help strippin' the stalls this evenin', but I told him I didn't. I do need to go over there to the corral, though, to feed and check on the horses."

"Maybe he wanted to help. Maybe you could have told him that you need help."

"But I don't," Corrine said, a little confused.

Aunt Marilee said nothing more.

Corrine wondered why Ricky Dale couldn't just come to the corral because he wanted to see her.

Later on, as they were preparing lunch, Corrine's mother and aunt asked her to tell the story of tending Melissa's nose, so Corrine knew that Jojo had told them. She was glad. Her mother and aunt both hugged her and complimented her ability in a crisis. They did not seem competitive in their attention to her. At least not much.

As it was quite cold and damp and with a good wind, Corrine's mother drove her over to the corral. It was her last time with the horses before Leanne returned. Corrine looked forward through the windshield and wished so much that the weather had been nice. She imagined riding the mare and playing tag with the filly. Even with the poor weather, she might have done those things with the horses, if she had been able to come alone.

When the car drove up to the corral fence, both horses, who had been in the same stall, came racing out and prancing around. Corrine said she would hurry and for her mother to stay in the Cherokee, but her mother got out to help anyway. Corrine worried a bit that her mother might get stepped on by the horses, who were frisky in the cold weather. But her mother proved perfectly all right with them, petting them while Corrine went to the bin to get grain.

"Sweet Sugar will find it in my pocket," Corrine said, showing her mother how the filly smelled the bit of grain she had slipped into the pocket of her coat.

Her mother wanted to brush the horses while they ate, so

Corrine retrieved brushes for each of them. She was a little surprised at her mother's ease with the horses and finally had to comment on it.

"Oh, Louis keeps horses down in Lu'siana," she said, but nothing more on that subject, saying then, "You could have let Ricky Dale come help you. Wouldn't that have been nice?"

"I didn't really need his help," Corrine replied, thinking how her aunt and her mother had obviously been talking about her, which of course they would.

"Well, you enjoy his company, honey, and he would have liked to come."

"If he would have liked to come, why didn't he just say that?" Corrine said. "He was just bein' nice. He likes Melissa." Instantly, she wished she had not said that. She felt transparent and hated it. She couldn't look at her mother but kept brushing the mare with firm strokes.

"Oh, I don't think he likes Melissa so much," her mother said. "It's Melissa who likes him. And he's like any male— he enjoys the attention she gives him."

Corrine looked over the filly's back at her.

"Males bask in the attention," her mother said with a knowing grin. "Melissa is one of those girls who likes boys in general, and likes to flirt and carry on. She's gonna be noticed, and boys are gonna respond to her, but it doesn't mean they like her all that much.

"He asked if you needed help because he wanted to come over here with you."

Corrine looked at her, wondering. She didn't know why he wouldn't have just come, then.

"I saw Ricky Dale lookin' at you a lot at church." Her mother smiled a knowing smile that caused Corrine to look away and to wonder if what she said could possibly be true.

"Honey, all you'd have to do is give him a bit of attention, and he'd come on the run."

Corrine focused on brushing the filly's tail, but dared to ask, "How do I give him attention?"

"When he asks if you need help, say yes, and let him help you."

Corrine thought this seemed silly, and like lying. She just didn't like it.

"And just go up to him sometimes, smile at him and ask him how he's doin'."

Corrine thought about how she had met up with him in the hallway on Friday. Maybe he had seemed interested in her, but not all that much.

"Ricky Dale has eyes for you. Give it a try a couple of times and see."

Corrine thought for several minutes; then, throwing their brushes in a bucket, she said, "It sounds like a lot of trouble to me."

Her mother laughed. "You just keep that attitude all the way through college, at least, and Marilee and I will be very happy."

Just as they were coming out of the corral, Leanne's big truck pulled into the yard. Leanne hopped out and strode over to them.

Corrine introduced her mother and Leanne, who said, "I think I remember you from school. A few years ahead of me, and one year you were Homecoming Queen?"

Corrine's mother laughed and said she had been.

Then Leanne thanked Corrine profusely for caring for the horses the past week and went on to brag to her mother how much Corrine had helped her all year. "I sure don't know what I would have done without her," she said.

Corrine was pleased and embarrassed by the compliment; she didn't know how to act or what to say.

Then Leanne said, "I guess Corrine told you that I'm movin' and sellin' the filly."

"Yes," her mother said. "I heard that you've gotten a place a bit north of here."

Both women's gazes came round to focus on Corrine. Leanne gave the directions to her ranch, and Corrine's mother knew just where it was, and they talked about that for a minute.

Then Leanne said, "I've sold the filly, Corrine. To Mr. Littleton who you met last week. He'll be coming to get her on Monday, and I'll be movin' the mare up to my place on Tuesday."

"Okay," Corrine said, as the woman gazed at her intently.

Her throat got thick. She would not cry. She would not.

"I know you'll miss them. You can have your mother or Marilee bring you up to my place to see the mare, if you want. Anytime."

Corrine didn't know what to say to that, but her mother said quickly that maybe they would just do that and put her arm around Corrine's shoulders. Corrine wished she wouldn't. When Leanne stuck out her hand for a handshake with her mother, Corrine slipped aside and away from her mother's touch.

Then Leanne shook Corrine's hand, too, and said she would be sure to pay her what she owed her. She would drop it at the newspaper.

"Thanks," Corrine managed to say and even to smile.

Then she and her mother got into the Cherokee and drove home.

"I know you'll miss the horses," her mother said.

Corrine shrugged. "Yeah." Her throat was so thick she could hardly breathe. She kept her face turned to look out the window of the door, where beads of moisture formed on the glass.

"Perhaps you can get your own horse before too very long," her mother said in a hopeful manner, as if it could really happen.

"We don't have anywhere to keep a horse," Corrine said. She wished her mother would shut up.

"Well, arrangements can be made. And you won't be living in the apartment forever. Marilee and Tate are plannin' for a house in the country in the next couple of years."

Corrine did not reply. She just looked out the window, thinking that a couple of years was a lifetime.

When they reached the apartment, she was heartily glad that Aunt Marilee was on the phone with Grama Norma from Europe. Stretching the cord of the phone in the kitchen, she called Corrine's mother immediately to come talk to their mother, who, she said in a hoarse whisper, "has decided to stay in Italy for Christmas with a friend...at a villa!"

It seemed that Grama Norma had made the acquaintance of royalty and had been invited to stay at their home. It also seemed there was, "a man involved," as Aunt Marilee put it in a way that Corrine took to mean that she and Willie Lee weren't supposed to fully know about that part of it.

To Corrine's great relief, this bit of news drew attention from herself, and she stayed in her room until supper, and then went back to her room right after the meal. She didn't even help clear the table or clean the kitchen. When Aunt Marilee came in to check on her, she had the light out and pretended to be asleep. She thought that if she had to talk to anyone she would shatter into a million pieces.

The apartment was quiet, everyone asleep, even the hamsters. Willie Lee's faithful companion, Munro, wasn't asleep. He was looking at Willie Lee, who put his finger to his lips and whispered, "Shusshh."

Reaching for his glasses, he carefully put them on and then slipped from his bed. He pushed his bedroom door closed, but not fully, so as to not make the loud clicking noise. That would bring his mother right up out of bed. He knew there were certain noises that could do that. He turned on the overhead light and went to his coat on the hook, pulling a folded piece of paper from the pocket.

Gabby had helped him to start a letter to Santa Claus. She had said that she did not know if there really was a Santa, but she thought there was. And she liked to write to him. Willie Lee had asked her help, because he liked being around her and knew she liked to do things for him. Remembering now, he thought himself pretty smart.

He had decided that he wanted to send his letter to Santa, and without anyone knowing it. That would fool his mother for sure. And then he could tell Gabby that he had mailed it. That would please her.

He had to finish the letter, though, and it took a lot of work for him.

"Santa Claus knows who you are, Willie Lee," she had said. "He won't expect you to write perfect."

Just to be sure, he'd had her write the first part of it. She had insisted on drawing little hearts at the top of the paper. Willie Lee was glad to please her at the time, but now he hoped no one saw the letter and thought he was some baby girl.

Dear Santa,
Please bring me my pigun for Christmas. You will know the one I want.

Gabby had not known how to spell pigeon; he couldn't remember, either, but Santa should know. Gabby said if Santa knew all about what they did, then he knew about Willie Lee's pigeon.

Now, concentrating hard, he wrote as fast as possible what he wanted to add to the letter.

I hav ben a good boy mama sas. corrine has to pleas bring her a hors. mama wans a babe boy or a prcha swing. Papa tate sas hs best prsent is a rasn pie. We movd to thu roms on top of the nwspapr. I am Willie Lee James Holloway

He wished he could write better. He thought that if Santa knew the pigeon he wanted, then Santa probably knew they had moved from the house where they had lived last year, but people did forget things. He liked writing his name. He wrote his name very well, his teacher said. It looked good to him.

Leaving on his pajama top, he changed the bottoms for jeans and put on socks. Then he put on his coat, took up the letter and turned out the light, and slipped out of the room and down the hall, with Munro padding silently at his heels. His cat was lying on the rug at the opening to the living room, and he tripped on her. She let out an angry squeak.

He froze, quite expecting his mother to appear out of her bedroom. When she did not, he stood listening.

He heard his mother's faint snores. He knew that was his mother and not Papa Tate. His mother did not like anyone to tell her this.

Going on tiptoe to his mother's desk, he slid open the small top drawer where he knew she kept envelopes. He looked down at Munro and heard, *Don't risk the light.*

Good idea. Having very poor vision without his glasses, Willie Lee was used to finding things by feel. He reached into the drawer and located an envelope fairly easily. Carefully, he folded the letter and put it into the envelope, and tucked the envelope deep into his coat pocket, along with a pen from the container atop the desk.

He and Munro went to the door, and Willie Lee very, very carefully pulled down the latch handle, opened it, got his shoes and stepped out into the stairwell. Closing the door as quietly as he had opened it, he sat down beside Munro to put on his shoes; then it was down the stairs as quietly as possible and out the door to the sidewalk.

He had made it! He stood there, hardly daring to breathe.

Then his eyes popped wide, as he was looking right across the street at the police station. Light shone from the door. The entire corner was very light, with streetlights and Christmas lights. Somebody in there might see him!

He scurried into the darker shadows next to the building, then across the narrow alleyway and down the sidewalk past the café. Munro followed right behind him.

The wind had quit, and the night was all quiet and cold. Being out in the night alone did not frighten Willie Lee. When they had lived on Porter Street, he had often sneaked out in the night. He enjoyed being alone a lot. He didn't feel so stupid when he was by himself. His mother always acted like he could not do a lot of things, and sometimes Corrine did, too. Papa Tate let him do a lot of things, but sometimes Papa Tate thought he could do things that he could not, and then Willie Lee felt he disappointed Papa Tate. Sometimes his angel came when he was alone. And Munro was always with him.

All he had to do now was head for the corner at the end

of the street, cross over to where the bank was and come back to the post office. He could do that easy.

As he went along, he stuck out his tongue to feel the cold. He lingered as he passed the store windows. Then he remembered that he had to get down to the post office and hurried along, but again got sidetracked by looking in the windows. A car came past, and he flattened himself against the bricks of the old Opry. The car did not even slow.

He came to the corner and crossover place with a little surprise. He looked carefully either way, as his mother and Corrine always told him to do, then crossed the street. He made it to the other side and stepped up on the curb, which seemed quite high. As he headed for the post office, he saw a figure walking toward him. He stared at the figure with curiosity. It was a man, walking sort of hunched over. Using a cane.

It was Mr. Winston!

"Well, Mr. Willie Lee, what are you doin' out in the middle of the night?"

Willie Lee stared at the old man and thought he could trust him. "I am mail-ing my let-tur to San-ta." He was pleased to tell the old man.

"I see...I see. I'm proud of your initiative."

Sometimes Mr. Winston said things Willie Lee did not quite understand, but he sensed the man was pleased.

"And this is a secret mailin', right?"

That Willie Lee understood, and he said that it was. He put his finger to his lips.

"Mum's my word. I won't tell," Mr. Winston said. "And good for you on the endeavor."

"What is en-deav-or?"

"The brave act of believin' in Santa Claus."

"Oh." Willie Lee felt he was doing something awfully good.

They shook hands, and Mr. Winston went on past, and Willie Lee headed for the post office. At the glass door, where light glimmered through, Willie Lee looked back to see Mr. Winston turning the corner around the bank.

He had not asked Mr. Winston why he was out in the

middle of the night. He wondered about it as he went into the post office lobby.

There was Santa's mailbox sitting underneath the small light in the ceiling. Because he couldn't reach the tall table against the wall, Willie Lee sat on the floor in the glow of the light, took out the envelope and pen and wrote: To Santa Claus. He made the letters very carefully.

Getting to his feet, he deposited the envelope in the little slit in the Santa mailbox.

He rather expected some horn to sound. Something to indicate that his letter had gone somewhere.

But there was nothing. He was a little disappointed.

Then he thought of Gabby. He could tell her he had sent his letter, he thought proudly, imagining her reaction. She would likely clap for him. Gabby clapped at a lot of things.

He pushed out the door and ran down the sidewalk toward home. Too late, he realized that he was going to go right in front of the police station.

With great daring, he crossed the street before getting to the corner. He ran as fast as he could, and he didn't trip on the curb. He got through the stairwell door, then up the stairs and into the apartment and to his room, forgetting to leave his shoes at the door. Oh, well. Coat and shoes tugged off, and Willie Lee hopped into bed.

He had made it! Cool, as the big boys said.

He never saw Winston, who had turned to peek around the corner and watched until the boy had gotten through the door to his apartment. When the door had closed, Winston came back down the sidewalk very slowly, as his joints had stiffened in the cold. He ended up stopping at the police station and asking Deputy Dorothy Jean Riddle, who was on desk duty, to drive him home.

The Valentine Voice

Christmas About Town
by Marilee Holloway

Just in time for Christmas—the Cut and Curl beauty salon is now offering massage therapy! That's right, Oralee Beaumont has returned and is now a certified massage therapist. If the holiday preparations have you on your last nerve, treat yourself to the healthy benefits of a relaxing massage. This may just help you get through the season.

The IGA deli has everything you need for three different and fairly healthy meals, and, at least for the following 2 weeks, they offer in-town delivery! The phone number is 555-YIGA.

I call your attention to Charlotte Conroy's column on page 3, *Top Ten Web Sites for Christmas Gifts*. You can pick out and order your gift and have it mailed directly to the recipient. Now that is easy living. A complaint about this procedure is that it is impersonal. Let me just say that you can spend as much time and care choosing the correct gift in this manner as you would running your legs off. Returns may be a bit more difficult, however, so keep this in mind when choosing.

Belinda Blaine's Professional Shopping Service is a big hit. For a small fee, Belinda offers an initial consultation to help you get started, or you can hire her to do your buying. Home delivery and wrapping are available for an extra charge.

Here is the result of our latest sidewalk poll of the most desired items for women: gift certificate for Blaine's Drugstore, fine fragrance (meaning expensive), silk long underwear, cashmere sweater, slippers, leather coat, book or gift certificate to a bookstore, gift certificate to Home Depot (yes, this was from a woman), a Victoria's Secret nightgown, feather pillows, bird feeder and bird seed, and one woman wanted the Merry Christmas All-Male Maid Service prepaid for six months.

The result of the poll for men: big screen television with surround sound, gift certificate to Home Depot, deer rifle, ticket to the NASCAR races at the Dallas Raceway, rechargeable cordless drill, leather work gloves, and one man wanted the Merry Christmas All-Male Maid Service for his wife.

I only report these poll results, I do not make them up. It does seem to me that our mindset is running on the material side. I'm not suggesting we give up the idea of the electric drills or cashmere sweaters, but perhaps our thoughts might run a little deeper to things that money cannot buy. Gifts that are of our heart and bring us together. Such gifts cannot be bought but require a giving spirit, the expenditure of time and love. Just a thought.

Monday—that's tomorrow—is the deadline for entering the Outstanding Christmas Yard award. Entry forms for nominating yours or your neighbor's yard can be found at the IGA, the Quick Shop on Main Street, and here at the *Voice* offices. Winners will be announced on Wednesday.

Our recipe this week comes from Ms. Judith Beckett, who reads *The Valentine Voice* from all the way out in North Carolina. Valentine is sure a small town in a great big world. I've already tried this recipe at our table, and it is voted a winner. Thank you, Judith!

Congealed Cranberry Salad

2 packages cranberry Jell-O
2 cups boiling water
8 ice cubes
1 can whole cranberry sauce
¹/₂ cup chopped nuts
1 large can crushed pineapple, including juice

Dissolve Jell-O in the 2 cups boiling water, then add 8 ice cubes and stir until ice cubes are melted. Refrigerate until mixture thickens, almost set. Then add cranberry sauce, nuts and pineapple with juice. Mix and pour into mold or flat dish to congeal.

Due to high call volume and the busy-ness of these weeks, the *Voice* will be relying on voice mail and e-mail only until after the New Year. We trust you understand that we are attempting to keep our sanity and will cooperate.

19

Candles were everywhere in the sanctuary, and someone
had put up a Christmas tree since the previous morning. It
was tall and wide and glowed magically in the ethereal light
of the sanctuary. At the top was a beautiful golden angel.
The sight of it sparked Corrine's interest out of her misery
about the horses. She could hardly take her eyes off of it as
she went up to the altar for communion.

This is my body, which was broken for you....

Her mother, who had joined them that morning, knelt at
the altar, and Corrine went down beside her, catching the
scent of Shalimar. Then Aunt Marilee and her C'est La Vie
knelt beside her on the left. Corrine felt like a creamy center
sandwiched between two crispy, aromatic crackers.

This is my blood, which was shed for you....

Reverend Smith moved in front of her. His shoes, scuffed
and worn loafers, peeked out from beneath his black robe.
From previous communion services, Corrine recognized
them. She thought he needed to get a new pair. She opened
her palm to receive the pinch of bread he deposited there
and took the tiny glass of sacrament juice from the silver tray.

For the forgiveness of your sins...

She never could think of her sins to confess to God while she was trying not to drop the bit of bread or spill the little jigger of purple wine. She had once thought to make a list before church, but when she got up to the altar, her mind went as blank as a fresh blackboard, and it was impossible while juggling the bread and wine to whip out and consult the piece of paper. She decided God knew everything anyway, so she didn't need to tell Him.

Her riding the horses when she wasn't supposed to popped into her mind. This brought anger. She wasn't sorry she had ridden them, and she would not be sorry. She squeezed her eyes closed. *Why did You have to let the horses go away, God?*

She blinked, and then found herself looking at the figures and faces around the curve of the altar. On the other side of Aunt Marilee was Papa Tate, with his arm around Willie Lee, whose head was bowed and hands tightly clasped. His pale hair glowed like maybe he had a halo. He was as near to a saint as Corrine could imagine walked the earth.

There were the pastor's children in a line, and their mother guarding them from behind. Shad was picking his nose. Two old ladies, and then Jojo, petite and delicate looking, was squeezed between her mother and father...and there was Aunt Vella in one of her big hats that she wore to church, with Uncle Perry, who was making a rare appearance at services, and Mr. Winston and Granny Franny...and there was Ricky Dale beside his sister and mother and father. He had his head bowed low.

Passing her gaze back quickly over everyone, she experienced an emotion she couldn't quite name. It was a bit of wonder at these people who made up her life, and a bit of fear that they would be snatched from her.

She glanced over to her mother's graceful hands, folded in prayer.

Reverend Smith began praying. As she bowed her head, she saw his worn shoes again and thought about his big family, and his voice just then flowing out over them all.

Our Father, who art in heaven...

Pastor Smith finished and smiled, as he always did. They all rose and, with shuffling and a few coughs, filed back to their pews. Aunt Marilee went ahead of Corrine, and her mother came behind.

In their pew, Corrine got the hymnal and opened it to the page she had bookmarked earlier.

Joy to the world, the Lord is come...

Her mother's hand came out and took hold of the book on the left, and then Aunt Marilee's hand came out and took hold of the book on the right.

"And heaven and nature sing," the three of them sang.

After services, some ladies came over to speak to her mother and Aunt Marilee. Two of them, friends of Grama Norma, were quite elderly; they welcomed Corrine's mother to the church. "Aren't you glad to have your mama here?" one of them said to Corrine.

Corrine, preoccupied with watching Ricky Dale, said that she was.

Papa Tate and Willie Lee slipped off. Willie Lee went to play with Gabby Smith, and Papa Tate went up to the Oakes' pew and was visiting with Ricky Dale's father, Sheriff Oakes. Ricky Dale was standing right there, too, looking bored. Corrine thought eagerly that with Papa Tate there, she had the perfect opportunity to go speak to Ricky Dale. She had a good opening for conversation, too; she could tell him about the horses leaving. She hesitated with the thought of the horses, wondering if she could speak of them without crying.

That hesitation cost her, because Melissa Pruitt hollered to Ricky Dale from the center aisle.

He went right over there to her, of course.

Disappointment fell all over Corrine, as she watched them laughing and talking.

Turning, she strode out the side door into the hallway. She didn't know what to do once she got there.

Wandering on into the kitchen, she found the two older Smith girls cleaning up the communion dishes, and Willie

Lee and Gabby sipping all the extra blessed wine out of the plastic container used to fill the little glasses.

"I don't think you should be drinkin' the wine, Willie Lee," Corrine said with some alarm.

One of the Smith girls said, "Oh, it's only grape juice. See—Welch's." She held up the bottle.

"Oh," Corrine said, quite surprised.

"It's 'cause all are invited to the Lord's table," the other Smith girl said. "We can't have drunk children all over the place."

Corrine observed the girls and her cousin and wondered at the propriety of the children drinking what was supposed to be sacred. It seemed awfully odd, all special one minute, and just plain old grape juice and bread another.

There was nothing in the kitchen to occupy her, and she wandered back to the sanctuary, where she ran into Jojo.

"I was lookin' for you. Here, wanna' orange slice?" Jojo offered Corrine candy from a bag she pulled out of her little purse.

"I haven't ever had these," she said, taking one of the candies.

"You haven't?" Jojo, chewing on a big bite, looked at her like she was from the moon.

Corrine shrugged. She didn't want to say the truth of it, that Aunt Marilee didn't allow them to have much candy, except chocolate. Since Aunt Marilee was such a chocoholic, she couldn't very well keep it from them.

It came to her that Aunt Marilee kept her and Willie Lee awfully sheltered.

This thought didn't get much exposure, though, because she glanced over to see Melissa moon all over Ricky Dale.

Jojo was now asking about Corrine's mother. "Did she come for Christmas?"

"Yeah." Corrine didn't figure she needed to explain that maybe her mother would stay in town. Probably she wouldn't, anyway.

Jojo, on her knees in the pew, just like a little child, gazed at Corrine's mother and said, "She sure is pretty."

Corrine started to tell her not to get her sticky hands on

the pew back, but then Jojo said, "You look just like her, too."

Corrine's response was to look at her mother, who was talking with Jojo's mother. Her mother was pretty, and in the low-lighted sanctuary, she did look beautiful. Corrine could not see herself in her mother. She wondered if what Jojo had said could possibly be true.

"How come you don't live with her?" Jojo asked.

Corrine didn't know what to say. "I..." She looked at the orange slice in her hand. "She got sick and out of work, so I came to live with Aunt Marilee. Then Mama moved to New Orleans, and I don't much want to go there." She shrugged and stuffed the candy in her mouth.

"Well, my dad run off," Jojo said.

"But..." Perplexed, Corrine looked at Jojo's father, who was in the knot of men where Papa Tate was talking.

"Oh, Mason's my stepdad. My real dad run off. He might be dead for all we know. No one's heard a peep from him in over a year now. Everyone says I look like him more than my mom. I guess I do."

She dug into the bag and handed Corrine another orange slice. Corrine said she rather liked them, but that they were awfully sweet.

Then Jojo said, "Mason's really great. I love him. He's been in prison, so he knows sufferin'." She drew out the words and leaned toward Corrine. "He killed a man."

Corrine did her best not to display a rude reaction to this amazing piece of information.

Jojo bit into an orange slice and continued, "It was an accident back in his torrid youth. It was over a woman. His first wife. He clobbered the man with a boot and killed him dead. Now Mason won't hit anyone, and he don't hardly raise his voice, either. Sometimes he fills in as a temporary deputy, but he won't carry a gun. Mama says no woman or man is worth somebody losin' their life over."

While she was speaking, Jojo held the bag of orange slices toward Corrine, who took one without thinking, because Jojo was continuing on with telling about her Uncle Freddy. "My Mama's brother..." who'd had a breakdown and had to go to the psychiatric ward at the hospital, and when he got out, he had moved off to Palm Springs, because his wife wanted to get out of Valentine. From there she went on to relate about her Aunt Rainey, who had married a man from a rich Houston family—Harry—a doctor who'd had, "something of a breakdown and become a psychiatrist."

"I had to go to Harry and talk sometimes, after my dad run off," she added. "I saw angels once. Have you ever seen any?"

Corrine stared at her. "Maybe," was all she could think to say.

"Harry says that children can see and hear things grown-ups can't. He didn't think it was strange that I saw angels."

"Oh."

Corrine, studying Jojo's sweet face, thought that she was getting information overload. She also had to decline any more candy, because she was feeling sick to her stomach.

Just then Jojo's father—or Mason—hollered for her and Charlene to come on and go home. He called Jojo, "Sweetheart," and Jojo said a quick, "See ya'," and scurried off to him. He looked at Jojo like she was ice cream or something and put his arm around her.

Watching his every movement and his face all grinning at Jojo, Corrine could not imagine Mason MacCoy as some criminal out of prison. He was the ex-rodeo cowboy who had reined in Melissa on her runaway horse that day during the Fourth of July Parade, and she had been crying and had fallen into his arms, and Corrine had watched him carry her like a baby doll.

Right that minute, as she watched Jojo go off with him, Corrine longed for a father as she never had before. Her gaze moved to Papa Tate.

Going over to him, she slipped up beside him very quietly and stood there. He glanced down at her and smiled, while continuing to talk with the sheriff. She got really close to him, and he put his arm around her and drew her right against him. She hardly dared breathe. He never did make any big deal out of it, and she was glad.

Later, as she followed her Aunt Marilee and mother to the

car, she looked at the other people getting into their cars and driving away. A quietness, like a sheltering warm blanket, came over her. It seemed like somehow she just knew and understood that how people looked and seemed on the outside might not be exactly how they were on the inside. It was as if she knew in that moment that people carried secrets inside, just like she did.

She thought about how Willie Lee had healed the pigeon, and she was the only one to have seen and to know. What if stuff like that happened all over, and no one knew, because no one ever told about it? Just like no one knew who was giving out money to people who needed it.

She looked at her aunt's and mother's heads in the front seat, at their shiny, soft hair, and listened to their voices talking about this person or that person, giving their true opinions of them, and private facts, such as this one wasn't speaking to her sister, and that one had to put her mother in a nursing home and was heartbroken over it.

Quite suddenly Corrine caught sight of herself in the rearview mirror. She felt older, and she thought she looked it, too. Especially with her ears pierced.

In Corrine's thoughtful state, she soon remembered the horses and became very sad. She wanted to go home, to her room, but she went along with everyone to the drugstore soda fountain, because if she didn't, Aunt Marilee would quiz her about why she wasn't feeling well, and likely she wouldn't get to go home and be alone, because Aunt Marilee would come to look after her, make her something hot to drink and fuss over her.

When she trailed into the drugstore behind Willie Lee and Munro, she breathed in the familiar scents of musty wood mixed with barbeque and coffee, and now Aunt Vella's latte. It was a scent that made her feel snuggled. She set herself down at the rear table next to Uncle Perry, who was already there and who winked at her and said, "Hey, you." They sat there together and watched people just streaming in and streaming out.

The drugstore was three times busier than normal, and

Aunt Vella said she praised God that people needed to shop and eat themselves into aspirin and antacid. Several times Uncle Perry was called on to get up and help someone pick out a remedy of some sort. Mostly he offered aspirin to everyone. "It's as good a remedy as anything...that or a nap," he said.

Willie Lee took the nap advice to heart. He went to Uncle Perry's old recliner chair in the back of the pharmacy and went to sleep.

Belinda, doing her work of shopping, had the television hanging over the soda fountain going on one shopping channel or another; she kept changing it when something was offered that didn't interest her. A woman Corrine knew only by occasional sight had set herself down on a stool at the fountain and was using her cell phone to do her shopping along with Belinda. She got a little annoyed when Belinda changed the channel when she wasn't ready.

The girl who was working at the soda fountain was about to run herself to death, so Aunt Marilee and Papa Tate pitched in to make their lunches and ended up working behind the counter for half an hour. Papa Tate loved it. He kept getting all the customers talking, so it took him twice as long to get people served and out of the way. Once there was a line three deep all along behind the counter stools.

The conversation centered around the mystery gifts of money and lots of wild speculation as to who was the mystery Santa.

"I figure it's somebody new in town," said Deputy Lyle Midgette, and he looked at Corrine's mother, who had on her fur coat and did look awfully rich right that minute.

Her mother laughed a big laugh and said that she would love to be the Santa Claus giving out money. Then Papa Tate reminded them all that the first money had been given out well before Corrine's mother had come to town, and anyway, a stranger in town would not know all that the Santa appeared to know about the people who were getting the money.

Someone said maybe the mystery Santa was Papa Tate. He

said, "I thank you for the compliment, and I wish I were. And my banker wishes I were, so I could pay off my debts."

Corrine thought that Papa Tate would do something like giving away money, if he had it to give. The memory came to her of the time when Aunt Marilee had sent her to his office to tell him that supper was ready, and she had stood in the door and seen him bent over his computer, a horribly worried look on his face as he worked on balancing their bank account.

Papa Tate hid his worry, she realized, watching him at that moment laugh and talk. Only if you caught him by surprise would you see his worried side.

When the mayor came in for two lattes to go, someone asked him if he was the mystery money-bag Santa. "My wife'd kill me if I tried somethin' like that," he said, as if speaking of something illegal. Corrine thought the answer so funny.

She laughed and looked over to see Uncle Perry laughing, too, in a quiet way. Then he winked at her.

As the mayor left, the sheriff came in. He was so big, he took up the whole door, and right behind him came Ricky Dale!

"There hasn't been proven to be a crime with this thing. There's a lot of speculation, but that's all, so I'm not investigatin' anything," the sheriff said, when he was questioned right off. "Gerald's runnin' a few serial numbers from George Mann's money. That's all I know." He seemed a little tired of the matter. He told Papa Tate that he wanted eight barbeque sandwiches to go.

Ricky Dale didn't seem to see Corrine, who kept her gaze downward while stirring the straw around in her Coke. With covert glances, she saw him go over to the magazine shelves.

Okay, Melissa isn't here now.

She got up and crossed the room to the magazine rack that was near the window. Halfway there, she wished she had put on lip gloss. Thinking of her pierced ears gave her courage. She wasn't some little kid.

"Hey," she said.

"Well, hey, Corky." He was surprised, and he seemed pleased, too. "What's up?"

Well, now what was she supposed to say?

"Just hangin' out." She saw he held a motorcycle magazine. "Is that what you want for Christmas?" She indicated the motorcycle on the cover.

"Yeah," he said. "I can't drive one of these yet...not a real cycle, but I can a little scooter. You know, one like Jim White's got. I've been on his a time or two. It makes gettin' around a lot easier."

She nodded and said that she imagined it would. "Is it hard to ride?" She didn't think it would be, but the question was all she could think to say.

"Oh, no. It's real easy. Just like ridin' a bike," he said. "You could do it."

Corrine figured of course she could do it, but she didn't say this. She said instead, "Leanne's sold the filly. The man's comin' to get her tomorrow, and on Tuesday, Leanne's movin' the mare up to her place." She was annoyed with herself for bringing up the subject.

"Oh." His green eyes clouded, and he frowned. "Well, it was cool this past year, takin' care of them."

"Yeah, it was."

"Remember that day that Willie Lee saved the filly?"

She nodded, and then she found herself gazing into his green eyes for long seconds, sharing the stream of memory without words.

Just then his father called him to leave. "See ya' at school tomorrow," he said, moving quickly, because when the sheriff said move, you moved.

"Yeah, see ya'."

She went back to the table where Aunt Marilee and her mother were now sitting with Uncle Perry. They gave her speculative looks and smiles, and she felt silly. But not as silly as Ricky Dale, who popped back in the door and hurried over to the cash register to pay for the motorcycle magazine that he had accidentally carried out and forgotten to buy.

He cast her a wave as he left that second time.

* * *

She thought about going to the corral to say goodbye to the horses, but she decided against it, mostly because the weather was still cloudy and cold, and if she went to the corral, someone would have to take her, and she couldn't bear for anyone to be with her when she told them goodbye. Better to not go at all. Likely the horses would not notice.

She profoundly regretted her choice and the missed opportunity the next afternoon, when she and Willie Lee were coming back from the post office with the mail and chanced to see the filly being driven out of town.

She and Willie Lee were waiting to cross the street in front of the police station when the Littleton Ranch truck and fancy aluminum horse trailer pulled up for the stoplight. Wade Littleton was in the driver's seat. Corrine could make out a horse head through the smoky plastic window of the horse trailer, or at least she imagined that she could.

Just then the horse whinnied. It was Sweet Sugar's whinny.

"That is the fil-ly," Willie Lee said.

"I know." Corrine kept staring at the trailer and watched as the truck crossed the intersection and headed away, taking the filly.

Sweet Sugar was gone. And she hadn't said goodbye. How could she have done that?

On their way up the stairs to the apartment, Willie Lee said, "You could write a let-ter to ask San-ta Claus to bring you the fil-ly. That is what I did." Then he put his hand over his mouth.

Corrine only faintly noticed that Willie Lee looked odd and what he had said. "I guess," she said.

Willie Lee told Aunt Marilee and her mother and Papa Tate, too, who was in the kitchen, about seeing the trailer taking the filly away. Her mother asked if Corrine wanted to drive up and see the mare.

At first Corrine shook her head, doing her best to act unconcerned as she dug into the refrigerator and brought out a bottle of juice.

Then, standing there and gripping the bottle, she said, "Yes. I'd like to go see the mare. She's alone now."

Her mother and aunt about knocked their chairs over getting up. They looked so horribly distressed that she wished she had never let on. Both of them got their coats and took her. At least they didn't say anything to her. Not a word on the way there, although she caught her mother looking anxiously at her, and Aunt Marilee looked at her in the rearview mirror.

Leanne's red pickup was in the yard, but she was not in sight. The mare was trotting back and forth at the fence, snorting in agitation. She gave a distressed whinny when Corrine got out of the car. Thankfully, her aunt and mother remained in the car and let her go alone.

Corrine climbed up on the rails, and the mare came over to sniff her. "Oh, Miss Queen." She reached out to pet the mare, but the horse allowed only a swift caress before she ran along the fence again, stretching her neck, looking for the filly.

Leaving her alone, Corrine went into the corral and filled the water tank and did a swift job of cleaning the stall. Just before she left, the mare came over and allowed her to hug her neck.

"Goodbye," Corrine said softly, her heart breaking into a thousand pieces.

Turning, she hurried out the gate and over to throw herself into the car, where she slammed the door and said, "Don't ask me if I'm okay."

The Valentine Voice

Christmas About Town
by Marilee Holloway

Good News! Santa Claus is alive and well in Valentine! That big jolly old elf has been spreading his cheer all over town with surprise gifts. A few to receive gifts are Mayor Upchurch, who found a beautiful gold pen on his desk; the Richard Hardy family, who received a Christmas tree, fully decorated, on their front porch; and Mrs. Minnie Oakes, who found a kitten in a basket on her back step. Each gift came with a note that said, *Merry Christmas, from Santa.*

To help all of Santa's helpers, we have some good suggestions for gifts for that special woman in your life: gift certificates for ballroom dancing lessons at Myerberg Dance Studio and for a pedicure from the Cut and Curl Beauty Salon, basket of massage oils for feminine feet (available at Blaine's Drugstore) and the promise to give the massage once a week, a Sunday drive in the country, and my favorite idea of the magical bath, which consists of a fragrant, hot bubble bath with lit candles all around the tub, soothing music and big warm towels, all prepared and waiting for the woman in your life. Believe it or not, ladies, this idea was phoned in by a man. He did not leave his name, but Charlotte and I shall be listening to voices to see if we can identify him.

Ideas for men are running thin. Only two men phoned in suggestions, and so Charlotte and I went out and asked. The results are: five men wanted cordless drills, and they each already had drills but said one could not have too many drills; six men named various computer gadgets and accessories; four men wanted automotive accessories, and two said they'd like sets of action movies. One said he wanted anything that wasn't underwear or touchy-feely stuff, and another's suggestion cannot be printed here, so use your imagination.

Congratulations to the winners of the Outstanding Christmas Yard Awards! First prize goes to Odessa Collier, Second prize to Iris and Adam MacCoy, and Third prize to Stella and Leon Purvis. Honorable Mentions go to Ms. Lila Hicks, Mr. and Mrs. Jaydee Mayhall, and the J. Macomb family. We at the *Voice*, and personally the Holloway family, thank you all for your hard work and imagination in decorating and thus providing a feast for the eyes and spirit for all people in our community.

If you have not visited around town to see the light displays, you're missing a real treat. Afterward, our family recommends a stop at the Main Street Café for a hot drink and pie.

Our recipe today is from Mrs. Franny Holloway, who says she has always made this for the men in her life on Christmas Eve. She said that if the man who suggested the romantic bath identifies himself to her, she will make him a big bowl.

Heavenly Ambrosia

3 large oranges, preferably navel variety, peeled and sectioned
3 bananas, firm
1 small can pineapple tidbits, or fresh equivalent
1 red delicious apple, chopped in small pieces
1 1/2 cups shredded coconut

Mix the pineapple tidbits and chopped apple together; helps to keep the apple from getting brown. Using a dish that is not too deep, or individual cups, layer alternately each fruit, topping each layer with the shredded coconut. Sprinkle coconut on the top and add mint leaves for decoration.

Note: Franny said every day's a new day for her, and she was guessing at the measurements for the ingredients.

Our thanks to all for sending recipes. We do not need any more for this column; however, we've accumulated so many wonderful ones, that we have decided to begin work on a cookbook that will be a fund-raiser for our planned new library. We'll begin with recipes for salads. Please send those you want to share to Charlotte, either by e-mail at charlotteconroy@thevalentinevoice.com or by regular mail to the newspaper. We are not taking recipes by phone, as they tend to lose ingredients and measures in the shuffle. Thank you for your cooperation, which we know you mean to give but often forget.

20

∞

All the mystery gifts of money had seemed to spark a lot of gift-giving in general, some recognized and some anonymous.

When the news got around about how little Kevin Mann had written the letter to Santa, asking for help for his father so that he wouldn't worry so much, and how the family had lost their wife and mother in a car wreck that had incurred sizable medical and funeral debt, everyone was touched. People and stores all over town were giving the Mann family all sorts of things.

Wilson's Christmas Tree Farm gave them a free tree, and Aunt Vella admitted to pitching in with ornaments. The IGA delivered several boxes of groceries and a certificate for a free large Christmas dinner, and Fayrene called Mr. Mann and told him to bring his children in to the Main Street Café for a free meal to celebrate. They came and had the meatloaf special, and Fayrene sent them home with two pies, raisin and apple. Everyone said Fayrene was the most generous woman in the country. Then the Community Bank, whose slogan was "The bank that cares," announced a beginning savings account for each of the four children, for their college education, in the amount of $50 apiece.

Aunt Vella rolled her eyes at this news. "Who does Gerald think he is foolin'? It's the bank's own money stayin' at the bank. Why didn't he make himself look better by making it a hundred dollars a child? He still wouldn't be out any real money."

In the midst of all the giving to the Mann family, reports began to surface of people receiving other types of secret Santa gifts. The mayor, the Hardy family and Miss Minnie were only the beginning. By Wednesday afternoon, Corrine had heard that Miss Laura Dewberry had received, wrapped on her desk, a full-color glossy art book, and that Becky Rhudy's grandmother had come home to find her yard raked and fig tree covered for a hard winter, and Jaydee Mayhall's secretary had received a basket of essential oils along with a candle burner, which she was crazy over. Along with each gift had been the little note from Santa.

Papa Tate made it his business to go see all the notes that he could, and reported back that some read, *from Santa* and some, *from Santa Claus*. Some had been handwritten and some were typed, and one was print cut from a publication. He did not find that any of the handwritten ones appeared similar.

Lots of the kids at school were still talking about writing letters to Santa, asking for money for this or that, and when Corrine and Willie Lee stopped in to the IGA on their way home from school, the checkout girl was telling the Coca-Cola delivery guy about having written her letter to tell Santa that she wanted to go to college, just like the Murphy girl had done. The checkout girl was so intent on the delivery guy, who was quite a hunk, that Corrine didn't see any need in mentioning that it was only the little Mann boy who had written to Santa and not any of the others who had received money. Corrine did not think the girl would appreciate being interrupted. As it was, Corrine had to wait for her change while the girl tore herself away from pushing her rather sizable breasts out at the muscular delivery guy in order to count the money into Corrine's hand.

Corrine found that all the talk and speculation about the secret Santa did help her not to think so much about her sadness over the horses. She had, in fact, begun to find herself caught up in the notion of writing her own letter to Santa Claus, which she kept telling herself was a really stupid thing to do. There was no need to believe she would get a horse that way, and thinking so would only lead to more disappointment. There was no money for a horse and nowhere to keep a horse, and the entire idea was only a stupid fantasy.

And any time she thought of another horse, besides the mare or the filly, her heart did a deep dip. It was possible that all of her life she would want those two horses and that no others would do.

Just then Willie Lee said her name, and she realized that he had stopped behind her. He needed her to help him open the package of his Bama pie. She gave him hers that she had already opened but not yet bitten out of and took his.

As she went to open the package, she caught sight of Uncle Perry's big black Cadillac gliding through the rear entry of the IGA parking lot and over to stop in front of the mailbox.

As Uncle Perry got out, Corrine tapped Willie Lee's shoulder. "Come on. Uncle Perry will give us a ride down to the drugstore. Hey, Uncle Perry!" she hollered to him.

He looked around at her, and the next instant he tripped and was falling forward. His arms flailed out, reaching for the fender of his car but missing, and he went tumbling to the pavement, his knees hitting first.

Corrine raced to him. "Uncle Perry...Uncle Perry, are you all right?"

He had tripped over the concrete parking barrier. He was braced on his knees and one hand and one elbow. He was breathing hard, and the back of his neck, which was the only place she could see very well, was bloodred against his white hair. She bent to try to see his face, and at that moment he let out a painful, "Ohhh," and turned to drop on his bottom.

One good look at his flushed face, eyes squeezed closed,

and trembling arms, and she told Willie Lee to go into the IGA and tell them to call the paramedics. Willie Lee went immediately, and Corrine hollered after him, "Go to the girl at the checkout."

As Willie Lee ran in his awkward gait, she had the thought that she should have gone instead. She sure hoped the girl wasn't still captivated by the Coca-Cola guy.

"Uncle Perry, maybe you should lay down." Crouching close, she touched his arm. His eyes were still closed in pain, and his hands were braced on the rough pavement. The flush was leaving his face, draining away, except for his nose, where the veins were bloodred.

Oh, if only she hadn't hollered at him. He wouldn't have tripped.

"No," he said in a breathless manner. Then his eyes opened. "My letters..." He looked around. "I had..."

"There they are. I'll get 'em for you." She scrambled to get the two envelopes scattered some feet away, wanting to do anything she could to ease his distress.

"Mail 'em," he said to her in a hoarse voice. "Get 'em in the mailbox." He gestured and winced as he did so. "Get 'em in!"

"Okay. I will," she said, eager to please. If he'd asked her to jump ten feet in the air, she would have done her best to do it in that moment.

She went to the mailbox, and just as she lifted the envelopes into the opening, she looked at them. They were padded manila envelopes of the five by seven size. She felt them at the same time that she looked at the addresses, which were typed.

It was the money.

Well, one surely was money. The other maybe not.

Uncle Perry was the Santa Claus money man?

She read the addresses: Billy Gomez on one, and Mrs. Rose Fletcher on the other. She repeated the names, pressing them into her memory, as she dropped the envelopes into the mailbox.

Returning to Uncle Perry, who had gone frighteningly

white, she looked up and saw Willie Lee running toward them, hollering, "They are com-ing!"

When he reached them, he went on his knees and said hi to Uncle Perry, who attempted to grin at him.

Uncle Perry was breathing in an erratic manner, and Corrine had the awful fear that he might be having a heart attack. She looked at Willie Lee. "Do you think you could..."

But Willie Lee shook his head. "I can-not with-out Munro."

"Munro?"

Willie Lee nodded.

Just then they heard the siren, and seconds later the red paramedic truck came pulling into the lot at the same time that Mr. Juice Tinsley, owner of the IGA, came running out of the store with his stained bakery apron flapping in the air. "That girl just now told me!" he said. "Hey, Perry...man, we're gonna get you taken care of."

Just as the paramedic truck stopped and two paramedics hopped out, Aunt Vella's Land Rover pulled into the lot. She was going so fast that for an instant Corrine was afraid she might crash into the paramedic truck. The Land Rover's wheels squealed as Aunt Vella stomped on the brake.

In the kitchen, Corrine poured them each a glass of milk. She looked down at Munro, who was lying on the rug in front of the sink. "Munro helps you heal animals?" she asked Willie Lee.

He nodded as he drank from his glass. "Yes. Mun-ro does it with me."

Corrine looked again at the ragged little dog lying curled on the rug and then at her cousin, who had a white milk mustache over his lip.

She was badly tempted to tell him about Uncle Perry being the Santa money man, but doubts had begun to assail her. It would be really bad to tell Willie Lee or anyone and then be wrong. Besides, Willie Lee had enough secrets to handle.

She got the mail from the post office and came back across the street in order to pass by the saddle shop. The colorful

Christmas lights up and down the street were becoming very bright in the growing dimness, and with the holiday shoppers, there was a lot more traffic, both vehicles and pedestrians, flowing up and down the street.

A car driving past slowed, and the woman on the passenger side hollered a merry Christmas to a woman who walked ahead of Corrine. The woman called gaily back: "Merry Christmas to you!"

"What is Santa bringin' you for Christmas?" asked the woman in the car.

"Well, you know what? I got a gift from Santa...." The woman walked to the car that had stopped in the middle of the street. People stopped on Main Street to talk all the time.

Corrine wondered what the woman had gotten.

Then she was at the window of the saddle shop and stopped to look in, gazing at the saddle of her dreams while melancholy memories of the horses washed over her, and she told herself, "Someday, I will...someday." Someday seemed not only very far away but impossible.

Tearing her gaze from the saddle—which she noticed remained at the same price, unlikely to be marked down any further, and what did she care anyway?—she saw that a number of small and inexpensive items had been added to the front of the window. There was a leather hair clasp, a small billfold, and several knives in leather holders to go on the belt.

And there was a small pocketknife. Price: $10.

After biting her bottom lip and studying the knife for half a minute, she then hurried inside and pointed out to Mrs. Silverhorn what she wanted from the display window. Mrs. Silverhorn even wrapped the knife for her, and Corrine came out of the store with the small package safely tucked into her jacket pocket, while her mind went over possible ways of slipping it to Ricky Dale as a secret Santa gift.

"Corrine!" It was Leanne hollering from her big truck. Her horse trailer was hooked to the rear—and the mare was there and whinnied.

Corrine's step faltered, and then she ran out to the truck. Leanne scooted over to the passenger window. "Here, hon. I have your payment that I've been meanin' to drop off at the newspaper."

"Thanks." Corrine reached up and took the envelope.

"Oh, honey, it's I who thanks you. You took such good care of the filly and mare." Leanne jerked her thumb in the direction of the trailer. "You want to go speak to her?"

Corrine nodded and went back to the trailer and stepped up on the running board. The mare peered at her through the slats.

"You take care of yourself," Corrine said in a ragged whisper. "I love you." She hopped down and ran forward to the passenger window, where she called thanks again, then waved as she raced between the parked cars and hopped up on the sidewalk.

The big diesel truck chugged as Leanne hit the accelerator. Keeping herself from turning to look at the trailer, Corrine ran the opposite way down the sidewalk and into the stairwell to their apartment, where she threw herself down on the steps and tried to muffle her sobs in the sleeve of her jacket. She was sure mad at having seen the mare again, after she had already told her goodbye at the corral.

It struck her with a suddenness that she loved the mare most of all. The filly was fun and Corrine loved her, but the mare had been a patient guide and teacher. And now she was gone.

She slipped quietly into the apartment. The television was on but no one in sight. Someone was in the kitchen, likely Aunt Marilee. Laying the mail on her aunt's desk as she passed, Corrine went on to the bathroom to wash away the traces of tears with a cold rag.

When she removed her jacket, the envelope Leanne had given her fell out of the pocket. Opening it, she found a check for two hundred dollars.

Well, it looked like Leanne was *her* Santa money man.

Willie Lee was in his room, asleep on his bed, with all his clothes on. It wasn't Aunt Marilee in the kitchen, but Corrine's mother, who was making a good attempt to cook supper.

It was a sight that opened Corrine's eyes and made the thought of telling about Leanne's generous check fly right out of her mind: her mother with gold filigree earrings swaying, a denim apron covering her silk blouse and wool trousers, moving around the kitchen in her patent leather shoes.

She said to Corrine, "Oh, I am so glad to see you. I've had the greatest idea! Let's do one of those baths for your Aunt Marilee like she wrote about in her column. Have you read her column?"

Corrine said that she had read the column. She stood there blinking. There was flour on her mother's nose. Her mother was about as happy and excited as Corrine had ever seen her.

"We'll surprise Marilee with supper and the bath," her mother said. "She won't have to do anything when she comes in. Won't that be fun?"

Corrine didn't want to spoil her mother's happiness, so she said yes, she thought it would be fun. She thought but didn't say that she hoped the meal would be edible. The lamb chops looked on the well-done side to her. She pitched in to do what she could with the meal and the dirty dishes. It looked like her mother had used every pan and every available inch of counter space. It was going to take hours to clean the kitchen, a job she knew would fall mainly to her. Luckily she knew herself to be very capable for the endeavor.

Shortly, however, Corrine found herself having the most fun she had ever had with her mother. They put their minds together on making the elaborate meal and decorating as if for a party, and in the process they even began to finish each other's sentences.

Together they set the table with the good linen and china and silver, and then they created a decorative centerpiece of a ring of goblets with candles floating in water. When Aunt Marilee telephoned that she was on her way from the hospital, they hurried to the bathroom to get it prepared for the "romantic bath experience," as her mother referred to it.

Papa Tate came to the doorway, having come up from his office, where he'd been working on his book. He had brought pages and held them in his hand, looking expectant for someone to hear what he had written.

Paying absolutely no attention to his hopeful expression or the pages in his hand, Corrine's mother said to him, "Tate, you can use the bathroom, but don't mess up anything we've done in there."

At that moment Willie Lee appeared and wanted to use the bathroom, so Papa Tate took him downstairs to the one in the *Voice* offices. Ten minutes later, the two reappeared, running up the stairs and through the door and calling in hushed voices, "She's comin'," then sat themselves out of the way at the table, where they could watch.

When Aunt Marilee came in, Corrine's mother stood ready with slippers and a robe, while Corrine waited to take her aunt's coat to hang up.

Aunt Marilee looked quite surprised, and then she laughed and waved away the robe. "Oh, it's very nice of you, but I…"

Something stopped her. Perhaps it was the way Corrine's mother was gazing at her, or perhaps it was that she could hear Corrine's loud thoughts: "Get in the dang robe and don't ruin it all."

"Oh, I can use this," she said with appreciation as she slipped into the robe and slippers, and then, on sight of the table, "Thank you…well, my goodness…my goodness."

Luckily her chair faced away from the kitchen doorway. Corrine had not gotten the mess cleaned up very well as yet, and her aunt wouldn't have been able to stand it.

"Uncle Perry'll be in the hospital for a few more days," Aunt Marilee told them over supper, which, surprisingly, had not turned out all that badly.

She went on to explain that not only did he have a broken ankle and cracked wrist, but further tests were to be done.

"Uncle Perry has had some vertigo over the past few months, and it looks like his blood pressure is dangerously high. You know he won't ever go to the doctor. Well, anyway, they're goin' to run tests while they have him."

Papa Tate mentioned that he had noticed Uncle Perry's

forgetfulness and that he'd seen the man fall once a few weeks back.

To that, Aunt Marilee said firmly, "It isn't anything serious. The doctors just want to be thorough."

Corrine saw Papa Tate and her mother exchange glances.

She wondered about Uncle Perry really being the Santa money man. Her doubts had grown, and she began to think she might have jumped to conclusions. She kept seeing his white face in memory and hoped he was going to be okay. Her worry about this escalated at a rapid rate to imagine Uncle Perry dying and the effect this would have on Aunt Vella and then on Aunt Marilee.

Imagining her aunt's upset caused a little panic. Corrine felt responsible for the whole thing, but then her aunt was saying, "It was very fortuitous for you two to have seen him fall." She smiled at Corrine and Willie Lee with a great deal of pride and asked Corrine to tell what had happened.

Corrine collected herself to act perfectly natural, because if she got upset, Aunt Marilee would be upset. The story was easy to tell, minus her part of mailing the envelopes. There were two strong voices in her head, one saying she should always tell the truth and must tell about the envelopes, and the other saying not to do that and blow Uncle Perry's secret. Her loyalty to Uncle Perry won out. He should be the one to tell, if he wanted. She hoped Aunt Marilee couldn't read her mind, and as a diversion, she made a big deal of how Willie Lee had been the one to get the girl to call the paramedics.

"The girl would not lis-ten to me, but the man in the Co-ca-Co-la shirt did," he said.

Aunt Marilee stayed in her romantic bath for almost an hour. After helping clear the dishes, Corrine's mother went to check on her and did not return. Going to check on the both of them, Corrine lifted her hand to knock on the door, but the sound of the women's light laughter caused her to pause. She tilted her head closer to the door, captivated by the low and warm tones of the voices on the other side.

Her mother and her aunt together, enjoying themselves.

Aunt Marilee laughed. Water splashed. Her mother hollered, "Oh, no...I'll get you!" More splashing water.

She returned to the kitchen and told Papa Tate, who was typing away on his novel, that he was out of luck for the bathroom any time soon.

Papa Tate answered the phone, and Corrine heard him say, "Good evenin', Miz Julia," and all but stretched her ear a foot. Within a few words on Papa Tate's part, her mother and aunt shut up and listened, too, as it appeared certain he was learning of more money gifts.

He said, "I see," and "They didn't mind?" and "Did you notice the dates? Ah, yep. Thank you, Julia."

When he hung up, Papa Tate said with pure delight, "Well, our Santa Claus has been busy again. Miz Julia found two envelopes she suspected as being from this secret Santa in today's mail and made a special delivery of each of them and had the recipients open the envelopes in front of her, in order to see if she was correct."

"Boy, talk about goin' above and beyond as a postmistress," Corrine's mother commented.

"And aren't we glad?" Aunt Marilee said, praising the woman for a change.

Corrine said somewhat breathlessly, "So, who got it and for how much?"

"Mrs. Rose Fletcher...five hundred dollars..."

Corrine watched Papa Tate's lips keep on moving, but her mind sort of took over with, *ohmygosh, ohmygosh!*

"Who got the other envelope?" she asked, regarding him intently.

"One Mr. Billy Gomez, who got fifteen hundred that'll get him some new teeth that..."

Oh-my-gosh! Uncle Perry really was the secret Santa money man! She had been correct after all.

Immediately, with the thought, she checked herself to make certain she appeared unruffled. She listened to Papa Tate add the further information that the postmistress said the money was old, some being silver certificates. And that she had come to believe the envelopes contained money by carefully feeling them. She had assured Papa Tate that she did not usually snoop. He said this with great amusement, and Aunt Marilee and Corrine's mother laughed outright.

"This is great," Aunt Marilee said happily. "There's a Santa Claus. There is," she said to Willie Lee, who grinned at her.

Captivated by the news, her mother decided to stay for another cup of coffee and to speculate at length just who might be giving away the money, and where such money had come from.

Corrine, safeguarding herself from saying anything that might give Uncle Perry away, took herself off to bed, where she lay listening to the murmur of the adults' voices from the dining room. She tried to stay awake and listen as long as possible. She wanted to hear them be content with each other. If she could hear them be content, even happy, with each other and with life at the moment, then she didn't have to worry about them. And hearing them be content with each other comforted the hole in her heart that losing the horses had caused.

She kept her attention on the adults' voices and drifted into sleep.

"Perry? Sugar, are you hurtin'?"

He cracked his eyes to see Vella's face peering at him. He was startled to see that she looked so old. He must have said this, because she said, "I *am* old, dear."

Then she went away. He blinked and saw her at the mirror over by the sink.

Then it came to him that he had been dreaming, and in his dream he had been a boy and Vella a girl. Just kids, as they had once been. He was annoyed at her for waking him up.

She returned and asked him again if he was hurting.

"Not till you leaned on my leg," he said.

"I'm not leanin' on your leg, Perry. Are you sure you're okay?"

"I'm in the hospital with broken bones and doctors thinkin' I'm losin' my mind," he said. "No, I'm not okay."

She patted him. He hated it when she patted him. "They do not think you are losin' your mind." She sounded tired.

It shook him when Vella sounded tired, which she was doing more and more.

He closed his eyes and heard her move over to the recliner, where she was spending the night. Imagine, a recliner in the hospital. The hospitals he recalled didn't have those. And relatives didn't get to stay.

Perry had never been in the hospital himself. He had dispensed medicines for over forty years and knew what to take and what not to take, and he credited that with keeping himself out of hospitals.

But here he was.

They did think he was losing his mind, and he thought he might be, too. It scared him something awful. He'd been looking back at his life a lot for the past year, as he'd finally retired and found himself going headlong through his seventies. He had not liked what he had seen. He had never done anything. He had gotten Vella pregnant and married her. He hadn't even gone to war; he had slipped through with having two children and being necessary to his father at the pharmacy. Having sex with Vella and them not being married was probably the most daring thing he had ever done, and if truth be known, he had not had much say in it, as it was Vella who had led him to it. In all his life, he had only had sex with one woman, and that was Vella.

Of course, she had really been something in their prime years.

But he'd not had enough get up and go to keep getting it up. That had been a major disappointment to Vella. He never found that he cared very much, except for disappointing her. And he knew that he had been a big disappointment to her. He was a disappointment to himself.

The passion that other people—Winston, for instance—had was a mystery to him. Winston had gotten in more fights as a teen and had enjoyed women all over the place. Perry had been born a boy who went along and grew into a man who went along. It had all seemed perfectly all right all those years, but then, when he thought he might be losing his mind, he had gotten this very empty feeling about his life.

Then the money had come to him, and he'd started giving

it away, and he felt so great about that. It was like a gift from God, a second chance at experiencing life as he wished he could have lived it.

It was over now, though. He didn't even get to finish it before he got finished. He was going to die, and they were going to find what was left of the money and the envelopes underneath the seat of his Cadillac. Everyone would know then that he'd been the Santa Claus. He guessed that was something.

Maybe they wouldn't find the money. Maybe they'd sell the Cadillac and eventually it would get to the junkyard, and the money would rot away, and no one would ever know.

This thought was so depressing that it threw him back to sleep, where his dreams were better than his life.

He stood on the sidewalk of Main Street, and the wind was blowing hard. He had trouble getting to the door of the drugstore. It was time to open the store, and he was late. He saw his reflection in the glass of the door. He was surprised that he had so much hair, and it was dark.

Then he was in the drugstore, and sitting right there at a table in the soda fountain was Santa Claus.

"Hello, Perry, I've come to get your Christmas list."

"I don't have one."

"Oh, sure you do. Tell me what you want."

Perry told Santa that he wanted a new television and VCR. Santa smiled and nodded and said, "What else."

Perry did want something else, but he couldn't remember what it was. That made him mad.

But Santa just smiled and nodded, like he had heard and said, "You've been a good boy.... God bless you, son." And he patted Perry.

Then he was awakened by the fool nurse who was patting him and saying it was time to take a pill. Dang fool hospitals could kill a person, and that pill-taking could *definitely* kill a person. He thought to ask her what sort of pill he was taking, but he didn't have the heart to care.

21
∾

"I've had an idea," Aunt Marilee said to her. "Tomorrow is your last day of school before Christmas break. Let's celebrate by goin' out and stayin' the night with your mother at the motel. We can have a sleepover party and eat popcorn and chocolate and paint our nails."

Corrine had forgotten that Friday was the last day of school. Quite suddenly she saw the vacation yawning wide before her, and without the horses.

Then she realized her aunt was looking at her with high expectation, so Corrine said, "O-kay," then, "But there's only one bed in her room."

"Oh, her room has a connecting door to the room next to it. She already told me. I'll call out there and reserve it, and then we'll tell your mother our surprise tonight."

Corrine didn't think it was much of a surprise, but she didn't say this. Her aunt was terribly excited and said, "Won't it be fun?"

Corrine agreed it would be fun, and, in fact, she found herself looking forward to the experience. A little later, though, as she was heading out the door for Papa Tate to take them to school, a thought popped into her mind: Which one of them would she sleep with?

This was a daunting thought. If she chose Aunt Marilee, her mother would feel left out, and if she chose her mother, Aunt Marilee would feel left out. Her enthusiasm for the sleepover began to slip.

Maybe the adjoining room would have two double beds. She sure hoped so.

Immediately at school, she heard from Jojo, who came up to Corrine's locker, about several students receiving secret Santa gifts.

"A girl in my English class, Penny Lewis, got a bead necklace," Jojo said. "She found it in her desk, and it had the note from Santa, and so did the cross necklace Darla Rae found in her home room desk this mornin'. But Cory Gilbert found a harmonica in his tennis shoe after he took a shower after gym, and it didn't have a note, just the harmonica. He asked around, thinkin' maybe someone had lost it, but I mean, how would someone lose it in his shoe?" She shook her head.

With a small thrill of excitement, Corrine put her hand into her denim vest pocket and felt Ricky Dale's present. "I gotta get to class," she told Jojo as she saw Ricky Dale at his locker. She headed away, intending to pass by, maybe nudge him and have to apologize, although that idea didn't seem too reasonable at the moment, as the hallway was not too crowded. She hesitated, and with that hesitation, she lost her opportunity, because Ricky Dale slammed his locker closed and headed away down the hall. Then first bell rang, and Corrine had to get herself to her own class.

She kept a lookout all day, waiting for her chance, which began to seem less and less promising, as she had little reason to be around him. Surely she could go up and talk to him. Or maybe she could get to the desk he used in home room.

By algebra class that afternoon, which they shared, she had worked out the strategy of asking him to explain a problem they were to have done for that day. She hurried over

to him before the bell and asked. He looked at her oddly—
she never had trouble with a problem—but he went over
the figures with her. The entire time, she tried to figure out
how to slip the present into his coat pocket without anyone
seeing.

"Got it now, Corky?"

"Yeah, thanks."

"You bet. Glad I could help." He really did seem thrilled
to have helped her with a problem. Corrine thought maybe
she was beginning to understand what her mother and aunt
had been trying to tell her. Except she felt as if she had been
lying to him by saying that she couldn't do something that
she could do very well, and she didn't see why she would
have to act stupid to make a boy interested in her.

The bell rang, and she still had the present in her pocket.
She was thoroughly disgusted. She sat in her desk two rows
over from Ricky Dale's and considered the situation.

Then, barely five minutes into class, a great thing happened. The fire alarms started going off.

Corrine about jumped out of her chair, and someone
screamed, and there was a bit of scuffling as everyone got
up. No one was in much of a hurry, though, as they all
figured it was just a fire drill.

The substitute teacher they had for the day didn't think
this. She got a little hysterical at everyone's slowness and
began yelling for them all to get moving. She ran out when
only half the kids were through the door.

Corrine saw Ricky Dale leave his desk, and leave his school
coat hanging on the back of his chair. He didn't come back
for it.

Hurrying the two rows over and up past his desk, she pretended to stumble and bent low enough to drop the small
package into the pocket of his coat.

She could not believe it had been that easy.

The alarm turned out not to be a drill after all. When she
finally got outside with all the other kids, a fire truck and
the sheriff were wailing up to the front, and firemen in
heavy gear and carrying an ax or two went trooping inside.
The kids and teachers watched with wide eyes, and some

kids clapped. Then they had to stand outside in the wind for about twenty minutes, while the firemen and then the sheriff searched all over the place for the fire.

Paris Miller said, "I'm out here...I might as well go on home," and she headed away down the sidewalk. If any teachers saw her, they didn't stop her.

Corrine, in her vest over her shirt, wasn't too cold, but a lot of the girls just had on little T-shirts and short skirts. Those girls huddled together and either held down their shirts or their hair in the wind.

It turned out there wasn't a fire. Gideon Brown, Anson's brother and fellow wiseman player, had pulled the alarm. He had been seen by another boy, who told on him. Boy, did Gideon get in trouble. Principal Blankenship came out and jerked him by the arm into her office, and then the rest of them were allowed to go back to their classes.

There really wasn't much school work done after that, though, because everyone was ready for Christmas vacation.

The next day was really one long day of being in school and doing nothing but Christmas partying. To head off a repeat of the previous day, the superintendent gave an announcement over all three schools that if anyone pulled the fire alarm, they would be subject to expulsion and their family fined. He added, "And be sure: We Will Find You."

Corrine would have just as soon stayed home, especially after she found out that Melissa was pretty much taking credit for giving Ricky Dale the pocketknife.

She was passing Melissa and two of her girlfriends who were in a huddle in history class, when she heard one of the girls say, "Okay, girl, did you give Ricky Dale that pocketknife?"

And Melissa said, "Maybe," real cute-like and sat down.

Corrine sat in her seat. A moment later her gaze met Melissa's, and she read in the girl's eyes the knowledge that the girl knew that Corrine had given Ricky Dale the knife.

That girl sure did like to act the angel.

Leaving Willie Lee at the drugstore with Corrine's mother, who was helping out at the fountain, and Gabby Smith, who had come in with her mother and brothers, Corrine and Aunt Marilee drove up to Aunt Vella's house to see how she was making out with getting Uncle Perry home from the hospital.

Corrine couldn't wait to see Uncle Perry. She didn't know if she would say anything to him about him being the Santa money man. She sure couldn't speak of it with anyone else around.

Uncle Perry was sitting in his recliner in front of a portable television that Aunt Vella had rolled up into the middle of the living room. That she would do that for him was testament to her care of him; Aunt Vella had banned television from their living room.

His injured foot was wrapped up and lying on a pillow. One of his wrists was also bandaged. He said it didn't hurt too much.

"I reckon not," Aunt Vella said. "They got him doped up." The woman looked more wrought up than Corrine had ever seen her. Her hair was fairly sticking out.

Aunt Marilee sat on the edge of the sofa and exchanged a few comments with Uncle Perry, all the while doing a thorough inspection of him. Corrine did that, too. She did not think he looked too good, but she noticed that he did hold the television remote in the hand that wasn't bandaged and had it pointed right at the television. She took this as a good sign.

Then Aunt Marilee and Aunt Vella went off into the kitchen, and Corrine felt obligated to tag after them. When Aunt Vella poured coffee, though, Corrine offered to take a cup in to Uncle Perry.

"Well, that might be nice for him, sugar," Aunt Vella said, as if Corrine was a pure angel and not the nosy child that she really knew herself to be.

Aunt Vella poured a cup of coffee, and Corrine carried it very carefully in to Uncle Perry. But he was asleep, his head back and mouth open slightly. His hand had dropped the television remote control onto the floor.

Rats. Now she had no chance at all to ask about him being the Santa money man.

She picked up the remote control and carefully laid it in the old man's lap, to be there when he woke up. Then she backed up and gazed at him for a full minute in which she studied his face, trying to see in him someone who would give away thousands of dollars.

No wonder no one suspected him.

She went out to the car in Aunt Vella's driveway, while Aunt Marilee remained up on the porch, still talking to Aunt Vella. Generally, the two would say goodbye about three times before actually parting. Once they had hit a record of seven times; Corrine had counted.

All of a sudden, she was gazing across the small meadow that separated Aunt Vella's house and Mr. Winston's and staring at the horse corral.

Rays from the late afternoon sun fell on the roof of the barn. The big bale of hay remained, half eaten. Already, she thought, the empty corral looked like it was going to ruin.

Corrine stared and stared and had the oddest feeling that the mare was going to come out of the stall just any minute, and the filly would follow, and Corrine would holler to them and wave. She didn't realize how close she was to tears until Aunt Marilee came, getting into the driver's seat, and said, "I'm ready, sugar."

Jerking her gaze from the sight, she got into the car and would not let her head turn to look again. Only a few yards down the street, and the corral was safely hidden by the cedar trees lining Mr. Winston's yard.

On the drive out to the Goodnight Motel, Corrine hugged her feather pillow to her chest and thought that she was glad to be going, and glad that Aunt Marilee was going with her. She should have thought at the very beginning of asking her aunt to go out to stay with her mother at the motel, and then she never would have wasted all that time of worrying about going out there alone.

There was, however, the continual and growing anxiety about possibly having to choose which woman to sleep with, should the room have only one bed. Finally she grew so anxious, she asked, "Does the room have two beds?"

"Well, I don't know, honey. I didn't think to ask. I'm sure it has one big enough for both of us."

Aunt Marilee assumed Corrine would sleep with her. What if Corrine's mother assumed the same?

Corrine imagined telling both women to double up, so that she could sleep by herself.

It was dark already, and the lights of the motel glowed yellow, like a beacon.

"Mama's waitin' on us," said Corrine, who saw her mother standing in the wide-open doorway of her room.

Even before Aunt Marilee stopped the BMW beside the Cherokee, her mother came hurrying out to the car as if it had been days, instead of about an hour, since she had seen them. "I've been airin' this room out," she said.

Corrine knew it was because of the cigarette smoke. Her mother's room now was fresh smelling, but down to forty degrees, which might prove equally as hazardous as smoke.

Aunt Marilee went down to the office and came back with the key to the adjoining room. While she unlocked the door, Corrine moved from foot to foot, anxious to see if she would have to make a choice between which woman to sleep with.

The door swung open, and Corrine saw two double beds. She went quickly to the first one and dropped her feather pillow, then fell back on it with great relief.

However, while she did not have to choose which woman to share a bed with, she soon realized that she still did have to make a lot of choices between them. There was the question of what type of pizza—the works, as her mother wanted, or just hamburger and extra cheese, as Aunt Marilee wanted?

"Let's get one of both," Corrine said.

"Good idea," said her mother, who was ordering.

Aunt Marilee investigated the movies on the cable television. She wanted one, and Corrine's mother wanted another. Which one did Corrine want to watch?

Corrine looked at the women. "Why don't we just watch Nickelodeon?"

Minutes later her mother hopped out the front door of Corrine's and Aunt Marilee's room in order to wait for the pizza delivery boy and to have a cigarette, leaving the door open so as to holler back comments.

After pizza, they each got showered, and both women left the doors of the bathroom open and called out comments. Corrine had to keep moving from room to room, as she heard, "Corrine, honey..."

Then they did each other's nails. Corrine's were first, and her mother, positioned to do Corrine's fingernails, chose one color, and Aunt Marilee, getting ready to do her toenails, chose another. Corrine, unable to abide two different colors, even if they were widely separated by her body, firmly chose a color, but then she had to decide which woman would get to go first. She handed the bottle to her aunt and volunteered to remove her mother's nail polish.

During the entire evening of such interactions, Corrine came to realize just how much Papa Tate and Willie Lee eased the burden of attention for her when in the presence of her mother and aunt. They drew the heavy focus off of Corrine. This night there was only herself to see to the two women.

She got so worn out trying to split herself that she finally lay on her bed and feigned sleep. She heard her mother and aunt whispering about her and felt them gazing at her, and indeed, when she dared to pretend to stir in her sleep, she peeked and saw them looking.

Rolling over, she pulled the pillow over her head and escaped into sleep.

She awoke twice in the night. Once when her aunt got up to go to the bathroom, and another time when she found everything dark and had trouble remembering where she was.

Then she smelled cigarette smoke and the realization of being in the motel with her mother came to her. She opened her eyes a slit and saw her mother in the doorway between the rooms. Silvery flickering light from the television behind her illuminated her mother's form. She was just standing there, looking in, in the same manner that Aunt Marilee always did when bed-checking.

The next morning, when Corrine awoke and looked into her mother's room, she found her mother's bed empty. She assumed her mother was in the bathroom, but after cautiously approaching the opened door and listening, she then looked in and saw the room empty.

She stood, looking around the motel room. It smelled of tobacco and Shalimar, she thought. She liked the scent. Her mother's fox fur was thrown over the chair. She went over and ran her hand over it, enjoying its silky softness. Her gaze fell to the drawing tablet that she had given her mother, lying on the small round table in front of the window.

Cautiously, ears listening for her mother's arrival, she lifted the pages of the tablet and looked through. She had expected to see only the first couple of pages with the drawings her mother had played with at the apartment. But there were more. Many more than the two her mother had done right first thing when Corrine had given her the tablet. There was a drawing of the Shalimar bottle; Corrine liked that. And an attempt at a horse. It was pretty bad, except for the head.

Why, her mother could draw. She really could.

Corrine felt suddenly ashamed of not having asked her mother about her drawings. She had not really shown any interest in her mother's life at all.

The telephone on the nightstand rang, and she about jumped out of her skin. Aunt Marilee was still asleep, doing a little whooffling snore. She just hated to be awakened by a ringing phone. Corrine hurried to the connecting door and pulled it closed.

The phone rang two more times, before Corrine finally answered it, fully expecting to hear Papa Tate's voice.

But it wasn't him.

It was Louis. She recognized his voice immediately, but he did not recognize hers.

He said, "Oh, I apologize. I must have gotten the wrong number."

"No," Corrine said quickly. "This is Louis, right? This is Corrine."

"Well, hello, Corrine." Surprise. "How are you?"

"Okay. I don't know where Mama is right this minute. Maybe she went to get coffee at the office." Her mind filled with the question: And just why are you calling?

Then the front door of the room was opening, and she said, "Oh, wait! Here's Mama."

Her mother came in, balancing a tray of foam cups and doughnuts. Corrine held the receiver toward her. "It's Louis."

She hoped her mother wasn't angry about Corrine being in her room. She didn't seem to be. She cast Corrine a bright smile, set the tray aside and, coming with the faint scents of Shalimar and tobacco, took the phone. She called Louis darling. "Hello, darlin'," she said. And her face looked really happy.

Corrine busied herself appearing not to listen, while selecting a doughnut and debating about getting away with taking one of the cups of coffee. She decided the dark coffee was not her style anyway and took up the cup of milk that was obviously for her. She slowly went away into her and Aunt Marilee's room. By the time she was out of earshot, the most she had heard from her mother's end of the conversation was her mother calling Louis darling and asking how the week had gone and saying a lot of, "Uh-huhs." Her tone was warm and sympathetic, though.

Corrine sat on her bed and ate her doughnut—a powdered sugar cake doughnut, one of her favorites—and wondered how her mother would stay in Valentine, if she and Louis were still together.

She heard her mother say goodbye and hang up, and the next instant her mother came in to Aunt Marilee's bed and bravely cried out, "Get up, get up, you sleepyhead. Get up and get your body fed!"

"Oh, my God," Aunt Marilee said, coming up from the pillow.

"Are you praying?" said Corrine's mother, laughing, then telling Corrine, "Your aunt Marilee used to wake me for school with that little ditty. Got you back," she said to Aunt Marilee and rocked the bed.

Corrine regarded her mother and aunt with a little apprehension, but her aunt only threw a pillow at Corrine's mother.

As she had driven out to the motel with Aunt Marilee, Corrine thought she should ride with her mother on the way back to town. She got into the front seat, and her mother gave her a lovely smile.

Thoughts tumbled over Corrine's mind as she sought something to chat about. She wanted to express interest in her mother's life in some way. In the effort to get her things all together and leave the motel, she had forgotten to ask her mother if she could see her drawings. She wanted to look at them with her mother's knowledge, so she wouldn't feel as if she were sneaking. Also, she wanted to compliment her mother. She was annoyed with herself for forgetting to ask.

Another question on her mind was about her mother's relationship with Louis. She was uncertain about asking about him, though. Some trepidation held her, while the question of the man became bigger and bigger, until it finally popped out of her mouth.

"Are you and Louis still goin' together?" She was instantly sorry she had asked. Her mother gave her a curious glance, and Corrine hoped she wouldn't ask why Corrine wanted to know, because Corrine wasn't certain why she wanted to know.

"We are good friends," her mother said, in the slow manner that adults use when being careful of what they said. "I wouldn't call it going together. Louis has...obligations. But we've remained friends."

"Oh." Corrine knew that Louis had a wife who was in a psychiatric hospital. "Is his wife still in the hospital?"

Her mother's eyebrow rose, as if maybe she had forgotten that Corrine knew about Louis being married.

"Yes," her mother said then, giving a nod. "She will likely be there the rest of her life." It was as if a great sadness came over her, and her expression took on a faraway look. Then she glanced at Corrine and said, "So he needs his friends."

Giving a nod, Corrine jerked her gaze and face around to look out the passenger window and all the Saturday shoppers on the sidewalk of Main Street.

There was to be a full-dress rehearsal of the Christmas pageant at the church that afternoon, so Corrine hurried down right before lunch to get the mail. She passed the saddle shop and gave only a fleeting glance into the window, just enough to see the saddle was still there and still not marked down any further. She didn't know why she should want it marked down. She still couldn't buy it, and she had no use for it, without a horse.

She thought of what her mother had said about Louis keeping horses in New Orleans.

What if her mother decided that she wanted to return to New Orleans to be near Louis? Would she require that Corrine go with her? Although still anxious about the idea, she was also now curious. She imagined Louis's horses on some big old Southern plantation with white painted fences.

Yet she could not leave her Aunt Marilee and Willie Lee. No, she couldn't do that.

But neither did she want to lose her mother now.

She tried to imagine her mother living in Valentine. This seemed very odd. How could her mother live in town and Corrine not live with her?

She felt a very confused, anxious feeling. She was afraid for her mother to go, and afraid for her to stay.

"You have a package," Mrs. Julia Jenkins-Tinsley called to her from the postal counter, catching Corrine on the way out after having retrieved the wad of mail from their P.O. box. "I didn't get it into your box, but it's here."

The woman disappeared behind the wall as Corrine came to the counter. She anticipated something that Aunt Marilee had ordered, but the small padded envelope the postmistress handed down to her had Corrine's name on it. There was no return address.

"Why don't you open it up right now?" the postmistress

said. "I'm needin' a break. These Saturday hours are killin' me." Her eyes danced with curiosity.

And curiosity overcame Corrine's urge to get away from the woman. In fact, it was sort of fun to share opening the package with her. The woman even handed her scissors to cut the end off the envelope, saying, "Law, people all over the place are gettin' secret gifts."

A secret gift? For her? Corrine couldn't believe it. Probably there would be a name inside. Probably Granny Franny had ordered something for her.

But there was no name, just a small silver foil box.

The postmistress told her, "Well, go ahead and open it."

Corrine used her newly painted fingernail to cut through the clear tape and pulled off the little box top. Inside, there was something wrapped in white tissue paper. That something was a pair of small earrings. Very dainty, they were black glass, or maybe plastic, nuggets hanging from blackened silver posts. She recognized the earrings. She had seen them at Wal-Mart, on the rack of teenage jewelry.

"Well, aren't those pretty," the postmistress said.

Corrine checked again the address on the front of the envelope. It was handwritten, but oddly, as if concealing the handwriting.

"Do you know who sent them?"

"No, ma'am."

"Well, another secret gift."

"I guess so," Corrine said, thoroughly amazed. "Um... Merry Christmas, Mrs. Jenkins-Tinsley."

"Merry Christmas to you, too, Corrine." The woman smiled, and Corrine took note for the first time of the antlers on top of her head.

She hurried out of the post office and down the sidewalk for home, wondering who in the world could have given her the earrings. Aunt Marilee or her mother, she guessed. But on second thought—the earrings were cheap, not something Aunt Marilee or her mother would send her. In fact, Aunt Marilee probably wouldn't like them.

This proved the case for both her aunt and her mother.

"It's our age, Marilee," her mother said.

"I know," her aunt replied with a sigh.

Corrine, gazing at herself in the earrings in the dining room mirror, thought she liked them. But she wondered if really they looked silly.

She turned and checked her appearance in her aunt's and mother's eyes.

Both women smiled and said, "They are nice on you," and, "Yes, they suit you...they do."

The knot in Corrine's stomach eased, and looking again in the mirror, she thought that she liked the earrings more and more. Someone had sent her a secret gift. Imagine that.

"Can I wear lipstick?" she asked.

To which both women replied, "No."

Aunt Marilee said, "Anita, don't let me forget to get down to the IGA and get those avocados and shrimp for Franny, so's she can make her shrimp avocado cocktails for tomorrow night's party. Juice has it all saved in back for me."

"Look who you're askin' to remind you. I'll do my best."

"What party?" Corrine asked.

"Why, honey, the party over at the MacCoys' house after the pageant. Didn't I tell you?" Her aunt looked dismayed. "I'm sure sorry. I meant to tell you."

"Oh, yeah," Corrine said. "Are you goin'?"

"Well, yes, honey. We're all goin'."

"I thought it was just for the cast," she fibbed. She really was going to have to stop this lying, but she felt pressed to give a reason for her question.

Aunt Marilee shook her head. "No, honey, it's for you and me and all the parents of those in the pageant, too. Your mother's goin', aren't you, Anita? I guess anyone in the church who wants to go is invited."

"Oh." She couldn't imagine the whole church. But then, she had seen the MacCoys' house from the outside. It looked pretty big.

Then she had another worry. "What should I wear?"

Well, this was a thing to ask both women, who marched themselves into her bedroom and began to coordinate her outfit for the party. They held everything in front of her, in order to check it with the new earrings.

22
∾

Corrine felt she could safely rule out Papa Tate and Willie Lee as the secret Santas who had given her the earrings. They each were polite but showed little interest, despite Aunt Marilee making a big deal about it all to Willie Lee.

It appeared that secret Santa gifts were becoming commonplace. Papa Tate and Aunt Marilee had gotten several from people about town, and it was fairly obvious that Papa Tate had given Aunt Marilee a box of chocolates, and she had given him a box of his favorite roller ball pens. Willie Lee and Corrine had both received candy canes on their pillows, and to that Aunt Marilee said, "Santa Claus strikes again," as if she hadn't done it. Even Willie Lee knew she had done it, but he played along with her.

When Papa Tate came up from having coffee at the Main Street Café, he said that Fayrene Gardner had now received two secret Santa gifts, a Christmas bell pin and a James Taylor CD that had her in a flutter, because she felt certain it was from some man. According to her account, the CD had been packaged romantically, and the note from Santa looked romantic, too. The café cook had gotten a bag of

Hershey's Christmas Kisses that Fayrene swore were not from her.

Corrine began to feel badly about not thinking at all to get Jojo a secret gift, or any gift, for that matter. The prospect of Jojo maybe being the one to have given her the earrings seemed more and more possible, and Corrine felt more and more badly about overlooking the girl, whom she had grown to like a lot. And she needed to get something for Granny Franny, too. How could she have forgotten her? Oh, and Aunt Vella and Grama Norma, too. And Uncle Perry. She wanted to get a gift for Uncle Perry since he had given so much to so many others, and she was the only one to know about it. It seemed like God had selected her to get him a secret gift.

It was a good thing she had gotten the money from Leanne.

Her mother went to take care of Uncle Perry, so that Aunt Vella could come assist—visit, would have been a better word—at the pageant rehearsal. Corrine would have liked to have gone with her mother. Maybe she would have been able to speak a private word to Uncle Perry about him being the Santa money man. She still wasn't certain what she would say to him, though. Saying, "Okay, I know you are the Santa givin' out all this money. Where'd you get it?" didn't seem quite right. In addition to her curiosity about the money, she wanted to tell him how great she thought he was. But she couldn't seem to find the words for that, either.

Besides, her curiosity over her earrings edged everything else out. She had to go to the rehearsal and see if she could tell if it was Jojo or Ricky Dale who had given them to her.

The more she thought about it, the more she thought it could very well have been Ricky Dale. His sister could have helped him pick out the earrings. Although, would he have noticed that she had pierced ears now? This did not seem likely. She would like it to turn out to be Ricky Dale who'd sent them, though.

Unfortunately, and surprisingly, neither Jojo nor Ricky

Dale gave any indication of being her secret Santa. Jojo was preoccupied with getting her Mary's head covering to stay in place. When Corrine had taken care of that with two bobby pins, Jojo said with great excitement, "Everyone is comin' to our party. Just about half the town!"

Ricky Dale appeared inordinately absorbed in acting nutty with Anson and Gideon. They were more like the Three Stooges than the Three Wise Men. He didn't even seem to pay a whole lot of attention to Melissa Pruitt, who said her lines perfectly and was annoyed at anyone who did not. She said things like, "I wish you people would pay attention," and "I don't know why people don't learn their lines, Miz MacCoy."

Corrine spent most of her time over at the light switches on the wall, turning certain directional lights on and off according to Charlene MacCoy's hand signals. This job kept her all alone, and no one even seemed to look her way.

It appeared that although Corrine finally had her dangling pierced earrings, her life had not changed one bit. All of Aunt Marilee's worrying had been for nothing.

"Corr-ine!"

She jumped and realized it was Melissa screaming at her. Preoccupied with her thoughts, Corrine had leaned against the switches and turned out the spotlight that was supposed to be on the girl for her final narration. As it was cloudy outside, the spotlights were showing up a little.

"Sorry," she hollered back and flipped the switch, illuminating the golden-haired girl, who called out grandly, "Peace on earth and Merry Christmas to all."

"Honey, it's, 'and goodwill to all people,'" Mrs. MacCoy corrected.

"Peace on earth and goodwill to all people everywhere," Melissa said with feeling.

Corrine stood with her finger on the switch, awaiting Mrs. MacCoy's hand signal. However, Mrs. MacCoy turned away to consult with Aunt Vella and Aunt Marilee, and Melissa screamed, "Now, Corrine!"

Corrine flipped off the switch.

Later, as everyone was leaving, Melissa came up and said,

"You'd do best to pay attention and not turn that light out on me tomorrow night, Corrine. You'll be in big trouble for ruinin' the whole pageant."

Tongue-tied, Corrine stood there while the girl walked off. Then, just as the girl reached the door, Corrine called, "You should remember that I can do that, if I want."

Melissa whirled, stared at her, then huffed out the door.

The knowledge that she was the most important person in the pageant came over Corrine. She had the power of light.

She was a little shocked at her attitude. It was her earrings, she thought, feeling them sway.

Who could have given her the earrings? Could she have been wrong in thinking that Jojo hadn't done it? If not Jojo or Ricky Dale, who? It wasn't like she had a lot of people in her life to choose from.

"I'm moving over to Aunt Vella's," Corrine's mother announced, coming into the kitchen where Corrine and Aunt Marilee were wrapping up gifts for the *Voice* staff, as well as some toys for the Chamber drive. Corrine enjoyed wrapping packages with Aunt Marilee, because Aunt Marilee really loved wrapping packages. She loved curling ribbon and making each little thing pretty and festive.

Aunt Marilee, her eyebrows rising in surprise, while she was trying to get a bow tied as perfectly as she liked them tied, questioned Corrine's mother. Her mother said that she was very worried about Aunt Vella and Uncle Perry, and described how Uncle Perry just sat and stared at the television.

Aunt Marilee pointed out that that was normal behavior for Uncle Perry.

"It's depression," Corrine's mother said flatly. "I wouldn't doubt that he's been depressed for some time. He's sunk, and Aunt Vella is followin' after him."

"Vella seemed fine today at the pageant," Aunt Marilee said, casting an uncertain glance at Corrine. "She was chipper and laughing."

"Marilee, if there's one thing I know, it is depression." Her mother let that sit there for a moment, before continuing. "Vella's of stout will. She's not goin' to show her depression in public, but it's there. She's forgettin' to comb her hair, doesn't care what she's throwin' on, and when I went over there, her sink was full of dishes, and she hadn't cleared breakfast from the table. Does that sound like Aunt Vella to you?"

"No," Aunt Marilee said, clearly paying attention now.

Corrine's gaze moved back and forth between the two women, who gazed at each other for a long moment with a common bond so strong Corrine felt the air swirl.

Then Aunt Marilee finished taping paper on a box, leaned back against the counter and looked at her sister in such a way as to say, "Okay, I'm ready. Tell me. What are we dealing with here?" Corrine expected to be sent from the room, and indeed, her aunt's gaze flickered on her, as if assessing and apparently deciding that Corrine should stay.

Her mother, who never gave any thought to what Corrine should or should not hear, said, "Uncle Perry doesn't hardly say a word."

Corrine thought that Uncle Perry rarely said a word, so this could not be used as a dire prediction.

"He's sleeping hours on end, and when he isn't sleeping, he's focused on the television. He's withdrawn, and even when Vella goes at him, she can't seem to get a rise out of him. He's got high blood pressure that should have been treated years ago, and he's possibly had some mild strokes. Vella said he's been forgettin' things, like asking her for a sandwich, and then not remembering he asked. All of this, well, it's natural for them to be depressed."

Aunt Marilee was nodding right along. "I know. I know," she said. "Vella mentioned about him forgetting things. I just put it down to him bein' retired and not needin' to remember like he used to." She rubbed her forehead.

"Depression really means adjustment. That's what they're dealin' with," Corrine's mother said. "And that's what we can help them with."

Corrine had never seen her mother be so in command,

and she could tell that it was even having an effect on Aunt Marilee.

Aunt Marilee said, "Well, it'll make a much better Christmas for Vella and Perry, anyway, with you over there."

"Maybe somebody should call or write to Margaret," Corrine offered. Although speaking with hesitation, she had been worrying for some time about the matter of this daughter Margaret, who Aunt Vella had cried over.

"Margaret? Law, I'd forgotten about her," her mother said in a tone Corrine had not heard her use often.

Aunt Marilee nodded and seemed very pleased at Corrine's taking part. "I don't have her phone or address, but I'll get Tate to convince Belinda to contact her. He can convince anyone of anything."

Corrine had forgotten all about Belinda also being Aunt Vella and Uncle Perry's very own daughter. She wondered how Belinda would take this action on her mother's part.

Wanting to alert them to possible difficulty, she gave voice to the wondering, and her mother said, "Oh, if Belinda is anything, she's a realist. I imagine Belinda will be relieved that she doesn't have to take care of them."

"If Belinda and Aunt Vella had to spend too much time together, one of them would go to prison for murder," said Aunt Marilee.

Her aunt and mother laughed, and Aunt Marilee hugged Corrine.

A few minutes later, as she was getting her coat on to go start moving her mother from the motel, Corrine thought about how the three of them had been, there in the kitchen. Together, that was how they had been.

Maybe it would work out, after all, for her mother to stay in Valentine. Maybe her mother could live with Aunt Vella.

It would still seem strange for her mother to be here and Corrine not live with her. What would she say when someone asked why she didn't live with her mother?

Every time she thought of the situation, she felt anxious. She wished she knew what was going to happen. She was about to the point of saying that if her mother wanted her to live with her, then they needed to get to it. But she couldn't leave Aunt Marilee and Willie Lee. She felt like crying.

Her mother threw things into her suitcases, but all that had come out of them would not go back in.

"Oh, here. You're only goin' into town," Aunt Marilee said, and hurriedly began stuffing things into plastic trash bags. In the way Aunt Marilee had of knowing about contingencies, she had brought the box of bags from home.

They helped Papa Tate pile all the cases and bags into the Cherokee, drove over to Aunt Vella's and began unloading them, trooping into the house like worker ants, Aunt Marilee said. Even Willie Lee carried things.

Uncle Perry started to struggle up out of his chair, saying, "I'll help you all," but Aunt Vella said with a mixture of helplessness and annoyance, "Perry, sugar, you can't get on that ankle."

Uncle Perry went back down in the chair like the air had gone out of him.

Aunt Marilee cautioned them all to avoid running into his foot and possibly getting hurt, or hurting the foot. She instructed Papa Tate to move Uncle Perry across the room and out of the traffic area.

Corrine didn't think anyone was helping the old man with his depression.

Pretty soon the Cherokee was empty and Aunt Vella's guest bedroom was full. Papa Tate and Willie Lee went off to get a supper from the IGA, while the women worked to get Corrine's mother settled in. Aunt Vella was definitely looking picked up; the three women were acting like they were having a sleepover party.

Corrine, standing near the bedroom door, realized that Uncle Perry, the reason for all of this moving in, was alone downstairs.

Backing from the room without the women noticing she was gone, she crept down the stairs. Uncle Perry was awake, sitting there watching the television with the remote in his hand. He looked like he had shrunk.

"Hey," she said, going up to the side of the chair.

"Hey, you," he said and made an attempt at a smile. Then he returned his gaze to the television, which was tuned to a program about the history of beer.

When she continued to stand there, he looked at her.

She said, "You know those envelopes I mailed for you the day you fell? Well, they got where they were goin'." The disturbing thought jumped into her mind that maybe he didn't remember having her mail the envelopes. Maybe he didn't remember the envelopes, or being the Santa money man.

But then she saw a spark of life in his pale eyes that cut over to her.

"So I heard," he said, gazing at her.

She lowered her voice. "I won't tell anybody that you're the Santa Claus. I promise I won't."

Watching his eyes get sharp, she realized how much she wanted to make up to him somehow for causing him to fall. If she hadn't called to him, he wouldn't have tripped.

The next instant, he startled her by flopping down the foot of his recliner and struggling to get up. "He'p me up here."

"I don't think you should get up on your ankle…. Aunt Vella is gonna—"

But he flapped his hand at her. "Shussh!" Then he leaned on her shoulder. He was heavy, just as she had known he would be.

"Get me that wheelchair over there."

Following the direction of his gesture, she saw a wheelchair folded up beside the door to the closet under the stairs.

She got the chair for him, unfolded it, and he got settled in, with his leg propped up like an aimed rifle.

"Come on," he ordered. "Get me to the back door."

He started to push himself with one hand, which made him look so helpless that Corrine was compelled to take hold of the wheelchair handles and roll him through the house. The entire time, she kept thinking that she was about to be responsible for him harming himself in some way, and she expected to hear Aunt Vella's loud voice calling from behind them.

They were both going to get in big trouble.

But the voice never came. Aunt Vella and the other women were having their happy time upstairs.

When they reached the back door, Uncle Perry again hauled himself up and balanced on his good leg. By holding on to her, he got himself out the door and down the three stairs. The sun had set, and the pole lamp came on when they reached the patio. Uncle Perry grunted something awful, and then said, "That's why I got those pain pills, dad-gummit."

She maneuvered the wheelchair down the steps as fast as possible, and he plopped in it, and she was certain he was going to have a heart attack, and it would be all her fault, but then he said, "Get around to my car," and gestured for her to hurry up.

She hesitated, but figured doing what he wanted was better for him than arguing with him. She rolled him on the concrete sidewalk to the edge of the house, where a light came on up at the eaves. It caused her to jump. It must have had a motion sensor.

Uncle Perry said, "Get in there and get that bag and the envelopes from under the front seat, and put them under the seat of Marilee's car."

She looked at the car, wondering if she should be doing any of this.

"Go on."

He was an older relative, and it was his car and his things. She did as she was told, opened the door of the Cadillac, got down on the floor and peered into the darkness under the seat. She felt underneath and pulled out first a bag, which she knew instantly contained money. There was printed on the bag: First National Bank of Caldwell. *Ohmygosh. Uncle Perry had robbed a bank?* Then she reached under again and pulled out a crackling package. It was padded envelopes.

Uncle Perry was gesturing and telling her to hurry up.

She ran to the Cherokee sitting behind the Cadillac and stuffed the envelopes under the front seat. *Oh, God, please don't let anyone look under there.*

Then she ran back to Uncle Perry in the wheelchair. He was already turning himself around. He told her to wheel him out further on the patio. "I'm sick to death of that house."

She did as he said, and then he told her, "I want you to mail out that last bit of money from Santa Claus for me. Do you think you can do that?"

"Uh…I guess so." It was beginning to seem as if she had no choice.

"Divide what's left of the money between the two envelopes. The addresses are already on the envelopes, but you'll have to make up the Santa notes, and you'll have to get the postage on them. Two dollars in stamps ought to do each envelope."

"Did you steal that money, Uncle Perry?"

"It's stolen, but I didn't do it. It was…"

The back door opened, and Aunt Vella stepped through. "Well good heavens, here you are. How did you get out here?"

"How do you think?" Uncle Perry called back.

"Well, you two don't even have any coats on. Get in here."

"I guess I can get in when I'm good and ready," Uncle Perry answered, and for a moment Aunt Vella was quiet.

Then she said, "Maybe you can catch a cold out there, Perry Blaine, but Corrine doesn't need to get one."

Uncle Perry gestured for Corrine to head for the door. "We're comin'. Keep your pants on."

Rats! She wanted to know about the money.

Getting back into the house proved a whole lot more difficult for Uncle Perry than had coming out. Corrine imagined this was because he didn't want to go back inside nearly as much as he had wanted to come out. Papa Tate, who had returned with supper, came out and helped.

Corrine thought Uncle Perry looked to have grown back to his original size, however, once he was inside in his wheelchair. He even joined them at the dining room table.

He winked at her a couple of times, and Corrine quit looking in his direction. She was afraid he was going to make everyone suspicious that something was up.

There was a bit of a problem. The money was now out of Uncle Perry's Cadillac and into Aunt Marilee's Cherokee, but the Cherokee was going to stay right behind the Cadillac, because Corrine's mother was driving it, and she was staying at Uncle Perry's house.

Corrine thought of this as they were getting ready to leave. Luckily Aunt Marilee always had to say goodbye to Aunt Vella a number of times before she actually managed to get broken away. Corrine hurried out to the cars at the side of the house, got the money and envelopes from beneath the Cherokee seat and stuffed them underneath the seat of the BMW, which wasn't easy, as there wasn't much room. She had just slipped into the back seat when Willie Lee and Munro and her mother came to the car.

"I didn't get my hug good-night," her mother said.

Corrine hugged her tight.

Boy, she felt as if *she* had robbed a bank.

She hoped she couldn't get arrested for handling stolen money.

The Valentine Voice

Christmas About Town
by Marilee Holloway

In case you haven't realized, there are only 5 days left until Christmas. Here's a checklist:

* Anyone you want to remember with a card? You can still send cards in town, although I do say give it up at this late date, except for really special people in your life. You might want to hand-deliver, too.

* Make a list of the people to whom you want to give a gift. Everyone covered?

* Check the wrapping situation.

* Food. Do you have everything you want for the Christmas dinner? Have you accommodated each person's favorites and made provisions for drop-in guests?

For last minute cards, gifts and wrapping supplies, Blaine's Drugstore and Soda Fountain is having 40% off all their holiday stock, and this includes the perfumes.

We have given up with any further gift ideas, except to say that now is the time to make full use of the gift certificate idea. The Cut and Curl Beauty Salon is offering lovely gift certificates for perms, styling, complete facials, manicures and half-hour massages. You really can't go wrong with one of those gift certificates for the lady in your life.

Another good idea for man or woman is a gift certificate to *The Valentine Voice*. Six-month and one-year certificates are available. Drop by the *Voice* this week. The coffee's always hot.

For the men, The Quick Shop Video rental is offering gift certificates for action adventure movies, and the saddle shop is having a sale on leather wallets.

The Christmas Cottage will have its annual Christmas Sale Day on Tuesday. Everything will be 60% off.

Tonight the United Methodist and First Baptist churches will each be celebrating Christmas with pageants and parties. Reverend Smith of the United Methodists and Reverend Phelps of the First Baptists apologize that no one thought to check each church's schedule and the pageants ended up on the same night. As the First Baptist starts first at 6:30 p.m., and the United Methodist comes after at 7:00 p.m., perhaps those of you who have family performing in each event can divide your time and see half of each.

The United Methodists have agreed to hold their production up for 10-15 minutes. Charlene MacCoy says that they never start on time anyway.

This will be the last night of the live nativity at the Sons of Light Church, located in the old Hardees building. Make sure you get over to see it, but Reverend Rooney requests no honking to show appreciation while driving past. They have had several catastrophes with the frightened cow.

For those of you who have been phoning each day to ask, we have received a new shipment of *Voice* mugs and will be mailing them to those who are due one for their kind donations to our Chamber toy drive.

Our recipe today comes from Fayrene Gardner, owner of the Main Street Café, and who our dear Editor begged to give out this recipe. I don't know why anyone would want the recipe, when all a person needs to do is go down and buy the pie at the café.

Fayrene Gardner's Raisin Pie

2 heaping cups of raisins.
Fayrene says she really heaps these cups, so the amount is closer to 3, but she wouldn't swear on it.
1 cup water
1 cup orange juice
1 tablespoon lemon juice
1/2 cup brown sugar
1/2-1 teaspoon cinnamon
2 tablespoons cornstarch

Reserve 1/2 cup of the water, and put the raisins and the rest of the liquids into a saucepan. Simmer for at least 5 minutes. Add brown sugar and cinnamon and mix, still simmering, until the sugar is melted. Use the 1/2 cup water to mix or shake with the cornstarch until all lumps are gone, then pour into saucepan mix. Stir until thick. Allow mixture to cool slightly before pouring into pastry.

Fayrene says you're on your own for the pastry. She is keeping her recipe secret. I recommend my method, which is to buy the frozen pastry dough.

Better yet, get yourself down to the Main Street Café and have a cup of hazelnut coffee and a piece of raisin pie already made. Now that is easy living.

Charlotte is going on vacation starting tomorrow, so hold up your recipes for our upcoming cookbook until after Christmas. Please limit your calls to the *Voice* to emergency news items only.

23

The house was quiet in the early morning hours. Corrine, in robe and slippers, debated going to get the money and envelopes. Her aunt slept the soundest in the morning, she thought, and got her book bag.

She slipped out the back door and down to the BMW.

Well, rats. Of all the times for Papa Tate to lock the car. And Papa Tate was not like Aunt Marilee, who laid her keys down wherever. He usually kept his in his pants pocket.

When she went to the kitchen to make the morning coffee, she found Willie Lee there, with Munro beside him, looking out the east window.

"What're you guys doin'?" She went to look out the window, too, thinking there was something going on in the street. The Christmas lights were growing dim as the day brightened.

Her heart did a jump. Christmas was less than a week away now!

"I was watch-ing for my pi-geon to come back." Her cousin sighed a great sigh of disappointment.

"Oh," Corrine said. There didn't seem to be anything else to say to the matter.

She went to the refrigerator, opened it and stood there looking in. "Want some cornbread and honey?" She wanted to perk him up.

"No, thank you," he said.

After a minute, she asked, "Did you ask Santa Claus for a pigeon?"

He said with some righteousness, "It is se-cret."

"Oh."

He returned to gazing out the window, and she stared for long seconds at the back of his head.

She closed the refrigerator door and headed for the bathroom to get a shower before the morning rush. Aunt Marilee and Papa Tate's bedroom door was pushed to, but not closed tightly. Hearing whispering from the other side, she leaned her head close. Maybe they were speaking about Christmas presents!

"What if...Corrine..."

At the sound of her name and the concerned tone in her aunt's voice, she caught her breath and listened harder.

"I asked her...and...reverse the adoption. I can call...but it could...and that's sticky. If she would just...patience. We have...and leave it to God. It'll be..."

It was about her adoption. Was there some problem? Was her mother going to make them give Corrine back to her?

As much to get them to stop talking as to tell them what she needed to tell them, she knocked on the door. The whispering was cut off as if strangled. Then Papa Tate said, "Come in."

"I need to break up whatever you were whisperin' about to tell you somethin' you might have not noticed. I don't know how you wouldn't notice, but just in case." She paused, watching their faces. Aunt Marilee, her silky gown falling off one shoulder, was calmly propped against her fluffy pillows, and Papa Tate was lying at her feet, massaging them. She had a twinge of embarrassment at seeing the two so intimately together.

"What is it, sugar?" her aunt asked.

"I think Willie Lee asked Santa for a pigeon for Christmas." She had lived with Willie Lee long enough to be able to read his mind in the same way that Aunt Marilee read hers—and everyone's, really.

Both of them looked dismayed, but neither questioned Corrine's discernment of the situation. "I don't see how we can do that, Tate," Aunt Marilee said. "Where would we keep it?"

Papa Tate said, "I'll work on it."

Corrine nodded. She wanted to ask what they had been discussing about her, but she felt too ashamed to let on that she had been listening. And too ashamed to know that once again she was the cause of trouble.

To explain why she was taking her book bag to church, she worked out a story. "Jojo and I are exchanging books. She's bringin' me a couple, and I'm taking some to her. You know, sort of like a lending library."

She carefully put two books in the bag, but planned to tell Aunt Marilee four titles. She ran it over in her head, so that she could convince herself and her aunt's radar for truth would be confused. She sure would have something to confess at communion, and she wouldn't have to write it down to remember it.

Then, after all that trouble, Aunt Marilee never even noticed the book bag. She was going around happily singing Christmas carols and intent on prodding the rest of them to join in.

"We wish you a merry Christmas…" She grabbed Willie Lee and danced him around. "Come on, all you Scrooges. Sing!"

So they all sang as they went down to get into Papa Tate's BMW, where Aunt Marilee made Papa Tate wait before driving off so that she could apply her lipstick.

In the usual manner of adults, her aunt wouldn't have noticed if Corrine had horns coming out of her head. And of course the only thing Papa Tate was likely to notice was tears.

When they arrived at church, there was a crowd of people on the lawn. It was a beautiful day, and the congregation was swelled by those people who came for this Sunday before Christmas but not the rest of the year. All the people were a great draw for Aunt Marilee and Papa Tate, who quickly went off greeting everyone, shaking hands, kissing and hugging. Gabby Smith came running over to take Willie Lee by the hand and haul him off.

Corrine slipped back to the BMW and dragged the money bag and envelope package from beneath the front seat. A quick glance into the money bag and she saw several clumps of bills wrapped together. She wondered how much it was but wouldn't take time to count, and it was a good thing, because she had no sooner stuffed the money and envelopes into her book bag than someone spoke from behind her.

"Hey, Corrine."

She about jumped out of her skin. "Ricky Dale! You scared me to death."

"I...I'm sorry. I didn't mean to." He sort of shrank back, and she felt aggravated at herself. Couldn't she say anything right to him? Besides, she was awfully glad it was him and not her mother or Jojo, both of whom she felt would notice her messing with her book bag and ask about it. A guy wouldn't notice anything.

She said, "Oh, it's okay. I just wasn't expectin' you." She sure hadn't been. What was he wanting of her, anyway? It wasn't like him to come around her. "What do you need?"

Even as she asked this, she had the strong urge to tell him about Uncle Perry and the money right that minute in her book bag.

He shrugged. "Oh, nothin'. I just saw you over here. We just got here."

"Oh." Of course she would not tell him about the money.

They headed toward the front steps, where Ricky Dale's mother and father were talking to Aunt Marilee and Papa Tate. Seeing Ricky Dale, Aunt Marilee waved and said, "You're gonna be great tonight."

He looked embarrassed.

"She's excited about the pageant," Corrine told him.

"It's just another church pageant," he said, but she thought he was pleased.

Corrine had been keeping an eye out for Melissa. Not see-ing the girl or her parents anywhere on the lawn, she thought maybe she and her family were already inside.

The bell started ringing, and Ricky Dale's daddy and the other men instantly went to stubbing out their cigarettes as everyone began filing up the steps.

In a wild impulse, Corrine said, "Would you like to sit with us?"

"Sure," he said.

Boy, was she surprised. And just wait until Melissa Pruitt saw.

Only Melissa Pruitt didn't see, because she wasn't there. The place where Melissa and her parents usually sat was empty.

Well. Her spirit dropped, and she looked at Ricky Dale, thinking to tell him that he might as well go sit with his mother. She didn't care to be second fiddle. But then, sitting up straighter and feeling her earrings sway, she decided that she didn't need to cut her nose off to spite her face, as Aunt Marilee would say.

Also, just then Aunt Vella came rolling Uncle Perry up and parked him right at the end of their pew, beside Papa Tate, then scooted herself down to sit beside Corrine.

"Your Mama is stayin' home and restin'," Aunt Vella said. "Hello, Ricky Dale."

Corrine was leaning around Aunt Vella. She waved at Un-cle Perry, who winked at her. She wished he wouldn't keep winking at her. Somebody might notice. But then, they would just think he was being friendly, or, more likely, that he had a twitch.

The music started, and she grabbed up the hymnal and shared it with Ricky Dale. Even if she was second fiddle to Melissa, it was nice, him being there. Before she knew it, she had smiled at him, and he smiled in return.

"Are you goin' to the MacCoys' party tonight?" she whis-pered.

"Yeah. Mom and Dad and Raetta are goin', too. Are you?"

She nodded. "All of us, too."

And right there, with the preacher giving his message,

Corrine began to have a fantasy about getting alone with him at the MacCoy's party and giving him a kiss.

When they had communion, which they were having each Sunday of advent—there were so many people, and Pastor was trying out all kinds of ways with the service—she definitely had transgressions to confess.

"Push me to the car while your Aunt Vella's jackin' her jaws," Uncle Perry said.

Corrine took hold of the handle and pushed the chair to the center hallway that led to the disabled ramp at the rear of the church. His leg sticking out the way it did made her worried that she might bump it against something.

"Did you get the money home?" Uncle Perry asked, when they were out of everyone's earshot.

"Almost," Corrine said. She was relieved to be safely through the doors and not have clipped Uncle Perry's foot. "It's in the car. I'll get it to my room when we get home."

"You'll need to get it in the mail tomorrow."

"I'll try."

"Call me when you get the thing done."

"Okay." Corrine felt like some sort of spy. She slowed in the middle of the parking lot. "Where'd the money come from? Is it really stolen?" What would she do if she found out that Uncle Perry was a thief? Oh, she shouldn't have asked!

"I guess it's stolen. I don't know why anyone would hide it in the wall, if it weren't stolen," he said.

Relief swept her. Uncle Perry hadn't stolen it.

"I found it in the wall behind that old air grate, when I had to tear everything out for the broken pipe. That grate'd been painted a hundred times and made part of the wall," he said, giving a shake of his head. "Near as I can figure it, some bank robber put it there. There was a time when, when Bonnie and Clyde—you know who they were?"

Corrine nodded. She seemed to remember seeing something about them on the History Channel on television.

"Well," Uncle Perry drawled, "those two, along with three other fellas, come stoppin' into our store once back in '33,

I think it was. I was just a little boy, but my dad told the story lots of times. He knew who they were, but nobody else in the store did, and they didn't believe my dad, neither. The store had just the one rest room in those days, men and women alike. The way I figure it, it could be that one of that bunch stuck the money in there, intendin' to come back for it. Only they never got back. Or for all I know some other fool bank robber came through and stuck it there, or my own uncle who owned the store put it in there. He was a little strange," he added.

Corrine thought it was the most wonderful thing she had ever heard. But something occurred to her. "Wouldn't the bank where it was stolen from want it back?" It seemed the honest thing would be to give it back.

Uncle Perry said, "Nah. They probably got some sort of insurance, and givin' it back would mess up everything. Beside, there's a statute of limitations. That money's been on the premises of a building I own for over seventy years. I'm claimin' it."

That made perfect sense to Corrine, who was imagining the bag to contain at this moment thousands and thousands of dollars, but then Uncle Perry was saying, "There's three thousand left in that bag. You divide it between the two envelopes. You'll have to get stamps. Here." He pulled bills from his pocket.

"I can do it. I have some money," she said. She wanted in this thing. She wanted to be Santa, too.

He looked at her and put the money back in his shirt pocket. "Okay. You're handlin' it. Now, after you get it done, you burn that money bag."

She did not even question how she was going to burn it. She just knew she was going to get it all done.

"I think we should lay down and rest this afternoon," Aunt Marilee said on their way into the apartment. "It's goin' to be a long evenin'."

"I'm goin'," Corrine said with feeling and took off for her room, where she shut the door and leaned against it.

She looked down at her book bag, then took it to her closet and threw it inside and shut the door.

Lying on her bed, she listened to the apartment getting quiet. There wasn't a lock on her bedroom door. Anyone could come in and catch her when she had the money out.

She took her little flashlight and went into her closet. Squeezing down beneath her clothes, she got the money out of the bag and counted it. She stared at it and felt it. It was not enough to buy the filly, even if the money was hers.

She divided it between the envelopes, as Uncle Perry had said, and then—ohmygosh! She almost sealed the envelopes without the Santa note.

At her desk, she grabbed a piece of drawing paper, but then realized she should use notebook paper that anyone would have. She carefully wrote the notes with her calligraphy pen: Merry Christmas, from Santa Claus. They looked pretty, and not like her handwriting.

Back in the closet, she slipped the notes into the envelopes, sealed them, and then looked at the addresses. One was to a Mr. Delmar Kidd. She didn't know him; he lived on a street she thought was out by the cemetery. But the second one was to Joe Miller, on Spring Street.

That was the street Paris Miller lived on.

Hearing someone go into the bathroom, she quickly stuck the envelopes down into her book bag, which she left in the closet.

Crossing her room in sock feet, she jumped onto her bed and yanked the blanket over her. She intended to pretend sleep, should Aunt Marilee look in, but quite quickly she fell fast asleep, dreaming of Christmas trees and angels and a wonderful horse, with wings.

There was a knock on her door. It was her mother, with, "A little something early for Christmas." She handed Corrine a wrapped box.

Coming right behind her mother was Aunt Marilee, who had brought a small wrapped box, as well.

The two women grinned at her with anticipation. She knew she had better act happy and surprised, and she also knew that the boxes contained clothes. She hoped they weren't too old-fashioned. She prepared herself to act happy, no matter what was in the boxes.

Her mother had given her the most wonderful red velvet peasant top. "It's just like the one I saw in *Seventeen!* Oh, Mom, thanks!"

"Well, a girl needs something new for a party."

Corrine checked Aunt Marilee's expression; it was calm and patient. Corrine made a big deal about tearing into the box. "Oh, wow." It was a small black patent leather purse on a long strap.

"Look inside," Aunt Marilee said.

It was a tube of pink lip gloss. "Oh! Oh, thank you!"

She hugged them and thanked them again, and they urged her to put on the velvet top.

They all agreed that her earrings went wonderfully with the outfit.

When the women left, Corrine stood in front of her mirror again and looked herself over very carefully.

She was growing up. She really was.

The pageant went off better than Corrine had ever imagined it would. The lights of the sanctuary were turned very low, and candles flickered all over the place. Of course, Aunt Marilee went around to inspect each of them and ended up blowing out five that she deemed unsafe for one reason or another.

Corrine's mother and Papa Tate stood at the front doors and handed out the programs Papa Tate had printed up. Corrine handed them out to anyone who they missed; then she took up her place beside the light switches. She was not going to make any mistakes and ruin the pageant, as Melissa had said. She listened carefully to Mrs. Hicks at the piano. Since they were stalling for time, the woman was playing a medley of Christmas music, and Corrine was waiting for the first chords of "It Came Upon a Midnight Clear," which would be her cue to turn on the first light. The instant Mrs. Hicks looked at her and nodded, Corrine put her finger on the switch, and at the first chord, she flipped on the direct light that lit the sparkling star that Aunt Marilee and her mother had finally gotten hung above the stage only just before the pageant. Everyone oohed and aahed.

When Charlene MacCoy came out to stand in front of the piano, Corrine flipped on the light above her and turned the knob to lower the other lights of the sanctuary almost off.

The lighting truly made all the difference. Right then the star looked all magical, and the velvet covered partitions looked like black night, and Mrs. MacCoy was beautiful and glimmering.

Corrine held her hand near the switches, and just as Mrs. MacCoy finished and bowed her head, Corrine flipped off all the lights and the place went dark, except for the candles. An "oohhh" rippled softly through the room. It was great.

Then Mrs. Hicks began playing, and Corrine flipped on the light for Melissa, who stood there looking every bit like a fairy princess.

Gazing at the girl, Corrine's finger lingered above the light switch. Then she sighed and removed it and awaited another cue.

She had a great time working the switches. She was queen of the lights, which were the main players, really, and she never had to get up in front of anyone.

The pageant was a hit. When Melissa ended with her "Peace on earth and goodwill to people everywhere from God, our Father in heaven"—Corrine had thought Mrs. MacCoy might have to drag the girl off—everyone began to clap and even to stand up.

"By, golly, I sure enjoyed that."

"I do believe that was the best pageant they've done in this church, no offense meant to Reverend Smith, but his weren't worth a flip."

"Wasn't that beautiful?"

"I never in my life..."

"You missed the procession of the angels, gettin' here late. I wish you woulda' seen it."

"I thought it looked a little Catholic. All those candles."

"Oh, it did…it was beautiful."

"Did you see the mustaches on those boys? What a hoot."

"That announcing angel was wonderful. Mrs. Pruitt, you have a budding star there. We're gonna see her out there in Hollywood, I'll bet."

"My favorite was the shepherd boy with his dog."

"That was Willie Lee Holloway. Hasn't he grown up?"

"Who were those three angel singers? I couldn't see for the woman with big hair sittin' in front of me."

"Bill Pruitt takin' all those pictures annoyed me, but maybe I can get some prints from him."

"It was beautiful…yes, it was."

"We got to have Charlene MacCoy di-rectin' this show from now on."

After all the compliments all over the place, all the players went back in the kitchen, hootin' and hollerin' and patting themselves on the back.

The three wise men tore off their headgear and said, "Whew, that's done."

The shepherds played a game of tag with Munro, who chased them and pulled at the hems of their robes.

The singing angels sang over and over, "Peace on earth, peace on earth, peace on earth."

And Melissa Pruitt sat down and cried.

Seeing this, Corrine got really worried, thinking maybe she had made a mistake and turned the light off the girl when she wasn't supposed to. But she didn't think she had, and she prepared to defend herself, if the girl said she'd ruined the pageant. She was relieved when she heard Mrs. Pruitt tell Aunt Vella that Melissa always cried after a performance because she was so high strung.

Then everyone was gone and the church was quiet. Her mother, Papa Tate, Willie Lee and Munro had gone on to the car. Aunt Marilee was making a round of the church, to be sure no one had left a candle burning somewhere it wasn't supposed to be, or anything else that might prove a calamity. "Now, Tate, you know how fires are a problem at Christmastime. It won't take a minute for me to check."

Corrine, who had unplugged the lights of the Christmas tree, stood looking around the shadowy sanctuary. Moonlight came through two windows at the rear.

It was fun. And I didn't mess up. Oh, thank you, God. Now let me do okay at the party, please.

She wished someone would have said that the light girl did a good job, she thought, giving a sigh as she walked out into the hall. But it was okay. She knew she had done a good job. And God knew.

"Okay," said Aunt Marilee, putting on her coat as she came into the hall. "All the candles are out and the building secure." She grinned at Corrine. "You did a great job on the lights, sugar. Just great."

Wow. Corrine looked at her with surprise, then grinned in return. Had God really done that?

Aunt Marilee put her arm around Corrine, and Corrine slipped hers around her aunt's waist as they walked out to where the others waited in the car.

The MacCoys' house was lit up and could be seen from far down the road. Cars were streaming up the driveway. It was a brick entry with an iron gate. Corrine had seen the house before, of course, and knew it was big and fancy, but somehow it looked a whole lot bigger and more impressive at night. Jojo never acted stuck up, but her house was sure something. It was new, maybe not a year old. Papa Tate and Aunt Marilee told Corrine's mother all about it, how Charlene and Mason had a fairy-tale romance and were madly in love even after being married, and how everyone in town saw it; and how they had built that senior living community and Mr. Winston could live really nice there, but he wouldn't go, and he wouldn't go live with Charlene, either, and she was really worried about him living alone.

Aunt Marilee broke off worrying over Mr. Winston to be thrilled with the Christmas lighting everywhere, all along the fences and outlining the house. There was an enormous cedar tree decorated, and a lit-up nativity scene, and a Santa Claus on the roof.

"Oh, Tate, we can put a Santa Claus on our roof next year. You've been up there now."

"Who's gonna see it on our roof? You'd have to crane your neck up."

Aunt Marilee might have argued the point, but a really cool looking guy appeared at Papa Tate's window. Papa Tate lowered the glass, and the guy said, "We're parkin' the cars, sir, what with the crowd and all."

He was about the most handsome guy Corrine had ever in her life seen. His short hair was streaked blond, and he had an earring in one ear. He wore a jean jacket over a starched shirt.

"Oh...you bet," said Papa Tate. "Everyone out."

Corrine wished she could have gotten out the side where the guy was. Behind them, two other cars were stopped, and two more young men were parking them, too. She wondered if they were friends of Jojo's brothers. She knew that one of Jojo's brothers, Danny J., was in senior high and rode broncs. Her other brother was in college. Maybe that really handsome guy was him.

There were so many people! Corrine took hold of Willie Lee and kept them both inches away from her mother and Aunt Marilee, who saw all the candles everywhere and told them to be careful. "This place is a fire hazard. I guess we're lucky most of the fire department is here."

Corrine, who had never managed crowds very well at all, wished she had stayed home, even if she did have her earrings, a dynamite outfit and lip gloss.

There were Mr. Winston and Granny Franny sitting on a high-backed love seat near an enormous fireplace. They looked like the king and queen. They both saw Corrine and waved, and she waved back.

My gosh, there was Uncle Perry sitting in a recliner. And he called out to her, "Merry Christmas, you!"

Well, if he wasn't careful, people were going to catch on about him being the Santa. People would get suspicious with him being so jolly.

Aunt Marilee took Willie Lee off to the family room, where the smaller kids were gathered, and Charlene MacCoy took Corrine out the back door and pointed to the barn. "All the teens are out at the horse barn for a dance, honey. You go on out. Jojo's out there." And she went back into the house.

Corrine stared at the barn. A fancy horse barn, and all lined in blue Christmas lights, too. Would there be horses in there? Just then music started coming from the barn.

She looked down at herself, at her velvet blouse and black skirt. She would have felt better if she had worn her jeans. She felt sick to her stomach at thinking about going into the building full of people all by herself. But there wasn't anything else to do.

"Corrine!" Jojo greeted her. "I'm so glad you got here. Mama made us have the dance out here in the barn, so's the little kids could have the family room. It's pretty nice, anyway."

It sure was nice, Corrine thought, looking at the pine paneled walls, and the festive lanterns and Christmas lights strung above the wide area where kids danced on a concrete floor. It was even heated. Music played out of a large colorful jukebox of the sort that was in cafés and clubs.

Corrine's attention was quickly diverted, however, to the stalls that lined a concrete alleyway. "Are there horses in here?" She was already walking toward the stalls to look in.

"Nah. We put 'em out in the pasture. You can step out that door over there to see 'em if you want. But come on and get a Coke first." She took hold of Corrine by the hand and led her along.

There was a small kitchen, complete with refrigerator and counter and sink. Older kids were in here, and Corrine instantly felt self-conscious following after Jojo, who wasn't self-conscious at all.

"What'cha need, sis?"

Right there in front of Corrine, big as life on a bright day, was the guy who had parked Papa Tate's car. The most handsome guy Corrine had ever in her life seen.

He had called Jojo sis.

"We want a couple of Cokes." They had stopped at a big cooler on a stand.

"Comin' right up. And who is this pretty lady you got with you?" He smiled at Corrine, as he reached into the ice in the cooler and pulled out two small bottles of Coca-Cola.

"This is Corrine. Corrine, this is my big brother Larry Joe. Thinks he's a big shot, home from college and being our chap-er-one," she added in a smart tone.

The guy popped the tops off the bottles and handed over the drinks. "Nice to meet you, Corrine. Whatever Jojo tells you about me, don't believe it. She loves me."

Corrine never said a word. The best she could do was to nod and make herself quit staring at him, and turn to follow after Jojo.

"Every girl is hot for Larry Joe," Jojo whispered in an annoyed tone.

Corrine kept her mouth shut.

It was a Christmas party that Corrine would remember all of her life. The sort she would long for and likely never experience again, as this was a night of so many firsts.

It was her first time for seeing a young man who made her heart trip over in the same manner as did a horse.

It was her first time to wear earrings and colored lip gloss, a pretty outfit, and even a dash of Aunt Marilee's perfume, to a party where she socialized as a feminine young woman.

It was her first time to dance, which she did with Ricky Dale after watching on the sidelines and studying how it was done. She asked him to dance, when she realized that he and Melissa weren't having anything to do with each other. Melissa, it appeared, had become enamored with her friend Darla's older brother, Michael. Corrine feeling a little sorry for Ricky Dale for being so tossed aside was what gave her courage to ask him to dance in the first place. After that it was all very easy to dance with him and joke with him, and ask him to go out to look at the horses with her.

It was while petting the horses who came to the fence that she had her first kiss beneath the moonlit sky. She always would think of it as her kissing him, but she could admit that perhaps it was as much Ricky Dale's doing. His lips were warm on hers for lazy seconds, and then they were each a little embarrassed. But she reached out and took his hand, and he smiled eagerly at her and held her hand the rest of the night.

Somehow, with a few words, but mostly with unspoken yearnings, she told him that she had missed him, and he said the same. He said aloud, "Melissa's too much of a dang girl," and Corrine knew he meant it as a compliment to herself.

That night was the first time she saw what a lady her mother was, being surrounded by men who were drawn to her at every turn, but her mother kept them politely at a distance, while still entertaining them.

It was the first night she saw Aunt Marilee kiss Papa Tate in public, and the first time she came around a corner and caught a couple she barely knew in a passionate kiss—Pastor Smith kissing his wife Naomi in such a way that it was no wonder they had all those children. She was relieved that the couple did not see her, and Ricky Dale and Jojo, too, as they turned around and went the other way, Ricky Dale and Corrine slapping hands over Jojo's mouth.

It was the first time she ever walked along the top rail of a board fence, in earrings, skirt and dress shoes, leading a line of kids behind her.

It was the first time she ever sang Christmas carols at midnight in front of an enormous bonfire, along with a few adults who set down their beers long enough to fold their hands and listen to Mason MacCoy, who she kept remembering had been in prison, offer up a prayer that many said was powerful.

"By golly, that was a party," Papa Tate said when they left.

Everyone agreed.

And when Corrine drifted off to sleep in her warm bed, she thought of the most handsome guy she had ever in her life seen, Larry Joe Darnell. She thought maybe she would grow up and marry him.

Until then, there was Ricky Dale.

24
∞

The telephone woke Corrine at first light. Thinking every-one else still in bed, as usual, she hopped out of bed to an-swer it before everyone got awakened by the ringing, only to find Aunt Marilee already in the kitchen, dressed and drinking coffee, with the telephone receiver held between her neck and shoulder, while jotting notes on a pad in front of her.

When her aunt hung up, she said, "We have five days. Just five days."

The memory of the wonderful pageant and party went flying out of Corrine's mind. She had to get the Santa money mailed and buy all the presents she now wanted to make certain to give.

While Aunt Marilee was thus occupied with studying on her to-do list, Corrine slipped off to the bathroom to wash her face and brush her teeth. In the process, she left a Her-shey's chocolate Kiss on top of her aunt's makeup bag, to be a little secret Santa gift.

She wanted to get her mother a secret Santa gift, but she wasn't certain what it could be.

* * *

The first order of business was to get stamps for the Santa money envelopes. That was a snap. She often got stamps for the newspaper or her aunt, so Mrs. Jenkins-Tinsley's curiosity would not be aroused. It would be a bit more difficult to mail the envelopes and not have anyone notice her doing it. She would have to think on that.

On her way to the post office, she stopped into the *Voice* offices to speak to Papa Tate about taking her shopping at the mall. He said he would do so that evening, just like he always said he would do anything she asked him. She wondered in that instant if she dared ask him to go out and steal her a horse, since they couldn't afford to buy one.

"This evenin', you and me, gorgeous," Papa Tate said, giving her a wink.

"Yep," she said, smiling really big for him. He had never called her gorgeous before. She thought it had to do with her dressing up for the party the night before. She had never before felt as she had the previous night, and others had seemed to take notice, too.

However, as much as she had enjoyed that dressing up, she was sure glad to be in her jeans and boots this morning. She had worn her earrings, though, with her boots and jeans.

"Well, for heaven's sake!" Reggie Pahducony said loudly, just as Corrine was leaving Papa Tate's office. Reggie was manning the reception desk in Charlotte's absence, and she was on her feet, while a delivery girl from Grace Florist carried a big basket of flowers down the middle aisle of the long room.

"They're for Zona," Reggie said with wonder, staring after the delivery girl.

"Well, by golly," said Papa Tate, who had come up behind Corrine. His eyes, like everyone else's, followed the girl and the basket of flowers as they went to the door of Zona's small office.

"Did you do it?" Reggie asked, casting a searching gaze over at Papa Tate.

"I did not," he replied. "And I don't know who did."

Corrine believed him.

The girl couldn't knock on Zona's door with her hands holding the basket, so Leo Pahdocony jumped up to knock for her and said, "Miss Zona, there's somethin' here for you."

The door opened. The delivery girl went in. Everyone kept staring. The delivery girl came back out.

"Who sent them?" asked Reggie, as the girl came back up the center aisle.

"I don't know. They don't tell me who they come from, just who they go to. You know, I think that's the first time I ever saw that woman. She's little, idn't she? I wouldn't let her carry that basket. She might fall over."

As the girl went out, the UPS delivery guy, Buddy, came in the door. "Ho-ho-ho. Packages for everyone."

There was a long package for Papa Tate, who grinned a great big grin and told Corrine not to ask questions as he carried it away into his office and shut the door that was hardly ever shut.

"It's from Mama!" Imperia Brown called out about her box. "Her gingerbread cookies."

"It's my sexy black dress for my Christmas date!" Tammy Crawford said, dancing around.

"Everett Northrupt sent us all his yearly fruitcake," said Reggie Pahdocony. She dumped it into the trash.

But skinny June Redman ran over and grabbed it out. "Don't do that. What if he came in here? It'd hurt his feelings." She put the cake up on the reception counter and took several slices out, wrapping them in a Kleenex and putting those in the trash. "That way, if he sees, he'll think we're eatin' it."

Corrine wondered about this deception at the holiest time of year.

Outside, the street had the same feel of energy and excitement that Corrine had sensed in the *Voice* offices. Traffic and people were moving up and down the street. Corrine just about got run over, and she was crossing with the light.

"Merry Christmas, Corrine!" called Deputy Midgette as he came out of the police station.

She Merry Christmased him in return, and the next instant Jaydee Mayhall called from his car, "Merry Christmas, Deputy Midge! How's things at the po-lice station?"

"It's the Sheriff's Office. That's what it is," the deputy stated emphatically. Then he said to Corrine, "I don't know why everyone keeps callin' it a police station. I thought we'd gotten that straight." Then, "Ohboy, I'd better get down to MacCoy's and get one of those real pine wreaths I told my mama I'd get for her. They're a little cheaper than the florist."

Corrine was glad the deputy turned in his tracks and went the other way.

When passing the drugstore, she decided to go in and see if Uncle Perry had come down. He hadn't, though, and Belinda said all his activity of the day before had him laid out in his recliner at home. "Your mother is waitin' on him hand and foot," Belinda said, and Corrine couldn't decide if Belinda was glad or angry about it.

Then Belinda said, "Look at this," and showed Corrine the Christmas card that she had made out of Corrine's drawing. She had it displayed on the small perfume and gift counter, and there were packaged sets tied with a red bow. "They're such a hit that I began sellin' 'em," she said happily.

Corrine, looking at the card, felt odd. Happy, but it sure was odd to see her drawing displayed like that. It was a pretty drawing, though, she decided.

Down at the Senior Center, Mr. Winston and Mr. Everett were hanging two real pine wreaths with little American flags on them on the double doors.

"It might snow, right, Corrine?" Mr. Winston said as she came near.

"I guess it might," she said, not wanting to disappoint him with her true skepticism of the prospect. Right then the temperature was warm enough for her to be comfortable in her jean jacket.

"Twenty percent ain't much of a chance. Don't get your hopes up," said Mr. Northrupt. "And I moved down here to get away from snow, anyway."

To that, Mr. Winston said, "Let me tell you, ol' son, that

I've seen the day it was seventy degrees in the mornin' and by evenin' it was thirty-five and a blizzard a' comin' on."

As she walked on, she heard Mr. Northrupt telling Mr. Winston that the pine wreaths wouldn't last long on the door, if it stayed warm.

Then, just as she reached the post office, there was a man in a wheelchair being pushed out the door. A man with long, straggly brown-grey hair, whose legs were missing below the knees. Corrine saw the stumps and quickly looked away, not daring to look him in the eyes but keeping a smile on her face. Then she realized this was the man she had seen on Paris Miller's front porch, and it was Paris pushing the wheelchair.

"Hi, Paris," Corrine said, and grabbed hold of the door to hold it open.

"Hey…thanks."

"You're welcome."

Their eyes met. Corrine felt awkward, wondering if she should speak to the man in the wheelchair. She smiled at him. He nodded and looked away.

"See ya'," Paris said.

"Yeah, see ya'."

Their eyes met again.

Corrine went on into the post office, then turned and looked back through the glass, watching Paris push the wheelchair down the sidewalk. Funny how Corrine had not ever seen Paris with this man, or even hardly ever seen the girl anywhere.

Paris had looked at her oddly.

Paris had looked at her earrings.

Paris was the one who had given her the earrings.

The certainty stole over Corrine, as she remembered the way the girl's eyes had slid over her face and to her ears, then darted away. She just knew without a doubt that Paris was her secret Santa. For heaven's sake.

Then, bringing her mind back to her endeavor, she saw with relief that no one waited at the postal counter. Mrs. Julia Jenkins-Tinsley was there sorting through some mail.

"Who was that man who was just in here?" Corrine asked. "The one in the wheelchair?"

"What?" She looked down at Corrine. "Oh, hello, Corrine...that man, oh, that's Joe Miller. He had his legs blown off over there in Vietnam. He was returnin' some mail sent to his daughter, who is not livin' there with them anymore. She run off with some man to Phoenix and left Joe and her daughter. Just up and left—" the postmistress was shaking her head "—right at Christmastime, too. Joe hasn't lived here but maybe six months...and it's a good thing he's here, even though I think that his granddaughter takes more care of him than him her...but at least..."

"Uh, could I have four dollars in stamps?" Corrine said. She felt guilty for listening to gossip, and besides, she was really excited now, thinking about one of the envelopes going to the man. She couldn't wait for Paris and her grandfather to get their Santa money. What a miracle that she, Corrine, got to see that they got this money. She could hardly stand the wonderful prospect.

"Which ones do you want? The Santas or the angels?"

"The Santas, please."

She realized when the postmistress grinned at her that she was grinning really big.

"Merry Christmas, Mrs. Jenkins-Tinsley."

"Merry Christmas to you, sweetheart."

She suddenly wanted to get the woman a secret Santa gift.

She flew out past the Santa mailbox, out to the sidewalk and to the corner in front of the bank, hopping from foot to foot until the light changed and she could cross.

"Hey, Mr. Mayhall!" she called out, passing the man on the run and hearing his return greeting floating after her.

She remembered to slow down, though, in order to glance into the window of the saddle shop.

The saddle was gone.

She stopped and fully looked. The saddle stand now stood empty. They hadn't moved it and hadn't put another saddle on it yet.

Tearing her eyes from the window, feeling her flying spirit sink, she went on to the apartment. Her saddle, the one she had imagined as her own, was gone. Someone else would be riding in it. Likely it was a Christmas present.

She tried not to be too disappointed. After all, it was really silly to think that she would ever have gotten that saddle. She didn't even have a horse and wasn't likely to get one.

Get over it! she told herself.

Her mother had come. Corrine smelled her perfume and heard murmuring in the kitchen. Instinctively she closed the door quietly, crossed the living room and slipped up to stand outside the archway to the kitchen, straining to hear her mother's and aunt's voices.

"...Belinda's not...Perry is...he seems perfectly..."

"...we can tell Corrine...won't fight you...but I will not have that..."

"Oh, come on, Mari...give me..."

Were they arguing about her? But where did Uncle Perry come in? Boy, she hoped he hadn't told about being the Santa money man.

"Okay...that's just...careful, is all I'm sayin'. Lordy, I've got to get off my feet."

Footsteps started out of the kitchen, and Corrine turned and hurried back to the front door, giving it a slam.

"Well, hello, sugar," said her mother, coming out of the kitchen behind her aunt, whose gaze was surveying Corrine thoughtfully.

"Hey."

She thought her mother and aunt looked agreeable, not like they had been arguing. But there was something between them.

"Come on in here. Your mother has news from Uncle Perry."

Corrine's heart went to pounding. If Uncle Perry had told about being the Santa money man, it would ruin everything.

"Uncle Perry has decided to give everyone their inheritance from him for Christmas."

"Is he dyin'?" Corrine asked with alarm.

"Oh, no, honey. He just feels that he wants to see his

loved ones enjoying their inheritance while he's alive. Especially you and Willie Lee. You know, Uncle Perry doesn't have any grandchildren yet, and he thinks of you and Willie Lee as his own."

"Oh." She calmed down a bit. It appeared Uncle Perry's secret, and her own, was safe.

She was so preoccupied with this relief that she had to bring her mind back to what Aunt Marilee was saying about Uncle Perry giving Corrine and Willie Lee each ten thousand dollars. Her aunt and mother were thrilled and went on and on about how the money would be a good start of a college fund for her, and how Uncle Perry was very pleased to do this.

"You'll want to give him a big thank-you," Aunt Marilee told her.

Corrine said she would. She didn't say it, but getting money for college was like getting socks in her Christmas stocking. No matter how much they might be needed, it was just too practical to be any fun, and besides, college was so far away as to be totally irrelevant to her life at the moment.

She was glad to see her mother and aunt so happy, though. Talking avidly about the grand prospects of her future kept them occupied while she went off to her bedroom to get the stamps on the envelopes and figure out how to get the envelopes into the mail without anyone noticing her.

"I'll go for your groceries," Corrine told Aunt Marilee, who was fretting over time.

"Oh, honey, that's a pretty good walk."

"I don't mind," Corrine said quickly and grabbed up the list from the table. "I'll charge them." Without waiting for an okay, she raced out of the kitchen and to her bedroom, where she tucked the Santa money envelopes into the waistband of her jeans and then put on her coat.

Then, just as she came out of her bedroom, there was Willie Lee. "Munro and I will go, too." He had his coat on.

Rats. She couldn't tell him no.

She would work it out, she thought.

"Marshmallows...the tiny ones," Aunt Marilee called to them as they were going out the door.

During their walk to the IGA, Corrine discarded the idea of simply going over to the mailbox and dropping in the envelopes in full view of Willie Lee. Not only did he know what the Santa money envelopes looked like, but he might tell someone about Corrine mailing envelopes. Of course, it wasn't likely anyone would connect Corrine with the Santa money, but the necessity to keep a secret led her to wild imaginings about being discovered. She could fairly see the sheriff grilling her as to where she'd gotten the money and just what did she think she was trying to do by pretending to be Santa Claus? She would just die if the identity of Uncle Perry as Santa came out. She saw herself as heroically carrying this secret to her grave. Keeping secrets obviously led to anxieties, she thought, as she walked all the way to the IGA and then home again with the envelopes tucked into the waistband of her jeans and scratching her skin.

"Telephone, Corrine. It's Ricky Dale."

"Hey," she said, thrilled to think he would call her. It had been a long time since he had called her on the telephone.

"Hey, Corky. What's up?"

"Oh, just hangin' out."

"My brother and his girlfriend are goin' up to the mall this afternoon, and I was wonderin'...well, do you think you might wanna go up there with me?"

Ohmygosh! She had to ask Aunt Marilee, of course. She was glad her mother was not there, because then she would have been caught between who to ask. As it was, Aunt Marilee got herself on the phone to speak to Ricky Dale, asking about who all was going and making certain Ricky Dale's brother, Junior, would be with them all the time, not just dropping them off.

"You have her home here no later than 8:00 p.m., Ricky Dale, or I'll send your daddy after you all."

Corrine was surprised her aunt didn't require Ricky Dale to have a tracking device on him.

She was thrilled to get to go, so thrilled that she forgot all about her date with Papa Tate, until she was getting dressed, and then she came racing out to ask Aunt Marilee to explain to Papa Tate.

Okay, God. If You mean these envelopes to get mailed today, You have to handle it. She tucked them again into the waistband of her jeans, covering them with her thick coat.

"Oh, my baby's first date," her mother said, when she came into the living room. Aunt Marilee had called her, and had also summoned Papa Tate, who said, "I've been thrown over for a younger man."

Good grief. They never used to go on like this when Ricky Dale stopped by to get her to go to the corral.

"Now, here, take my cell phone." Her mother showed her how to work it and then tucked it into her little black purse. "You can call anytime from anywhere. So much better than what we had for a date, right, Marilee?"

"It's not a date," Corrine said. "We're just goin' to the mall."

She looked out the front windows and saw Junior's black truck pulling to the curb. "They're here," she said, hurrying for the door.

"Wait! I want a picture."

Corrine, hand on the doorknob, turned and shot a smile at Aunt Marilee, who had the little Canon to her eye. The flashbulb went off.

"See ya'!" And she raced down the stairs before Ricky Dale could come up and see everyone making a big deal out of the whole thing.

As she climbed into the back seat of the pickup, the envelopes tucked into the waistband of her jeans scratched her skin. What was she thinking, carrying them around like this?

Somehow she just had to mail them.

Ten minutes later, and halfway to the mall, the cell phone in her purse began ringing. She about jumped out of her skin.

It was her Aunt Marilee, who said, "We just wanted to make sure the phone worked."

Corrine was a little annoyed. Junior and Cindy were laughing, and Ricky Dale's face was red.

A few minutes later, though, as she looked at Junior and his girlfriend, Cindy, Corrine was rather glad to know her aunt and her mother were only a phone call away. She felt totally a child, standing in an opening into the future life that awaited her. It helped to know she could reach out and touch those who loved her.

"You want to leave your coat in the truck?" Cindy asked her.

"No. I'll just wear it."

She felt like a nerd. Possibly this was because she was a nerd, who was wearing her heavy coat, while all the other teens out of school for the week and cruising the mall were in T-shirts.

She was glad Junior and Cindy went their way, leaving Ricky Dale and Corrine to themselves. Ricky Dale hit her shoulder and said, "Beat you to the top of the stairs."

Corrine gave the sprint a good go, but was too afraid to give full effort, as she feared the envelopes might fall out of her jeans.

After two hours of pinball in the arcade and shopping, they stopped to get pizza and soft drinks. Ricky Dale bought them. She had money out to give to him, but he said in rather a masterful fashion, "I'll buy. Why don't you get us a table?"

She was glad to do so, because she just had to get out of her coat. Keeping an eye on Ricky Dale, who had his back to her, she tied the arms of her coat around her waist, covering and anchoring the envelopes against her at the same time. She could not believe she had gotten herself into this situation, carrying them around. She just had to get them mailed.

Here came Ricky Dale, bearing a tray of food. He looked really cool, with his styled hair and his earring. He sat down across from her.

They *were* on a date. She didn't think she liked the thought.

Quickly aiming, she blew her straw paper at Ricky Dale and hit him right in the forehead. In retaliation, he blew his back at her, she ducked, and the straw paper went over and hit a woman in the back of the head, sticking in her hair without her knowing.

It was great. It was like old times, only better.

She looked up and saw her chance—a mailbox in the wall in the alcove to the rest rooms.

"I'll wait when I come out," Ricky Dale said. "You girls always take so long."

"Okay." She kept herself from shoving him into the rest room.

She entered the ladies' room, then pivoted and came right back out, raced over to the mail slot, jerking out the envelopes as she went. One got stuck. In her haste, she about tore her shirt. She got the envelopes in the slot and turned to find a lady giving her a curious look. The lady was on her way to the ladies' room, and Corrine shot around her and entered, because she didn't want Ricky Dale to catch her out there.

Some twenty minutes later, when she got a minute to herself, while Ricky Dale was again enamored with the pinball game at the arcade, she used the cell phone to call Uncle Perry. She sure hoped he answered, and if he didn't, she would hang up really quick.

Uncle Perry did answer!

"It's me, Corrine," she said, making certain she was far away from anyone else. "The packages are in the mail."

"Right. Good work," Uncle Perry replied in the same manner.

She put her coat on for the drive home and discovered an object in her pocket. It felt like a pocketknife. When Junior stopped to fill up with gas and Ricky Dale got out to wash the windshield, Corrine drew out the knife and looked at it in the yellowy gleam of the convenience store lights.

It was a small, even dainty, pocketknife, with a pearl handle.

The knowledge that Ricky Dale somehow knew that she had been the one to give him a knife stole over her, bringing a warm delight. Slipping the knife into her coat pocket, she closed her hand tightly around it.

She didn't say anything to him, just as he had not said anything to her. She sat close to him, with her arm rubbing his. He carefully extended his arm on the seat back, and she moved closer to him, recalling having seen Junior and Cindy in the restaurant, and Junior putting his hand on Cindy's breast.

When she got home, and finally—after telling the adults that yes, she'd had a wonderful time, and not to ask about the gifts in her bags—she was alone in her room, she looked again at the knife in the warm light of her desk lamp.

Some girls might like a bottle of perfume, or earrings or a necklace, but this gift was perfect for Corrine. And it was a perfect thing for Ricky Dale to give, too.

Her heart filled with all manner of hopes and dreams for her future as a woman. She saw the years ahead as if rolled out before her, and seeing it all like that served to make her tremendously glad that her first date was with Ricky Dale, with whom she could still be a child. She knew, in the instinctive manner that she knew many things about life, that Ricky Dale would give her a safe place to grow and blossom, until they both went away to college, she to art school, which would take her away from his scientific mind of veterinary medicine. And she would see places, like New York City and Paris, and then she would return home to Valentine, a woman full grown and ready for Larry Joe Darnell, who she already loved and who, even if he didn't know it, was just waiting for her to grow up.

The Valentine Voice

Christmas About Town
by Marilee Holloway

We have come to our final *Christmas About Town* column. What a month this has been.

The Delmar Kidd and Joe Miller families want to thank Santa for his latest gift of cash. We could not begin to print all the thank-yous from people who have received all manner of gifts; however, *The Valentine Voice* family wants to thank Santa for reviving the spirit of giving all over town, and a big appreciation to those of you who have shared with us your experiences of receiving gifts.

Those Santa helpers who sent me the pound of chocolates, the box of gourmet cocoa and the chocolate Santa, have my sincere gratitude. I'm set for several weeks. The Editor says a big thank-you to the Santa helpers who sent him the book of Mark Twain essays, the light-up pen and the musical toilet paper roller.

Okay—are you one of those who has waited until the very last minute to get some, or any, of your gifts? I will not point out your error. We all make mistakes. Do not despair. See the article our Editor put together for last minute gift ideas. There are a number of electronic gadgets on that list, and the Editor assures me that everything on there will especially suit the younger generation. That means I'm of the older.

No matter the age, here are two things that will save you from appearing like Scrooge: gift certificates and food. If you want to make it especially easy, you could give gift certificates of food from Tinsley's IGA.

In cooperation with the Valentine Homemakers, the IGA now has gift baskets of food items, as well as a posting of a list of suggestions of food that makes good gifts. Also posted by the Valentine Homemakers is a list of easy recipes for breads, cookies, candies and canned relishes that make excellent and appreciated gifts. The list contains many sugar-free, gluten-free, egg-free and milk-free recipes to suit every need and desire.

We can thank high school home economist Mrs. Peggy Sue Langston for having the idea, and Doris Northrupt, an expert on gourmet allergy-free cooking, for getting the recipes together at the last minute. It is the spirit of giving at work, and speaking as one who is not wild about cooking, I know gifts of food are welcome gifts indeed, most especially to women who work outside the home. I also call your attention to the recipe for building a gingerbread house, something enjoyed by children and adults alike.

Our final recipe for the season comes again from Mrs. Julia Jenkins-Tinsley.

Pep-Up Drink for Easy Living

1 cup polite words.
Choose and measure carefully those ripened on the positive side.

3/4 cup each hope, humor and humility
1/2 cup each honesty and compassion
1/2 cup generosity
Prayer to suit
Pinch of faith. Only a pinch is required, but
make it pure.

Cook the first six ingredients over a steady flame of difficulties.

Sprinkle in generosity and prayer, then add the pinch of faith in God. Simmer until faith has expanded to double the mixture, then sip it up and feel the courage and gratitude lift you up and have you skating through life.

And don't forget to make everything easy on yourself by relying on your United States Postal Service to get your letters and packages where they need to go and when they need to be there. Even through rain, sleet, snow and muddy roads, the USPS gets it there!

We invite everyone to drop in to the *Voice* offices the rest of the week. We're serving coffee and cookies, some of these sugar-free and gluten-free, courtesy of Doris Northrupt. And in your buying of gift certificates, don't forget: A gift certificate to *The Valentine Voice* shows how much you care!
Merry Christmas!
Love to all.

When Marilee finished writing her column, she put her head down on her arms. She had gotten out another column, here at the last minute. Writing was so hard for her. Tate, he could just pound out everything on his mind, but she had to think and think and prod herself along. She wasn't even certain what she had written. She was afraid she sounded too silly, especially when putting in that recipe from Julia Jenkins-Tinsley.

Only a real ass would fail to appreciate a person who could think up something so sweet as that Pep-Up Drink for Easy Living. Okay, maybe Julia was just a little too peppy, but God help her, Marilee would appreciate that woman in the future. And He *would* have to help her, too.

When she lifted her head, there was a Hershey's chocolate Kiss sitting on top of the keyboard of her computer, and she heard Corrine's sweet voice in the kitchen singing, "Joy to the world…"

25

As a result of Aunt Marilee's final *Christmas About Town* column, they received several applesauce cakes, zucchini bread, cranberry bread, about a half a dozen gifts of cookies, fruit butters and pickles and casseroles, an entire gingerbread house, and a couple of things no one could safely identify and so didn't want to taste.

There were a few dishes from people they didn't even know, and Aunt Marilee refused to let anyone touch these. She threw them away, in secret, wrapping them in old copies of the *Voice* and securing them in plastic bags, then carting them out to the Dumpster at midnight.

She wrote thank-you notes for each thing and had Corrine help her to make up cute scenarios of how their family had enjoyed the particular food.

"Aren't you teachin' me to lie?" Corrine said.

"In a good way," Aunt Marilee replied.

It was the magical and exciting final days before Christmas. They didn't wait until Christmas Eve to have their stockings hung by the fireplace with care. Aunt Marilee, saying that since they didn't have a fireplace, it didn't matter, had already hung them up on the wall beside the Christmas tree, and with pretty strong hooks, too. She'd gotten out her power drill and sunk fasteners in the Sheetrock, so they wouldn't have an accident of a stocking falling down once it was full.

"Darlin', I hope you didn't just make it so that a piece of wall is pulled out by a falling stockin'," Papa Tate said.

And to that Corrine's mother said, "Y'all are sure plannin' on full and heavy stockings."

Willie Lee piped up and said, "We have been good, Aunt A-ni-ta," and grinned his cute grin that made Aunt Marilee hug him. She was thrilled that he had abandoned his stance on no Santa Claus and had fallen into pretending right along with the rest of them.

When they made one of their quick trips to the Wal-Mart and the same Christmas Santa was at the entry of the big building ringing his bell for money, Willie Lee said very pleasantly, "Mer-ry Chris-mas, San-ta."

Recognizing Willie Lee, the man tried to pull his hat down more over the strings that held on his beard—it was hopeless, but he did try—and said, "Merry Christmas, little boy."

Aunt Marilee made out her last minute forgotten Christmas cards, and Corrine mailed them, along with the Christmas card with her own drawing that she had bought from Belinda and sent to Mrs. Jenkins-Tinsley, signing, *From Santa Claus*, because she rather thought that the postmistress handled everyone else's mail but didn't get much of her own. Corrine had overheard two ladies talking at the drugstore about how Mrs. Jenkins-Tinsley was married to a man fifteen years older than herself and had no children, and not even any sisters. Corrine thought maybe this was why the woman was always so curious about everyone's mail.

She also mailed the pair of earrings that she had bought for Paris Miller at the mall. She signed the note *From Santa Claus*, and made certain to disguise her handwriting. It was great fun, and in her enthusiasm, she put the scarf she'd had Belinda buy for her mother in a padded envelope and mailed it to her mother, signing it from Santa, too.

Her mother received it the very next day and brought it

around to show them, wondering who could have sent it, naming everyone from Aunt Marilee to Aunt Vella to some handsome man who had been passing through town and come into the drugstore soda fountain and flirted with her.

That Corrine could have been the one did not seem to occur to anyone. Corrine found this fact at once thrilling and annoying. Why would they not consider that she could be a secret Santa? More than once she had to bite her tongue to keep from blurting out, "I sent it, you nuts." Basically, though, she didn't want to point the finger at herself, since she had not gotten a secret present as equally nice for Aunt Marilee but kept giving her aunt chocolate Kisses. The little candies were her aunt's favorite, after all.

When she helped Aunt Marilee and Papa Tate deliver the *Voice* food baskets to certain needy families, leaving them anonymously whenever possible, she wished they could have taken one to Paris's house. Not that Paris probably needed it so much now, after getting the Santa money, but still, Paris was the only needy person she knew.

Experiencing the excitement of pretending to be like Santa Claus, Corrine quite suddenly wanted to give things. She remembered, sometimes with a sinking feeling in the pit of her stomach, how she had felt when she and her mother lived in Fort Worth, and they had often been very needy. She never wanted to go back to that again.

Whenever she thought of perhaps having to go live with her mother again, she would worry about them being poor and needy again. She would be fearful that perhaps her life would never go anywhere helpful, that she would never get the horses and home that she wanted. Giving stuff and signing it from Santa helped to distance her from that fear.

Yet, as Corrine gazed at the gifts under the tree, she wished she could be more excited about Christmas and getting presents. She fretted over what could be wrong with her that she wasn't all aglow about the whole matter.

Aunt Marilee was sure glowing about it. She always did, and, as always, had gone overboard. There were about a dozen wrapped presents each for Corrine and Willie Lee beneath the tree. From past experience, Corrine knew that there would be other unwrapped gifts from Santa on Christmas morning, not to mention full stockings that would contain things like hair clips, gloves, fingernail polish, coloring pens, possibly a pocket radio or electronic toy of some sort, chocolate bars, apples and oranges.

Corrine wasn't certain why Aunt Marilee always put food in the stocking. Maybe she wanted to make sure no one went hungry in case of some emergency.

Sitting there, thinking about it all, Corrine thought that Aunt Marilee bought all this stuff in order to make up for her own disappointing childhood Christmases. Aunt Marilee seemed to love Christmas more in an attempt to make up for how hard it had been not only for herself, but for Corrine's mother and for anyone she ever heard about, too.

Corrine prepared to be very excited about it all on Christmas morning, so as not to disappoint Aunt Marilee and her mother, and Papa Tate, too.

But she would be glad when this Christmas was over and she could get on to finding out if she was going to be staying with Aunt Marilee or going to live with her mother. She was surprised that she had come to the point where maybe she didn't really care which one she lived with, just so she found out. She had come to the point of thinking it wouldn't be bad at all to be with her mother, if only she didn't have to leave Aunt Marilee and Willie Lee. It would be okay, if her mother stayed in Valentine.

And she wanted to get on to being older, too. She wanted the years to fly by so that she grew up and never again had to wait on grown-ups to decide her life. She was not going to rely on anyone else, not ever. She was going to make her own money and fashion her own life, which would include horses and a big place to keep them, and no one would ever take any of it from her, either.

There was a voice inside that whispered this time would never come. But she told herself that it would. She would make it come. She would never have to wait and hope on anyone else, other than herself, when she finally got to be a grown-up.

* * *

Corrine went with Aunt Marilee around to all their friends and neighbors, delivering gifts of sweet breads and fudge, teas and coffees, with the *Voice* mug and various handsome table linens. Aunt Marilee only made the fudge. The rest she bought. Aunt Marilee was not one to make presents, but she greatly enjoyed devising unique wrapping. She believed that the beauty of the presentation was part of the gift. This year she had gotten struck with the idea to use wicker baskets for gift containers. That way, she said, she didn't have to be bothered much with paper, and people got two gifts in one. She filled the baskets, covered them with toile fabric and a bow, or else just a bow. Her bows were things of grand designs.

When they took Fayrene Gardner her basket, the woman almost cried. She said, "I won't be able to touch that basket. It's too pretty. I'm settin' it up here as a decoration."

Aunt Marilee was thrilled. "Well, I'm not much of a cook or handicraft person, but I can sure make a pretty gift box," she said, in the manner of Corrine's own mother's attitude about always writing pretty.

Mrs. Julia Jenkins-Tinsley got all excited about her basket and showed other customers in the post office, and then had to come clear out from behind the counter and hug Aunt Marilee, who hugged her back in a most tender manner and even said, "Thank you, Julia, for all your kind attention to our mail. It's a help to our family."

Corrine watched this exchange with quite a bit of fascination.

Then, when they got outside the post office, Aunt Marilee breathed really deeply and said, "Whew, that's over."

When they didn't get an answer at Mr. Winston's front door, Corrine suggested going around to the back door. It was an excuse to give her the opportunity to see the horse corral. It seemed a stupid idea, since the horses were gone, but she still wanted to see it.

It turned out that Mr. Winston was in the back, splitting a piece of firewood into small kindling pieces atop an old thick table just outside the back door. Corrine was amazed that he could do this, but his hands did seem strong. He showed her how to do it. It was a surprisingly easy action. Then he and Aunt Marilee left her there and took his basket gift, which was fruit, fancy coffee packets and a *Voice* mug, into the kitchen.

As soon as they went in the door, Corrine turned her gaze to the corral. Sunlight filtered through the bare limbed trees and made patterns on the board fencing. She saw like a fast-moving film the day she had first seen the corral and the horses and heard Ricky Dale instructing her, as he liked to instruct, on how to approach them. She thought of all the months of coming here. It was like her corral, and it felt strange to be staring at it and know it wasn't.

Just then Aunt Marilee came flying out the door. "Are you being careful with that ax?"

"Yes, ma'am." And Corrine hit the small split wood, neatly breaking off a thin piece.

"Handy girl," Mr. Winston said.

One of their last deliveries was to the MacCoys, where Corrine gave Jojo her gift of two Saddle Club books.

"Thanks," Jojo said, her eyes round. "I don't have anything for you."

"Doesn't matter. Thanks for havin' me to the party the other night. It was fun."

Jojo looked at her. "I didn't think you liked me much...you know, at first."

Corrine didn't know what to say to that. She shrugged, then managed to say, "Well, I guess I didn't know that I did."

Jojo laughed merrily at this, causing Corrine to laugh, too.

Then, with her normal joyous expression that Corrine liked to see, Jojo took Corrine out to see her horses in the daylight, saying, "We'll go ridin' sometime. My mare is gonna foal in February, so I'm not ridin' her now, but after she has the baby, you can ride her, and I'll ride my brother's old horse."

"Okay," Corrine said. Wanting to express the knot of anticipation, she managed to say, "That'd be really great. Thanks. I don't have a saddle, though."

"It's okay. We got Larry Joe's saddle. He don't use it much anymore."

Larry Joe's saddle. She just about died.

A new saddle sat in the window of the saddle shop. It was a roping saddle, big and dark and with a thick horn.

Corrine gazed at it for long seconds and then moved on, stuffing her hands in the pocket of her coat. It was steadily growing colder, too cold to ride, anyway, so she wasn't missing much. Even if the horses had still been at the corral, she wouldn't have spent a whole lot of time over there.

On the morning of Christmas Eve, while not yet having had a full cup of coffee, Aunt Marilee got a call from Grama Norma. Corrine, who answered the phone, felt hesitancy about giving the call to her aunt. She said, "Can I have her call you back? Aunt Marilee is just wakin' up."

"No, you cannot. I've been on a plane all night. I'm at a pay phone at the airport in New York, and I need to talk to her now before I collapse."

At the word "collapse," Corrine got moving. "I'm gettin' her right now, Grama Norma." Corrine took the phone to Aunt Marilee, who was propped up in bed, and said, as a warning, "It's Grama Norma. She says it's important."

Aunt Marilee pressed the receiver to her ear. "Mama? What..." was all she got out, and then Grama Norma's voice could be heard. A couple of times Aunt Marilee broke in to speak, but the most she would get out was, "I don't..." and "Well, I..." Finally she said, "Yes, Mama, we'll take care of him. Okay, you call from Chicago."

When she got off the phone, Papa Tate and Willie Lee had joined them in the bedroom.

"Mama's on her way home. She's at JFK, waitin' on her flight. She called home and found out that Carl got arrested for public drunkenness again last night, and she wants us to go get him out."

"I'll handle it," Papa Tate said.

"Bless you," Aunt Marilee said.

Corrine wondered if there was anything Papa Tate

couldn't handle. She figured the only thing might be Aunt Marilee.

"I've got to get their presents wrapped," Aunt Marilee said, slinging back the covers.

Corrine's mother came flying in the door. Clearly aggravated, she yanked off her fluffy fox fur coat and threw it on the couch, saying, "Didn't Corrine tell me that Fayrene sent over two raisin pies? I need one bad."

"A whole pie?" Aunt Marilee said from the kitchen doorway.

"A piece of pie, Marilee. Don't be ridiculous."

"But you said…"

"Now is not the time to tell me what I said. I haven't had a cigarette in four days. Just use common sense, okay?"

Corrine, ever mindful of hoping to calm tension, was already getting her mother a healthy slice of pie.

Her mother sat herself at the table. Aunt Marilee brought her coffee, and Corrine brought the pie.

"Margaret just called. Finally," her mother said, cutting into the pie and shoving it into her mouth. "She's down in St. Thomas with her boss. When she found out that I was helpin' out at Aunt Vella's, she said that was wonderful and that she thought maybe she could get home for New Year's, but right now she had work to do and just could not get away."

Corrine was amazed that a woman as graceful and beautiful as her mother would shove food into her mouth in such a manner.

"With her boss…right, and I'm Queen of Sheba," her mother added, then sighed and looked forlorn. "I've gained five pounds tryin' to quit smokin'."

Aunt Marilee touched her hand. "You could always use a bit of weight, honey. You're lookin' great."

"Well," Corrine's mother said, looking at the now empty plate, "I made it through that one."

On Christmas Eve, the Christmas tree lights stayed on all day, and Aunt Marilee played only Christmas music on the stereo, and they only watched Christmas programs on television. All the gifts that needed to be wrapped were wrapped, even the ones Corrine had bought for Aunt Vella and Uncle Perry and Granny Franny. And the extra one she had gotten her mother—a china cup printed with "I love you, Mother." She couldn't wait for her mother to open it.

She was all set with her gifts, except now something for Grama Norma and her husband, Carl. She didn't think Grama Norma would notice. She would just make sure that she gave her gifts to the other adults when Grama Norma wasn't around.

Papa Tate had called and said that he had Grama Norma's husband, Carl, out of jail and was going to make him a good meal before coming home, and maybe pick up the house a little bit. When Aunt Marilee got off the phone with him, she told them that Papa Tate had said that Grama Norma was going to have a fit over the state of her house.

"Well, she went away for over a month. I don't know what she expects," Corrine's mother said.

Just then the telephone rang again.

"Corrine, are y'all home?" It was Mrs. Jenkins-Tinsley.

"Yes," Corrine said, which seemed a little unnecessary, as the postmistress was speaking to her.

"I have an Express Mail delivery for Willie Lee. I'll be right there."

The phone clicked dead before Corrine got out another word.

"I wonder what this could be?" Aunt Marilee said with high curiosity that Corrine thought was real.

They all went to the front windows and looked down to see the postmistress carrying a box down the sidewalk, followed by one of the mail carriers, Dwight Willis, who carried a larger box. Corrine suggested they go meet them and save them a bit of the trip, but Aunt Marilee said that Mrs. Jenkins-Tinsley would be disappointed not to deliver the boxes and see what was in them.

It turned out that the postmistress knew what was in one of the boxes, as the contents were marked on the side: Adult

Fowl. Pigeon. Transport With Care. There were air holes in the box, too.

"Yes, ma'am, the USPS delivers pigeons," the postmistress said in response to Corrine's surprise. "Regulation 546.41. Adult turkeys, guinea fowl, doves, pigeons, et cetera, provided they are in an approved container. The USPS can handle just about every transport need there is. Open it up, Willie Lee, I want to see it. Who'd send you a pigeon?"

"Maybe Santa Claus sent it," Aunt Marilee said with expectancy.

Corrine thought her aunt did a good job of being surprised. Maybe she really was surprised.

Willie Lee was quite excited. His eyes got really big when he opened the box and saw on the top a big note that said, *Merry Christmas, Willie Lee. I had to send this by postal service. We're overloaded this year, and I wanted to make sure the bird was cared for. Your friend, Santa Claus.*

It was so cool.

But then Willie Lee drew out the pigeon, petting it and holding it close, and he said, "This is not my pigeon."

"Well, yes it is, hon," Mrs. Jenkins-Tinsley said. "It's addressed to you. Right there. See?"

"No," Willie Lee said. "This is a nice pigeon, but it is not the one I wanted."

"Oh," Aunt Marilee said. Trying very hard not to be disappointed, she added, "Well, honey, maybe this was the best Santa could do."

"It has a return address on it, Willie Lee. Do you want to send it back?" asked the postmistress.

"No, he doesn't," Aunt Marilee answered for him.

Corrine hoped there was a pigeon coop in the other box and suggested they open it.

A cage was in the other box. They put the pigeon in it, and put the cage in the small laundry room, because Aunt Marilee didn't like the idea of the bird being in Willie Lee's room. She felt she needed to know more about pigeons first. Any time they wanted to wash clothes, until they could get a pigeon coop built somewhere, they were going to have to move the pigeon's cage into the hallway. Aunt Marilee was not too keen on allowing the pigeon out much, so Willie Lee was in the laundry room when Papa Tate came home and found out about the pigeon's delivery, and how Willie Lee knew it was not the same pigeon that he had been looking for.

"Well, Marilee, I couldn't get that other pigeon," Papa Tate said, his frustration causing him to spill it all out in front of Corrine, who was eager to know all about it.

It turned out that Papa Tate had succeeded, through the leg band, in locating the pigeon who had kept using their windowsill as a motel and had tried to buy it; however, the man who owned it was recovering from triple bypass surgery, and his son, who was caring for the man's birds, would not sell the bird—a champion racer—without discussing it with the elder man, and his son didn't want to upset his father just yet. So Papa Tate had bought this one.

Papa Tate went in to speak to Willie Lee, going into the laundry room and shutting the door, even, so that Aunt Marilee and Corrine didn't get to hear.

When Papa Tate returned to the kitchen, he said, "I told him the truth, that I was the one who sent the bird, and that I'd tried to get the other bird, but this was the one I could get."

"Oh, Tate," Aunt Marilee.

"Well, it's better that than have him believin' Santa Claus is inept and uncaring."

Corrine decided that this thing with Santa Claus was tricky business.

"Corrine, this is your grandmother Norma. I'm callin' from Chicago. Is your mother there?" The woman was talking loud enough to be heard from Chicago.

"No, she left a while ago. Aunt Marilee's in the shower, but I can take the phone to her." Anticipating that the woman would bite her head off if she didn't get the phone to Aunt Marilee, she was already walking that way.

"No. Just tell your mother that Chicago is socked in with snow, and when I called home, some strange man answered and said Carl was not available. A strange man in my house.

I don't know when I can get home to take care of that. I'll probably die before I can get home. Just tell her I called." Grama Norma was clearly distraught.

Corrine hung up and wondered if she should have told the woman she hoped she didn't die. She felt she should have said something more positive than just saying, "Okay. Goodbye."

When she relayed the message to her aunt, her aunt said, "She's been gone four weeks, and now she's worried about him having a strange man in the house?"

But then she got to worrying about the possibility of the strange man being some disaster, such as a burglar or killer.

"Oh, I forgot to tell you, what with the pigeon crisis and all," Papa Tate explained, "but I called a friend—Shaw Tuttle—to look in on Carl and help him out until Norma got home. Carl was pretty shook up about her coming home, I guess."

"Oh," Aunt Marilee said, her mind obviously clicking along and maybe thinking that Grama Norma could produce anxiety.

"It's Christmas Eve, Marilee. The man doesn't need to be alone in his home, at least not the way it was, on Christmas Eve."

"You're special, Tate Holloway."

Watching from the dining room, Corrine saw her aunt wrap her arms around his neck.

"I think so, too," Papa Tate teased, while his hands went up and down her back. "We're almost through it, darlin'," he said and then he kissed her in a way that caused Corrine to turn away, as it didn't seem the sort of kiss a child should view.

But it made her heart glad.

Aunt Marilee put a red bow on Munro for going to the candlelight service at church. Papa Tate wore a tie and his best Irish tweed sport coat. Willie Lee wore a sweater over his starched shirt, had his hair slicked back, and carried a present for Gabby, one he had picked out himself. Corrine wore a black sweater, black skirt and her black earrings.

Every time she looked in the mirror, she was struck by how dramatic she looked with her dark hair and eyes. She kept checking, certain that she was missing something, that she couldn't possibly look that good.

The church was a blaze of lights. It seemed like the glow met them nearly down at the corner when they turned from Main Street. People came streaming in, speaking softly for a change.

"Merry Christmas," was repeated over and over, bringing the response of, "Merry Christmas to you."

Corrine passed out the taper candles with their drip guards. Ricky Dale, in his too-big sport coat, came to help her, and they moved to the front doors to pass out the candles to the later arrivals.

Jojo came bouncing in the door. She was all in red and said she felt like a Christmas apple. Corrine told her that she looked really pretty. "Really?" Jojo said with skepticism. Corrine nodded, and Jojo gave her funny little grin.

And then there was Larry Joe, so cool and handsome that Corrine could only stare. "Hey, pretty girl," he said.

Corrine handed him his candle. His hands were tough looking.

She got to hand a candle to Melissa, who was wearing a white rabbit fur coat and had her hair in a mass of curls. She looked like a model out of *Seventeen* magazine, and Corrine was struck with instant envy. The girl smiled at Ricky Dale, and he said hello, but he didn't leave Corrine's side.

Where was her mother? Corrine wondered, peeking out the door. She had, in fact, grown worried about why her mother had not shown up. Maybe it had finally happened that her mother had said she was going to come but would not. Maybe her mother had even left town. This idea came in a whisper that gripped her. It was crazy, she told herself. Surely her mother would not just up and leave.

Would she?

Another look out the door into the cold night, and she saw Paris pushing her grandfather up the disabled ramp. Quickly alerting Ricky Dale, they opened both doors wide for the wheelchair to come easily through the doorway.

The older man was freshly shaven and his long hair pulled back into a ponytail at his neck. He wore a white starched shirt and sport coat. Corrine wouldn't look at his legs.

She gave him a candle, and he said, "Merry Christmas," and winked at her.

Then she handed Paris a candle. Paris had on her black lipstick, heavy eye makeup and the long beaded earrings Corrine had sent her.

"Hey, kid," Paris said. And she smiled.

"Hey, kid," Corrine said back to her.

Paris raised an eyebrow but kept on smiling.

Mrs. Hicks began playing "Noel."

"Come on, Corky," Ricky Dale said. He took her hand.

"Wait...I'm waitin' for my mother. You go on."

He looked hesitant and didn't go. She checked out the door again and saw the Cherokee pulling into the parking lot. "There she is!" She waved Ricky Dale away and stood waiting for her mother with a tremendous relief washing over her. Her mother had come, as she had said she would. She had not left Corrine.

But not only did her mother get out of the car, a man did, too.

It was Louis. Corrine recognized him with a bit of a shock, when the two came into the light. Tall and slender, dark hair carefully combed back, long black leather coat.

"Hello, sugar. Look who's here." Her mother, in her fabulous fox fur and full makeup, was beautiful, gleaming and hugging on to Louis's arm.

"Merry Christmas, Corrine," Louis said. He smiled in a warm way. He had always been nice to her. She liked him. But right that minute she didn't want him to be here.

Had he come to take her mother back to New Orleans?

Her mother put an arm around Corrine on the way to their pew. They slipped in, and Corrine sat between her mother and Aunt Marilee.

Several times she looked up at the women. Aunt Marilee looked the same as always, lovely. She smiled encouragingly at Corrine.

Her mother, Corrine thought, looked happier than she had seen her since her arrival.

She noticed once that Louis held her mother's hand.

She wanted to jerk her mother away from him.

Watching television and the lights of the Christmas tree, Corrine listened to the voices of the adults visiting at the dining room table. Occasionally she would watch them from beneath her heavy eyelids. The east windows reflected their images.

Louis never put his arm around her mother, but sometimes he touched her hand. He could not take his eyes off her.

Aunt Marilee and Papa Tate liked him. Aunt Marilee had not wanted to like him from the first, and she admitted this and then said that she couldn't help but like him, because there was something about him that was very likable. Louis was, Aunt Marilee had said in the past, so much like a little boy in a sophisticated, even intimidating, man's body. He had been the one to give Corrine really nice presents when her mother had still been giving her things for a little child. And it had been Louis who had taken care of her mother before she had gone to the rehab hospital. It had been Louis who had encouraged her to stay there.

"He's a good man," Corrine heard Aunt Marilee tell Papa Tate later, when they thought she was asleep on the couch, after her mother and Louis had left.

"It's just such a shame about his wife. I just wish that Anita would find someone without problems."

"Darlin', we all have problems," Papa Tate said.

"But Louis can't give her..."

"They're good for each other right now," Papa Tate broke in. "And in any case, it isn't our business."

Corrine wished Louis had never come. Now her mother wasn't looking at her but was just looking at him. Just the way she always had, when she got a man.

Then Aunt Marilee was shaking her, and she pretended to come awake. "Have to get you to bed, sweetheart. Santa Claus won't come until we're all in bed and asleep."

As her aunt tucked the covers around her and murmured that it was going to be very cold that night, Corrine wanted to say, "I don't want to go with Mama and Louis. Don't make me go. I don't care how good he is. Don't send me away."

But what good would it do? It had not mattered in the first place that she hadn't wanted to leave her mother. And it wouldn't matter now, if her mother wanted to take her away with her and Louis. She was a child. All they would say to her was that it was for her own good.

She didn't care if Louis had horses, either.

26

This Christmas day, as on the previous ones that Corrine had spent with Aunt Marilee, her aunt accomplished the once a year feat of being the first one awake. When Corrine rose, she smelled the aromas of coffee, sausage and cornbread. In the living room, she found the tree brightly lit, Gene Autry singing about Rudolph from the stereo, full stockings sagging on the wall and a few Santa gifts under the tree, and a fireplace blazing on the television.

"Isn't it great?" Her aunt beamed, when Corrine commented on the television fire. "Your Papa Tate misses a fireplace something terrible, so Santa brought him this authentic video fireplace. He's gonna love it.

"Here, have a piece of cornbread, but you can't touch any presents until your mother gets here," Aunt Marilee informed her. "Then, after we get done here, we'll go over to Granny Franny's, and then to Aunt Vella's for Christmas supper. You might want to pace yourself on the food," she added, giving the pan of cornbread a skeptical eye.

From past experience, Corrine understood that they were going to eat, carol and unwrap their way through three Christmases, starting with the one at their apartment. Aunt

Marilee couldn't have been more happy and excited if she had been ten years old again.

"Joy to the World" came on the stereo, and Aunt Marilee began to sing. She snatched the cornbread away from Corrine, took Corrine's hands and danced her around the kitchen, while they both sang. One just couldn't be around Aunt Marilee on Christmas and not get a bit joyous and excited.

They waited on Corrine's mother before touching any presents, even the ones that were laid out by Santa Claus. This was especially hard on Aunt Marilee, who kept saying, "She said she'd come by seven." At fifteen after, Aunt Marilee said, "I'll call her. Y'all go on into the living room," and shooed them out of the kitchen. Corrine figured Aunt Marilee didn't want to be heard giving Corrine's mother the what-for.

But a minute later, Corrine's mother arrived. "Please," she said, not even saying hello, "I need a cup of coffee."

"I was just callin' you."

"Well, I'm here, so you don't have to."

Corrine watched the two women and held her breath. Aunt Marilee simply said, "Merry Christmas," and disappeared into the kitchen.

"Where's Louis?" Corrine asked.

"He's out at the Goodnight. He'll join us later."

Corrine took this news with relief and the happiness that she would have her mother's undivided attention.

And then her mother surprised them all by having on pajamas beneath her fur coat. "I wanted to fit in," she said.

This touched Corrine so deeply that she experienced the really odd sense of wanting to cry and had to turn away quickly.

Aunt Marilee was particular about the production of opening presents. Using the fine Christmas china, she made certain everyone had their coffee, and Corrine and Willie Lee their hot chocolate, and Corrine's mother her pie. She put Christmas carols on the stereo, sat herself down and said, "Okay, Tate, pass our stockings first."

In an unbelievably short amount of time, this orderly procedure gave way to the living room looking as if it had exploded, with torn paper and bows everywhere, and barely a spot on the rug uncovered. Willie Lee lost Munro and found him under several sheets of discarded wrapping paper. When Aunt Marilee had to cross the room in order to get more coffee, or to answer a phone call, she clutched her robe and stepped carefully, as if avoiding land mines.

The phone call had been from Grama Norma. "She's made it to St. Louis but is socked in with snow again," her aunt reported and looked worried before being distracted by Papa Tate and his Schwinn bike, to which he was attaching the wheels.

"You aren't gonna ride it in here, are you?"

"No, of course not. But we have to get them ready. It's just like the one I asked for in my letter to Santa when I was a kid," Papa Tate said to Willie Lee, just as thrilled as if he had not put the bikes under the tree himself. Willie Lee and Papa Tate each got Schwinn bikes. Willie Lee's was modern and had special training wheels, and Papa Tate's was a classic, meaning it was old and used but looked new.

Finished with attaching the training wheels to Willie Lee's bike, he helped Willie Lee atop the seat and went to instructing him on how to ride, receiving much caution from Aunt Marilee.

"Tate, don't ride inside the house. You are goin' to break his neck."

"We're not ridin', honey. We're just gettin' the feel."

"You better not ride. You're liable to break one of *our* necks."

"We-are-not-riding," Papa Tate said in a measured tone, appearing exactly like a middle-aged man who didn't need to be told how to handle himself.

Among the many things that Corrine received were new boots from her mother and a wool coat with horses on it from Aunt Marilee.

"They're just so great," Corrine said, smiling bright and happy and staring at the clothes.

"Try 'em on, sugar," Aunt Marilee said.

"Yes, hon...try 'em on," her mother said.

There was nothing else to do but try them on. She flipped off her slippers and tugged on the boots, put the coat on over her pajamas, then posed, being as bright and happy as she knew how to be. It wore on her nerves.

Everyone thanked everyone for their gifts. Corrine was pleased, because she could tell her items went over well. Papa Tate immediately began to read aloud quotes from the famous Texans, and Willie Lee used the small folding binoculars to study each of their faces. Her mother kept saying, "Oh, Corrine," and looking at the drawing pad and wooden pencil box engraved with the words, "Mama's Pencils" that Corrine had gotten at the mall. Aunt Marilee had said, "Oh, darlin', just what I wanted," and dabbed on the perfume with great satisfaction. Corrine thought the two women were equally satisfied.

Then, when they were all sitting there, regarding the mess, "So This Is Christmas" began to play from the stereo, and Papa Tate, Aunt Marilee and Corrine's mother laughed and began to sing with it. The next instant, Willie Lee's new pigeon came flying across the room and perched on a Christmas tree limb, causing a shiny red ball to fall on the floor and break, and then here came his cat, making a dive for the pigeon. The tree might have gone, with Munro cowering beneath it, but it was safely anchored to the wall.

"See," Aunt Marilee said, after all the commotion had settled. "It's a good thing I anticipated a possible disaster."

"Come on, y'all, we've places to go." Aunt Marilee prodded them up and to getting dressed. Corrine's mother headed back to Aunt Vella's, while the rest of them piled presents into the BMW and drove over to Granny Franny's, where they enjoyed lemon cake and warm apple cider, and destroying her living room with crumbs and dribbles and wrapping paper all over.

Corrine gave Granny Franny a small stained-glass suncatcher, which she seemed to really like. "Just what I wanted!" Granny Franny said, which was what she said with every one of her presents.

Corrine said, "Wow, these are great," about the Western-style leather gloves that Granny Franny gave her, although she wondered where she would wear them. She didn't see wearing them to school.

In just a little over an hour, they gathered up the rest of the gifts and Granny Franny and headed for Aunt Vella's and Uncle Perry's house. Papa Tate got almost backed out of the driveway, when Willie Lee shouted, "Wait!"

They had left Munro up on the porch.

Willie Lee opened his door, and Munro came running. Then it was off to Aunt Vella's house, where they launched in again.

Corrine watched Uncle Perry take up her gift. She suddenly felt shy; her gift was small. He read the tag through his little half glasses, then raised an eyebrow at her. "For me?"

She nodded and watched with anticipation as he pulled out the tissue paper and unwrapped the bright red stocking cap.

"Well, hey, you, thanks." He put the cap on and grinned at her. Their eyes met with a shared secret.

Aunt Vella passed out cherry pie that she had made from real cherries saved from summer. "Be careful," she cautioned. "My pies are like life. They have an occasional pit."

"Willie Lee and Corrine, did you hear that?" Aunt Marilee said, as if they were deaf. "Be careful with the pie."

Corrine looked at hers and felt as if she might not want to eat it now.

Louis showed up with his arms full of packages. He was dressed as if he was going to the opera or something, in a suit and a blue silk shirt and gold cuff links, and when he smiled, his teeth were all white and even. He was from a rich family, and Corrine's mother always said she could tell a wealthy man by his perfect teeth. Probably this was what had drawn her to him in the first place.

Corrine didn't know why she felt so hateful toward him,

but she sure did when her mother, dressed now in a deep crimson velvet dress and with rubylike earrings at her ears and deep red lipstick, came out of the kitchen and saw him and went right to him and kissed his cheek and said "Merry Christmas" in her sultry, just-for-a-man tone.

Aunt Vella was falling all over herself in being nice to him, too, welcoming him and getting him coffee, and even Aunt Marilee said, "Oh, Louis, you are so handsome, you make a woman's teeth ache."

It was disgusting. Corrine would not ever be that stupid over a man.

Larry Joe's image popped into her mind. He had lovely teeth, too. But maybe she wouldn't marry him after all, she thought.

"How are you this mornin', Miss Corrine?" Louis said to her in a very warm and friendly manner. "Has Santa Claus been good to you?"

"Yes," she said and sat herself in the space on the other side of her mother on the couch, so Louis couldn't sit there.

He simply perched himself on the arm of the couch, where her mother put her hand on his thigh, right there in front of everyone.

Aunt Vella was going over the packages Louis had brought. He had something for everyone. He sure wanted to be liked. He must have given Corrine's mother her present earlier, because she didn't get one, but there was a basket of fruit for Aunt Vella and Uncle Perry, oranges so big and perfect they looked fake. Granny Franny got a fancy candle. Aunt Marilee opened her package and pulled out a genuine cashmere shawl, in bright Christmas red. It looked beautiful on her, but Corrine didn't think Louis should give Aunt Marilee, a married woman, such a present.

Papa Tate's was a fancy pen, which he likely wouldn't ever use; Papa Tate was a computer man. Willie Lee's was a watch with a compass on it. Willie Lee was tickled crazy over it.

"He already has a compass," Corrine said, feeling the need to point that out.

Then Aunt Vella put a large square box in Corrine's lap, saying, "Sugar, here's yours from Louis."

Corrine looked at the box and then at Louis. *Why'd he have to go and give her a big present?* she thought, eyes back on the box. As irritated as she was at him for even bringing her a gift, she was curious to discover what was inside.

It was a cowboy hat.

She stared at the hat, still in the box, not knowing what to say. It was a really nice felt Resistol, with a woven horse-hair band and chin strap. Probably cost a bundle. But what was she supposed to do with a cowboy hat? She kept her eyes on it, trying to cover how stupid she thought it was, until she could finally say, "Thank you, Louis."

They made her put it on.

She did like it. But she couldn't figure out where she would wear it.

Everyone fell to talking, and Corrine put the hat back into the box, then rose to begin picking up the discarded paper. The room got quiet. She looked up to see everyone looking at her. She wondered if she had been rude to have put the hat back into the box, but she sure had no intention of wearing it around all day.

"Corrine, honey, you haven't opened your present from me and Uncle Perry," Aunt Vella said.

"I..." She looked at Uncle Perry, who grinned at her. Everyone was grinning at her. She felt foolish, thinking she was supposed to know something that she didn't know. She had thought Uncle Perry's college fund money was her present. But Aunt Vella and Aunt Marilee were shoving forward an enormous box that had been sitting back near the wall.

Corrine's eyes widened. *That was for her?* She had seen it earlier and thought it had to be for Belinda.

The two women backed away, and everyone was gazing at her. Feeling terribly shy, she slowly removed the paper, until Aunt Vella said with impatience, "Sugar, we don't want to be here at New Year's. Tear that paper off."

Tearing off the paper, Corrine saw a plain brown card-board box. Papa Tate used his pocketknife to cut the tape holding the flaps, and then Corrine was staring into the box.

It was a saddle.

Oh-my-gosh, *it was the saddle from the saddle shop.*

She had the thought that she was going nuts or seeing wrong. And she didn't want to look up at anyone, because she didn't want anyone to see her. She just wanted to disappear.

Finally, when she did look up, it was at Aunt Marilee, and she knew by looking into her aunt's eyes that there very probably was a horse.

Papa Tate was saying, "Well, by golly, a saddle. Do you think there could be a horse around here somewhere?" He took hold of her shoulders and directed her to the window, pointing toward the corral behind Mr. Winston's house.

She saw first Leanne's truck and horse trailer.

And then, there, tied to the corral fence, was a black and white paint horse that looked just like the mare.

The mare!

"Is she…?"

Papa Tate's blue eyes were innocent. "Well, I don't know…but you are the only one here who got a saddle."

Before he had finished, she was already running, through the dining room and kitchen and out the back door. Aunt Marilee's voice came after her, but she didn't stop. She raced over and ducked through the fence to the small pasture, across it and into Mr. Winston's backyard and over to the corral, where she stopped short, overcome with emotion in front of the horse.

It *was* Miss Queen. It *was!*

Glancing over her shoulder, she saw figures streaming from Aunt Vella's house and across the small pasture toward her, Aunt Marilee and her mother, side by side, coming with hurried, long strides, then further back Willie Lee, Aunt Vella and Granny Franny.

Whipping back around, Corrine ran to the fence, climbed up on the rails and put her arms around the mare's neck.

"Oh, Miss Queen. You're home."

She could not believe it. She clutched the mare, certain that it was all a dream or a mistake. Nothing so wonderful could possibly happen to her.

Then Aunt Marilee was there, holding out Corrine's coat and insisting she put it on. As Corrine slipped her arms into the sleeves, she asked, "Is she really mine? Really? Who gave her to me?"

And her mother said, "Honey, I see a note there in her mane."

Corrine got the note and read it aloud, "Merry Christmas, from Santa Claus."

She looked at her mother and aunt through vision blurred by tears. She hugged each of them, and then she was back up on the rails hugging the mare.

Leanne appeared, bringing a bit and headstall and a bucket and brushes. "Merry Christmas, cowgirl."

Louis came driving up in his Lexus, with Papa Tate and Uncle Perry and Corrine's saddle.

"No saddle until I get some trainin' on both Corrine and this mare," Leanne said and had Louis cart the saddle to the small tack room at the side of the barn.

"Will I be able to keep her here?" she asked.

"I'm sure we can work somethin' out with Winston," Papa Tate said. "But you'll be responsible for her care."

"Oh, I'll take good care of her. I *will*." She pressed her head against the mare's neck.

"Thank you," she remembered to say at last, but the words seemed so small.

"Thank Santa," her mother said.

Her mother's eyes were so tender that Corrine had to look away, while wondering which one had done this thing and still feeling as if it were all an incredible dream.

She was barely aware of the others leaving, while she exchanged breaths with the mare and walked and enjoyed the mare following her and sniffing at her coat pocket and tickling the back of her neck with her velvet nose. She pressed her cheek against the mare's strong, warm shoulder and ran her hand over the animal's broad back. She remembered and was remembered.

Quite suddenly she realized it had begun to snow tiny white flakes. She looked around to see that her mother, Aunt Marilee and Willie Lee were the only ones left at the fence. Snow was flecking their hair and shoulders.

"My goodness," Aunt Marilee said, looking upward. "I think it may snow after all."

"It *is* snow-ing," said Willie Lee, who was climbed up on the fence. Turning his face upward, he stuck out his tongue.

"Can I stay a while longer?" Corrine asked, anticipating her aunt's cautious ways. "I have to get her water tank filled and the stall ready and feed her. Ohmygosh, is there food?"

"Well, I don't imagine Santa would bring a horse without food, do you, Anita?" Aunt Marilee said and pointed at the big bale of hay once again in the corner of the corral. "We'll help you." She began to climb through the rails.

"No. I mean...well, I'd like to do it." She didn't want to hurt their feelings.

"Of course you would, darlin'," her mother said, putting a staying hand on Aunt Marilee, who looked hesitant.

"Willie Lee can stay and help me," Corrine said quickly, seeing his disappointment.

"I will," he said, coming down from the fence rail.

"Here, take my gloves," Aunt Marilee said, pulling them off and even putting them on Corrine's hands before turning to tie Willie Lee's hood up around his head.

Corrine's mother pulled her woolen scarf from her pocket and wrapped it around Corrine's head. It smelled of Shalimar.

Then, with the mare breathing on the back of her head, Corrine watched her mother and Aunt Marilee, arms linked, head back for Aunt Vella's house through the snowflakes that were growing larger.

Blinking away snowflakes, she thought of how handy the cowboy hat would be to keep snow out of her eyes.

"Can you teach me to hear what Miss Queen says?" she asked Willie Lee as they made the stall nice and fresh with pine shavings.

"You just lis-ten," he said, as if anyone could do it.

Corrine set aside the manure rake and went to the mare. "I'm so glad you're back," she said, then listened.

The mare blinked her big dark eyes, and the next instant,

she pivoted, lunged away and pranced around the corral in the softly falling snow, with her tail arched high and proud.

Corrine laughed. "She said she's glad to be back, too."

Willie Lee laughed, too, his rare laugh that always caused Corrine much delight. "And that she is glad to be a-way from a bos-sy horse at Le-anne's."

"Did you make that up?"

"No, I did not," he said seriously, shaking his head.

The ground now had a thin covering of snow. Willie Lee kept lifting his face to the falling flakes as he and Corrine headed across the small pasture toward Aunt Vella's house, where the glow of lights had begun to show faintly at the windows, and Christmas could be heard from there, too.

Corrine was filled with gratitude for the entire world, as well as determined to be good as gold so as to repay this wonderful gift she had been given. She also did not want to do anything that could possibly get her grounded from the horse, or maybe even cause the mare to be sent back. With this idea, she made herself small and invisible, getting Willie Lee out of his coat and then putting their coats on Aunt Vella's washing machine, so as not to drip snow on the floor.

Aunt Marilee and Aunt Vella were their happy selves, flitting around the steamy kitchen, the both of them singing Christmas carols. Aunt Marilee's face was flushed, her lips red as cherries. Corrine's heart swelled to see her.

She slipped on into the living room and saw her mother sitting with Louis on the sofa, her hand on his leg, and talking to Papa Tate and Granny Franny. Louis's arm was on the back of the sofa, his hand on her mother's shoulder.

Her mother looked beautiful. Her eyes kept returning again and again to Louis. There was a man in her life. She was happy.

Uncle Perry had Willie Lee on his lap. Corrine slipped up on the other side of his chair and gave him a hug. "Thank you for the saddle," she whispered.

"You bet, you," he said. "Thank you for the hat." He still had it on his head.

Corrine got the good china plates from the corner hutch. She was careful to carry only two at a time, so as not to take a chance of breaking any.

Mr. Winston came in the front door, knocking snow from his little roadster cap. "We're gonna have us a white Christmas!"

"Winston Valentine, did you walk down here?" said Granny Franny, who had gotten up immediately to help the old man out of his coat.

"I did. I had to wait for Charlene to leave after she dropped me off, but then I walked on down here in the snow. I haven't walked in the snow in ten years." Grinning broadly, he grabbed Granny Franny and waltzed her around. He was so unsteady that he knocked over a lamp, but luckily Louis caught it.

Corrine had the table almost all set when Aunt Marilee came from the kitchen and saw it. "Well, sweetheart, you are such a help," she said.

"What about me?" Papa Tate said, then held a piece of mistletoe over her head and kissed her.

Louis asked for the mistletoe and held it over his own head. Corrine's mother kissed his cheek.

Apparently taken by this behavior, Aunt Vella went over to Uncle Perry and kissed him, too.

Corrine watched them all.

They were about to sit down when Grama Norma arrived with Grandpa Carl, who came in with an umbrella over their heads. "Merry Christmas!" Grama Norma hollered. "I made it!"

"Mama, are you hearin' okay?" Corrine's mother asked, after she'd hugged the woman.

"Oh, it's the jet planes. I can't hear a thing after all those hours on jet planes. I swear, I'm about to collapse."

Corrine, who was squeezing two more place settings at the long table, saw Aunt Marilee virtually take herself by the collar and go over to give Carl a hug. Carl looked stunned, but then he nodded and patted Aunt Marilee's arm.

Aunt Vella was choreographing the seating arrangements, when the front door burst open and Belinda and Deputy

Midgette came in, and with them was a woman Corrine had never seen before. She looked like one of those women who sold makeup on television and wore designer suits.

"Margaret!" Aunt Vella breathed the name.

"Hello, Mama. Surprise."

"She just said that about St. Thomas so as to make this a surprise," Belinda said to Corrine's mother and all of them.

Aunt Vella and her daughter Margaret cried together, and then Aunt Marilee and Corrine's mother and Grama Norma were crying.

Corrine turned from the sight and went to get the card table from the closet under the stairs. Granny Franny and Papa Tate helped to get it set up as an extension of the dining table. When everyone was getting sat down, Corrine maneuvered her way to sit between her mother and Aunt Marilee.

She held her breath and looked at the door, expecting someone else to pop in, although she didn't know where they would put them.

"Winston, would you say a prayer?" Aunt Vella asked.

Mr. Winston got to his feet. He seemed suddenly quite a bit smaller and more bent over than Corrine could recall.

"Let's all join hands."

Corrine's mother took her hand; her mother's was warm and soft and pale in the light of the chandelier. Corrine took Aunt Marilee's hand, which her aunt wiped on her apron first. She saw her Aunt Marilee's other hand reaching for Grandpa Carl's, which was shaking.

Mr. Winston prayed, "Thank you, Lord, for all of our blessings...."

Corrine peeked and saw her mother's left hand enveloped by Louis's much bigger one, and Willie Lee's hand was in Papa Tate's, and there were Aunt Vella's fingers holding on to Uncle Perry's. One of Belinda's was under the table with Lyle's, and her other one was on the table and not touching her sister, Margaret's.

"Thank you mostly for good friends and family...and Santa Claus."

Corrine saw Uncle Perry give a little grin. She was the only one to see this, because no one ever paid him any attention. She grinned at him, and he winked.

Corrine was awakened by her aunt's bed-checking. For the first time, she got up and padded silently through the living room and into the kitchen, where her aunt sat with a cup of coffee. Her aunt was concerned about Corrine being awake, as always, but then she said the most amazing thing.

"How 'bout joinin' me for a bit of coffee?" And she got up and poured Corrine a half a cup, then set the sugar and cream beside it.

Corrine sat down and fixed her coffee rich with the cream, as she liked it; then, lifting it with both hands, she asked in a casual manner who had gotten her the horse.

"Your mother did," Aunt Marilee said with only a moment's hesitation. "Oh, me and Papa Tate helped a little, but it was your mother who did it. Don't you tell her I told you. You should know, but don't spoil it for her."

Corrine saw clearly how her aunt's heart's desire was to make everything right for everyone.

How had her mother paid for the mare? Didn't she cost a lot? It was from Louis, wasn't it?

Aunt Marilee cocked her head and said very possibly, but what did it matter?

Tears welled in Corrine's eyes. She tried to stop them, because Aunt Marilee could get panicky with their tears, but she couldn't seem to stop.

Aunt Marilee saw and cupped her chin, "What is it, sweetheart?"

"I...I don't deserve the mare. I've been so mad at Mama, and I don't..."

"Oh, honey, the mare is a gift. When you give a gift, don't you want the person you gave it to to enjoy it?" She passed Corrine a napkin. "A gift is about the giver, not about the one who gets it. The giver wants so much to give something. Your mother wanted more than anything to give you that horse. And you know what you give her? You give her the gift of accepting. This is the greatest gift of all. A giver can't have any fun unless the person they're giving to accepts the gift and is happy."

Corrine was able to smile at this idea.

She knew now, with the horse, that she wasn't going to have to leave Valentine, but she wondered if her mother was going to stay in town.

"That's something you'll have to ask your mother," Aunt Marilee said.

After this, Corrine sat there quite a while, sipping her coffee and recalling the Christmas dinner and how Aunt Marilee had been so very nice to Grandpa Carl, who Corrine knew Aunt Marilee could not stand, and how Grama Norma clearly favored Corrine's mother and ignored Aunt Marilee when she was around, and how Margaret, Aunt Vella's long lost daughter, had all but thrown herself at Louis and Papa Tate both. She didn't want to speak of any of that, but she could mention about Mr. Winston and how he was so happy about the snow, which was still coming down.

Aunt Marilee smiled broadly at this. "Turn the light out.... Let's see what it looks like in the street."

Corrine did as she was bade, and Aunt Marilee threw up the window, and my gosh, there was the pigeon!

"Lord 'amercy!" Aunt Marilee said in a breathless tone. "*Now* you come? We already have a pigeon."

But she drew the bird inside.

"There's a message," Corrine pointed, so excited she could hardly contain herself. "See. That capsule. Messages go in that capsule. I'll bet it is for Willie Lee."

"What makes you say that? Maybe it's for someone else."

"Well, if it is, we can put it back in and send the bird on its way."

"Okay. Let's open it."

Heads together, they got it open and drew out the tiny piece of paper.

Merry Christmas, Willie Lee. Love, Santa Claus

"Willie Lee!" Aunt Marilee cried, jumping up with the bird and running through the apartment to his room, shaking him awake to show him the pigeon, who was a little perturbed at such handling.

"This is my pig-eon," Willie Lee said quite factually, holding the bird.

Corrine asked him if he was surprised, and he said, "No."

Aunt Marilee had made so much noise as to awaken Papa Tate, who appeared with sleepy eyes at Willie Lee's door. His eyes popped wide-open with the news.

They all went back to the kitchen, and after they had thoroughly marveled over the bird and the message, they turned out the light and looked down onto Main Street and *oohed* and *aahhed* over the Christmas lights glowing through the silently falling snow.

Papa Tate, standing behind them, said very quietly, "I know we all like this view, but I think we'll have to take Winston up on his offer."

"What offer is that, sweetie?" Aunt Marilee asked, not taking her eyes off the street.

When Papa Tate didn't answer right away, Aunt Marilee turned to look at him, and so did Corrine.

Papa Tate swallowed. "He's offered us his house. We could live there with him and take care of him, so Charlene wouldn't be so worried. In exchange, we get rent-free living, in a house with a yard large enough to accommodate pigeon coops."

That basically was the end of any sleep for Papa Tate on Christmas night.

27

It snowed off and on all the next day, and by Monday morning they had registered over eight inches, enough for children to make snowmen and snowballs. The city workmen kept the two crews going, attempting to clear the streets, no easy task with road graders. The city had no snowplows and no parking ordinances for times of snow, so there were a lot of parked vehicles in the way.

The Main Street Café did a bang up business with feeding the city workmen and people gathering to talk about the weather and tell of their Christmas celebrations. Vehicles were parked up and down the café side of the street, causing the driver of the road grader to holler with aggravation as he came along.

When the sun came out on Monday, Corrine and Willie Lee made angels and snowballs and cleaned the sidewalk in front and around the side of the *Voice* building. Corrine felt she owed Papa Tate, because while her mother had given her the horse, Papa Tate was going to be paying for feed. She had overheard him say this to Aunt Marilee. He wasn't aggravated or anything; he was just on the lookout for hay at a good price. It was true that Corrine had received a gift that would keep on costing.

She was able to earn twenty-five dollars cleaning the sidewalk in front of the café and the saddle shop and over in front of Blaine's Drugstore, because of Aunt Vella being her blood kin. Ricky Dale, enterprising as always, cleaned most all the others. When she was about to give out cleaning in front of the drugstore, he even came and helped her, and he let her keep the five dollars Belinda gave her. By pointing out that the others had paid her ten, she was able to wrangle free hot fudge sundaes out of Belinda for them both.

They were sitting at the soda counter when two men in suits and long tan coats came in and ordered Cokes, and then brought up having heard that a number of people in the community had received money in the mail from an anonymous donor. They wanted to know if Belinda knew any of them.

"Oh, yeah," Belinda said. "I've seen each one of them a time or two. They've all come in here for prescriptions or over-the-counter medication." She said that she personally knew Joe Miller, that he was a decorated Vietnam hero and had an account there at the drugstore. "We deliver to him for free, since he lost his legs serving our country."

The men wanted to know if she had seen any of the money.

"I may have. I didn't pay attention." She wasn't paying all that much attention right then, as she was jotting down notes about the outfit for sale on the shopping channel.

"Didn't you notice anything about the money?"

"It was cash. I was glad to have it."

"You didn't know that it was money from the thirties? Possibly stolen money?"

"I never thought about it being stolen. Where was it stolen from?"

"I didn't say it was stolen."

"Oh, I thought you did."

The man looked at her.

"Well, it was from Santa Claus. You can ask anyone."

The two men blinked. "Santa Claus?"

"That's what the note said. I saw a couple of the notes. They for sure said that. You can ask anyone."

"Uh-huh."

"If you'll excuse me, I'm workin'," Belinda said and turned her attention to the television.

Shortly the men left, but only minutes later, Mrs. Julia Jenkins-Tinsley came in to get a cup of latte to go and to say that there had been men—"Looked like government types, and since I'm with the Postal Service, I do know that type"—asking around town about the Santa money.

"I asked Gerald over at the bank, and he said somethin' about a routine investigation, since it was old money, but I don't know what that's about."

Belinda nodded and said the men had been in the drugstore. "I told them the money came from Santa. They didn't seem to believe me."

Mrs. Julia Jenkins-Tinsley smiled. Belinda smiled. Then Corrine and Ricky Dale smiled to see the women smiling at each other. Corrine thought that Belinda had sure been a surprise just about all Christmas. She had definitely come into her own, as Aunt Vella was telling everyone.

Just as Ricky Dale and Corrine were leaving, Mrs. Naomi Smith and little Gabby came in.

"See what Santa gave me!" Gabby said. "He gave me just what I asked for—see." She opened her coat and displayed a glittering pink ballerina dress. She did a pirouette and then shoved forward a Game Boy. "Just what I asked for," she said again. "Where's Willie Lee? I want to show him."

"He's up at Mr. Winston's," Corrine told her, admiring the little girl's gifts, while listening to the exchange between her mother and Belinda over at the soda fountain.

"Belinda," the pastor's wife said in a manner that drew the eyes of everyone in the shop and had Belinda come up straight, "you advised my husband for his Christmas buyin'. You told him to get me that chair and ottoman at the Morris Brothers that cost a thousand dollars."

By this time the woman was coming around the end of the counter, and Belinda was sort of backing up.

"He wasn't gonna do it, but you told him it was the perfect gift." The next instant Mrs. Smith threw her arms around Belinda, who by this time was backed up to the counter. "Well, honey, thank you...thank you. By the time he bought it, it was on sale for fifty percent off. Oh, you're a great shopping consultant!"

Corrine was awfully happy for Mrs. Smith, because she obviously had very much wanted that chair.

"I'll look around for some hay for you," Ricky Dale said when they came out on the sidewalk. Giving a wave, he headed in the opposite direction.

She watched his saunter with appreciation, thinking she was a real horse owner now. She headed around the corner and onto Church Street, walking easy through the slushy, melting snow and looking at all the lights and decorations, her heart filled with gladness to be in Valentine.

A pickup truck came up and stopped. It was Wade Littleton's green truck, and Leanne called at the window, "Hey, hon, come on and we'll give you a ride."

When Corrine got in, Leanne was sitting close up to Mr. Littleton. It looked like she at last had a prospective husband. She asked Corrine how she was getting along with the mare and talked about how good the filly was doing down in Texas at Mr. Littleton's place.

Pulling into the driveway, they saw Mr. Winston in a rocker on the front porch, and Aunt Marilee and Willie Lee in the swing, and Papa Tate shoveling the snow off the walkway to the house.

"Mr. Northrupt says he'll pay you to clean his front walk, Corrine," said Aunt Marilee, who was wrapped in a blanket and moving the swing back and forth in a contented manner.

"Good deal! I sure hope we get some more snow." She waved and headed around to the corral, where she checked Miss Queen's water tank and cleaned the stall a bit before going to scrape Mr. Northrupt's walk.

Louis's gleaming black car pulled up at the back door of the house, and he and her mother got out. He waved, then went in the house, while her mother came to the corral gate.

Corrine crossed the corral, with Miss Queen coming at her shoulder.

"You two are a pair," her mother said, smiling and reaching up to pet the horse.

"I'm awfully glad for her," Corrine said, mindful of what Aunt Marilee had told her about not spoiling her mother's happiness by saying she knew that her mother had been the one to give her the horse. "That Santa Claus is a pretty cool guy."

Her mother smiled.

"There were two men in town looking for Santa Claus just a while ago," Corrine said.

At her mother's puzzled expression, Corrine explained about the men who had been in the drugstore asking questions and how Belinda had answered. "Well, Santa is safe in Valentine," her mother said.

She gazed at Corrine, then said, "And you're safe here, too."

Corrine knew what her mother was going to say.

"I'm goin' back to New Orleans with Louis."

Corrine nodded.

"I'll come back for your birthday in three weeks."

"It's just over two weeks."

"Ah, that's right. Well, I'll be back, for sure. And when Easter break comes, you can come down to New Orleans to visit me, if you want."

"Okay. I want," she added.

Her mother looked pleased. And then she said with a hopeful and excited expression, "I've decided...I'm going to be a schoolgirl, just like you."

Her mother was going to college to get her degree. She wasn't certain exactly what area as yet, but she leaned toward business. She could go to school so much easier in a city like New Orleans. And she already had a job waiting for her there, and Louis needed her to help him with running his house and entertaining, as he was becoming much more prominent with his firm.

"He needs me," she said, possibly not realizing how this was the heart of it for her.

Corrine understood now. While she couldn't put it into words, she understood that somewhere during Christmas, she had grown up. She didn't know exactly what had happened to her, but she sensed a shift inside of her in which she had a certain understanding that life was never quite as one thought it was. But it would all be okay, and sometimes, when you least expected it, and only for a brief period, it would be really good.

It was the same about people, too, she thought. No one was exactly as you expected, and at any given time people would either be more than you'd ever hoped for or a disappointment, but somehow people were always just what they were supposed to be.

She knew that she had received a heart's desire in the mare. The mare was the first thing she had ever really let herself want, besides her mother. She had gotten the mare, just as she had imagined her. And maybe she had gotten her mother, too, after all. Her mother and Aunt Marilee together were the perfect mother.

And as she watched her mother and Louis, she knew that Louis needed her mother and her mother needed Louis, but her mother didn't so much need Corrine. Her mother loved her. You could love someone but not necessarily need them right there in your life. Maybe her mother had just needed to know that she hadn't ruined Corrine's life, and that Corrine was just fine where she was.

This was okay, because Aunt Marilee not only loved Corrine but needed her, and so did Willie Lee. And even Papa Tate, and Mr. Winston, and Granny Franny, and Aunt Vella, and Ricky Dale, and Jojo, who came running up the stairs to find Corrine in the bedroom that was going to be her very own, with a bathroom to share with Willie Lee. A whole bathroom for just the two of them.

"We brought you over a bale of hay," Jojo said, dragging Corrine to the window and pointing to the corral that they could see through the bare tree limbs. "You know, you guys are gonna have to get a tractor now. Grampa's tractor can't hardly get that bale off the trailer. Larry Joe's havin' a devil of a time."

It was Larry Joe, in a cowboy hat, on the seat of the rusty red tractor.

"I can come over here and stay sometimes," Jojo said. "It's gonna be so cool. I brought my paint box to show you. Isn't it great? I just about died when I saw it. Will you help me learn to draw horses as good as you do?"

"Sure. You can do it easy."

They spent an hour drawing, and Corrine realized that she had gotten a lot of things that Christmas that didn't fit under a tree. She had friends in Jojo and Ricky Dale, and Paris, too. She and Jojo said they'd be friends forever.

The next evening her mother called from New Orleans to say that she and Louis had arrived safely. She chatted at length with Aunt Marilee, and neither of them said a cross word. Then Corrine spoke with her mother and told her all about finally moving in to her room at Mr. Winston's house and how she and Jojo were going to ride horses the next day, as the temperatures were going to get warmer. She talked about fifteen minutes almost nonstop.

Then, when she said goodbye, she said, "I love you, Mama."

"I love you, too, sugar," her mother said.

She knew that her mother had loved her enough to give her what she needed, which was her home and family right where she was.

Corrine turned from the phone and went to set the supper table for Aunt Marilee.

Author's Afterword

Dear Reader,
As I write this, I'm thinking ahead to when this book finds its way into your hands. I imagine many of you will be like I am in the fall, beginning to dream, hope and plan for the holiday, thinking, as I always do, that this year I'll be prepared. I approach the season with high hopes of organization.

Thinking of it now, though, what I feel may be more helpful is to be prepared to be unprepared, and to get through and enjoy so much of it anyway. Accepting being unprepared is a recipe for living life on good terms.

I want to thank my family for the recipes in this book.

Valentine's Frances Kinsey's Fruitcake comes courtesy of my dear mother-in-law, Frances Kinsey Matlock, who has for years now delighted her children and friends with it each Christmas.

Aunt Lizzie Lee's Cornbread, a genuine deep South bread, is provided by my cousin Mary Frances Eves Williamson, and was her Aunt Lizzie Lee's, of course.

Cousin Judy Johnson Beckett provided the delicious Congealed Cranberry Salad recipe. From the first time I made it for this book, I became addicted to it.

Naomi's Turkey and Fruit Salad, and Aunt Vella's Holiday Candied Sweet Potatoes, are two dishes I myself make, having arrived at the general recipes over many holiday meals.

The Heavenly Ambrosia is what I've made for years and called fruit salad, until I found a similar recipe entitled Ambrosia in a very old Southern cookbook that once belonged to my grandmother, Anna Johnson Wentworth. My mother's word on this is: "Ambrosia is highly overrated."

The raisin pie filling is also my own. My husband's favorite, it is a symbol of Christmas in our home.

Food is very much a part of living and loving down through the generations. From the moment of birth, we are comforted by food. Making favored dishes is how we women display love to our families, especially on special occasions. I can invite my son to a regular meal, and very often he's too busy. Invite him to a "family supper," though, and he comes on the run. Is it because he knows that for these meals I will be serving his favorites, and love and memories, too?

In the recent years, however, I have had to adapt many of my treasured recipes, as my mother and I discovered that we have a little known but not uncommon condition called celiac disease and could no longer eat wheat flour.

Celiac disease is an inherited condition in which the body's immune system produces a toxic response to the gluten found in all forms of wheat, rye and barley. The only remedy is not to eat the offending grain, which is poison to the body in any amount.

While widely recognized in other parts of the world, celiac disease has for years been overlooked and under-diagnosed in the United States. A landmark study released in February, 2003, concluded that celiac disease affects 1 in 133 people in the general population in this country.

If you or someone you know has any of these symptoms: abdominal pain, cramping and bloating, chronic diarrhea or constipation, anemia, fatigue and lack of energy, depression, weight loss with a large appetite, or weight gain, osteopenia, bone or joint pain, please visit the following organizations to find out more.

The Celiac Disease Foundation at www.celiac.org

The Gluten Intolerance Group at www.gluten.net

The Celiac Sprue Association at www.csaceliacs.org

My sincere gratitude to these organizations and to the many celiac sufferers who have gone before and so generously pass on the knowledge of this disease and how to live healthy and very happy with it.

All the recipes given here, except Frances Kinsey's fruitcake, are gluten-free. For Frances's fruitcake, simply exchange the regular graham crackers for gluten-free ones, and you have a gluten-free fruitcake. Other suggestions for substitutions are gluten-free cornflakes or gluten-free gingersnaps. I have not yet tried these substitutions, but will endeavor to do so by the time *Recipes for Easy Living* reaches the bookshelves, so as to give a good report on the results.

Years ago a dear friend, Cleo Farris, kindly gave me her never-fail pie crust recipe, which I shared in one of my earlier Christmas books. Many readers wrote then to say they used it. It is with great delight that I now share a new recipe adapted from that one with all of my fellow celiacs out there, or those of you who simply would like to try this great delicacy in making my Fayrene's raisin pie. My family swears they like this gluten-free crust better. Thank you, Cleo. I'm still making pies.

Curtiss Ann's Reliable Gluten-free Pie Crust

1 cup white, brown or sweet rice flour

1 cup tapioca flour

1/2 cup cornstarch

1 teaspoon xanthan gum (can be made without, but is helpful in making pastry stick together.)

1 cup shortening

1 egg, beaten

1 teaspoon baking powder

1 tablespoon apple cider vinegar
2-4 tablespoons ice water
Powdered sugar for rolling

Whisk together the flours and xanthan gum. Cut short-ening into the flour mixture with a fork or pastry cutter. In a measuring cup, break the egg and beat slightly. Add vinegar and baking powder and two tablespoons ice wa-ter. Add liquid mixture to the flour mixture, mixing un-til the pastry holds together and forms a ball. You may need to add 1-2 more tablespoons of ice water.

Form two balls, one slightly larger than the other, the larger one for the bottom crust, smaller for top. Set the balls back into the bowl; cover and chill for at least 15 minutes before using.

The dough will not roll out exactly like wheat dough, but it will roll. Place the ball of dough between two sheets of plastic wrap that are dusted lightly with pow-dered sugar or rice flour. Roll lightly and carefully. When correct in size, peel off only the top plastic sheet and invert the crust into the pie dish (yes, this is tricky), pressing gently into place, before removing the second plastic sheet. If dough cracks, just pinch it back to-gether. And don't worry if you need to start over and even moisten just a bit. I haven't found that this hurts the finished crust at all.

I make a simple edge with the tines of a fork. For raisin pie, I cut four large triangles out of the top, to give a lattice effect. A sprinkle of granulated sugar adds sparkle and liveliness.

I wish for each of you a loving and merry Christmas.

Curtiss Ann Matlock

USA TODAY **bestselling author**

STEF ANN HOLM

Deputy Lanie Prescott is ready to leave her ho-hum life in Majestic, Colorado, for an exciting job in the city. Paul Cabrera, her tall, sexy replacement, is looking for just the opposite.

But when Lanie's job offer falls through and an unthinkable crime rocks her small hometown, she's back on the force and sharing close quarters with Paul, turning what started as an arresting attraction into an affair of the heart.

Maybe life in Majestic isn't so bad after all….

Undressed

"Stef Ann Holm will make you laugh and cry and fall in love again."
—*New York Times* bestselling author Jill Barnett

Available the first week of October 2003, wherever paperbacks are sold!